DREAMKEEPERS
From the Oneirolepsy series

.▪.₀.▪° ★ ▪.▪☆▪.▪°.₀.

ONEIROLEPSY: DREAMKEEPERS
By
Y. X. Winters

NOTE: This novel contains content that might be troubling to some readers, including, but not limited to depictions of and references to violence, death, gore, and sexual assault. Please be mindful of these potential triggers.

.˙₀.˙° ★ ˙.˙ ☆ ˙ ˙₀.

Chapters: 30/30
Part 1 of the Oneirolepsy series
Word count: ~110k
Of Dreams and Nightmares, 2023

ISBN: 9798872107200

Oneirolepsy: Dreamkeepers

To those who dream of a better future

※★ ✦ ★※
Chapter 1: Magician

The car drove for what seemed like a century, and Raine had to recall how to breathe steadily again. Her playing cards rested at the tips of her fingers, and she shuffled them subconsciously as her eyes focused out of the car windows, tapping her feet every few seconds.

"I've never seen you so nervous before, Raine." Sitting next to Raine was her close friend and manager, Soraya Synns. Her long hair segregated into shades of blonde and brown, and she had been watching Raine fidget nervously ever since the two started travelling to the Dream realm. "I know you mostly perform at Summer's pavilion, but it's not going to be any different in the Dream realm. You'll be fine."

Raine closed her eyes and realised that Soraya was right. Most of her magician shows were performed in the Mainland, her homeland where Rhea, her ever-loving, raised and took care of her. Summer's pavilion eventually became Raine's second home, with all the performances and practice tricks she'd executed there. But now, she was deviating from her usual scene.

Well, to be exact, Summer's pavilion was a third home. Even though Rhea had a nice home in the Dream realm, Raine lived in her very own treehouse in the Mainland, surrounded in a large rainforest that nobody could access but Raine herself. "What if I make a fool of myself? I know the place itself won't affect my skills, but it doesn't help that I'm still nervous."

As much as Raine wanted to become a famous magician, her title as Revieras, the custodian of all the dreamers in Oneirolepsy, overshadowed her dreams into nothing more than a little 'hobby'.

She had never asked to play the role of Revieras, but she never complained about it, because as far as she knew, she was still able to live her life freely and as normal as she could. At least, she thought so, anyway. Although Raine didn't really like carrying the role, she still didn't want to embarrass herself in front of all the dreamers during her performances and have it undermined.

"Hey, the Dream realm is one of the friendliest realms in Oneirolepsy, not trying to throw shade on the other realms," Soraya laughed. "Don't worry so much, Raine! You've performed flawlessly countless times, you'll do fine! It's not like the president is watching you or anything."

Raine gave Soraya a forced smile. "Yeah, I guess." At least Rhea wasn't attending her show, Raine thought. If she did screw up in front of everyone, she'd prefer her mother to be absent when she did. Despite Rhea's initial excitement about Raine visiting and performing in the Dream realm, the venue was placed so ridiculously far away from Rhea's home that it might as well have been planned on purpose. Raine had told Rhea not to worry so much and that she'd be fine without her in the audience, and when Rhea finally accepted that she wouldn't be able to attend the magic show, Raine hid her relief with feigned sadness.

Raine calmed herself and kept her playing cards in her tailcoat. She was dressed as a typical magician, except for the over-the-top tophat and a magic wand. She used to wear them in the past, but stopped when she started being ridiculed for looking silly and childish for her age.

Raine had always found magic tricks to be more intriguing and fun than real magic. Dreamers were able to do incredible things with their dream energy - manifesting them into real life creatures, controlling the environment around them, manipulating the elements, and much more. But there was something Raine always found interesting about the execution of a simple card trick by diverting an entire audience's attention. How clever contraptions were constructed and established to execute a flawless show of wonder. The fact that there was no actual magic in magic tricks made it more magical, and her belief became her reason for why she had been learning how to shuffle cards from a very young age.

Soraya was one of Raine's only and closest friends who accepted her as Raine, rather than Revieras. They had met soon after one of Raine's earlier magic shows, in a café which would soon become their frequent meeting place. Soraya, despite being strangers then, helped to chase away another dreamer who was incessantly pestering Raine. From the very moment Raine saw Soraya appearing out of nowhere and using her bare hands to shoo the aggressor out the café effortlessly despite him being twice her size, and then offering Raine a free drink, she decided to befriend her right then and there.

Soraya's long eyelashes complimented the soft round shape of her eyes, and whenever Raine looked at Soraya's emerald eyes, she swore that her friend was a princess in her past life. Soraya gazed at Raine with a serious expression and spoke in a stern tone. "Raine, look at me. I don't want you to think pessimistically. Don't worry about screwing up. Just focus on *not* screwing up, and you'll do okay. Understand?"

Raine nodded, feeling slightly intimidated by Soraya. Although Soraya was friendly and light-hearted at times, she was still Raine's manager for a reason. Soraya could easily switch from being a joking friend to an authoritative manager. Regardless, Raine knew that both versions of Soraya cared about her equally, and Raine felt moved by her words. "I understand. Thank you, Soraya."

Soraya's face softened, and she turned away from Raine, less serious now. "That's good. Oh, by the way, after the performance, do you want to get lunch? I'll give you time to change out of your outfit, and we can spend some time in the Dream realm. It's been a while since I've left the Mainland." Soraya looked out of the window and her eyes widened. "Oh, we're arriving."

The hub came into view as Soraya and Raine arrived at their destination Dreamer's Cove, one of the largest places in the Dream realm built for recreational activities. It had a large and curved exterior with windows. As a popular tourist place, Raine would always find pictures online of dreamers posing outside the establishment with the beautiful northern lights at nighttime. Thanks to the early time, the place proved to be less crowded, much to Raine's relief.

Although Raine had the title of Revieras, she had never been treated like a celebrity, with the exception of the Ambition realm, of course, but other than that, Raine had never experienced being bombarded with interviews or paparazzi.

The car came to a halt, and Soraya escorted Raine out of the vehicle, and both stepped out onto the pavement. Mountains could be seen from every direction and faded into the distance. The most unique thing about the Dream realm besides the fact that it had the most mountainous landscape out of all the realms was how the sky always remained in a state of dark purple, casting the illusion of perpetual night. With the cooling air, Raine felt like the entire realm was being tucked into bed with a blanket over its head.

"Come on, Raine, we still have to set up and meet the others," Soraya said, pulling her phone out and texting those who were in charge of the venue that

Raine would be performing at. Raine followed Soraya into the hub, and there they began their work after searching for the venue.

As the two entered Dreamer's Cove, the air conditioning inside blasted them with a cold and soothing environment, assuring Raine of her decision to wear her triple-layered magician's suit even before the show had started, for unlike Soraya, who shivered in the cold, she was spared from frost.

Following the directions of the nearby signs in the hub, Raine and Soraya made their way to the stage, and where the audience would be. The room stretched far - twice as spacious as Summer's pavilion. Raine began to feel nervous again, but sought to distract herself by admiring the cleanliness of the environment. The velvet curtains appeared brand new, and the stage had decorations to appeal to the audience.

There were cushioned seats that complemented the curtains on stage, and were aligned perfectly with spaces between each row to make walking through them comfortable. The air conditioning in the room was just right - not too cold, not too warm, and the lights weren't blaring, but also made sure no space was dim or hard to see.

Raine started setting up her tricks while Soraya met up with the supervisors from Dreamer's Cove and discussed administrative things. She went through the routine she had meticulously planned in her head over and over again, worried that she had missed something. Even the smallest of nuances was crucial in her performances.

The clock struck nine in the morning, and after ensuring that every single thing, down to the tiniest of details, was perfect, Raine stood backstage, hiding behind the curtains, listening to the flood of footsteps as the seats in the audience began filling up. A host would arrive and welcome the guests, then Raine would begin her magic show after introducing herself - not that she needed to, anyway.

Soraya ensured order within the audience, leaving Raine backstage by herself. Soon, the host showed up. He was a well-dressed Pure dreamer who had studied in the Subliminal realm, his face often appearing behind many sponsors for awards, celebrations, and charity events. In fact, he was probably one of the most famous masters of ceremonies in the Dream realm.

"Hey Revieras. Ready for the show?" The host asked, with a polite smile. The two met backstage, and the accent he picked up from abroad leaked through his enunciation of his words.

Raine gave a smile in return and nodded. She thanked the air conditioning which cooled the sweat emerging from her nervousness. Her legs had stopped shaking, but her mind was still ablaze with thoughts. "I'm ready to start anytime."

The host soon left backstage, ripping the curtains aside as he walked on stage, allowing Raine to catch a glimpse of the filled seats. He picked up the microphone that laid idly on stage that had been prepared and tested an hour ago, and his voice boomed through the speakers, grabbing everyone's attention. "Ladies and gentlemen, I hope you're having a fine morning! Thank you for coming out at this hour; I can see you're all on time. We have a very special guest today for this event, and she'll be coming out on stage very soon. But first off, I'd like to give a few words about the event..."

As the host started talking to the audience, Raine listened intently, waiting for her cue. She fidgeted endlessly until finally, after about five minutes, she heard the host shout: "Everybody, give it up for Revieras!"

Raine ignored the fact that she was called Revieras instead of her own name and walked out onto the stage to a large applause. All eyes were on her now, and from her peripheral vision she could see the host walking off the stairs on the side of the stage and claiming a reserved seat in the front row. She picked up the microphone the host had left on stage before he walked off and cleared her throat, trying to exert as much energy as she could. She learned that she shouldn't sound too tired or too obnoxious, as how she spoke could easily influence her audience. "Alright, who's ready for some magic?"

※ ※ ※

"Oh, what's this?" Raine pulled a card from the deck she held in her other hand. Among the many diamonds, hearts, clovers and spades, the single card she excluded from the pile consisted of a single raven. The audience watched intently as Raine continued to speak. "A raven! What bad luck! This needs to be fixed!"

It had been about ten minutes since Raine first appeared on stage, and she eased significantly when she found the audience to be reciprocating actively with great interest. They ranged from small children to working adults, paired with their parents or siblings, and Raine found it easy to communicate with them whenever she gave a one-off comment or question to grab their curiosity.

Raine flicked her wrist as fast as possible as she swapped the card of the raven with another card. She held out the new card to the audience, directing their attention as she discreetly kept the raven card with her other hand. "A dove! Now isn't that cool?" She spoke. Raine then gestured to the audience, "But you know what'll be cooler? Pulling out a real dove from this very card!"

"That's impossible!" She could hear a young member of the audience shout out.

"But is it? Are you ready?" Raine took a deep breath as she prepared for the trick. The great risk of failing and the consequences of it always worried her - she didn't want to throw away her reputation and reduce it to nothing but a failed illusionist. Some prior tricks

included duplicating money from the air and Raine
had even invited a few audience members on stage to
create a levitation illusion. Now, one of her final tricks
was to pull a real animal from an inanimate card with
a cartoon drawn on it.

Raine waited for when the suspense peaked at just
the right moment, and then executed her move.
"And...Presto!" Raine quickly lit a flash paper and
pulled out a white-feathered dove out of her sleeve.
The dove flew out, its wings hiding Raine's hand as
she flipped the dove card to an empty card frame. The
audience gasped their loudest and applauded, and the
children cried with joy and amazement. The dove
circled around the audience's heads, before it finally
landed on Raine's arm, waving at the audience with
its wings.

Raine let the dove soar above the audience once
more, and while the audience continued to marvel at
the single bird, another white dove flew in, and then
another, and then another. Not only had Raine
managed to create the illusion that she had
summoned a bird from a card, but she also made it
look like the dove had multiplied. Raine gave a heave
of relief when the trick was executed flawlessly, and
nobody seemed to suspect that she had hidden the
several doves in her costume the entire time.

"Alright!" She called out, signalling the four doves to
return to her. A jolting sound of the door bursting
open echoed out as several individuals entered the
venue just then. Raine was too preoccupied with

starting a new trick to see who had entered, only
assuming that they had probably broken the doors
with the amount of force they used to enter the room.
Maybe they were worried about being late, Raine
thought, then went back to her tricks. "Now, we're
going to-"

A group of people screamed bloody murder, echoing
throughout the entire room. Caught off-guard by the
sudden shriek, Raine immediately put her trick on
hiatus, tiptoeing to see what was going on at the back
of the audience. She gasped audibly into the
microphone when she saw the group of individuals
who entered just a few seconds ago carrying all sorts
of weapons and beating up whoever was closest to
them in the audience. Everyone began shouting and
trying to leave their seats, but with the number of
dreamers and small children running around, it
caused more chaos and prevented anyone from
properly exiting the scene. Raine froze on stage,
refusing to believe that her show had been interrupted
by what seemed like a planned attack.

Soraya and a few other representatives called
security and tried to escort everyone to safety and
arrest the aggressors. Some brave parents and
guardians in the crowd had taken it upon themselves
to protect the children and were fighting back against
them, and Raine quickly left the stage to help the
audience.

A dreamer around the age of a university student had
her body mercilessly trampled by the crowd. She was

shoved and pushed like a pinball, and Raine managed to catch her before she got crushed, pulling her to safety by the side. "You can leave through the backstage," she instructed. The dreamer nodded and left. Raine guided more audience members to the exit from backstage and helped them to safety.

Raine caught the sight of a dreamer on the floor. He was an older gentleman, with his body covered in blood and bruises. Immediately, Raine went over to the gentleman and bent down to check on him. "Hey, hey, are you alright?" She called, even though the answer was obvious.

A cough came out from the gentleman. "I got attacked by one of their knives," he whispered weakly, revealing a gash on his torso and arm. Raine gasped. She wanted to pull him somewhere safe, but worried that moving him would cause more injuries. She hoped nobody would come after Raine or the gentleman and used her ability.

Raine closed her eyes and gathered all the dream energy from her surroundings. The power seeped into Raine's body, and she released them out to her fingers as she healed the injured dreamer, and as Raine slowly opened her eyes, she saw the bruises and wounds on the injured dreamer patch themselves up, and the bleeding stopped. The gentleman recovered his strength, and he slowly got up with Raine's assistance. "Thank you," he said, before fleeing to safety. Raine watched him leave, glad to have made use of her ability to heal.

About ten security guards busted into the room and with even more shouting, detained the group of angry attackers with much struggle. Soraya instructed everyone else to leave the room, leaving only her, Raine, the host, and the security guards while the rest of the staff left to help the confused and scared guests.

The group of assailants were pinned to the floor with their hands behind their back, and Soraya tried to identify them while the guards remained tense, standing next to her in case anything happened. Raine walked over to Soraya in search of context, but a sudden sickness hit her when she stood right by the aggressors.

Soraya noticed Raine clutching her stomach and frowned when she limped over to her. "Are you alright? Did you get injured just now?" She scanned Raine's body for any bruises or wounds, but Raine shook her head.

"No, nothing of the sort. Just bad timing for a stomachache, I guess. Who are they?" Raine gestured at the arrested individuals. There were about seven of them, and all their faces were flat on the floor, weapons dropped and confiscated by security.

"You wouldn't believe it," Soraya muttered.

"What?"

"Nightmares."

Blood drained from Raine's face. She took another look at the seven individuals on the floor and realised that the sick feeling in her stomach was caused by the nightmare energy radiating from the seven of them.

"But...how? The barrier isn't supposed to let black-dreamers leave the Nightmare realm-"
 WEEEEEEEAAAAAOOOOO!!!!
 A piercing noise interrupted Raine. It sounded as if it was being played by every speaker in the world, and Raine felt her ears being torn apart by the sound. It only took Raine a second to realise that it was, in fact, a worldwide emergency siren. "Attention, all dreamers! This is not a drill! The barrier separating the Nightmare realm from the rest of the Dream realms has been completely broken, and Nightmares are now swarming all over Oneirolepsy! Please seek shelter immediately, and do not attempt to engage with any nightmares! I repeat, do not engage!"
 The announcement played on loop, its booming voice adding a layer on top of all the noise. Raine heard more screaming from afar and jumped when she felt something tap on her shoulder. She turned around and saw that it was only Soraya, who was already making phone calls. Using her free arm, she threw Raine's bag at her.
 "We need to leave. Now." Raine managed to catch her bag before it landed on the floor. "Quick! We need to head back to the Mainland! It's not safe here!" Soraya shouted, holding her phone up to her ears with her other hand. Doused in cold sweat, Raine recalled that the Dream realm was located closest to the Nightmare realm, and Dreamer's Cove was located in the far north, subjecting her to even more danger. "Hello? Is Mom okay?" Soraya's panicked voice could

be heard over the siren as she left the room in a hurry while on call.

Mom! Raine felt something carve a hole into her stomach as she imagined what could've happened to her mother. She ripped out her microphone headset as she dashed towards the exit, leaving the doves behind.

Exiting the hub, Raine was shocked to see the entire Dream realm flipped upside down. Scanning her surroundings and seeing groups of black-dreamers that seemed to have appeared out of nowhere evoked panic and stress. Raine grew increasingly worried. Rhea resided in the south, and Raine needed to get there to check on her ageing mother. She knew Rhea had the bad habit of leaving her doors and windows unlocked, and now, her home was ripe for a black-dreamer to break into.

Raine looked around, trying to find the fastest route to get to Rhea's home. Soraya had long gone, and any public transportation by now would have been either flooded by other dreamers or infiltrated by black-dreamers. There was no way Raine could get anywhere without relying on her own feet.

With no choice, Raine dashed towards Rhea's home, hoping she wouldn't suddenly get attacked. She then remembered her magician's outfit included a cape-looking cloak that allowed her to turn invisible with the help of optical cloaking. Raine did exactly that, and now to the whole world, she was invisible.

Fortunately, Raine found a bicycle lying on the pavement nearby after ten minutes of non-stop running. After ensuring nobody would miss the bicycle, she claimed it as her own, and began cycling.

It took Raine about an hour and a half on the bicycle before she reached Rhea's home. The surrounding buildings and roads were not any prettier in the south, and although there were relatively fewer black-dreamers around, the air was still heavy with tension, and it didn't help that it was dark out, making any ambush significantly easier.

Raine threw herself off the bicycle and dashed toward the humble cottage that Rhea lived in, her palms and forehead dripping with sweat.

Her legs stopped working as soon as she reached the front door of Rhea's house. The entrance to the humble abode of Rhea's showed signs of wreckage, its front door already wide open. The living room could be seen from the outside. All of the furniture appeared in disarray - the sofa had been dragged outwards, with the floor rug folded by the edges, but that didn't matter. Raine wheezed as she ran inside, still out of breath, trying to find Rhea.

The sound of a kettle reaching its boil could barely be heard, muffled by the loud siren. Whoever oversaw them probably lacked the opportunity to turn it off. Raine's ears had gotten used to the siren by then and quickly made her way to the kitchen, almost tripping over her own legs.

Raine's eyes grew wide and tears began to form as she saw her mother on the kitchen floor, a stab wound in her chest allowing blood to gush out and pool around her. Raine's heart sped up as Rhea's slowed down.

"Mom!" Raine screamed and ran over to Rhea's side, ignoring the icky sensation of the blood seeping into her pants as she kneeled next to her. "Please just hang in there! I'll heal you with my ability!" Frantically, Raine attempted to channel her dream energy from within, but she couldn't feel a speck of dream energy at all. She was too exhausted. Instead, Raine traded her invisibility cloak for a tourniquet, and attempted to stop Rhea's bleeding. She carefully tied the makeshift tourniquet, but her hands were still shaking.

Just a second after Raine finished tying the tourniquet, Raine's instincts immediately told her that something was wrong, and she quickly moved away from Rhea.

In that very split second, a black-dreamer jumped out from the corner and swung her machete at Raine, its blade missing Rhea and Raine by just an inch. Raine grew numb and got to her feet, taking a knife from the counter and holding it close to her chest. The black-dreamer's clothes were stained with red, her sharp and apathetic eyes landing on Raine. She dared to smirk. "You did this, didn't you?" Raine cried, filled with rage. Emotion overtook her mind, and she felt like something had possessed her into a defensive stance. She was ready to fight.

The black-dreamer chuckled, her fangs showing as she spat, "That old hag deserved it! It would've been better if she bled out years ago, before she decided to house a freak like you!"

Raine's face contorted in disgust. She knew that the black-dreamers had a vendetta against Revieras, as her generation was said to have curated the barrier in the first place, but for this to happen...

The black-dreamer's unkempt brown hair moved along with her skinny body as she charged again at Raine with her machete, stepping over Rhea's legs. Raine didn't dodge the black-dreamer's attack, but instead swung her knife too, and at the same time swung her fist at the black-dreamer with her other hand. The two blades hit each other with a clunk while Raine's punch landed on the black-dreamer, who yelled as the force of the punch pushed her out of balance, and she knocked over the boiling kettle whilst falling onto the ground.

The kettle spilt its contents on the ground, the water mixing with Rhea's blood. Raine's mind blanked out as the hot water made contact with Rhea and the black-dreamer, scalding them both. The black-dreamer dropped to the ground in shock from the boiling water, and Rhea's scream tuned out as Raine took the opportunity to swing and stab her knife with all her might at the black-dreamer. The knife landed directly in the black-dreamer's chest, and she yelled as the knife deeply inserted into her body.

Once Raine came back to her senses, she realised that she had just killed somebody with her own hands, and her mother was dying in front of her eyes. Raine had caused her even more pain by spilling burning water on her, and she began to cry when she fully processed what just happened in the last few seconds.

"Raine..." Raine almost missed Rhea's whisper of her name, her sobs louder than the chaos around her. Raine abruptly stopped her crying and ran to Rhea's side, avoiding the water. "It's too late for me...But you...Have to save everyone else..." Rhea muttered, almost incomprehensible.

"Don't say that! I can still save you! I can use my healing-" Raine started, but her voice got caught in her throat when Rhea coughed again, choking on her own blood as she tried to speak.

"You have to...find the map...and save Oneirolepsy...I love you, my little rainflower." Rhea's eyes closed, and they never opened again.

Raine felt her heart break, and she wailed for the next few minutes, refusing to believe what was happening. Just a few hours ago, she was waving goodbye to Rhea whilst nestling her five doves in her palms. Now she would never hear Rhea's voice again.

From the open window of the kitchen, Raine heard wailing aside from her own. Much younger and untamed sobs, sobs that belonged to a child. Someone whose childhood would be ruined thanks to the outbreak.

Raine stopped crying. She needed to ensure no other dreamers faced what she had just witnessed. She ran her fingers gently through Rhea's grey hair and whispered, "I love you."

As Raine left the kitchen, she noticed a vase on the living room table. It was miraculously left untouched amidst the chaos around. A bundle of blooming, white petals, its shape is that of a raindrop, hence the term 'rainflower'. Rhea had always used the term as an affectionate nickname for Raine. Much like Raine, the flower had healing properties utilising dream energy to help dreamers recover from any injuries or ailment. It would've been useful about three minutes ago, but there was no way Raine could've rushed into the living room to grab the flowers while taking on the machete-wielding black-dreamer.

Raine took the bundle of rainflowers and shoved them into her bag, noting that she would probably lose her healing capabilities like what had happened not too long ago. Raine zipped up her bag while her mind raced. *I have to get the map...? What does that mean?* Raine thought to herself, trying to piece back what Rhea had said in her last moments. She tried hard not to think about Rhea's death, and focused on what she had said.

That was when something clicked in her mind. A few years ago, when Raine was turning eighteen, she had started to get really interested in the geography and history of Oneirolepsy. She wanted nothing more than an adventure, and Rhea had fed into Raine's obsession by giving her a map on her birthday, alongside ten other overbearing gifts and a large cake.

"This map is very special. It's more than just a normal map," Rhea had told Raine. "When the time comes, you will need this map to find your way through the darkness."

"Darkness?" Raine had asked. She was still new to the concept of black-dreamers and had never met one before.

"You'll be the light to guide others in the darkness, just like these candles." Rhea pointed at the striped-coloured candles on Raine's birthday cake, their flames burning bright and strong. "Now blow out the candles and make a wish, dear."

Raine's tears snapped her out of her memories. *That's right! I left the map at the treehouse!* It was her second home located within the rainforest in the Mainland. A private forest where Raine had the privilege to access as the successor of the dreamers' leaders. She left Rhea's house in search of the map.

Raine gasped and stopped dead in her tracks at the very moment she stepped out onto Rhea's front yard. There was so much going on outside that Raine wanted to just curl up into a ball and disappear. She could see a dreamer in his car trying to hide from a pair of black-dreamers, who were puncturing the car's wheels and trying to shatter the glass windows with their fists. A few unlucky dreamers were caught out in the open, and their bodies were left on the ground with blood splattered everywhere.

Raine suppressed the urge to collapse. Tension hung in the atmosphere, and the air felt stifling. Quickly, she hugged her bag to her chest as she unzipped its contents and took out a rainflower. She held the flower close to her face as she smelled the flower, slowly regenerating her dream energy.

Raine pushed against the walls of the surrounding buildings while holding onto the rainflower for dear life, hugging her limbs close to her body to make herself hidden from the black-dreamers' sight. The last thing she wanted was to get caught.

The Mainland extended beyond the Dream realm, its name granted for its centre location connecting all the realms. Tall intimidating mountains filled the Dream realm, but it served no problem for Raine, who had a keen sense of direction, to navigate around. The rainforest called out to her, and subconsciously she could feel its presence all the time. Still, Raine wished she had a better method of transportation aside from her weary legs. She flinched multiple times as she heard cries from dreamers and yells from black-dreamers.

After a long time, Raine finally stepped into the invisible line dividing the Mainland and the Dream realm and continued making her way toward the rainforest. She saw the tall buildings of apartment flats built by the Mainland, a contrast to the relatively short houses back at the Dream realm, where most of

the houses had pointy roofs. The Mainland was
desolate, and everyone hid in their homes. Raine tried
to look past the buildings to catch a glimpse of the
greenery of the forest's trees, but couldn't see
anything past the smoke.

Wait, smoke?

Raine ran west, where the rainforest anticipated her
arrival.

The white petals of the rainflower turned into an ugly
shade of grey as smoke particles landed onto the
delicate plant, and Raine started to cough. She looked
up and saw bright orange overtaking what used to be
a calm and serene rainforest.

It took Raine longer than needed to realise her
rainforest had been set ablaze, leaving her jaw agape.
Something about the fire seemed unnatural, and it
bothered Raine enough for her to concede. She
backed out with her shaky legs, accepting the loss of
her home. She had already lost so many precious
things to her, including Rhea, and she didn't want to
add her own life into that list.

"Nope...Can't do this...I'll just go to an emergency
bunker or something. I'm not cut out for this..." Raine
muttered to herself as she stepped away, but then she
heard a voice in her head.

*You need to save Oneirolepsy. The map will guide
you. Find it.*

Raine stopped moving, and wondered if the voice she
heard was her first symptom of going crazy.

This is your calling, Revieras. Listen to it.

"Why should I listen to it? How am I supposed to do anything on my own, much less save the world?" She called out to nobody.

It's your responsibility, Raine. The voice called out to her again, emphasising on her name. It would've been more convincing if it was Rhea's voice, but instead, it was another female voice that Raine had never heard before. Something about it persuaded Raine nontheless, and she decided to take on the role of Revieras.

She gripped onto the rainflower and clenched her teeth. *The voice is right. It is my responsibility. I need to save Oneirolepsy. I need to rescue my people from the black-dreamers.*

Raine held the stem of the rainflower with her mouth and fumbled about in her breast pocket, releasing a soft exhale as she felt a piece of fabric. She took the fabric out, revealing a handkerchief that Raine had used for one of her disappearing acts during her show. Raine then took out her water bottle and unscrewed the lid. The water poured down like a waterfall and seeped into the handkerchief, which absorbed some of the water. Most of the water trickled off Raine's palms and landed on the dead grass, and Raine quickly moved her boots away to prevent them from getting wet.

Raine removed the rainflower dangling from her mouth and kept it in her now empty breast pocket, screwing the lid back onto the bottle. It was a large container, and Raine had been too busy to remember to hydrate herself. She covered her mouth and nose with her wet handkerchief, unsure if her tactic was actually useful, but it gave her assurance of easier breathing, and would increase her chances of survival once she did enter the burning rainforest.

Counting down from five in her head, Raine prepared for the worst, and when she reached one, began running headfirst into the rainforest.

★ ✦ ★

Chapter 2: Rainforest

Navigation became a challenge in the obscured path ahead, the smoke and the identical trees with the lack of a clear path proving to be a formidable opponent against Raine's desire to reach her treehouse. But none of these factors deterred her.

The smoke grew thicker, and Raine's handkerchief hardly helped, save for muffling her coughing. Somewhere in her mind, Raine felt the treehouse calling out to her, whether because of the map or because of the Old Tree's dream energy she didn't know. The Old Tree, being known as an immortal tree and a core source of dream energy, was rooted somewhere deep into the rainforest, accompanied with an ever flowing river rich in clean water. Youthful grass and healthy rainflowers grew in its vicinity as well, the refreshing air always a pleasure to take in. In the past, Raine would rest against the bark of the Old Tree and write in her dream journal, taking in the scent of the rainflowers and fresh nature.

Rhea had told Raine before that the special map she received on her birthday was created from the Dream Weavers themselves, after planting the seed of the Old Tree, blessing both the tree and the map with dream magic and divinity, allowing them to be practically indestructible. Raine's treehouse was quite the distance away from the Old Tree, but the latter served as a landmark to guide Raine around the forest. In

fact, Raine was probably the only person in
Oneirolepsy who knew how to navigate around the
large rainforest.

Too much ash piled onto the handkerchief, and it
proved to be redundant to carry around. Raine
dropped the handkerchief and used her arm to cover
her mouth instead, which only blocked her already
hazy view of where she was heading. By some miracle,
though, a flight of man-made stairs caught Raine's
attention. She was reaching the treehouse.

It was a magical place that Raine lived in, nestled
high among the lush canopy of towering trees. Its
wooden structure blended seamlessly with the
surrounding foliage, safely built and decorated with
vines, flowers, and plants, the height offering a
breathtaking view of the rainforest and the sky itself.

The Old Tree was the tallest and most majestic tree
in the rainforest, but Raine always liked the tree her
treehouse was built on more, despite it lacking any
defining or fancy features. Even though she had to
climb a ridiculous number of stairs to reach the
treehouse, the open-air living space with wide,
weathered planks always made the exercise worth it.

Unfortunately, in this case, there was nothing worth
climbing a tall flight of stairs in the middle of a forest
fire. Raine somehow wished she could exchange her
ability to heal with the ability to fly, or at least turn
into a bird at will, but she had no choice but to climb,
working her legs to death.

Raine felt herself burning up, but she finally reached the entrance. She opened the front door and immediately shut it behind her to block out all the smoke from flowing into her home. There was just barely enough protection to keep out the fire from completely burning up the treehouse. Nostalgia choked Raine as she remembered how she would spend her time with Rhea in the treehouse all the time, but something else choked her even more - the suffocating smoke from all the fire. Raine's treehouse was open-spaced, and the smoke had welcomed its way in despite the door having been shut completely.

Raine dropped her heavy bag onto the floor to move faster, and like a burglar, began to tear the whole place down. Even though Raine liked to think of herself as an organised person, she could never find anything she searched for on the first attempt. She rummaged through her cupboards, drawers, desks, and even under her bean bag chair, only to find it under her pillow after ten minutes of searching. Raine gave herself a lecture about her lack of tidiness causing such an inconvenience before going back and retrieving her bag and keeping the map inside, where it was safer.

Not wanting to be in the burning forest any longer, Raine departed from the treehouse. Just as she sped down the stairs, her peripheral vision caught a silhouette moving from down below.

Raine froze.

Initially, she presumed it was an animal attempting to escape, but the shape of the silhouette suggested otherwise.

Assuming that she was just hallucinating, Raine fled down the stairs. A branch had fallen just an inch away from her, and Raine was glad she chose not to hesitate, although now she had a feeling that there was a new threat to Raine's life other than the forest fire.

A bright amber light suddenly appeared, grabbing Raine's attention. Distracted, Raine took a misstep, and tripped over something, possibly a rock, and tumbled down to the dirty ground. Raine let out a gasp, only to start coughing, and struggled to get up with her bag. She turned to see what had distracted her, only to find nothing but more fire. The silhouette was nowhere to be found, and Raine wasn't sure if she should feel scared or relieved.

Raine began treading carefully without making any noise, sacrificing her lungs for stealth. Her eyes grew watery from holding in her coughs, and her vision left her in the smog.

Swerving around a tree, Raine almost had a heart attack when she saw the silhouette just in front of her. She hid back behind the tree and crouched down, squinting her eyes to see what the silhouette really was. She was practically blind by that point, but she could see that it was another person. Whether or not it was a black-dreamer Raine couldn't tell - there was no presence of any nightmare energy. But Raine

figured that a normal, sane, dreamer wouldn't ever be
in a burning rainforest, so she had to assume it was
either a black-dreamer with weak nightmare energy,
or a dreamer who had escaped from a mental asylum.

Both options didn't sound very safe, so Raine tried to
find an alternative route. But her eyes were glued to
the silhouette - as if she was watching a spider on a
wall in her room, making sure it didn't suddenly run
off and end up killing Raine. She could only see their
short and wavy titian hair, an orange ombre fading
from the edges, with the top of their head covered by a
black cap. Raine's eyes travelled to their arms, where
both had been wrapped in dirty gauze bandages. Their
entire jacket was black, and Raine couldn't tell if it
was its original colour or if it was the ash staining
their clothes. The person thankfully faced away from
Raine's direction, and they were making some sort of
gesture with their hands outwardly to the fire.

Raine was convinced that the person was completely
unhinged, and began to retrace her steps. *I can't risk
getting caught. I'll just move somewhere else-*
  RIIIIIIING!

The ringtone belonging to Raine's phone called out
to the mysterious figure, easily distinguishable from
the cackling sounds of fire. Raine immediately
jumped and fumbled about to grab her phone. It was
Soraya calling her. Dismissing the phone call, Raine
saw that the person had gone missing.

Raine felt her heart attempting to jump out of her
chest, and she wished she could burrow herself into

bedrock and disappear. Her lip trembled and her hands were clenched, knowing that she was now exposed and out of hiding.

Within a second, the person jumped in front of Raine, their amber eyes meeting Raine's, allowing her thoughts to scatter everywhere like sheets of paper. She let out a surprised yell and stepped back, but a fallen tree blocked her escape.

"Woah? Another person here? And a dreamer, no less! Tell me, dreamer! What are you doing here in this world of flames? Have you come to seek the fiery thrill of pyrotechnics?" Their loud voice boomed out to Raine, clearly unbothered by the smoke and ash around them.

Raine managed to get a closer look and realised it was a black-dreamer, although he seemed to lack any nightmare energy. He also didn't appear to recognise Raine as Revieras, and instead talked to her casually with a bright grin. "Oh, do you happen to be a fire elemental as well? You look like one of those funny magic people. And you look like you're about to have an aneurysm any second now."

Raine furrowed her brows. "Um...I assume you're the one who started the fire?" She asked, mildly concerned about offending the black-dreamer. "Why, though?"

"I'll ask you a better question: Why not? If I have fire powers, then of course I'm going to use it! And what better way to use it than against an unsuspecting forest in the middle of a dream realm? I heard this

place is where Revieras is-" the black-dreamer cut
himself off, as if he had just realised something.
"Wait, *you're* Revieras, right? I didn't think any
dreamer would be cool enough to walk into a burning
forest. Hoho! Have I caught you off-guard while you
were resting peacefully in your bird's nest?"

Raine wondered if she should start preparing to run
away from the black-dreamer. "Uh, no, I actually ran
in here," she replied, not wanting to elaborate any
further.

"Well, that doesn't sound like a smart idea, but hey! I
don't judge. Fire is pretty great."

"So...you're a black-dreamer who's a fire elemental?"
Raine asked slowly.

"Black-dreamer? You mean nightmare? Is that some
dreamer euphemism or something?" He chuckled.
"It's stupid, just call us nightmares! Hell, we don't
care what you call us. And duh, I'm a fire elemental."
His face lit up again, but this time, it was more of a
malicious smirk than one of sudden realisation. "That
being said, since I already have Revieras in my trap, I
wonder what I should do with you? Maybe I could
roast you alive! What do you think of immolation
right now? I'll give your ashes to the King of
nightmares for his birthday. Except I don't really
know when his birthday is."

Unsure what to say, Raine remained quiet, and
looked about, trying to find the black-dreamer's relic.
They were what stored the essence of a
black-dreamer, and every black-dreamer had one.

They were essentially their weak spot, but Raine couldn't find anything resembling a relic, and instead got dizzy.

She inconspicuously unzipped her bag to take another rainflower, but the black-dreamer suddenly moved his hand in Raine's direction, and by impulse, she threw the phone that was still in her hand at him - a pitiful attempt at defense, and began running in the opposite direction.

"Hey, what gives? You missed, by the way!" His voice faded out as Raine continued to run, immediately regretting her decision to part with her phone. She took out a rainflower and consumed it, ignoring the bits of ash that landed on the petals as she stuffed them in her mouth. She felt her dream energy replenishing by a bit, and then a thought struck her mind.

I shouldn't be running away from the fire elemental, Raine thought, her legs moving faster than her mind. *It's bad if I leave the rainforest while he's still running around free. He might hurt the other dreamers! But I can't do anything in this situation-*

Raine failed to see where she was going and ended up tumbling over a slope. It wasn't too steep, but she still ended up on the floor, and got back up, only to get kicked down by the black-dreamer, who had appeared seemingly out of the fires. "You know, it's kind of a shortcut when you can walk through the flames." He let out a boastful laugh, keeping Raine on the ground. "Oh, right, you dropped this." He dropped

Raine's phone on top of her, and she let out a sharp
exhale as the phone hit her head. She winced as the
throbbing pain lingered in her head, sucking the
non-existent air through her clenched teeth.

The phone dropped next to Raine on the ground, and
she was more surprised it hadn't melted in the fifteen
seconds it had been with the fire elemental. "Damn it!
What do you want from me?" She asked, more
annoyed than afraid.

"Nothing, really. Koshalv wants you dead though. I
might as well do that, since y'know, he's the King and
all that," the fire-elemental gave a perfunctory shrug.
"Besides, I'm not just going to leave *Revieras* alone
without doing anything. I'm not letting this rare
opportunity fly past me."

Raine began sweating as she realised she might not
make it out alive. She didn't like what the fire
elemental was implying, and began struggling to get
up from the ground. Her torso was being locked in by
the fire elemental's feet and she couldn't properly
stand up, but it gave her enough freedom to move her
arms out from under her chest. She still couldn't pull
or attack the fire elemental with her bare arms alone,
though - she was out of reach.

Raine remembered that she had an extra piece of
flash paper hidden under her sleeve. It was meant for
a dove trick that she never got to execute because of
the interruption, and now that she thought about it,
there were only four doves that she pulled out and left

behind at Dreamer's Cove, when she had prepared *five* in her sleeve.

Raine pulled the flash paper out and linked it with the lighter contraption by pulling her two sleeves together, her years of being a magician allowing her to pull the move off within less than a second, and without any suspicion. In that small flash, she pulled out a fifth dove from her sleeve, which immediately flew in the fire elemental's face, stressed from the sudden heated environment.

The fire elemental let out a surprised yell as the dove that appeared seemingly out of nowhere began pecking at him ruthlessly. "Hey, what the heck?" The fire elemental stumbled away from Raine and started using his hand to shoo away the dove, which was in his face and refusing to fly away. Raine felt a little apologetic for the dove, but quickly got up, grabbed her phone, and fled to where the Old Tree was.

The Old Tree was a source of dream energy - the opposite of nightmare energy. Even though Raine wasn't able to detect any nightmare energy from the fire elemental, she was sure that he was still a black-dreamer, and dream energy was the black-dreamers' kryptonite. She hoped to lure the fire elemental into the dream energy core and stop him from there.

Catching a glimpse of the dove finally flying away into the sky, Raine heard footsteps behind her, and recognised it as the fire elemental being on her tail. *Now I just need to get to the Old Tree.*

After several turns and swerves, a river connecting to the Old Tree came into view. Raine was relieved to see that the water was still flowing through the river, a true miracle with the help of dream magic. The Old Tree refused to falter from the fire, chasing away the flames with its dream energy. Its leaves were as green as ever, and it stood tall, showing no signs of defeat from the flames, which were nowhere to be seen in the area.

Raine ran up to the Old Tree, seeking for fresh air. She placed a palm on its trunk and let out a sigh, then taking a deep breath for oxygen. The fire elemental stopped before the river, reasonably confused by the presence of water.

"That doesn't seem right," he frowned, looking at the Old Tree. "How is that even possible?" The fire elemental summoned a ball of flame from his hands, but it fizzled out as soon as it reached the radius of the Old Tree.

Ignoring the dream energy around the Old Tree, the fire elemental walked closer to the tree, mildly fascinated and at the same time annoyed. Raine felt surmounting panic when she realised he wasn't affected by the dream energy at all. "Wait, aren't you supposed to fall under dream energy? How are you able to even get remotely close to the Old Tree?"

The fire elemental chuckled, and Raine took a few steps back, feeling her heart pounding at her chest. "You think I'll crumble over some dream energy?

Hohoho! You are severely misunderstood, Revieras, for I, the magnificent fire elemental-"

It started to rain.

Raindrops started to pour down Raine's face, cooling her down almost immediately. The downpour was heavier than usual, but it wasn't enough to put out the entire forest fire. Still, it sufficed for the fire elemental to start panicking and cursing in pure terror as he got doused in rainwater.

Raine watched the fire elemental running around trying to find non-existent shelter. She sighed, feeling half relieved that the weather had saved her, but she also felt half bad for the fire elemental. "Um...Do you need help?" She asked, reluctantly.

The fire elemental didn't stop running about, and for a second, Raine doubted if he had heard her, but then he glared at Raine. "What? No! As if I'm going to accept help from Revieras!"

Raine crossed her arms and watched him run about in vain for a few more seconds before the fire elemental spoke again. "Okay, fine! Fine! Get me out of this rain!"

Taking off a layer from her magician's outfit, Raine walked over to the fire elemental and threw her jacket over his head as a makeshift umbrella. "My treehouse isn't too far off. Now if you promise not to hurt me, I'll-"

"Yeah, yeah, fine, just go!"

Raine rolled her eyes and began running to where the treehouse was, leading the fire elemental along

the way. *What am I doing?* Raine recollected
everything that just transpired half an hour ago,
hugging her bag which contained the map as she ran
to her treehouse, while ignoring the fire elemental's
wailing.

* * *

The fire elemental skipped up the stairs leading
toward Raine's treehouse, and immediately burst
open the door to seek shelter. Raine followed behind
sluggishly, ignoring the fact that she probably needed
new hinges for the door now. The heavy rain had
extinguished the fire surrounding the treehouse,
although she wasn't completely sure if the other areas
had cleared up. Regardless, she welcomed herself
back inside the treehouse, and found the fire
elemental taking off his hat and jacket, cursing to
himself about his wet clothes. Raine was convinced he
was a minute away from having a panic attack over
being caught in rain. "Are you alright?" She asked.

"No! Of course not! You wouldn't ask a drowning
man if they were okay, would you?" Even though the
analogy didn't match up, Raine sighed and took back
her jacket which the fire elemental had thrown on the
ground. She unhooked the lighter contraption from
the jacket's sleeve and dried it so the lighter could
work again.

The fire elemental immediately took the lighter from
Raine, who then went around to close every door and

window so that the rain wouldn't spill inside her home. "I have a feeling you're going to try to kill me again," she commented, watching the fire elemental messing with the lighter. "What happens if you get left in the rain? Do you die or something?"

"Well, no. But it'd definitely interfere with my elemental powers. And I hate the feeling of getting soaked, okay? Don't judge me here!"

"I'm not. In fact, I'm the one that should be ridiculed for helping you out." Raine rolled her eyes. "Look, this is my first time dealing with a black-dreamer by myself, and I don't want to hurt you or anything, but I also don't want you going around causing fires with your elemental powers."

"Well, too bad. I'm not planning on stopping anytime soon."

Raine frowned. "Do you need me to book you a therapy session for your pyromania? Is that it?"

The fire elemental snapped at Raine. "How dare you! I control the fires, not the other way around." He crossed his arms, pouting. "I'm the best fire elemental there is! I don't need anyone telling me what I can or cannot do. It's called freedom."

"It's called being an arsonist."

"Pssh, same thing."

Raine rolled her eyes. "Why do you even want to set fire to everything, then, if it's not caused by pyromania? There's no point in destroying everything. You have nothing to gain from it."

"Not everything is about gaining or losing. I'm doing this because I want to, and I like it. I don't care what anyone else thinks."

Raine couldn't believe how selfish the fire elemental sounded. "We all live in the same land, the very land that you're destroying. And anyway, what will you do if there's nothing left? When everything turns to cinders, will you really feel satisfied knowing that you've destroyed the world and those who live in it?"

The fire elemental let out a chuckle. "Me? Setting fire to the whole world? Oh, that sounds incredible! Besides, I would much rather live a fun and unrestrained life than a boring one without fire. I mean, there's so many rules! Oh, you can't set fire to this or that, you can't hurt another dreamer because that's *wrong*."

"We have rules for a reason. It's to have a peaceful life."

"A peaceful life is nothing compared to fire."

Raine felt like she was trying to convince a crack addict to give up on drugs, except it was a fire addict instead. "You're ignorant and missing out on a lot of great things in life because of your pyromania. But I guess you can enjoy the lesser things in life and get arrested, I dunno." Raine pretended to shrug dismissively.

"I am *not* a pyromaniac!" shouted the fire elemental, allowing Raine to confirm the fact that he was, in fact, a pyromaniac. "And you're just lying. There's nothing in life that can beat fire."

"There are a lot of things in life greater than fire," Raine stated confidently, arousing the fire elemental's curiosity. She saw his dubious expression and elaborated. "I'm not lying. I can show some of them to you. How about a proposal?"

"A what, now?"

"Y'know, like a business proposal."

"Oh? I'm listening."

Raine sighed. "Listen. As Revieras, I have to restore the barrier and stop whatever the black-dreamers are doing. If we can just have a truce and agree to work together, I can let you in on an adventure to save the world. How about it?"

The fire elemental considered. "Saving the world? Isn't destroying it more fun?"

Raine looked over her room and saw a potted plant resting on a table. "Take that pot over there. Sure, it'll be fun if you knocked it over and broke it. But isn't it more interesting and fun to try to revert it back to how it usually was? But it's more than just a potted plant. We're trying to save the entire world. And you've already been destroying things for a long time. Why not try something new? It'll give you more thrill and entertainment than any fire can. And you said you weren't a pyromaniac, so you can prove that to me by joining my side and promise not to set fire to anything unless it's necessary. So, you won't be completely banned from using your elemental powers." Raine watched the fire elemental's expression carefully, trying to gauge if she was succeeding in convincing him. "I'll protect you from the other dreamers who'll try to capture you, and we can save the world together."

Silence struck as the black-dreamer's face lit up, admittedly impressed by Raine's speech. Raine prayed for him to accept her offer while the downpour simmered down into nothing but a tiny drizzle, waiting impatiently as he considered the proposal.

Finally, after what felt like an entire hour of silence, much to Raine's relief, the fire elemental smiled. "Alright, I'm in. But don't pull any dreamer tricks on me, Revieras. Especially no doves."

※★✦★※
Chapter 3: Egotism

Raine couldn't help but smile. She had succeeded. "That's great to hear! I promise you won't be disappointed. We'll need to leave this place first. The rain should have stopped by now. Follow me. I know the way out." Raine walked to the exit and waited for the fire elemental to put his hat and jacket back on, throwing Raine's lighter back at her. As Raine reattached the lighter contraption back to the sleeve of her jacket, she gained two realisations: One, she should probably invest in a blow dryer. And two, the fire elemental would have probably gotten himself trapped in the burning rainforest if Raine hadn't offered him the route out.

Fire and smoke refused to depart from the forest, even with the rain attempting to chase them out. However, they dwindled significantly enough for Raine to walk back to her treehouse with less difficulty than before, having the fire elemental be surprisingly cooperative in following her. She still didn't know if he was just tricking or using her, and even though she knew it was a horrible idea, she decided to place her trust in him. She couldn't do much either way - she could only heal and shoot little bullets of dream energy, and given that the fire elemental had hardly been fazed by the Old Tree, Raine didn't need to be tested to know she wouldn't be able to fare against him alone. She just thanked the unpredictable weather for saving her life and tried not to die subsequently.

Raine and the fire elemental made it out of the burning rainforest after what felt like an hour of constant walking in the rainforest. She was surprised she had managed to escape such a place in one piece and even somehow teamed up with a black-dreamer, who stretched his arms once he got out, seemingly happy from the adventure he just had in the forest.

"You're not able to extinguish the fire, are you?" Raine asked, once her view was free of smoke and ash. She felt glad to be able to breathe and see clearly again.

"Even if I could, why would I do such a thing?" The black-dreamer responded, admiring his work. Raine rolled her eyes at his response and watched the poor rainforest still burning.

"Jeez, okay. I'll just call the firefighters." Raine kept the remaining stalks of rainflowers in her breast pocket and took out her phone.

"Firefighters?" He asked, as if he had never heard of such a term. Raine ignored him and dialled the number for the firefighters, putting the call on speaker. The fire elemental stared at the phone like a curious child, ignoring Raine's side eye.

An unusual sound of static started playing on the call, sending chills down Raine's spine.

"Two...Two...One...One...Four..." A robot's voice played over the static, reciting an unknown number.

Raine's grip on the phone loosened, and an urge to find out what the number was.

"Maybe I'll call the number? Let me write it down..." Raine murmured, starting to dial the number on her phone. The fire elemental slapped Raine's phone away, letting it soar into the sky before dropping onto the concrete ground.

"Hey! What was that for?" Raine asked, raising her voice. She ran over to pick up the phone, inspecting for any damage. "Oh, great, the screen protector has a crack now!"

"You're welcome, I just saved you from another nightmare," The fire elemental said, nonchalantly. Raine furrowed her eyebrows.

"A black-dreamer?" She rephrased, confused.

"You promised an adventure," The black-dreamer pointed out, refusing to elaborate on what just happened.

"Oh, of course. I'm not quite sure what I have to do exactly though, which is why I have the map." Raine rubbed the scratch mark on her phone screen before placing it back into the safety of her bag, and then took out the map. "You still haven't told me how you're able to handle dream energy," she commented, watching the fire elemental carefully.

"Yeah, don't worry about it," he replied, dismissively.

"It's still strange, though, that I haven't detected any extreme nightmare energy from you. You *are* a black-dreamer, right?" Raine asked, holding the map near her chest.

"And proud," he grinned widely.

Raine sighed and decided to carry on with inspecting the map. Part of it was burnt, though not from the forest fire. The map showed an outline of Oneirolepsy, along with a guided symbol of a compass. She turned the map around and found a paragraph of an old text in an archaic script called Orael. Raine frowned, never having seen the segment in all the while she's had the map. The paper had aged and the text was small, but Rhea had taught her how to read Orael since she was young. Despite Raine never having practised her proficiency in Orael, she tried her best to translate the passage.

"This map reveals the locations of the Dreamkeepers, whose souls contain a fragment of a key to...the ultimate weapon?" Raine paused, slowing down with her translation. "The ultimate weapon will be able to help restore what has been broken, and rescue the world from...danger," Raine continued, rephrasing some bits so as to not offend the black-dreamer. "There is a Dreamkeeper for each realm: Ambition, Subliminal, Dream. Revieras, the Keeper of Dreams, must locate each Dreamkeeper and unlock the ultimate weapon in Kolshav's Castle."

"Koshalv?" The black-dreamer asked, referring to the King of nightmares.

"Some of this text is illegible." Raine squinted at the text, skipping over the unreadable parts and continuing. "To reveal the Dreamkeepers' location, you must recite a spell: Irah salma iae abad."

As the last consonant left Raine's tongue, the text on the map glowed a golden yellow, blinding Raine. When the light faded, Raine turned the map, and found there was now a pinpoint on the map. The pinpoint looked like a token - a red symbol contrasting the musty brown of the map.

"The Ambition realm's emblem!" Raine placed her finger on the insignia. "But where are the other two? Never mind, we'll head to the Ambition realm first." Raine looked up ahead. The siren had stopped sounding a while ago when she was still in the rainforest, and it was quiet. "Maybe we can get to the Ambition realm through the Mainland. It's the fastest way there." She added.

"Alright! We're heading off then? Lead the way, Revieras!" The fire elemental announced, excitedly.

"Just call me Raine." She kept the map in her bag and began to walk forward, but then stopped, and turned to face the black-dreamer. "Oh, before I forget. What's your name?"

"Kegan. Glad to have Revieras on my side now, I guess. Oh, sorry, I mean *Raine*." Kegan sneered.

The realisation that Raine had befriended a black-dreamer sunk in, and she contemplated whether she should trick him into arrest, but for now she played along. "Okay, the Ambition realm is that way. Follow me."

Raine started making her way back to the town where she had last seen Rhea. Kegan was strolling along at a quicker pace than her, and went even faster after getting acquainted with the route they were going.

Meanwhile, Raine took out her phone, remembering that Soraya had called her not too long ago. She was a little annoyed that Soraya was the reason why Kegan had found her out in the first place, but decided not to hold it against her. Instead, Raine called to see if she was alright.

Raine dialled Soraya's number and held the phone up to her ear, only to face disappointment when she heard the same static noise and the eerie repetition of the number. There was something foreboding about the noise, and Raine quickly ended the call before something bad happened.

Did a black-dreamer hack all of our devices? She wondered. Raine sent Soraya a message instead, hoping it was just the call system that was hacked. She told of Kegan and what had taken place in the rainforest, and prayed for Soraya's safety. Almost immediately, the phone registered Soraya's acknowledgement of Raine's message, but there was no response. Raine started worrying about what had happened to Soraya, only for her train of thought to be disrupted by Kegan's loud voice.

"Hey, are dreamers usually this quiet? I don't see anyone here." He glanced in all four directions, in search of another being. Strangely enough, despite the wrecking in town, there was no one to be found.

"Huh. Strange. The last time I was here-" Her voice stopped for a second as she recalled what had transpired then. "There were a lot of people around. Maybe the dreamers are hiding safely, and the black-dreamers have already been taken care of."

"How weak. I wouldn't be hiding nor caught in some prison," Kegan scoffed.

Raine questioned how her sanity would remain with someone like him around. What if someone caught her hanging around with a black-dreamer such as Kegan, and even worse, a pyromaniac? She could be found as suspicious, and her position as the leader of dreamers would be on the line, not that she wanted to be in possession of such a title anyway.

The town was silent as ever, but as Raine and Kegan got deeper into the town, a static-like sound started blending into the environment. Raine didn't notice it at first, but it became obvious once she saw the many blaring screens hung around town.

Before Raine could see any of the televisions and billboards, Kegan had turned around and shoved his cap into Raine's face, obstructing her view with black fabric and the smell of ash. "Hey! What gives?" She yelled, trying to push the cap away. Her efforts were rewarded with a harsh slap on her arm.

"Don't look unless you want a nightmare to enslave you," Kegan said.

"What?" Raine's instincts wanted her to remove the cap, but her gut feeling objected. "Then what am I supposed to do? I can't see where I'm going!"

"Yeah, that's the whole point, idiot."

An arm grabbed onto Raine, but the coldness of the touch told Raine that the arm wasn't Kegan's. She yelled as she was helplessly dragged back, wanting nothing more than to throw the cap away to see what was happening.

"Woah, where did you guys come from?" Raine heard Kegan ask. Her clothes were tugged from the back by someone, their grip tight and suffocating. Nightmare energy radiated off of them, their cold breath causing strands of her hair to stand.

"The queen demands to see the two of you," They spoke monotonously. Raine's heart thumped against her suit.

"Queen? Who's the queen?" Her muffled voice was barely heard.

"Queen Vanity, Divine ruler of all nightmares, epitome of beauty and soon-to-be sovereign of the Mainland. She wishes to see you in person."

A black-dreamer? Raine thought.

"Where is she?" Kegan asked, his voice edged with excitement. Raine was about to refute, but decided it would be best to find the source of whatever was going on. After all, if a black-dreamer was involved, then the dreamers living in the town were definitely in danger, and Raine had to save them.

A much warmer grip held onto Raine's free arm. "What's happening?" She questioned, her legs moving without her realising. "Why aren't I allowed to see anything?"

"It's Vanity's ability. Anyone who sees her reflection will fall under her spell," Kegan explained, his voice suddenly much closer than Raine had expected. "Guess a lot of nightmares and dreamers fell victim to her. She probably hacked all the devices to show pictures of her."

"Then why aren't you affected?" Raine asked.

"I have the ability where no other abilities can affect me directly. Wish I could've gotten a cooler ability, but whatever."

Raine surveyed his answer. Both dreamers and black-dreamers had the potential to unlock an ability, though they tend to never be discovered by the individual throughout their life. It was considered rare to possess an ability, but Raine was lucky to inherit Rhea's gift of healing. She wondered how Vanity first discovered her ability.

"You seem quite excited to see Vanity," Raine said.

"Oh yeah. We're friends."

Raine fell silent, unsure what to make of his answer. "So...You're helping her capture me?"

"Why would I do that? We just started our adventure. And anyway, Vanity doesn't need any help. She can collect your head herself."

"My head?" Raine asked, baffled.

Kegan chuckled and said nothing more.

Raine's legs carried on mindlessly. At first, she was worried about bumping into someone or hurting herself somehow, but she had gone on for a while without touching anything so far. This caused Raine to feel even more tense, but that tension broke when somebody tugged at her clothes again, stopping her from moving. "We are here," The brainwashed black-dreamer said.

Kegan removed the cap from Raine's view, her eyes blinded by the drastic change in light. She took a deep breath and blinked several times. In front of her was a pearl gate. Beyond the gates was a giant mansion, and from the gaps in between the gates, Raine could spot flowing water from a fountain. The mansion was light grey with many arches and windows. She examined the height of the mansion and saw the flag of the Mainland on the rooftop.

"Wait, we're at the minister's mansion?" Raine questioned, both in awe and fear of what she was doing there.

One of Vanity's minions handed Kegan a phone, to which he gladly accepted. Raine tried to take a peek, but Kegan pulled the phone away. "Sup, Vanity?" He greeted, a warning in disguise for Raine not to come close.

"Kegan! There you are!" Vanity's accent and voice was alluring, and Raine couldn't help but imagine how her body would match her voice. Vanity sounded relieved at first, but then immediately followed up her sentence with a mocking tone. "Thought you got caught by the dreamers, which is something that I'd never let happen to me. I'm too great for that. Though, I can understand why they'd try to capture *this* beauty!" She let out a cocky laugh. "Oh, I look absolutely perfect. They should make me queen immediately! Oh wait, I'm already doing that, ahahaha! Beauty and brains, that's just how I am, perfect, as always. I bet all the dreamers are jealous that a nightmare can be so gorgeous!"

Kegan ignored everything Vanity said and gave no comment. "Right, anyway, I was just lighting things up as usual. Your followers brought us to a mansion. What's up with that?"

"I told you I was going to be queen. I'm going to rule over the Mainland. They should be happy that such a nightmare as I get to be their ruler! Why don't you come in and join me? I bet I'm a sight for your sore eyes, haha! Don't you just love how long my eyelashes are? How fair my skin is? How flawless my hair looks?"

The locked gates swung open, although Vanity was still droning on about her flawless beauty. Neither Kegan nor Raine bothered to pay any attention to her.

One of the minions took the phone from Kegan's hand, and the horde pushed them past the gate. As if a flip had been switched, the subdued followers broke out into angry groups, and began charging into the mansion. Many left behind to wreck the fountain and landscape. The silence was pierced by mad shouts and Vanity's cackle.

Kegan dragged Raine to the side of the mansion before she could be trampled over by the many followers. "Vanity should be somewhere over here," he said, trotting over to the back of the mansion.

"Wait, wait! What about Mr Jamison? He's not going to be able to handle all of those followers!" Raine turned her head around, only to see nothing but ongoing destruction.

"For all we know, that old man has probably already been cursed as well." Kegan rolled his eyes dismissively, but then someone caught his attention. Raine heard the sound of heels closing up to her and Kegan, and immediately buried her face into the crook of her elbow, leaving a small gap so she could just barely see Kegan.

"Vanity!" Kegan waved excitedly.

"Kegan, I was told by one of my followers that you were hanging out with that freak," Vanity said, in a displeased tone. Raine frowned when she realised Vanity was referring to her. "I assumed you had captured her, but the way you're holding her hand says otherwise," Vanity pointed an accusative finger at him. "This is treachery! How could you help out our enemy like that?"

"Yo, you don't have to hide from her," Kegan assured Raine, ignoring Vanity's warning.

"Are you sure? What about her ability?" Raine slowly lifted her face from her arm, and for the first time, caught a clear view of Vanity. Her several silver jewellery including necklaces and bracelets complemented her one-piece dress which was the colour of a raven's feather, and her long wavy black hair draped behind her back like a waterfall. Vanity's sharp glossy eyes met Raine's, the rest of her face covered by a mask. A golden crown rested elegantly on the top of her head.

"What have you done to Kegan? Have you brainwashed him with your dreamer tricks?" Vanity's brows creased. Raine opened her mouth to respond, but Kegan spoke first.

"I would never fall under anybody. You of all people should know that, Vanity," he shook his head and stepped forward, inching closer towards Vanity. "And don't accuse me of being a traitor. I was never loyal to Koshalv in the first place."

Vanity took a step back and averted her gaze. "Are you going to stop me then? Will you be going against Koshalv? Our very king?"

Raine felt an eerie sensation, as if she was being watched by pairs of eyes, and saw that many of Vanity's followers had surrounded the two and blocked the exit. "Kegan!" She alerted him.

"Normally I wouldn't mind, but you're trying to capture the someone who promised to show me something greater than fire. We may be friends, but that doesn't mean you can stop me from having some fun."

"Darn dreamer. You've blinded my friend with your hopeless light," Vanity grunted. She took and held out something before she threw it over Kegan's head. It dropped on the ground right in front of Raine's boots.

"No, don't look!" Kegan called to Raine, who gasped as she glanced at the object.

It was a polaroid of Kegan and Vanity together. Vanity's face was as clear as day, her eyes staring into Raine's soul, and her lips curled into a smile. The image of Vanity burned into Raine's brain, and the static noise returned all at once, amplified tenfold.

Kegan snapped his fingers, and the polaroid was promptly incinerated and reduced to a pile of ash. But it was too late. Raine felt her mind going numb, the only thing going through her head was Vanity's name.

※★◆★※

Chapter 4: Hijack

"Damn it, you idiot!" Kegan watched Raine as she lifted her head. She had the same emotionless expression as the rest of the followers, her mouth slightly ajar.

The circle of followers chanted Vanity's name, and she laughed. "Looks like your new friend has fallen under my spell!" She took out her keychain and slid it on her fingers, doubling as a spiky weapon. "Capture him!"

Several arms reached out to grab Kegan, but they quickly retreated when their fingertips started to melt off within an instant. Instead, about ten cursed dreamers jumped onto Kegan all at the same time. Surprised by their reckless attack, Kegan tumbled onto the ground, but managed to kick the dreamers away before they could grab onto him.

"Don't expect yourself to be welcomed by Koshalv when you inevitably return to the darkness," Vanity adjusted her crown and glanced at Kegan, who had gotten back on his feet and was now returning the favour of being thrown to the ground.

"I was never into darkness. The fires that burn brighter than the sun are more favourable," Kegan responded, throwing meteors of fire in all directions. They exploded into bursts of flames, and the cursed dreamers screamed bloody murder as their bodies melted, their faces drooping off.

Vanity glared at him. "Go to hell," she cursed, before running towards the entrance of the mansion. More of her minions marched towards Kegan like mindless zombies. He took care of them with little difficulty, his fire abilities overpowering them in an instant.

The back of the mansion was now back into the familiar state of burning with tall glowing flames, and just as Kegan launched another fireball, an explosion occurred midair as it made impact with something else.

Kegan sensed particles of dream energy lingering about in the explosion, and within the blazing field, he saw Raine.

Raine shot out pure energy blasts directly charged at Kegan, and he had to return the favour of shooting out fireball blasts to stop her attacks.

"I guess Vanity got into your head after all," Kegan sighed.

Raine stood silent, unresponsive. She then began to charge at Kegan. He shrugged and blocked her punches before throwing her on the ground, only to find that she had disappeared.

Feeling the presence of a dreamer behind him, Kegan turned around, but was too late. Raine appeared and attacked him with a blast of dream energy, and he ended up getting hit.

Kegan summoned a barricade of flames dividing the ground between Raine and himself. More of Vanity's minions were on Kegan's side now, and they were trying to grab onto him.

"Alright, that's enough!" Kegan shouted out,
preparing to incinerate everything and everyone in his
way.

*** *** ***

Soon after, Kegan left the back of the mansion,
leaving hundreds of charred bodies behind. The whole
landscape was set ablaze, but Raine was nowhere to
be found. "Ugh. Why do magicians always go for a
disappearing act?" He muttered to himself. As he
scanned the whole mansion, he heard a faint chanting
coming from inside the mansion. The main entrances
had been burst open, and he took a peek from outside
to see what was occurring inside.

"Vanity! Vanity!" Kegan could hear more of Vanity's
minions chanting her name. They were scattered
about everywhere in the mansion. But not a second
passed by when they were obliterated by the undying
flames, and their chanting of their leader was instead
replaced with blood-curdling screams.

The soft white palette of the mansion rooms was
replaced with a fiery orange, the stairs stained with
prints of ash. Heavy footsteps rang out as Kegan
chased after Vanity upstairs.

He felt a pull on his leg and fell back on the steps
with Raine throwing him down. He tumbled down the
staircase, but not before dragging Raine down with
him. Using her body as a cushion, he got back up and
encircled the mindless Raine in a ring of flames. The

flames rose to her height, and now nobody from the outside could see that there was anyone inside the hollow pillar of fire.

Kegan watched Raine walk through the fire as if it wasn't there, her body liquefying with the heat. But her hand reached into her breast pocket and she pulled out a rainflower, seemingly fireproof, and absorbed its dream energy. Combined with her healing ability, Raine became immune to the fire, her body unharmed.

Kegan shuddered at the thought of Vanity being competent enough to make use of Raine's ability, aside from the fact that he hadn't actually thought that Raine would walk through his fire barricade. Regardless, he ignored Raine's stunt and pushed forward in chasing Vanity. Her minions grew aware of his presence and scattered about, their intentions shifting.

The stairs led to a new floor, and across the less crowded hallway, Kegan saw Vanity. She shifted about in place, as if looking for something behind Kegan, but then stopped after a second. "Why are you siding with the dreamers? We could have ruled the realms together!" Vanity shouted instead. She was more upset than she was angry, her voice filled with conviction.

"Eh, I'd rather hang around and do whatever I want. Taking care of these brainless idiots seems boring," Kegan shrugged. "I don't care what you're gonna do,

Vanity, but I need my little tour guide. Unless you want to be incinerated, you should leave us alone."

"I-" Vanity was caught in between disbelief and sorrow, shocked at how her best and only true friend could threaten her as such. She cleared her throat. "Fine, do whatever you want. You're too pathetic to be a friend of a queen like me. I'm way out of your league."

Footfalls were heard behind the two, and there Raine was, except there was now some kind of a device strapped onto her body. A small red light flashed. Kegan realised what the device was and looked at Raine's expression. She had none.

"I'm not just a pretty face, you know," Vanity said. "There are thermal sensors in that bomb, so I'd recommend you not to go all fireball." And once that information had been disseminated, she ran. The bomb's constant beeping noise echoed throughout the hall, and more of Vanity's minions arrived.

Kegan prepared to chase after Vanity again, but another magic blast from Raine stopped him. He almost blew Raine up from his instincts and ended up getting hit by another oncoming blast.

The next swarm of Vanity's minions advanced onto Kegan, their numbers severely depleted. Unlike before, when they were wary of Kegan's fire powers, they were now completely surrounding him.

Kegan managed to slip out of their trance thanks to their lack of numbers, and noticed a nice potted plant by the side of the hallway. He took it and smashed it onto the ground, picking up a shard and claiming it as his weapon.

Having their shoes worn and torn from the previous battles, the remaining shards on the ground proved useful in slowing them down. Raine however, was still launching attacks from a distance, and Kegan had to swerve her blasts.

Eventually, the minions decided that their poor feet were worth sacrificing, and stepped over the shards. Slashing at them with the glass shard, the minions yelled as they were awarded with cuts for their relentless pursuit of Kegan.

Raine threw another attack, and Kegan used one of the minions as a meat shield. Waiting for their next move, he was understandably confused when several of them broke into dance.

"Dude...What?" Kegan watched incredulously while the minions moved their arms around like spaghetti, prancing around like they were auditioning for a cheerleading role. Even Raine, who was inching past the dancing group in order to attack Kegan, had her stoic lifeless expression turned into that of disgust and confusion. *Right, something is definitely wrong.* Kegan forced himself to turn his back on Raine and the funky minions, facing the empty hallway where Vanity once stood. *She's trying to distract me with their stupid moves in order to buy time.* Convinced by his assumption, he ignored all his potential enemies and pursued Vanity. Realising that their dancing has failed, the minions stopped dancing immediately and followed Kegan, trying to overtake him and slow his pace.

Resorting to physical attacks, Kegan kicked his enemies away, the beeping of the bomb reminding him constantly not to rely on his elemental powers as he usually did thoughtlessly. His fists were balled up and his jaw was clenched, bracing the impact of his enemies' hits every few seconds.

Raine, too, was chasing Kegan. The both of them knew that she was the only way to disable his elemental power, and using his lack of powers as an opportunity, Raine struck him with her own, summoning sphere blasts of pure dream energy.

A majestic door came into view at the end of the hallway. It was otherwise a dead end, and Kegan saw Vanity reaching for the doorknob. She shook it violently, the door refusing to budge. Kegan closed in on Vanity whilst she attempted to lockpick the president's door.

"How did you get here so fast? Did you actually kill Raine?" Vanity asked, surprised to see him.

"Course not, she's right here." Kegan finished his sentence and immediately ducked down, revealing Raine who was standing behind him. She had launched another attack whilst Kegan appeared to be distracted with Vanity, but he had already moved out of the way, giving way for Vanity to be attacked instead.

Vanity dodged the attack by a hair, and the blast made impact upon the president's door. It exploded and caused a huge gash in the door frame, rendering the lock useless. One could see the room from out in the hallway, and it was obvious that nobody was in the room.

"Of course he isn't here," Vanity deplored, realising her target was missing all along. Failing to notice Kegan creeping up on her, the crown on top of her head was snatched. Vanity let out a scream and turned to Kegan, who was now holding the crown hostage.

Vanity jumped out in an attempt to grab the crown. Kegan swerved around her arm and brought himself closer to her, ripping her mask off before moving behind her and kicking her on her back. She fell from the kick, allowing Raine and her minions to show her face.

Upon seeing Vanity, Raine regained control of her mind again, having barely any recollection of anything that had transpired. She heard the bomb's beeping sounds and glanced down, only to find a bomb strapped onto her torso. "Ah! Why is there a bomb on me? What happened?" She froze in place in fear of the bomb going off, her voice loud and shaky, but then she saw Kegan with a defeated Vanity in between. "Kegan?" She called, searching for answers.

"Oh yeah, I totally don't know how to disarm that thing, but you're welcome." Kegan grinned. He then pulled Vanity's hair and pulled her up. She was in a temporary state of unconsciousness. "Vanity's ability is disabled when her true face is shown to whom she brainwashes. It's kinda like catfishing, you know? You get immediately turned off once you see her for who she really is. Oh, right. You can have this." Kegan threw Raine the crown that Vanity owned. "It's her relic. Do what you will with it. Her ability won't be working for a while, so that stupid pretty face of hers won't be causing any harm."

"Why is there a bomb on me?" Raine yelled, ignoring everything he just spouted out.

The flash of several cameras was heard, and Raine saw that the other dreamers who had fallen victim to Vanity's ability had regained control of their own minds as well. They were now recording and taking photos of Raine, Kegan, and Vanity. Upon eye contact, they quickly scattered like bugs and vanished.

Vanity's eyes opened once she regained her consciousness, only to find her arms locked behind her back by Kegan. Noticing her relic in Raine's hands, she screamed. "Hey! You can't steal another nightmare's relic! Give it back!" She tried to break free of Kegan, but to no avail.

"Get this thing off me in exchange for the crown," Raine offered, trying to maintain her composure. She examined the crown in her hands, discreetly admiring its design and jewels.

This proposal rendered Vanity astonished for a few moments before she scowled. "Fine, get your hands off me! I don't want to get dirtied by you ugly commoners!"

Kegan released Vanity, who then went over to Raine and started to tinker with the device on Raine's body. While Raine and Vanity were throwing words back and forth at each other angrily, the bomb was eventually released from Raine's torso and dropped on the marble floor. Vanity then stretched her arm out expectantly with her palm in front of Raine, glaring at her as she waited for the crown to be returned.

Raine glanced at Kegan, and after he confirmed that she should respect the deal, she handed the crown back to Vanity. Vanity snatched the crown before anything could happen to it and she polished Raine's fingerprints off with her finger.

"Admit your defeat, Vanity," Kegan crossed his arms and looked at her disapprovingly.

Although it was obvious Vanity had lost, she still wore a smile on her face. She spoke condescendingly. "Do you really think going after that old man was my *only* trick? I have infiltrated this entire realm with bombs, and you don't even know it!" "Kill the nightmare!" Somebody shouted out.

Several gunshots fired from afar, and Vanity gasped. But just before the bullets could reach her, a sudden darkness engulfed the whole room, blinding everyone. It was only for a brief moment, and just as quickly as it appeared, the darkness faded. The light reflecting off a single bullet on the floor caught Kegan's eyes, and both he and Raine found that Vanity had vanished.

Upon seeing the bullet, Raine perked up and saw a tall man dressed formally in a black suit. His expression was stern, a gun gripped firmly in his hand. Unfazed by the mysterious and unnatural darkness that caused Vanity's escape, he walked over to Raine and Kegan, who both recognised him as an authority figure. Raine gave a small bow of respect and as a greeting while Kegan questioned his choice of shades.

"A nightmare attempted to overthrow the government and escaped - this is horrible news for Mr Jamison. Thank you, Revieras, for assisting us. We will do our best to help the public recover from this incident."

"Ah yes, no problem," Raine replied, knowing very well from Kegan's side-eye that she as a matter of fact had done the opposite of assistance. "If it's not sensitive information, where is Mr Jamison?"

"I was on a call with him earlier. Mr Jamison had left earlier to assist those in the Ambition realm. The situation there is much worse than it is here. At least the dreamers here are safe-"

Sounds of mayhem were heard, flooding from the giant hole in the president's room followed by shouting, instantly disproving the authority figure's words. He cleared his throat and directed attention away from the outside. "Anyway, we will be deploying more security measures to ensure the nightmares are taken care of. Would you like a personal bodyguard to protect you from any further harm, Revieras?"

"Oh, I already have one here." Raine pointed to Kegan, completely omitting the fact that he was a black-dreamer. Kegan gave a confident thumbs up to the authority figure, who was less than convinced. "Um, I'm currently looking for a way to head to the Ambition Realm. We have to find a Dreamkeeper in order to save Oneirolepsy," she added.

"Would you like a private ride there, then? Your friend can come along as well, as long as he doesn't set anything on fire." The authority figure swivelled and made his way back down the mansion, prompting Raine and Kegan to follow him. "I'll take you there, since I have to head to Mr Jamison as well. You may call me Mr Voss. I am the Minister of social affairs. As you know, in the Mainland, it is required for dreamers with special abilities to be officially registered in our records. My own ability grants me the knowledge of others' abilities from a single look at either them or their ability. As such, I am responsible for keeping all active ability users in check."

"You have my respect, sir. We appreciate your help," Raine gave another light bow whilst walking, a useless thing to do being behind Mr Voss. The three went down the stairs, only to find everything a mess, alongside the fact that the carpet was still on fire. Mr Voss sighed at the sight of other men in suits on the floor, their lives lost thanks to Vanity. Raine felt the need to apologise profusely, her knowledge of having been brainwashed by Vanity fuelling that urge rather

than excusing it. Instead, Mr Voss asked Kegan, "Are
you able to extinguish fires?"

"Seriously?" Kegan scoffed, annoyed by the repeating
question.

Mr Voss decided to ignore Kegan and changed the
topic. "Most of us were victims of the brainwashing
nightmare. Hopefully some lives and resources can
still be salvaged. We will be using a government
vehicle to make our way to the Ambition realm.
There's a secret underground driveway where several
vehicles are kept, though most have been used by
other officials." Leading to a new place with a
constructed elevator system, Mr Voss pressed the
button to go down.

Vanity had focused more on the higher levels of the
mansion since she was under the assumption that the
president would be there, and had neglected to spread
any chaos in the lower levels. Nobody had paid any
attention to the elevator either, but now that Vanity
was gone, Raine could finally appreciate the mansion
without having to worry about her.

The elevator doors welcomed Mr Voss and the two as
all three walked in, the elevator larger than usual one
would see in regular buildings. Mr Voss pressed a
button out of many, and the elevator doors closed
before travelling downwards, so elegantly that Raine
couldn't tell it was moving at all. Kegan stood in an
isolated corner lost in thought while she stood near
Mr Voss, relying on his leadership. She glanced at the
mirrored walls to keep an eye on Kegan without his

notice, thinking about how she would talk to him later about what had happened earlier.

Raine didn't notice that the elevator had reached its destination until Mr Voss walked out into a dark and moody private car park, connected directly to the underground driveway he had spoken of earlier. Lutescent lights emulating fireflies shone above, revealing empty spots where other vehicles had rested. There was only a single white car left behind. It was well kept, if not ominous with its single presence. Raine wasn't very familiar with cars, but it couldn't have been one of those specialised and ludicrously expensive ones.

Regardless, Mr Voss made his way towards the white car, taking out a keychain from his pockets. He opened the back door for Raine and Kegan before getting into the driver's seat himself.

The car was designed to fit around five passengers at the back, with two divided seats at the front and three attached ones at the back, linking to the trunk. Raine sat at the front seat where Kegan could sit without having to step over her legs, but instead he moved to the back seats. Raine moved to the other front seat to avoid seeing him from the rearview mirror, noticing a black bag placed at the front passenger seat. "I guess somebody was planning to escape, but failed," Mr Voss noticed Raine staring at the bag and commented.

"Ah," Raine replied, still suspicious. The car's headlights illuminated the underground and its wheels started moving as Mr Voss began to drive.

"It's surprising how a single nightmare managed to enslave most of the dreamers in the Mainland. If other nightmares are just like her, then Oneirolepsy is in a lot of trouble. I'm glad you're taking the initiative to help the world out." Mr Voss' calm and collected voice contrasted his sharp movement of the steering wheel, the car accelerating with every second. Raine could feel the car vibrating in her seat.

"It's what Rhea would've wanted me to do," Raine said, finding comfort in her toasty bag by hugging it in memory of her late mother. *Although I never wanted to be Revieras.* Were she not in a government official's vehicle, Raine would have rested her head on her bag and let out a heavy sigh. "I'm still worried though. Vanity said she had more bombs around. You didn't seem affected by her ability at all. Are there others like you?" She asked instead.

"Nobody as far as I know, but that nightmare's curse should have worn off by now. Unless they were injured or worse under her spell, everyone else should be fine," Mr Voss answered objectively. "Thankfully I wasn't exposed to her ability."

"I'm glad you were safe from Vanity," Raine replied, her tone empathetic. Hearing some ruffling sounds at the back of the car, she turned to Kegan, who was already looking at her. "Are you alright?" She asked, almost discreetly.

"You're the one who walked through pure fire and had a bomb strapped on her." Kegan was shuffling around, uninterested in the conversation between Raine and Mr Voss. "And I'm checking for any devices Vanity could have left. She once tried to put a tracking device on me."

Raine raised an eyebrow. "I thought you two were friends?" She recalled the polaroid Vanity threw at her before everything went blurry.

"Yeah, it was for a birthday surprise. She ended up causing a blackout and got in trouble for using her brainwashing on other nightmares." After ensuring there was nothing on Kegan, he sank back into the back of his seat. This prompted Raine to also ensure Vanity had completely disarmed everything off her body. "She's really arrogant and annoying at times, but she was an okay friend."

"She got in trouble?" Raine felt about in her suit and found she had one less rainflower than she remembered. "Do you black-dreamers have an actual justice system in the Nightmare realm?" Raine asked, forgetting that Mr Voss could hear her.

"Pardon me, Revieras, but your friend over there is a nightmare?" Mr Voss kept himself from swivelling in case he crashed the car, the speed limit completely thrown out the window by now. "And a fire elemental at that, are you sure he's a friend?" Raine covered her mouth quickly, wondering if it would be worse to look at Mr Voss in the rear-view mirror or to keep eye contact with Kegan, who was giving her an incomprehensible look, presumably intrigued in what she would say next.

The sunlight seeped into the car as it finally left the underground tunnel, the sun's rays bathing Raine in its warmth. She looked out the window and at the sky to prevent any odd looks from Mr Voss and Kegan, pretending to admire the sun's presence in such a predicament. "Well, he's helped stop Vanity from taking over the Mainland while I was...in hot water. He can be trusted." She stuttered. She peered at the rear-view mirror, and exhaled when Mr Voss gave a satisfied nod. Kegan sneered, both from Raine's response and the 'hot water' idiom which he found amusing.

"But still, others may see your friend as a threat. You should be careful not to be suspected of assisting the nightmares, and of his potential arrest," Mr Voss warned.

"I understand," Raine said, although she was sure Kegan could easily take care of himself.

The drive went on peacefully for a while before Kegan asked rather abruptly. "You said you could determine an ability from a single look alone?" It took a second for Raine to detect his provoking tone toward Mr Voss. "You said you weren't affected by her ability, but surely you know what it is?"

Mr Voss took a second to reply. "You and Revieras were closer to her than I. You should have seen that her ability to manipulate darkness has allowed her to disappear within it."

"Kegan, you-"

"Vanity doesn't have an ability like that. You sure yours is working right?" Kegan was now leaning on the edge of his seat, and Raine turned her body to face him, her expression of disapproval not stopping him in any way. "You mentioned you were on a call with Jamison earlier, but all the devices were hacked. You would've been subjected to Vanity's ability, yet you claimed you weren't."

"I called Mr Jamison after the ability wore off. What are you trying to imply here, nightmare?" Mr Voss' voice was growing dangerous.

"Raine," Kegan called, dragging out the vowels. "You should call back your friend from earlier, since phones are working again, apparently."

Raine pulled out the phone from her bag and did as told. "There's no service," she stated, after her call failed. Although Vanity's ability had worn off, she had hacked the devices in the Mainland, and it still hadn't been fixed. That was when it clicked. "Wait, excuse me, but how did you call the President if there was no service throughout this whole time?"

"That's 'cause he didn't," Kegan answered. "That's a fake Mr Voss."

Mr Voss sighed and took his shades off, revealing his eyes. They were that of a black-dreamer; lifeless, full of terror and anguish, pitch black.

There were three methods of identifying a nightmare: a relic, their nightmare energy, and their lack of white pupils that dreamers naturally had.

Raine hadn't noticed it until now, but it made sense why she was so tense. Her dream energy was constantly repulsing against Mr Voss', and he was always wearing his shades just as Vanity had always worn her crown.

The person in the driver's seat wasn't Mr Voss. It was a black-dreamer.

Kegan climbed out from the back seat and sat in the front next to Raine, pulling the car door. It was locked. "Where's the real guy at?" He asked, attempting to break the car windows.

"Mr Voss was eviscerated long before Vanity had stepped into the mansion," The nightmare stated, his hands free from the steering wheel and his feet on the accelerator. "And don't try breaking the windows. They're made of tempered glass. Just so you know, that bag over there is another bomb. Guess how it's triggered?"

"Alright, this is just getting annoying." Kegan crossed his arms and leaned back in his seat, obviously ticked off by his inability to use his elemental powers without blowing up.

"I have a manual remote too, so if you try anything funny, you'll all end up dead." The car sped faster and faster, and Raine felt the urge to throw up. She didn't like any of what was happening at all, unlike Kegan, who seemed to have casually accepted the fact that a black-dreamer was in control of the driving seat. "I wonder how it would feel to have a dreamer's skin," The nightmare continued, putting his shades back on.

"Would you like to see how well I can roleplay as Revieras? I've never disembowelled a dreamer before."

"Oh shut up, you don't sound cool at all," Kegan replied. "By the way, are we still heading to the Ambition realm? I'd be very unhappy with this ride otherwise."

The nightmare chuckled. "Many nightmares have already infiltrated the Ambition realm. I heard one of 'em's targeting a popular stadium. Lots of fresh bodies."

"Stadium? You mean that stadium over there?" Kegan pointed at the car's front windows, a large stadium coming into view. Raine looked at the side windows and quickly found they were already on the bridge that connected the Mainland and the Ambition realm.

Raine closed her eyes and took a deep breath, trying to ignore the fact that she was in a car with two sadistic black-dreamers. Remembering she had a final ace up her sleeve - well, it was much less an ace and more of a safety tool granting Raine full use of her ability - Raine took out the last remaining rainflower from her pocket. She covertly nudged Kegan, who was still busy entertaining the black-dreamer, and whispered to him. "Look, I know you've never explained why, but you won't get hurt from dream energy, right?"

Kegan looked at the rainflower in her hand and chuckled. "Yeah, go ahead. Do whatever you want," he replied, showing no care if the black-dreamer overheard him.

Go ahead, he says. He doesn't even know what I'm planning to do. Why is he acting so cool about it? Raine suppressed the urge to smack his face with the rainflower and whispered back, "Okay, I need you to trigger the bomb. Don't ask why, just do it. I promise we won't die."

Kegan's eyes flickered in surprise for a moment, but then he nodded, almost in excitement. Raine brought herself closer to Kegan, almost as if she were about to hug him, and Kegan responded with a nervous chuckle.

The black-dreamer in the driver's seat seemed to have caught what was going on between Raine and Kegan, but before he could confront them in an angry tone, Kegan shouted: "Hey, nightmare, I hope you're ready to blow up!" and with the flick of a wrist, he shot out a fireball at the bomb.

The black-dreamer could barely register his shock at the bomb being used as an advantage rather than a threat by the pair behind him when it went off with a boom. Its deafening roar and blinding flash almost led Raine to forget that she had wanted this to happen.

※★◆★※
Chapter 5: Stadium

Raine's ears were ringing. She couldn't see anything, and she couldn't tell whether she was on the ground. Her body burned with what felt like lava, a blinding white being all she could see.

She tried to piece her mind back together. She intended this to happen. Well, not the pain - she intended for the bomb to blow up. Obviously, she wasn't a reckless masochist like Kegan, and she knew that his anti-ability ability proved to be counterproductive when she conjured up her plan, but she tried anyway.

Maybe Raine was taking a huge risk by relying on a single rainflower to save two lives, but she tried anyway. She believed in her abilities as a dreamer, as Revieras. She closed her eyes and remembered Rhea, the one who had taught her how to heal.

Raine remembered the first time she saw a true miracle. She recalled running to Rhea crying as a child, sobbing about her injured knee. And when Rhea soothed her to calmness with her voice, proposed to the younger Raine a magic trick. Raine would then watch the ugly bruise on her knee disappear, and all the pain going away almost in an instant. Rhea then smiled and admitted. "There's no trick to it, dear. It was my love for you that healed you."

Raine didn't want to waste her life now. Not without saving Oneirolepsy. Right before the bomb went off, she had created a magical shield around herself and Kegan, as well as the bomb itself. She knew that the shield itself wouldn't be enough, so with the rest of her dream energy, she healed herself as well. She could feel a radius where ability worked to the maximum. Raine could almost feel Rhea assisting her healing ability. She had never used her ability in such a life-or-death situation before, but she grew more confident as the scorching hot sensation turned into a warm bath of sunshine, and the ringing in her eyes slowly faded away into calm silence.

Nothing moved, then all at once, the white light Raine saw began to fade, with darkness taking over. This initially worried Raine, who thought her ability had failed or stopped working, but then she realised it wasn't darkness she was looking at, but the back of her eyelids. Her body ached, but the aching soon went as well.

She reluctantly opened her eyes and allowed the sight of the sky to register in her mind. Well, for a second anyway. In the next, Raine saw Kegan looking down at her with an amused expression. He appeared unhurt, and Raine quickly sat up, wondering how long it had been since Kegan awoke before her.

Raine half-expected her body to refuse to move, but was pleasantly surprised to find that she was completely healed, and fine. She stood up and met eyes with Kegan, who grinned. "Wow, I can't believe you actually did that. Thought you actually wanted to kill us," Kegan laughed, pointing behind him with his thumb, and Raine turned to see what he was pointing at.

The car was now torn into shreds with many pieces of metal and glass everywhere. It looked as if a giant from beyond the Earth had brought down its angry fist on the meagre car and crushed it, causing the car to splatter everywhere on the bridge. Fortunately, the bridge was devoid of other vehicles or pedestrians, sparing anyone else from harm.

"How did you manage to heal me anyway? Abilities don't work on me," Kegan asked.

"Rainflowers aren't abilities. I also created a shield for us and the bomb to reduce the damage, which technically isn't directed at you either, so your ability doesn't counter it. Where's the other black-dreamer?" Raine asked. Looking at herself and Kegan, Raine would have never figured that they had been trapped in an accelerating car with a bomb and a black-dreamer just a few moments ago.

"Oh yeah, that nightmare got annihilated. Too much dream energy, y'know? The body most likely flew over the bridge," Kegan replied casually. Raine looked to her left and ran over to the railing of the bridge. Beneath stretched a vast ocean of blue, littered by the car's scraps. The explosion had caused enough force to launch several pieces and presumably Mr Voss' body into the ocean. "That was quite a risk you took there. Exploiting loopholes of my ability? Now that's something else."

Raine sighed. She knew that it would be her first and last time attempting to heal Kegan, considering how much dream energy it took out of her, not to mention her mental fatigue. She also didn't trust that she could ensure Kegan's safety a second time, granted that he was still a black-dreamer, and her ability was based on dream energy. "Is there a reason you won't tell me why you aren't affected by dream energy like the other black-dreamers?" Raine asked, again. "And don't say 'don't worry about it'. I want you to answer me."

Kegan raised an eyebrow. "You're still not over that? Jeez."

He certainly had all the characteristics of a black-dreamer, but Raine's intuition told her that something about him was different than the other black-dreamers, excluding his nature as a fire elemental. "Are you sure you're not just a dreamer pretending to be a black-dreamer or something?"

Kegan burst out laughing upon hearing her question. Raine shot him an unamused look, and she watched with annoyance while Kegan slowly calmed down. "Oh, that's hilarious!" He commented, before clearing his throat, saying in a more serious manner. "I don't really get all the nightmare and dream energy stuff. Energy is energy, y'know? I guess I don't really have a proper scientific answer if that's what you're looking for. But hey! It makes it much easier to deal with things when you're not constantly worried about it."

Raine left the edge of the road bridge and went back to where Kegan stood, feeling mildly uncomfortable by the absence of her bag. "So, what, you have neutral energy? Is that even a real thing?" She wondered if being an elemental had something to do with Kegan's strange nature, but decided not to question it further. "I mean, I guess you're right. It does make things easier."

"Yep. We're not dead. So all's good."

Raine scrabbled about her clothes and found that she had nothing at her disposal. Panicking, she fumbled around her layers of shirts and heaved a sigh of relief when she felt her one-of-a-kind heart-shaped necklace kept safely under her clothes - a special necklace bestowed upon her since birth.

Sudden collective sounds of explosions banded together to challenge the limits of the sound barrier, its impact so large and loud that it didn't feel real, until Raine saw from her peripherals that the ocean's water had flown up from the shockwave before landing with a crash.

Raine and Kegan turned back and saw that the faint overview of the Mainland had been replaced with triggered explosives and destruction, its high-rise buildings gone within an instant, smoke rising up into the darkening sky. "I guess Vanity had the 'If I can't have it, no one can' mentality with that place," Kegan quipped, almost immediately after the simultaneous explosions. Raine's knees gave out, and she slumped onto the road.

The Mainland had been bombed.

Kegan didn't seem fazed at all, and continued talking. "The Ambition realm is right in front of us, so we should-" Kegan stopped mid-sentence as tears falling down Raine's cheek caught his attention. He had failed to read the room, so to speak, and only realised how upset Raine was when he saw her crying silently. "Uh..." He looked around, as if that would help him figure out how to comfort Raine.

Raine couldn't answer Kegan. Her eyes fixated straight ahead, where the view of the beautiful Mainland once stood. She cared not for the tears that were dampening her face; her homeland had perished in front of her. Summer's pavilion, her treehouse, Rhea's home, the café that Raine and Soraya would meet up for breakfast every week, they were all gone. It all felt like a very, very bad dream.

Chattering and murmurings along with gasps and flash of cameras were heard and seen behind Kegan and Raine. A crowd of dreamers from the Ambition realm had gathered by the end of the road bridge to gawk at the Mainland.

"Well," Kegan started, after a long pause. "I know Vanity is awesome, but she isn't *that* awesome. I don't think she's able to wipe out the entirety of the Mainland with her silly bombs. Don't worry about it too much." Kegan's poor attempt at comforting Raine somehow worked, and Raine found the strength to stand up again. She wiped her tears away, dirtying her sleeve as she did so.

"Yeah, you're right," Raine replied, her voice cracking. She had at least five arguments in her head that could refute Kegan, but she didn't want Kegan to deal with anymore of her crying. She tried to focus on finding the Dreamkeeper instead of the hundreds of innocent dreamers who may have been caught up in the explosion. "I can't let this happen to the other realms. Let's find the Dreamkeeper." Raine tried to think of any positives but was quickly struck down by another thought. "Wait, my bag! That map was in it! Where's my bag?"

"Unless your bag is bomb-proof, I don't think you'll be finding it any time soon."

Raine let out a groan. She wished that the entire thing was just a dream and that she could simply just wake up from the whole predicament, but the movement of someone nearby distracted her from going into a downward spiral of despair. He stood a few feet away from Kegan and Raine, and unlike the other dreamers who were sensible enough to keep their distance, he strolled along the road bridge and towards the car wreck.

Raine and Kegan watched as the mysterious dreamer carried forward, ignoring both of them and the crowd of dreamers discouraging him from moving forward. Taking the initiative, Raine ran towards the dreamer. "Hey, excuse me!" She called.

The dreamer stopped, as if he had just noticed Raine's presence. His dark blue hair with several streaks of sapphire highlights brushed against his face, his overgrown bangs swept over his eyebrows with two locks of hair covering his ears and framing his face. His pale complexion complemented his formal (if not broody) clothes, and for a moment Raine couldn't tell if she should call him sir. He looked at her as if she was the one causing him an inconvenience. "Is this your car?" The dreamer asked, speaking as if he was reciting a poem. His accent told Raine that he wasn't an Ambition dreamer, but more so of a Subliminal dreamer.

Raine somehow felt more threatened by the dreamer's cold demeanour than when she first met Kegan. "Um, no, but you shouldn't go near it. There was a black-dreamer and an explosive there, and there's many dangerous shards on the ground, you'll get hurt!" Raine examined the dreamer again, assuming that he was only two or three years older than her. "Are you with anyone? You're not from the Ambition realm, are you?"

"Boris!"

A girl escaped the suffocating crowd of Ambition dreamers and ran out to the mysterious dreamer, her loose short low pigtails bouncing along with her pink hoodie. The girl wore brightly-coloured accessories and a clip on her dark hair, her short-sleeved salmon coloured hoodie paired carelessly with a grey skirt and red sneakers, giving her an overall childish and informal appearance. Raine noticed her mismatching socks and wondered if she had worn them like that on purpose. "Boris! What are you doing? We have to like, get back to the stadium- Oh, heya, Raine!" She waved at the puzzled Raine, who was wondering if she knew her.

The indigo-eyed dreamer, whose name was apparently Boris, waited for the girl to catch up to him. "Don't run off without me, okay? What's going on here anyway?" Her voice was boisterous and loud, her personality a sharp contrast compared to Boris.

Before Raine could say anything, Boris snapped his fingers, and all at once, the many scraps of metal and glass shards were brought together - even the pieces that were floating in the ocean - and reconstructed back into the original car, without any scratches. It was spotless, as if just newly bought. Raine stood, dumbfounded, allowing Boris to approach the rebuilt car. He opened the door to the passengers' seat and pulled out a familiar bag. Picking it up, Boris walked back to Raine and offered her the bag. "This is yours, yes?"

"Woah, you're so cool, Boris! You're like, going to go on camera and everything. Look, even the Ambition dreamers are recording right now!" The girl pointed at the crowd of Ambition dreamers, who were applauding and gasping at Boris. From her demeanour and accent, Raine deduced that she was also a Subliminal dreamer.

Raine took her bag from Boris and unzipped it, shocked to find all her items in one piece. "Wha- How did you do that?" She took another look at Boris, and it clicked.

"Wait, are you *that* Boris?"

He glared at Raine quietly, as if that was supposed to be a resounding yes.

Years ago, there was an incident involving the Subliminal realm and the Ambition realm, which had permanently caused a strain between the two. Even now, the two realms didn't get along very well. Many buildings and homes had been wrecked and thousands of bodies were piled up. Raine was too young to know of the incident back then and only after a few years had passed, stumbled upon an outdated article talking about a child in the Subliminal realm who had the powerful ability to contrive structures, mainly buildings, with dream magic and raw materials alone. He had helped restore what was lost in the incident, although there were speculations that the buildings were made from the corpses that amassed during the war, for the thousands of bodies were said to have disappeared. Although Boris was celebrated as a hero, Raine couldn't help but wonder if it was really healthy for a child to have gone through such a predicament.

It was strange to see two Subliminal dreamers in the Ambition realm, granted the incident was labelled as a war between the two realms.

"Hey, what happened to the Mainland?" The girl asked, before covering her mouth in shock. "Oh, sweet mother of dreams, don't tell me that sound from earlier was a nuke! Are the dreamers there alright?"

"Jocelyn, you're being inconsiderate," Boris told her.

"Oh, right! Raine! We need your help!" The girl, presumably named Jocelyn, ran over to Raine and clasped her hands together into that of a prayer. "Could you like, come with us real quick to Yeong-gu stadium? Please, please, please, please, please?"

"Um, about that..." Raine took out the map from her bag and took a glance at it. The pinpoint of the Ambition dreamer glowed brightly, and close to her proximity too. In her circumstance, Raine knew that a meagre second would be all it would take for the pinpoint to either vanish or reappear on the opposite end of Oneirolepsy. "I'm kind of busy at the moment, but-"

Like tearing a piece from a slice of bread, a large part of the stadium's infrastructure was ripped open and cut in half, a broken bit of heavy concrete towering over the crowd's heads. Before anyone could scream, the concrete dropped with a loud crash and crushed everybody in the crowd. Blood pooled and splattered everywhere, and the sound of a pin drop could have been heard. Raine, Kegan, Boris and Jocelyn watched from a distance, unable to process the sudden death of several unfortunate Ambition dreamers.

Jocelyn screamed immediately, only for her mouth to be covered shut by Boris. "Somebody has taken advantage of a weak spot within the structural elements of the stadium. Likely a nightmare." He said, letting his hand go from Jocelyn's mouth. Grabbing onto her arm, Boris dragged Jocelyn in the direction of the stadium. Raine watched the two of them step

over the bloody mess, unable to process what had
happened.

"Y'know, you're more incompetent than I thought
you were. Hurry up," Kegan said to Raine. He then
followed Jocelyn and Boris, who were making their
way to the entrance of the stadium.

Raine questioned why the others were so insistent on
heading towards danger, but knew she had to
confront the danger in front of her. With an exhale,
Raine ordered her legs to march forward, knowing
she was potentially walking into more trouble.

※ ※ ※

The entrance of the stadium was placed on the
opposite side of the bridge that Raine and Kegan were
on, and despite the large gap that appeared due to
unknown reasons, none of them were capable of
manoeuvring the piece of concrete that squashed the
bunch of unfortunate spectators, or at least they
didn't want to anyway. Raine was sure Kegan would
have hopped over the concrete and yelled "Parkour!"
or something of the sort, but he followed Jocelyn and
Boris to the actual entrance of the stadium.

Still, the mystery of Kegan's nature as a dreamer or a
black-dreamer was the least of Raine's concerns.
Pieces of concrete didn't just randomly fall on people
for no reason.

Raine entered the stadium, and noticed an
inexplicable change in the atmosphere from outside

and in. Despite being rather sporty and athletic, competitive sports was not her forte, and immediately she felt like a foreigner treading in unknown territory. The stadium had a retractable roof to prevent anything from flying out, but today the stadium remained open for the sun to shine down on, despite the potential danger around. Lights illuminated the stadium, which had yet to be torn apart by a gang of angry black-dreamers. The grass flourished in a healthy green, with the bleachers well arranged, and a baseball group congregated in the middle of the field. Their primarily black uniform and their team's logo revealed them to be the Diamond Cutters - a very popular baseball team in the Ambition realm. Raine was never into baseball, but she still felt the same sensation as one would when meeting their celebrity crush when she took a step closer inside the stadium.

Jocelyn met with the baseball players, whose faces were plastered with fear from the strange concrete that fell earlier. Boris, acting as if all the baseball players were infected with some sort of deadly contagious virus, watched Jocelyn by the sidelines as she interacted with the baseball team. Kegan waited by the entrance for Raine and walked along with her as she approached the Diamond Cutters, scanning the stadium as if it was his first time seeing one. The coach of the Diamond Cutters tipped his cap when Raine walked close enough for him to greet her without it being awkward, and some of the players began whispering amongst each other, questioning why Revieras was in a baseball stadium.

"We have no idea what happened. It was so sudden," the coach said, his intonation making him sound unintentionally monotonous. He had a tough build and looked younger than a stereotypical baseball coach Raine had in her mind. Were it not for his facial hair and hat, he could have passed for one of the baseball players. "We saw the faint trajectory of a baseball, and it somehow sliced through the stadium's walls. We have yet to find who did this."

"It was probably that guy over there," One of the players whispered to another, pointing at Kegan. "Eek, he's looking at us!" They winced in fear. Raine was surprised at how they managed to recognise Kegan as a black-dreamer, only to have a thought that it probably wasn't the fact that he was a black-dreamer that they were treating with such disgust.

"Ahem," Raine cleared her throat, and the two players flinched. "In any case, it will be considered an attack against dreamers, and whoever is responsible will be dealt with accordingly." Finishing her sentence, Raine felt both impressed and ashamed for how bossy she sounded, but to everyone else, they took it as a display of authority from a good leader, and they simply nodded before stepping away to have their little group meeting. Jocelyn stayed behind with one of the players who were excluded from said meeting while Boris inspected the damage dealt from earlier. Raine watched Kegan stroll over to Boris, feeling an urge to interfere with whatever black-dreamer-ish intentions he may or may not have with him. In the end however, Raine found herself walking over to Jocelyn, curious to know more.

"Jocelyn, I was so worried when we saw the concrete fall outside the stadium! I assumed the worst had happened to you," A baseball player hugged Jocelyn. She was small and petite, and her primarily black baseball uniform made Jocelyn's hoodie flash in comparison. Her charcoal pixie haircut gave her a tomboyish and rebellious look, but her soft and agitated voice barely made her intimidating. The way she was talking with Jocelyn made it obvious that the two were extremely familiar with each other.

Jocelyn wrapped her arms around the baseball player in a warm embrace. "I'm just happy that I got to see you again, So-hyun!"

Their sentimental moment was broken up when Jocelyn noticed Raine looking at them, and the two let go of one another, making Raine feel bad for being nosey. "Oh, sorry. I just wanted to check if you're alright. Death is horrible, and nobody should ever witness it," A surge of guilt made its way to Raine. *I should've done something about it. If only there was enough dream energy around, I would heal all the dreamers suffering right now!*

"Oh no, you're cool! We haven't met, right?" Raine was already confused by Jocelyn's informal attitude towards her, but having Jocelyn confirm her

non-camaraderie status made Raine even more
puzzled as to why she was treating her as if they had
been best friends for years. "I'm Jocelyn, a Subliminal
dreamer, and this is So-hyun! She's from the
Ambition realm and is with the Diamond Cutters.
We're both roommates in the Mainland and Boris is
my cousin." She held out her hand and Raine was
about to shake it, only for Jocelyn to clench her fist. It
took a second before Raine realised she wanted a fist
bump and not a handshake. "By the way, who's that
guy over there?" Jocelyn pointed over to where Boris
and Kegan were standing and squinted. "You're with
him, right? Should I be worried for Boris?"

Raine considered telling Jocelyn that Boris was
standing before a black-dreamer who not too long ago
had set fire to her home, but decided against it as she
didn't want to try to persuade anyone not to arrest
him. If Raine hadn't teamed up with Kegan, she
would have done so as well, though she knew he could
and would have melted off the hypothetical handcuffs
in an instant. "Yeah, he's...an acquaintance of mine.
Kegan's his name." She looked back at So-hyun.
"Anyway, it's nice to meet you, So-hyun."

So-hyun nodded and gave a distant smile, saying
nothing.

Kegan caught notice of the three and walked over to
them, dragging Boris along with him. "He wants to
use my ability to set things on fire," Boris said,
unamused. Raine stifled a giggle, marvelling at how

Kegan had somehow managed to befriend the evasive Boris.

"Oh cool! Can I join?" Jocelyn asked, her voice going higher the more excited she grew. But then her excited face turned into one of surprise, and she looked at Kegan. "Wait wait wait, hang on. Are you a nightmare? And did you say fire?" She showed no signs of fear or disgust, only curiosity.

"Surprised now, are you? Not only am I a nightmare, but I am also the greatest fire elemental you've ever seen! Want a demonstration?" Kegan held his hand out, but Raine slapped it away before he could set the whole grass field on fire. "Hey!"

"Oh my dreams, and you're a fire elemental too?" Jocelyn looked as if she was about to burst with excitement. "Dude! You are immediately my favourite nightmare."

"That's enough fire for today, thank you," Raine said dryly. Jocelyn looked disappointed, letting Raine realise that it was probably not a good idea for Jocelyn and Kegan to be left alone together. She glanced over at So-hyun and noticed she was subtly hiding behind Jocelyn away from Kegan. "Even if he is a black-dreamer, Kegan is on our side. Just try not to say that out loud," Raine added, lowering her voice.

"Oh yeah, the coach really hates nightmares," Jocelyn commented, failing to notice he was behind her.

"That's right. Those nightmares are nothing but evil and chaos," The coach said, his voice scaring Jocelyn, who jumped in surprise. She waited to be chided for talking about others behind their back, but instead the coach rambled on about his hatred for black-dreamers. "They're destructive and sadistic, and get sick joy from hurting others!"

"Speak for yourself, coach!" A female voice shouted from above.

A baseball shot by in a blur, shooting straight for the coach. Raine couldn't even register the baseball before it hit the coach. She had expected it to hit him in the stomach, and for him to fall over in pain - that was the standard expectation. Instead, the baseball sliced through the coach, creating a hole right in his heart. The baseball carried some of his blood as it continued flying past him until it hit the bleachers, leaving a trail of red behind the coach, who immediately fell to the ground.

The Diamond Cutters stood in shock, their eyes fixated on his corpse. It happened so fast that they couldn't even cry, and So-hyun clutched onto Jocelyn for support, just a mere second away from passing out. The more desensitised individuals, specifically Kegan and Boris, looked around the stadium to find the source of the cackling laughter that followed the flying baseball.

"There," Boris pointed.

A tanned female wearing a button up denim jacket the shade army green stood atop the highest of the bleachers, and despite the distance between her and the Diamond Cutters, her voice projected loudly.

"How's that for aim, huh? I told you you would pay with your blood! Ahahahaha!" The ends of her shoulder-length locks were dyed a lime green, and her black crop top was matched with ripped jeans. Her clothes were surprisingly clean, for now.

Another black-dreamer, Raine thought, her heart immediately beginning to race again.

Footfalls were heard by the entrance of the stadium, and about eight individuals with a similar jacket were seen with evil smirks and spiked bats.

"Hyrensia!" The captain of the Diamond Cutters, a tall blonde with hazel eyes, shouted in dismay, infuriated by the black-dreamer's presence. The other players who saw Hyrensia began shaking as well, including So-hyun, who seemed to be terrified in particular.

"Who?" Kegan asked.

But nobody was available to entertain his question, for Hyrensia had begun making her way down to the grass field by hopping over the bleachers. "The Emerald Justice shall assert their power! Attack!" She commanded. Hearing this, the eight individuals by the entrance screamed a war cry and charged at the Diamond Cutters, obviously not searching for a match of casual baseball, but one of a bloody beating.

"Everyone, follow me!" The baseball captain of the Diamond Cutters shouted assertively in an attempt to lead everyone to safety, but the other members were so panicked and afraid that nobody ended up listening to her. "So-hyun! You!" She called, referring to the latter as Jocelyn. "I need you to gather all the players over there." She pointed to the top left of the field. "The exit is there, but I want to make sure no one is left behind, understand?"

"Yes, ma'am!" Jocelyn shouted, giving a nod to So-hyun, before the two ran off to hunt for the Diamond Cutters.

Kegan and Boris were dealing with the Emerald Justice, and just as Raine was about to approach the baseball captain, she was met with Hyrensia. "Revieras. I don't know what you're doing here, nor do I care. But if you dare try to stop my revenge, I will not hesitate to plunge this baseball into your heart," Hyrensia hissed.

Raine threw a glance at the baseball captain, who spoke out her name as a quick introduction. When Raine couldn't understand what she said, she just sighed. "Nobody ever gets it right. Just call me Kalynne."

"Hey! I'm talking to ya over here!" Hyrensia shouted, pointing at Kalynne. "Do you know why I returned, Kalynne? It's because I have a score to settle with you, ya hear?"

"What does she mean?" Raine asked, getting ready to fight.

"Long story short, Hyrensia used to be in the Diamond Cutters while disguising as a dreamer. She got upset that I was chosen captain over her and she was eventually found out to be a nightmare. She got a strike and left quickly, now she's back for revenge,"

Kalynne explained, proving herself to be a good rapper.

"Strike?"

Hyrensia picked up a baseball bat that was lying on the grass nearby. It was a weapon dropped by one of the Emerald Cutters who had by now been taken away by either Kegan or Boris. "Shut it, Kalynne. Your life is over."

With a swing, Hyrensia charged forward at Kalynne, ignoring Raine completely. Raine watched in confusion as Kalynee struggled to dodge all the swings, while Hyrensia's eyes focused on Kalynne and nothing else.

Given the opportunity, Raine lifted a leg and kicked Hyrensia from behind while she was busy with Kalynne. Hyrensia let out a yell and fell. "I need to get back to the Diamond Cutters. They need me to lead. Distract Hyrensia, and don't let her shoot the baseball. If you can, give her a second strike." Without elaborating on what she said, Kalynne dashed away to where she told Boris and Kegan to bring the Diamond Cutters. There were about five of them now, idly waiting by the designated spot, hugging each other closely for support.

Raine was surprised at how quick Kalynne ran, only to remember she was a baseball captain with much training. Hyrensia got up from the ground and stared daggers at Raine. "You got in my way, Revieras," she said, almost in a low whisper. "You're next."

Raine immediately kicked Hyrensia down again, wishing she had plucked an extra rainflower from when she was by the Old Tree earlier for an extra energy boost. Unlike Kegan, Hyrensia posed a problem with her nightmare energy, although Raine was still able to handle it. Still, she was confused by what Kalynne said to her. *Give her a second strike? What does that mean?* She tried to remember the rules of baseball, but her mind went blank as Hyrensia got up and returned Raine's kick with a direct punch to the gut.

Raine resisted her knees from plummeting and winced as she clenched her stomach. *Don't let her shoot the baseball,* Raine remembered Kalynne's words. She decided the best way to prevent her from doing so was a close-combat fight, hand-on-hand.

Hyrensia clutched onto a baseball, and Raine assumed that she had multiple hiding in her jacket. From what she recalled, the first baseball she shot was thrown in almost a thousand miles per hour. Was that her ability?

Raine tried to hit the baseball away from Hyrensia, but she grabbed onto her arm and twisted it before throwing Raine to the ground. "I have been waiting for this opportunity for a long time, Revieras. I won't let you stop me!" Hyrensia yelled, kicking her multiple times while Raine was on the ground.

Raine rolled out from under Hyrensia's foot and in return, kicked her in the shins. As Hyrensia sank, Raine stood up, and turned to punch her in the face as hard as possible. *There's no way I can kill her. I don't think I want to, anyway.* Raine thought, feeling slightly remorseful with each punch. But with the scowl that Hyrensia wore as she fought back, Raine started to reconsider showing any mercy.

She caught a glimpse of Kegan carrying the body of one of the Emerald Justice players and was shocked to see a pile of black-dreamers stacked on top of each other on her right. She realised that an unspoken plan had been set in place, and she needed to figure out what it was.

※★ ◆ ★※
Chapter 6: Execution

The last thing Kegan expected from fighting a vendetta-fuelled nightmare with a history of throwing balls was manual labour with a stoic edgy dreamer who fit the label of a nightmare better than himself. He was content with throwing and shoving the bunch of minions led by Hyrensia when his new dreamer friend approached him and said, "Gather all the bodies over there," whilst carrying a nightmare twice the size of him.

Kegan swore that Boris was the coolest dreamer he would ever have the pleasure of meeting, but the chores assigned to him were still annoying. However, he knew an unspoken plan had been set in place, and he needed to figure out what it was.

Kegan and Boris were now at the bottom right of the field, where about six unconscious nightmares were laying. With a little effort, the number rose to eight. That was all of the Emerald Justice, excluding Hyrensia herself.

Boris threw the corpse of the coach from the Diamond Cutters, a large hole left in where his heart used to be. "Why him?" Kegan asked, puzzled.

"Precaution. It will not work if they are still alive." Boris said, referring to the unconscious nightmares. Boris had specifically told Kegan to knock them out, but not kill them, so they would still be fit to threaten

Hyrensia. He looked over to the side, where Raine was busy fighting with Hyrensia. "Does she need help?"

Kegan looked at Raine throwing Hyrensia to the ground and smirked. "Eh, she'll be fine," he shrugged, knowing it was probably only half-true. After all, how much damage could a healer magician do?

Raine saw Kegan and Boris standing by the mountain of bodies. She gave a look of disbelief and an exaggerated shrug, giving an obvious *what the hell are you doing?* in improvised sign language.

Kegan gave a thumbs up and a grin, hiding the fact that he had no proper reply. He could see Raine roll her eyes.

"Hey Hyrensia!" He heard Raine call her. He was too far away to hear the rest, but he could see Raine pointing at the bodies behind him and Hyrensia turning around to get a view as well. Kegan imagined Raine threatening Hyrensia to eliminate all her friends were she to try anything funny, and he prepared to let loose all his fire. Finally, he could set something on fire again!

Kegan gave a wave to Hyrensia in an attempt to tease and distract Hyrensia, which had somehow worked. Hyrensia walked closer to him. "You! You're a nightmare! You're not supposed to be helping the dreamers!"

"What was that? I can't hear you!" Kegan shouted, even though he had clearly heard Hyrensia. He grinned as he watched her anger rise.

Kegan saw Raine creeping up on Hyrensia and trying to take the baseball away from her. He couldn't see the rest, but then Jocelyn came up to him and Boris. "We have a plan, guys! I need to explain to you guys real quick." Jocelyn pointed to the baseball captain. "That's Kalynne. She's the baseball captain and has the ability to slow down an object she focuses on. So-hyun told me that Hyrensia has the ability where she's able to multiply the speed of whatever she's shooting by tenfold, but when she misses her target, she'll get a strike. Kalynne's ability helped Hyrensia to get a strike a long time ago, and it's permanent. We think Hyrensia will lose if she gets all three strikes, so we're trying to accomplish that."

"How?" Kegan asked, mildly interested by the concept of their abilities.

"We force her," Jocelyn said. "I don't know if you guys are like, telepathic or whatever, but creating a bait for her is a good idea," she gestured over to the group of bodies. "So-hyun is already telling Raine the plan. I'll call the police just in case anything happens."

And with that, Jocelyn left to find a safe place to call the police.

Kegan shrugged and turned to Boris. "So...what now?"

"They are horrible at crafting and relaying plan strategies," Boris answered. "Though I doubt they had a proper one in the first place. It is difficult to communicate in a situation like this."

Raine gave a vague gesture towards So-hyun and Jocelyn telling them to leave her alone with Hyrensia, who now had the upper advantage against her. "That's stupid, why would she reject help?" Kegan asked, but then she saw Raine getting thrashed by Hyrensia, and felt something instinctual within him when her head started to bleed. "Oh, shit!"

Within an instant, Boris and Kegan were encircled in a ring of flames. "Why," Boris commented, unfazed. The fire relentlessly devoured the stack of unconscious nightmares, and slowly, the bottom of the pile turned to ash.

The ground beneath Kegan shook, and suddenly shot up. Kegan shouted in surprise and fell as what looked like a tower appeared from beneath him and sharply rose to the sky. The fire below was now unable to be seen, and Kegan stood up and looked down from the tower. "What the hell just happened?"

Despite the tower having been constructed from the earth alone, it maintained a sturdy and firm build. Kegan could only assume that the tower was the product of Boris' ability, but that hardly waned his confusion.

In less than a second after the tower had been constructed, something struck against it, causing the structure to shake and wobble, but after a while it steadied again. "That was Hyrensia's second strike," Boris said.

Kegan couldn't hide his surprise. "You mean you predicted that she was going to shoot at us? And you knew when to use your ability?"

"Yes. That rumble just now was her baseball hitting the tower."

Kegan marvelled at Boris. He couldn't have created the tower in time without knowing precisely when Hyrensia would attack. He had made his moves in advance with the assistance of an accurate prediction. "Wait, so it's actually true that you create stuff out of corpses?"

Boris didn't say anything.

He frowned at the unsatisfying answer and assumed it was a yes. "So, are we getting down, or?"

"You said Raine could handle it. It is much safer here. There is no point to go down at this moment. Besides, Jocelyn has called the authorities, which should arrive soon. As long as the other dreamers are near Kalynne, they will be safe."

Kegan suddenly regretted answering Boris in such a non-serious manner. "Well, actually, I think I should go help Raine." He began descending the steep tower, but his leg slipped immediately, and he almost plummeted down, if not for Boris pulling him by the arm, assisting him back up.

"I think I just saw my life flash before my eyes!" Kegan commented, as he was dragged back to safety. He then turned to Boris. "Um, Boris? I think we have an issue," Kegan said, standing back up and pointing at below. "Y'know Jocelyn's friend? Yeah, I think she's in danger."

✳ ✳ ✳

I can't believe they just did that.

Raine had no time to admire Boris' tower, because before she knew it, Hyrensia had gotten her second strike, and Raine had a feeling that there was another side effect of Hyrensia's ability that she wasn't told about. It would have made more sense if So-hyun had told her, "Oh, right, the more strike Hyrensia gets, the more amplified her nightmare energy will be," but she had figured that one out by herself a little too late. Raine didn't really know what would happen once Hyrensia received all three strikes, but she knew it couldn't have been a good thing for her if she was *this* upset.

Now that Hyrensia had a second strike, her nightmare energy wasn't the only thing that had been amplified. Her anger had risen exponentially too, after witnessing her target of Kegan and Boris be replaced with a strange tower that appeared from seemingly nowhere, and she had decided to take her vexation out on Raine.

Her stomach already hurt from all the punches, and her neck and limbs were sore, but there was something intangible about the nightmare energy that caused the worst type of drowsiness and nauseousness. Raine felt the shadows around her take over her sight as Hyrensia walked closer to Raine, her eyes filled with fury.

"I'll kill you right here, then. That'll teach you dreamers not to disrespect my ability." Hyrensia took her baseball bat and prepared to swing it against Raine's head, an aggravated frown worn on her face.

"Hyrensia! Stop!" So-hyun's voice rang out from across the field. She was quite the distance away from everyone, and only Jocelyn stood by her side. "Don't hurt Revieras, please! This isn't how you solve your problems!"

Raine was spared from Hyrensia's continuous beatings. Hyrensia left Raine on the ground bleeding and confronted So-hyun by taking small steps towards her. Raine turned her body to get a view of what was happening, worried about So-hyun more than herself. She was out of dream energy, and couldn't move a muscle at all. All she could do was watch.

Jocelyn stuck to So-hyun like glue throughout the entire fight, leaning against her for support, the effects of the nightmare energy slowly crawling into her veins. But So-hyun was barely affected by Hyrensia's overwhelming nightmare energy at all. That was when Hyrensia spoke. "*My* problems? My problems were caused because of your stupid friend, Kalynne! I don't need a dream-blind freak like you to tell me how to solve my own problems when you were the ostracised freak that was only pitied by that stupid blonde, time-slowing witch of a backstabber!"

That seemed to have rendered So-hyun mute. Raine couldn't help but gape at what Hyrensia said. *So-hyun was dream-blind?*

Rhea had once taught her about dream-blind individuals. They were dreamers who, due to unknown reasons, couldn't dream at all. Raine had always wondered what it would be like to see a black and empty void instead of dreams, and the thought of it made her shudder every time. For dream-blind individuals, it was like a whole part of them was locked away; they could not detect, feel, or harness dream energy at all, and were essentially powerless.

Maybe that was why So-hyun was always with Jocelyn, instead of the other Diamond Cutters. From how Hyrensia spoke, she had probably figured out that So-hyun was dream-blind and managed to ostracise her from the rest of the members.

The only good thing about being dream-blind was that because they were immune and pardoned from dream energy, it meant that they were also free from the effects of nightmare energy, though it meant that they wouldn't be able to detect a black-dreamer from the nightmare energy they emit alone.

As Raine knew, Hyrensia already had a first strike when she first met her. Maybe that explained why her nightmare energy brimmed so potently. So-hyun had mentioned that Hyrensia used to be an active member of the Diamond Cutters, and nobody back then had found her out to be a black-dreamer. Could it be that she had no nightmare energy back then, because she had no strike? It would make sense why nobody noticed anything, and besides, the barrier hadn't been broken then, so they wouldn't suspect a black-dreamer being in the dreamer realms, much less a part of a baseball team.

Hyrensia's ability probably allowed her to pierce through the barrier with her speed. But just because she could throw things fast didn't mean she was infallible.

Raine couldn't think, though. She felt dizzy and light-headed, and had to make the conscious effort to not pass out.

"You know what?" Hyrensia said, catching Raine's attention. "Maybe you are right. Killing Kalynne isn't the solution to my problems," she said mockingly, before spitting out in a venomous tone. "I'll kill you, instead, So-hyun."

So-hyun's eyes widened. "W-what?"

"From what I remember, Kalynne's your only friend in the Diamond Cutters. You two were pretty close, always walking home together after practice, helping each other train." Hyrensia's lips curled into a wide, evil, grin. "Revieras and your friend next to you seem to care for you too. It'll hurt them and Kalynne more to lose you than if I just simply murdered Kalynne. Besides, you played a key role in exposing my being a nightmare to the coach, weren't you, So-hyun?" Hyrensia let out a menacing laugh. "You took the only thing I cared about away from me. Now I will do the same."

Raine tried to reach a hand out to stop Hyrensia, but nothing would allow her to move. She watched in pure horror as Hyrensia began to throw the baseball.

Kalynne ran towards So-hyun in an attempt to help her, but she was too far away to make it in time - her ability was out of reach, and she couldn't focus on the baseball which she needed to slow down.

Raine looked back at the tower. She could barely make out the figure of Kegan trying to shoot fireballs at Hyrensia, but he was too high up and couldn't reach her. She had seen earlier how Kegan had almost fallen from the tower while trying to descend, and knew that even if Kegan or Boris had tried, they wouldn't make it in time to save So-hyun either.

She couldn't bear to watch So-hyun die in front of her. And yet, she couldn't do anything about it.

But then she heard a rumble from the ground.

A FEW MINUTES AGO...

"You should not be worried about So-hyun. She is not the one in danger," Boris said to Kegan.

"Why? She's clearly going to be targeted. Hyrensia doesn't care about Raine, and she's already given up on trying to save the other members of the Emerald Justice. All Kalynne is going to do is slow down the baseball, and even then, she's surrounded by the Diamond Cutters. Hyrensia doesn't know Jocelyn. She won't go after her."

"Yes," Boris replied. "But Jocelyn is with her. The two are twin stars in a cosmic ballet, more than just friends. Jocelyn will not hesitate to trade her life to keep So-hyun's light in the galaxy."

It took Kegan a while to understand his metaphor, but once he did, he didn't respond positively. Even though he had only met Jocelyn a while ago, she was the first dreamer to have been enthusiastic and welcoming of Kegan's nature. Not to mention she was energetic, carefree, and chaotic. Just like him. He liked Jocelyn too much to not feel bad if she died. Plus, as stoic as Boris was, Kegan knew that Boris cared about her. The two were cousins, and were also close, despite Boris not showing it. Kegan didn't want to see the aftermath of Jocelyn's death taking a toll on his new friend.

He aimed at Hyrensia from above and shot out his flames. But they barely even touched the ground. "We're too high up! Maybe I can stabilise the tower with my fire, and then-"

"Time is not on our side," Boris interrupted. "They are already talking. Soon, Hyrensia will realise it is So-hyun she is after."

"What the hell do we do then?" For the first time, Kegan felt worried for the life of another. And much, worse, the life of a dreamer. *Damn it, Revieras! You're such a bad influence!*

"Do you know that some abilities persist after death?" Boris asked. Kegan figured he wasn't one for small talk, especially one that seemed out of topic. "I am an architect, much like Jocelyn. I liked creating structures, but I also wanted to be one with them. It's a fascinating yet abstract concept. We shape our buildings, and they shape us. Each piece of my soul has gone into everything I have ever done in my life."

Kegan retraced every sentence he remembered about Boris, and then realised where this was heading.

"My life will be demolished to pave a new land for Jocelyn. I may never see her art or sculptures, but if a little piece of me can remain in her heart, a brick that serves as a foundation for her future, then I do not mind the outcome." Boris looked at Kegan, his face as stoic and cold as usual, but his words carried a strange sense of serenity. "I want you to help build her way up to the sky and reach the gods themselves. Preserve her virtuosity - her spirit, and ensure that she will always have a world to be used as her canvas, where she will have the freedom to express her soul. My ability will work even after my physical body is gone. There is no other choice."

Kegan nodded. In all honesty, he would have preferred for So-hyun to die, and have Boris and Jocelyn live instead, but he knew it wasn't possible. Jocelyn was too cool to let a friend die like that, and Boris was even cooler to just let his cousin die like that, too. "I'll take care of her," Kegan promised.

Boris nodded and approached the edge of the tower. "Farewell, my friend." The words left his mouth like the last line of a poem, and as Kegan ran after him, he found that he couldn't see Boris anymore.

Kegan felt something stab at his heart. At first, he thought that a nightmare had attacked his chest from behind and turned. When he saw nobody there, he finally realised it was his own pain.

But he didn't like processing such emotions. Luckily, he didn't have to, because the tower began to shake again, allowing Kegan to experience what an earthquake felt like. The tower, as fast as it shot up, began to shoot back into the floor like some ground-dwelling mole, and before Kegan knew it, he was back on the grass field.

He searched everywhere for Boris, but he was gone. The fire and the bodies of the Emerald Justice were gone as well. Kegan looked at where Hyrensia and So-hyun were. Hyrensia stretched her arms out and threw the baseball, aiming at So-hyun's heart, despite Kalynne's panicked scream and Raine's desperate crawling.

As Boris had predicted, Jocelyn jumped in front of So-hyun, but before she could, the same tower that saved Kegan shot up from underneath So-hyun and Jocelyn, the platform providing them a safe space away from the baseball. Kegan couldn't help but notice that the tower was constructed even faster this time, and the baseball Hyrensia threw hit the tower.

But the tower, now stronger and more refined than ever, had the baseball ricochet off its walls, despite its inhuman speed.

And just like that, Hyrensia claimed her third strike.

* * *

Raine didn't know what just happened. A tower had just appeared in time, saving So-hyun and Jocelyn, and suddenly, all the nightmare energy around had disappeared, and as Raine managed to sit up, she saw that Hyrensia was no longer there. Only the baseball bat that Hyrensia had as a weapon laid there on the grass field.

Kalynne ran towards Raine. She didn't question the tower, nor asked anything of Raine. All she did was use her ability to help slow down the flow of Raine's blood to prevent her from bleeding out. "We're safe now," Kalynne whispered, the three words carrying much weight to them.

Five policemen entered the stadium, holding out their guns. Their jaws dropped when they saw the tower in the middle of the field, and an injured Revieras as well. About three paramedics from the medical team arrived too, and immediately attended to Raine.

With the help of the paramedics, Raine regained her strength after a while, and recovered enough dream energy to heal herself again. There was no sign of Boris around. She hadn't seen what happened then.

Three of the policemen had dragged Kalynne and the other Diamond Cutters away to safety, whilst the other two stayed to interrogate So-hyun, Jocelyn, and Kegan. Raine watched, slightly amused from afar as

Kegan hid his eyes from the policemen
inconspicuously with his hat.

"So, um, this is my...half-brother, from the
Mainland. He escaped before the place exploded and
came to Yeong-gu stadium to find me," Jocelyn
explained, lying through her teeth. She was nudging
her elbow against Kegan, who was desperately trying
to hold in a laugh.

"And how did the tower appear? Was it an ability?"
The policeman asked, somehow buying the story of
Kegan and Jocelyn being half-siblings, despite them
looking nothing alike.

Jocelyn's eyes lit up. "Oh! You remember Boris? He's
the one who- wait...Where is Boris?" She looked
around, suddenly unwilling to answer the policeman's
question. Sorrow slowly crept up to her face, and
that's when Raine figured just as much.

Boris died.

Ignoring the medical team's advice to stay still, Raine
walked forward to Jocelyn, who was now being
comforted by So-hyun as she cried. Kegan sighed. He
was the last person to see Boris, and Raine knew he
had to be the one to tell them all what had happened.
"Boris wanted you to live, Jocelyn," Kegan said, in an
uncharacteristic empathetic tone. "He knew you too
well. It was his choice to save you."

Tears poured out from Jocelyn and she started to
sob, falling down to the grass field and bawling in
front of everyone. So-hyun immediately sat down with

her and started patting her shoulder, before hugging
her again.

"I'll answer the questions, sir," Raine said to the
policeman, who had a flicker of sadness in his eyes as
he watched Jocelyn grieve over the death of her
cousin. But then he returned to a neutral expression,
one of pure professionalism.

"Sure thing."

Raine spent the next twenty minutes talking to the
authorities, telling them everything from when she
stepped into the Ambition realm with Kegan (except
for the fact that Kegan was a black-dreamer). When
Kalynne helped explain more of the past events that
happened with the Diamond Cutters, the policemen
were satisfied, and eventually left, while helping the
Diamond Cutters to leave the stadium as well.
Kalynne dragged her legs out of the stadium along
with her group. Even as a strong and bold leader, she
was still a regular dreamer, and all of them missed
their coach.

A policewoman with an out-of-place sling bag
approached Raine. She wore a helmet with a golden
symbolic badge embedded on it, her black uniform
making her look very professional and stern despite
the soft and inviting features of her face. She had
rounded cheeks and a smooth complexion with a
gentle appearance. "Good day, Revieras," she greeted,
despite everyone knowing that the day was in fact, not
good. "I was told you were present during the
black-dreamer's attack." The policewoman's use of

'black-dreamer' instead of 'nightmare' brought some sort of comfort to Raine. "May I ask what you were doing here and the events that occurred earlier?" She glanced at the giant structure of the dirt-hand and at the broken piece of the stadium's walls.

"I already told the other police everything with Hyrensia," Raine answered.

"No, not Hyrensia. I mean you. What will you do to save the dreamers?" The facade of her professionalism shattered. "Revieras, within this time, I saw my child getting murdered in front of my eyes, my parents burning in a building, and several other innocent civilians being tortured by the black-dreamers. If there is any way I can help you, I will. But I need reassurance that you know what you are doing."

Raine heard the crushed soul of a mother, daughter, and a dreamer all at once. She told her everything about the Dreamkeepers and how she planned to find them. She even included Kegan this time, although she tried heavily to refrain from using the words 'black-dreamer' and 'pyromaniac'. She spoke of Vanity and what occurred in the Mainland, and also Mr Voss, and how she had almost lost her life in an explosion.

The policewoman nodded when Raine was done with her long speech. "I see, I see. I wish you luck in finding the Dreamkeepers. Meanwhile, the Ambition realm's officials will take care of Yeong-gu stadium and its baseball team." Her stern tone softened to her genuine voice, a soft and relaxed one. "By the way, I

have something for you - think of it as a gift," she said,
almost in a whisper. She unzipped her sling bag and
pulled out a small plastic bottle. She unscrewed the
cap of the bottle and showed it to Raine.

  Inside the bottle was a pink liquid, smelling of
strawberries and dewdrops. Raine detected the
copious amount of dream energy emitting from the
liquid. It was so overwhelming and brimming with
energy that Raine almost felt sick. "Is that a potion?"
She asked, almost in disbelief. Potions were illegal in
all the dreaming realms because of the potential risks
they posed, and the way they were obtained were less
than humane.

  "It's confiscated from a criminal who took down an
elemental to create this healing potion," The
policewoman said. Raine gasped in shock - being able
to take down an elemental was an incredible yet
horrifying act of crime. "I hope this will be of use for
your ability. Be careful with it though, if you consume
too much at once, you will be poisoned. Dream energy
can be detrimental in large amounts." The
policewoman handed the bottle to Raine, who was
stunned by the appearance of the healing potion. She
assumed that a healing potion would look like one of
those fantastical round glass bottles with a cork, but
instead, it was just a regular small and opaque water
bottle. It had a thick layer and was cold to the touch.
"Don't worry, I was given permission to give this to
you." The policewoman smiled. "You're free to leave
now. Good luck on finding the Dreamkeepers. Stay

safe," she said, and then left Raine to find another
policeman who was inspecting the tower.

Raine wondered about the origins of the potion,
imagining what it was like to take down an elemental
and to create such a thing. She then remembered
about Jocelyn, So-hyun, and Kegan, and kept the
potion in her bag before running off to find them.

Jocelyn, So-hyun, and Kegan were still in the
stadium, standing by the exit. They had already waved
goodbye to the other Diamond Cutters, but Jocelyn
still remained in a heartbroken state, and the other
two were waiting for time to soothe her pain, while
So-hyun continued comforting her.

Raine slowed down as she saw Jocelyn's eyes all
puffy and red. She was still sobbing, her arm
smothered with tears. The moment Jocelyn saw her,
she immediately collapsed into Raine for a hug.
"What am I supposed to do, Raine? I miss him so
much," she sniffled, hugging tight onto Raine.

Raine returned the hug and patted Jocelyn on the
back. "He would want you to be strong and remain the
cheerful, bright Jocelyn that you are," she said. "I'll
save the world so you and your friends can live in it
without ever worrying about anything like this from
happening again."

Jocelyn gave a silent nod.

A couple of seconds went by, and Jocelyn let go of
Raine. Kegan looked at her as if he wanted to try
comforting her as well, but So-hyun was already back
by her side. Instead, he walked over to Raine. "You'll

keep that promise, right, Raine?" he asked. "I'm
beginning to feel bad now, thanks to you. You should
make up for it by finding the Ambition Dreamkeeper
now."

"That's right! The Ambition Dreamkeeper!" Raine
dug her map out from her bag. She had lost track of
her goal. Even though she had used much of her time
dealing with Hyrensia in the stadium rather than
hunting for the Ambition Dreamkeeper, Raine didn't
feel like she had wasted time at all. She unscrolled the
map and located the pinpoint of the Ambition
Dreamkeeper after a brief gaze, the neon dot catching
her eye easily.

Tracing her eyes to determine where exactly the
pinpoint was, a gasp escaped from Raine's mouth
when she saw where it was located - right in front of
her.

※★ ✦ ★※
Chapter 7: Ambition

Raine didn't know what the requirements were to be a Dreamkeeper. Logically, to be an Ambition Dreamkeeper, you would have to be an Ambition dreamer.

So when Raine saw the pinpoint right in front of her, where the only ones there were Jocelyn, So-hyun, and Kegan, it barely required a detective to figure out who the Ambition Dreamkeeper was.

Jocelyn still clung to So-hyun, and Raine noticed a baseball bat lying on the grass next to So-hyun's shoes. It was most likely Hyrensia's, and Raine assumed that So-hyun had reclaimed it as her own. "So-hyun, there's something I need to talk to you about," Raine started, her voice more serious than she intended it to be.

Jocelyn stopped crying, her misery now replaced with curiosity as she looked at her friend. "What is it?" So-hyun asked. Out of So-hyun, Jocelyn, and Kegan, Raine was most unfamiliar with So-hyun, and felt a little uncomfortable, unsure how to proceed with the conversation.

Luckily, Raine didn't have to continue. Kegan had peeked at the map and decided to suddenly be good at geography. Either that, or he guessed from Raine's expression. "Oh, she's the Ambition Dreamkeeper, right?"

Both Jocelyn and So-hyun's eyes widened at the suggestion. "Wait, what? So-hyun's a Dreamkeeper?" She asked, stunned. "You're talking about those special dreamers that have the potential to unlock control of the world and its gods? Those Dreamkeepers?" Her jaw dropped at her own revelation. "Holy macaroni! So-hyun!" She threw herself at So-hyun for another celebratory hug, squeezing the confused So-hyun half to death.

Raine would have never been able to tell that Jocelyn was just crying a minute ago. "How did you know all that?" She asked, wondering if Jocelyn, who was now shaking So-hyun like a maraca, had heard her question at all. She started to realise why the Subliminal realm was known to have the smartest dreamers out of all the other realms.

Jocelyn finally stopped shaking So-hyun out of sheer excitement and answered. "Oh! It's a very popular myth in the Subliminal realm! We'd always speculate on who our Subliminal Dreamkeeper could be back at school." The way she spoke and acted cleared all evidence of her breaking down a minute ago, and she was back to her agitated and cheerful self within a single revelation. "Wait, that means we can find the Subliminal Dreamkeeper too, right? That means I'll finally get to know who they are! Oh, I bet a hundred dollars that they're a guy! Who wants to join?"

Kegan shrugged. "Hell, why not?"

Raine doubted that Kegan even had a dollar to his name. She looked back at So-hyun, who was now free from Jocelyn's hug. "I'm the Ambition Dreamkeeper?" So-hyun asked Raine. "That...It doesn't sound right. I'm dream-blind. I can't be a Dreamkeeper. I can't even use dream energy at all."

Jocelyn placed her hands on each of So-hyun's shoulders respectively, her face plastered with eyes of confidence and a reassuring smile, as if she had spent ten years preparing to debunk So-hyun's claim. "So-hyun, you're one of the strongest and most ambitious dreamers I know. You don't need any dream energy to claim this awesome title of Dreamkeeper! You're already one of the very best! The world knew that you would be too powerful if you could use dream energy," Jocelyn sprinkled a bit of humour at the end, and So-hyun, who understood, smiled a bit. "I mean, look at you! You went through countless hours of baseball training! I know I would've quit within a month with all that vigorous stuff under intense heat. And the plan you came up with to Kalynne was-" Jocelyn gave a chef's kiss "-impeccable! Truly amazing! We survived a blood-thirsty vindictive nightmare thanks to you," she said, ignoring the fact that she'd just butchered the simplified version of Kalynne's name.

As if Jocelyn had spread her own dream energy to Raine and So-hyun, the whole atmosphere brightened up with Jocelyn's encouraging words, and all insecurity and fear crippled away within an instant.

So-hyun embraced Jocelyn into another hug, and
Jocelyn returned the favour too.

Raine smiled, too, and felt happy in knowing that
despite the horrible circumstances she was in, small
yet precious moments like this can blossom within, as
well.

※ ※ ※

Once So-hyun and Jocelyn broke free of each other,
Raine could see newfound determination swirling in
So-hyun's eyes. "I'm the Ambition Dreamkeeper," she
recited, as if trying to convince herself. "I need to help
Revieras save the world. And I will. For everyone."
So-hyun looked up at Raine with more confidence
than Raine had ever seen. "What do I need to do,
Raine?"

"Ah, well-"

Raine felt a surge of energy emitting from the map.
So-hyun's pinpoint, which originally had a white glow,
had turned into a bold red. It was as though the map
was trying to tell Raine that she had succeeded in
awakening the Ambition Dreamkeeper.

Apparently, the map also decided to reward Raine
for her endeavours by unlocking another pinpoint.
Raine had almost failed to notice it - the pinpoint
barely had its white glow and was almost transparent,
as if to say the Dreamkeeper's essence was slowly
wilting. Raine couldn't understand why the pinpoint
had such a weak glow, but then it made sense.

After all, the pinpoint was located in the Nightmare realm.

Raine's mind began to race. Is the map trying to tell her that she needed to go to the Nightmare realm to find the next Dreamkeeper? Why would the Dreamkeeper be in the Nightmare in the first place? Did something bad happen to them? For their pinpoint to be faint - it must be a sign that the Dreamkeeper is in trouble. Nightmare energy thrived in such a horrifying realm, and a dreamer's energy would easily be outmatched.

"'Sup?" Raine failed to notice that Kegan was peeking at the map Raine was holding. "You look worried."

"How observant of you," Raine quipped, trying to calm her mind. *Why wouldn't anyone be worried in this kind of situation?* Raine shook her head and decided to focus on So-hyun instead. "We have to find the other Dreamkeepers," she said, trying to plan out her next move. Surely it wouldn't be a wise idea if Raine decided to bring So-hyun and Jocelyn along to the Nightmare realm. Besides, they've already dealt with enough black-dreamers for a day, or rather lifetime. "The map shows that the next Dreamkeeper is in the Nightmare realm, so I think it's better if you two don't come along."

"That's a nice way to say they're weak," Kegan added.

Jocelyn's head perked up at the mention of the Nightmare realm. "I don't mind coming along." She turned to So-hyun. "What about you?"

So-hyun clenched onto Hyrensia's bat, unofficially claiming it as her new self-defence weapon. "Well, I won't be affected by the nightmare energy anyway. But we've already seen what Hyrensia did. We could potentially come across more nightmares and-"

"So-hyun! Jocelyn!" Kalynne came running over to Raine and the others, interrupting So-hyun's speech. "Oh, you're still here! I thought you'd already left."

So-hyun shook her head. "No, what's the matter? Didn't you all leave already?"

Kalynne looked surprised, but then she smiled. "Huh, you sound more confident now. I like it. Anyway, we did, but we all decided that we wanted to help clean up the stadium, y'know? With the tower and blood and everything? We could use your help as well," she said to Jocelyn.

"Do you guys really need to clean up the tower?" Jocelyn asked, as if the answer wasn't obvious. "That was like, the last thing Boris left, you know. I don't want to tear it down like it's an inconvenience."

"We'll figure something out. Maybe if you can pronounce my name right, I'd be more willing to help," she said, jokingly.

Jocelyn proceeded to spit out multiple poorly-made attempts at pronouncing Kalynne's name. "So-hyun! Let me borrow your tongue! You're the only one who can pronounce her name!"

"Um...I don't think I should," So-hyun replied, flushing.

Kalynne laughed. "I'm just kidding!" She looked at So-hyun, and then her eyebrows raised, giving So-hyun a knowing smile. "Ah, well, I'll put you two to work, and then the other Diamond Cutters will hold a funeral for the coach, sounds good?" Jocelyn and So-hyun nodded.

"Right! You all seem busy right now, right? I'll catch you later." Kalynne gestured to Raine and Kegan vaguely, before waving goodbye as she left.

Jocelyn sighed once Kalynne left, clearly disappointed. "I guess we don't have a choice in following you guys to the Nightmare realm. And I'll never figure out how to pronounce Kalynne's name!" An idea sparked in her head, and she jumped up in excitement. "Oh! How about this, Raine! when you find the next Dreamkeeper, come meet us back here at this stadium."

Raine nodded. "Sounds good." She was just about to ask whether they could exchange phone numbers in case of emergency contact, only to remember that Vanity's damage had still completely obliterated any use of technology.

"Be safe out there," So-hyun said to Raine and Kegan, before returning to find Kalynne. Jocelyn followed closely behind So-hyun after waving goodbye.

Raine waved goodbye in return, even though So-hyun and Jocelyn already had their backs turned. Nodding to Kegan, the two finally exited the stadium. She was happy not to be in the stadium anymore, and for the first time in a long while, optimistic. It was like turning over a page of a new book onto the next chapter. Although, she assumed the next chapter wouldn't be very nice, granted where they were headed. At least she already had a black-dreamer by her side. So it shouldn't be too bad, right?

Raine registered the location of the next Dreamkeeper before keeping the map in her bag. "Only problem is how we're going to get to the Nightmare realm from here. There aren't really any bus stops leading there."

There were lesser black-dreamers in the Ambition realm, and though desolate, it wasn't as if the whole city had been completely extirpated. Maybe the black-dreamers had calmed down, and the Ambition dreamers were unharmed. Maybe things could still function normally, and she could get some rest.

"Help!" Around the corner ran an Ambition dreamer. Her stylish overcoat and light skin was overshadowed by the fact that she was covered in blood. Horror and fear overflowed in her eyes, and the moment she saw Raine, she nearly collapsed. "Oh, Revieras! Thank the stars you're here! Please, help!"

Alarm bells immediately went off inside Raine's head. "What happened? Why are you covered in blood?"

"There- there was a nightmare."

Oh no.

"Don't worry. We'll take care of it. Right, Kegan?" She turned to Kegan, only to realise he was gone.

"Huh? Kegan?" She spun her head in all four directions, but Kegan was nowhere to be found. "Did you see the person with me go anywhere just now?"

"You're the only one here..." The Ambition dreamer said quietly, rather confused.

Oh no, again.

Raine sighed. Surely she could take care of a black-dreamer herself. How else could she call herself a custodian of Oneirolepsy? And anyway, she didn't like to think that she was depending on Kegan all the whole time. "Alright. Where's the black-dreamer?"

The Ambition dreamer pointed to one of the three sharp corners of the streets, the many buildings concealing whatever lay behind each route.

Raine nodded again. "If you need any help, there's plenty of dreamers in the stadium behind me. Take care." She made her way over to where the Ambition dreamer had pointed.

How did Raine fail to notice the gloomy atmosphere leaking out from the very ambiguous and suspicious corner? The moment that the sight of the stadium behind her vanished into the distance, it was as if she had accidentally walked into an alternate timeline where she stumbled upon the Nightmare realm instead of the Ambition realm. The whole pavement was smeared with blood, and it smelled like flesh and metal. There was no dream energy, no soul, no bodies present. Just an empty street.

Raine cautiously moved forward, leaving a trail of blood-stained footprints on the pavement. Her eyes darted everywhere, mind alert and body tense. She could be ambushed by any second now, and she didn't trust that she could let her guard down without encountering any looming threats. While Raine kept moving forward, she caught notice of a narrow corridor in between two nondescript buildings. She was just about to dismiss it as nothing more than a long path of nothing leading to a dead end, but then her whole body froze, and her mind was forced to process what she saw again.

The whole path had been painted with thin blood, as if a body had been dragged. And at the very dead end, a silhouette was crouched down. As soon as Raine caught sight of the silhouette, the clouds gave way to sunlight, and she saw a girl.

Consuming the body of a dead dreamer.

☀★ ✦ ★☀
Chapter 8: Split

After meeting a pyromaniac, a narcissist, and a vindictive black-dreamer, Raine assumed she would be prepared to take on a black-dreamer all by herself. She was incredibly wrong when she saw the very black-dreamer crouching in front of her, her lips smeared with blood and the body beneath her having its insides exposed. Some of its organs were even splattered around, like a picky child plucking out vegetables from their plate.

The black-dreamer was nothing short of a cannibal.

But why did she look so normal? Like a regular dreamer? Raine would have been less afraid of the cannibal if she looked like some sort of eldritch horror from the movies she's watched - but the fact that the cannibal appeared just like a normal dreamer from afar just solidified the fact that horrors like these were roaming around disguising as normal beings.

What was Raine expecting? It was a black-dreamer. She almost didn't want to label the black-dreamer as a cannibal as it would imply that black-dreamers and dreamers were one of the same kind, which might've been true, but Raine didn't want to be associated with them. Not anymore.

Technical terms didn't matter right now though, for the black-dreamer had her eyes on Raine, and her lips curled into a smile. Her dishevelled purple hair had blood dripping down from the strands, and onto the puddle of blood around her legs.

Raine began to tremble. Being eaten was the last thing she wanted to happen to her. But also, the fact that there was a circular saw next to the black-dreamer that had obviously been used prior to this encounter gave her the image of herself being dismembered alive, and that disturbed her deeply.

The cannibal wiped the blood away from her mouth and grabbed the saw. She stood up and muttered, "Well, if it isn't Revieras." Her voice shook Raine to her core. But more than that, she was feeling *ill*.

Maybe Raine had taken Kegan's lack of nightmare energy for granted, because now that she was facing a black-dreamer, much like Hyrensia, the cannibal's overwhelming energy easily took over Raine's dream energy. Raine couldn't think. Her eyes were fixated onto the bloody saw that the cannibal was holding.

"The nightmares in my realm tasted great, but oh, the dreamers here are much more...savoury. I wonder what you would taste like, Revieras. Well, should I find out now?" She continued, almost in a sing-song voice. It was like a terrorised sheep being preyed on by a hungry fox, and Raine didn't want to be eaten by a black-dreamer.

She quickly took out the potion from her bag. Well, as fast as she could manage the bag's zipper with shaky hands. Just as the cannibal started sprinting towards her, Raine took off the lid and threw it at her face, giving her at least a millisecond more to take a quick sip of the potion.

The liquid almost froze her tongue, giving Raine enough clues to suspect that the former elemental was probably that of ice. Regardless of the sudden cold that Raine didn't expect, it gave her a boost in dream energy, and as the cannibal's face flinched at the bottle cap being flung at her, Raine shot out an energy blast.

The energy blast hit the cannibal right in the stomach. Considering the direct opposition of Raine's dream energy against the cannibal's nightmare energy, she expected it to deal enough damage for the cannibal to back down. To Raine's shock, however, the cannibal brushed the attack off like a fly. Just how much nightmare energy did this black-dreamer have?

Raine maintained a distance between herself and the cannibal, in case the black-dreamer's nightmare energy decided to overthrow Raine's dream energy. She took a step back, not taking her eyes away from the black-dreamer. The cannibal was the one who stood at the dead end, and Raine could leave, even if she would end up being chased anyway. Raine didn't want to flee, however. She didn't want to leave a cannibal loose.

The cannibal let out a maniacal laugh before charging at Raine again. Raine dodged the saw by just an inch and she ran out of the corridor, not wanting to be trapped in a dead end with the black-dreamer. Her heart was pounding and while she ran, she continued shooting out more of her energy blasts. They didn't do as much damage as Raine would've liked them to, and the black-dreamer seemed unaffected, but they managed to slow the cannibal down, and Raine forced herself to take another sip of the freezing potion. She didn't want to use it all for this encounter, but she had little options. Her ability couldn't harm - only heal.

Wait, heal.

Raine's healing wasn't just about magically making wounds disappear. It was about channelling dream energy to turn it into a healing power. She had always used this on dreamers, but maybe her healing could work *against* a black-dreamer? It would make sense, after all. A black-dreamer had nightmare energy, and if Raine were to heal them, she would be channelling her own dream energy into their body. While the cannibal had a surprisingly high amount of nightmare energy, it did not match that of an elemental. The potion she had would be able to help her.

Raine bumped into a wall as she ran, failing to notice where she was running. She turned, only to realise she had been met with another dead end. The street was narrower than Raine recalled, and her intuition reacted after it realised her mind wasn't going to. She drank the potion in a large gulp, and at the same time, tried to distract herself from thinking about the saw by focusing on how she would probably lose her taste buds after drinking the potion.

The glimmering sensation of the dream energy quickly turned into a draining one; Raine's body was unable to contain all the dream energy she had just consumed. She didn't realise how generous she was when she drank the potion, but she was so quick and harsh due to panic that the potion was now practically empty.

Raine decided to dispose of the overwhelming dream energy by channelling it onto the cannibal, using her ability to heal. She didn't know what exactly she was healing, but she decided to heal anyway, hoping that it would work counterproductively on a black-dreamer.

The saw grazed Raine, ripping off a piece of fabric from her suit. The cannibal now stood directly in front of Raine, and she had reached her saw out, its blades spinning furiously. But the cannibal froze at that very moment, as if she was just shot. Raine ignored her own pain and focused on healing the cannibal, finding it ironic considering how she wasn't healing herself, the one who was truly in need of it.

The nightmare energy given out by the cannibal faded away, and Raine's dream energy spread across the whole streetway. The cannibal collapsed, and Raine stopped using her ability after healing her own wound from the saw's graze. For the first time ever in using her ability, she didn't feel drained. She wondered if this was how all elemental beings used their power without needing to worry about being drained of their energy.

Raine eyed the black-dreamer, who was now on the ground. Her saw, presumably her relic as well, laid just beside her. Raine's instinct told her to just take care of the black-dreamer, but she couldn't find it in her heart to eliminate life with her very own hands.

She took a look around herself. She was covered in blood, and she was alone. Just where did Kegan head off to?

A FEW MINUTES AGO...

Somehow, the loud engine of a dreamer's motorcycle hadn't caught Raine's attention. It was probably by pure luck that she had spun her head around the same moment the green vehicle zoomed past her, pulling the unsuspecting Kegan along with the driver.

The world was a blur for a moment, and Kegan was suddenly dropped somewhere far away from Raine. The environment was still very much ambition-realm like, but all the familiar landmarks that Kegan saw when he was with Raine had vanished. As a matter of fact, Kegan was in the middle of a wide road.

Kegan got his head to stop spinning and stood up. It was clear he wasn't alone, and when he looked in front of him, he saw a motorcyclist on her ride, dressed in black and green. The motorcyclist removed her helmet, revealing herself to be a brunette and Ambition dreamer, her eyes fixed onto Kegan.

"How dare you nightmares infiltrate our home. I'll bring the dreamers justice!" She shouted. Her motorcycle roared and she sped straight for Kegan.

Not wanting to deal with another speed-related ability-based opponent, Kegan lit the ground up in flames, and the blur that became of the Ambition dreamer was quickly thwarted by said flames. Kegan was close enough to grab the dreamer and yanked her down onto the ground, her head just a few inches away from the flames.

Her motorcycle veered and toppled over quite a distance away.

"You dreamers like to lose pretty quickly. It's almost anticlimactic," Kegan said, kicking the dreamer so that she wouldn't get up. He knew that a normal dreamer would never fare equally against an elemental, but still, if he was going to get dragged all the way to some unknown place, he would've liked a complementary challenge along with it.

"N- no wait! Don't kill me! I still have a future ahead of me! I'm a popular racer, and I can't let all my efforts go to waste!" The Ambition dreamer begged, her voice barely coming out.

"Oh ho, so you are. And so what? Your future was thrown out of the window the moment the nightmares escaped their cage you dreamers trapped us in." Although Kegan didn't necessarily believe what he was saying, he decided to have some fun as an oh-so-scary nightmare terrorising a helpless dreamer. He couldn't help but laugh as the dreamer whimpered, although he was slightly impressed at how the dreamer wanted to live solely because of her career. He supposed that was why Ambition dreamers were known as such.

He took a step back from the Ambition dreamer. She wasn't bleeding - at least not externally - but couldn't get up nonetheless. Kegan wondered if he should just incinerate her, but decided that Raine would probably chide him for that. Instead, he said, "I'll spare you, in exchange for something precious you have."

"What?"

Before the Ambition dreamer could say anything, Kegan walked away from her and towards the motorcycle.

Considering how motorcycles were just bicycles with engines, Kegan thought it would be effortless to steer one. He confidently mounted the now stolen vehicle, wanting to leave the Ambition dreamer cowering on the ground while he rode off in a cool fashion. Instead, he ended up veering and crashing into random walls and buildings at least more than ten times per minute. He wasn't particularly on a fixed route, since he had no idea where Raine was, but at least the detour was nice. His cap surprisingly made a decent helmet as well.

Naturally, Kegan rode into the part of the city where it was reeking of nothing but horror and blood. He noticed several eaten corpses with exposed organs scattered about and some bloody footprints, but he couldn't see or hear anyone.

That was until he sensed a familiar dream energy of Raine-ness nearby, more potent than usual, and made a sharp turn.

Raine had dragged the cannibal's body to a hidden part of the city and was trying to call the authorities, but her phone was still bugged by Vanity, and now she was just trying to ensure that the black-dreamer didn't suddenly wake up and start attacking her again.

It was very quiet with just Raine and the cannibal's unconscious body, until she heard the loud engine of the motorcycle and its wheels, but also Kegan's voice shouting, "Oh, Raine! Your ride is here-" before failing to hit the brakes and dashing right past her.

"Kegan! What- why do you have *that*?" Raine yelled incredulously, referring to his new motorcycle. "And where were you this entire time? You straight up disappeared!"

Kegan was too busy trying not to crash to answer Raine's question. He turned, or rather, spun, the motorcycle and sped back to Raine, managing to actually hit the brakes this time. "I got Kegan-napped by a dreamer. 'Sup with you?" He noticed that Raine was rather pale and had blood on her shoes.

Raine pointed over to the unconscious body of the cannibal.

Kegan's eyes widened slightly before he smiled. "Yo, is that Emeri?"

Based on his knowledge when he was in the Nightmare realm, he knew of Emeri as an infamous cannibal with her iconic weapon and relic - a circular saw which she's used every time she's victimised someone. Nightmares had no qualms killing or eating each other, and anyway, it was a good way to gain nightmare energy from someone. "I thought you would've ended up as her dinner," he said, mockingly.

"Yeah, me too. I was lucky, I guess." Raine kept the details to herself, and she looked at the motorcycle again before she gasped. "Wait, is that motorcycle from Jae?" She ran over to inspect the motorcycle.

"Who?"

"Jae is a very popular motorcycle racer known almost across all the dreamer realms. She's known for having an ability where 'her motorcycle goes as fast as how high her ambition is'. Basically, her motorcycle can go up to the speed of Hyrensia's baseball. In races though, she has to limit her ability." Raine explained. Kegan didn't really need Jae's backstory, considering how he thwarted her within three seconds, but acknowledged Raine anyway. "Was that how you vanished? She took you away on her motorcycle?" Raine gasped. "Did you kill her?"

Kegan laughed, wanting to say yes solely to see Raine's reaction. But instead, he told the truth. "She offered her motorcycle in exchange for her life." Half-truth.

Raine raised an eyebrow, obviously not buying Kegan's story. However, she just shook her head and sighed. "At least she's alive."

"Yup." Kegan looked at Raine expectantly. She was still standing next to the motorcycle, and she shifted about as if she was worried that Kegan would suddenly cause it to topple over and crash onto her.

"Well? Aren't we heading to the Nightmare realm?" He asked, when Raine didn't say anything.

"Now? On that thing?" She glanced at the motorcycle, worried.

"Yeah. Got a problem with it?"

"I mean, Jae is really cool on TV when she's on the motorcycle, but I don't think you're very fit to be in the driver's seat."

"Ouch. And you think you can drive better than me?"

"What? No? And anyway, I don't know if I should really head to the Nightmare realm." Raine glanced down to her boots, but decided to avert her gaze by glancing at the sky instead to avoid the unpleasant sight of blood. For the first time, Kegan realised that while everything that's happened prior was a normal day for a nightmare such as him, Raine was incredibly traumatised and tired. "No, we don't have time to rest. Anything bad can happen at any moment, and I don't want to be asleep when that happens. We have to find the Dreamkeepers fast to stop everything as soon as possible." She said, after a few seconds of silence.

"Right," Kegan replied, somewhat impressed by Raine's dedication. "Hop on, then."

Her expression changed. "I don't trust this."

"Would you like to walk there instead?" Kegan asked rhetorically, even though he knew that a lot of nightmares had spent countless hours on foot walking from one realm to another.

"No, on second thought, let me drive."

Kegan watched in disbelief as Raine smacked the glass screen on her phone several times, complaining about Vanity, when the internet was somehow restored. Thanking external circumstances, Raine decided to pull up a half-an-hour long video on the internet after searching 'How to ride a motorcycle for beginners'. Kegan sighed while Raine patiently watched the video, the voice of the instructor on the phone getting more irritating as each minute flew by. Raine fiddled with the motorcycle's features, and finally, once the video ended, Raine gave a sheepish smile and nodded to Kegan. The two got on the motorcycle and sped off.

"Kegan, should I be worried about being in the Nightmare realm?" Raine asked. She was constantly turning around in case Kegan either disappeared or was doing something that would make her roll her eyes again. They wore no helmets and the motorcycle barely fit the two, as it was most likely built for a sole individual, making Raine's constant head turns even more annoying with her hair flying into Kegan's face. He wondered if she would end up crashing after all.

Kegan considered Raine's question, thinking if he should be sarcastic or come up with a straight answer. "You probably should. Most nightmares hate anything that has to do with you or dreamers in general."

"But why though? I don't recall doing them any harm."

"Meh. Don't ask me."

"Why not? You're from the Nightmare realm and tried to attack me."

Kegan and Raine seemed to have recalled their first interaction differently. "No," Kegan said, slowly. "I was just having my fun with fire, and you stopped me, so I acted accordingly and attempted to eliminate the obstacle preventing said fun. Besides, you threw your phone at me first. You were actually the one who tried to attack me!"

"You caused a forest fire! And not just any forest - a forest that holds a very important energy core for the dreamers!" Raine raised her voice despite keeping a neutral tone.

"My point still stands. And besides, the Mainland got obliterated anyway," Kegan said. Raine sighed and decided it was pointless to argue.

There was silence for a while, except for the sound of the motorcycle's engine.

"Why do you keep turning around like that? I'll burn the edges of your hair strands if they keep flying in my face," Kegan asked, when Raine turned her head around for the millionth time.

"Keeping you in check," Raine replied, calmly. "It's very impractical and uncomfortable for the two of us to be riding together, so I prefer if you didn't try anything stupid."

Kegan frowned. "You're gonna end up crashing either way." He wondered if his presence was really so insignificant that Raine wouldn't notice if he was

suddenly yanked off the motorcycle again.
Considering this, he locked his arms around Raine.
"There. Now if I fall off or do something stupid, as you
say, you'll know." He grinned.

Raine went quiet for a while, and Kegan thought she
had just given up on the conversation and was now
staring blankly at where she was driving, but then she
replied after a while. "That doesn't really ease my
concerns, but thanks." Her 'thanks' didn't sound
sarcastic, so Kegan shrugged, unsure whether him
being considerate should be an insult. "I'm not really
used to being hugged by a black-dreamer. You're
quite hot, you know?" Raine suddenly said.

"Oh?"

"I mean, you're a fire elemental. Of course you're hot.
Just don't crush my stomach or anything." Raine
noticed the double meaning in her words and didn't
grow embarrassed. As a matter of fact, she had
probably done it on purpose. "But you know, I think if
any other black-dreamers tried to get near me, I
would probably scream."

"Why scream when you can beat them up?" There
was still a long way to the Nightmare realm, and
Kegan decided he was bored, so he decided to try
talking to a dreamer to see how one worked. Raine
was probably bored as well, anyway, considering how
she was starting to say strange things. "And why do
you keep referring to nightmares as
'black-dreamers'?" He suppressed the urge to add

another provoking comment at the end of his question.

Raine ignored Kegan's first question and instead answered his second. "Well, if you're familiar with the term 'black magic', then it should be easy to understand the meaning of 'black-dreamer'. It's just a synonym for the term, if not archaic. Besides, I don't feel comfortable calling them...that."

"So you're pitying the nightmares and calling them fake dreamers instead?" Kegan leaned closer to Raine, not because he was trying to threaten her, but rather due to a lack of space on the motorcycle.

Raine didn't hesitate. "I don't pity them; I hate them because they're cruel. I mean, I should be hanging out with my friend Soraya at a café, and instead I'm on a stolen motorcycle with you."

Kegan didn't refute.

The familiar sense of dread welcomed Raine and Kegan into the border between the Nightmare Realm and the other Dreaming Realms, with little particles of the barrier's magic lingering in the air like broken shards from a smashed window. The arrival of their destination allowed Raine to avoid continuing her conversation with Kegan, and she hit the motorcycle's brakes.

"Hang on," Raine said, when Kegan released his arms from her and was about to hop off. "I don't think it's very safe for us to travel on foot."

"Hm? Why not?"

"...Are you serious?" Raine gestured out to the Nightmare realm - it looked just about the same as before the barrier broke, if not more desolate, Kegan thought. He shrugged as he noticed numerous silhouettes escaping from his peripherals. The compelling nightmare energy seething from the place brought a sense of calm familiarity to Kegan, whereas Raine had to resort to using the remnants of her potion to get a boost of dream energy to protect herself. Kegan, having even less space with Raine moving her arm to reach her bag, decided to hop off the motorcycle.

"You'll be fine, there's no need to be paranoid." Kegan turned around to give Raine a reassuring and confident grin, but then he saw her body slump off the motorcycle, the weight of her bag dragging her down.

A tall figure appeared, dressed in a dark cloak with a clenched fist. The motorcycle stood idly between Kegan and the cloaked figure, before the latter spoke with a monotonous voice. "Cease, nightmare. For we are the Remnants of Keresius. Hand us your relic while we remain peaceful, lest you end up like Revieras."

Everything about the cloaked figure screamed 'cult member', and Kegan raised an eyebrow. He didn't even have a relic. Or well, he did, but that was for another story. "And where is Revieras ending up?" He asked, instead, feeling rather unthreatened.

Another similar monotonous voice responded behind Kegan. "You will find out." And with that, he was knocked over by another one of those cloaked figures. As Kegan landed on the hard and uneven ground, his vision began to blur. As intended, Kegan thought, before he went unconscious.

※★✦★※
Chapter 9: Remnants

Kegan decided that it was pathetic to stay unconscious from a tiny scratch on his head, ignoring how it could very well not be a mere scratch, but a concussion instead. The dimness of the room made it a little hard to discern between the lightless roof and the back of his eyelids, but his throbbing head and clutter of whispers everywhere reminded him of his consciousness, and he got up. The murmurings led him to believe that he had been kidnapped and placed into a library somewhere in the Nightmare realm, not that he knew any existed. Though if it did, Kegan doubted anyone would actually consider shutting up or returning any books they'd probably never borrow.

Anyway, he remembered that he had been very rudely hit on the head, and despite the fact that it was common sense not to deliberately give yourself a concussion, he had wanted this to happen, not because he was a masochist (which he totally wasn't), but because if Raine was going to be kidnapped by a bunch of random cloaked weirdos, it would only make sense if Kegan were to join her. He was convinced that Raine would've gotten herself killed otherwise, and Kegan would rather have his dignity stripped away from him by being attacked by an angsty nightmare than by defending a dreamer in his home realm. Although he didn't really care which side he played on, be it dreamers or nightmares, he wasn't willing to have the fact that he sided with Revieras exposed in case any die-hard supporters of the nightmares' monarchy decide to kill him for it.

The whisperings went away after a while. Kegan decided that his body was already well acquainted with cold concrete ground, and after a few seconds of ensuring that he could move without any of the cloaked figures screaming at his wake, sat up and glanced at his surroundings.

There wasn't much to look at, and even if there was, Kegan couldn't see. He considered turning himself into a makeshift torchlight, but decided that it would just attract any unwanted attention. After confirming a lack of Raines in the area, he carefully made his way towards the exit of the room.

An upsurge of nightmare energy took Kegan by surprise once he left, and Kegan reconsidered helping Raine at all if her dreamer nature was going to be absolutely annihilated by the sheer amount of nightmare energy in the place. He now strided along some sort of hallway, and despite the lack of light, he managed to not hit anything, and he let his gut instinct lead the way.

From the hallway, Kegan found another opening that emitted a faint light, attracting his attention. Peeking around the corner of the doorway, he found a typical ritual circle marked on the ground with white chalk - a weird yet familiar symbol drawn with many lit candles spread out evenly on the outline of the circle.

A few cloaked individuals were standing nearby, discussing with one another.

"...-and we'll be able to summon it sooner than we thought..."

"Yes, our work...relics...not in vain..."

"...King will..."

Kegan could barely make out what they were saying, and whilst eavesdropping, he seemed to have accidentally leaned too far away for comfort, and another cloaked member standing from an unlucky angle detected his presence. "We have an intruder! Over there!" The member shouted. All at once, every member in the room turned to Kegan and started shouting. Surprised, Kegan snapped his fingers and the candles' fire went out, snuffing out the only source of light in the room. Turns out, he was able to put out fires after all.

Unable to see anything, Kegan relied on his memory of the layout of the room and charged forward in the darkness, hoping not to trip over anyone or anything. There were a lot of noises of the members bumping into one another, and one of them even managed to pull at Kegan's jacket.

A hand grabbed onto Kegan from the front and yanked him away from the room. "Follow me, I know where Revieras is," a meek female voice whispered, almost mischievously. She began to walk forward while guiding Kegan in the dark.

"Oh, and who might you be?" Kegan asked, forgetting to keep his voice down. Thankfully, no

unwanted attention was caught. He didn't know if
whoever was leading him was a dreamer, a nightmare,
or another cloaked member who was either luring
him into a trap or turning against their own cult.

The individual didn't answer, but soon enough, the
two of them were led to a brighter hallway, and Kegan
could just barely make out the figure who stood
before him. It was a cloaked individual with a teddy
bear in one of her hands. "The Remnants of Keresius
want to use Revieras as their surrogate to summon a
being of pure nightmare. A real god created by pure
malice and darkness named the Eperlithian," she
explained, stopping in her tracks. She pointed to a
door in front of her. "Revieras is locked in there. We
need to be careful. The Remnants have accumulated a
large number of relics and have gained enough power
to-"

Kegan lunged at the locked door and kicked it open
whilst giving a dramatic yell, somehow succeeding in
doing so. He flew into the room, where he saw Raine
standing by a knocked-out member on the floor.
Raine was in the middle of freeing her wrist from a
knot of rope, and her face lit up when she saw Kegan,
only for it to be replaced with disapproval when
Kegan tripped over the uneven ground trying to walk
over to her.

"Kegan, what are you doing?" She asked,
unimpressed, leaving out the 'here' at the end of her
question on purpose.

"Why, I'm rescuing you, of course. You're welcome," Kegan replied, confidently. He earned a sigh from Raine and a giggle from the cloaked individual with the teddy bear.

Raine noticed the cloaked individual who had led Kegan to her. "Hey, watch out!" She pulled Kegan over to where she was standing, further from the cloaked individual, and took on a fighting stance.

"Oh! I come in peace." The cloaked individual put her hands up, surrendering. "I will help you two escape from this place."

Raine and Kegan exchanged glances. "Should we trust her?" Raine whispered to Kegan, still unconvinced.

"Well, she was the one who led me to you," Kegan stated.

"Why does she have that kid's toy, anyway?"

Kegan shrugged. "In any case, I can incinerate her if needed."

"Is your first instinct to set everything and everyone you see on fire?" Raine chided.

After a little back and forth between Raine and Kegan, the two finally looked at the cloaked individual again. "We accept your help. But if you try anything funny, you'll regret it." Raine went over to reclaim her bag, which was sitting on top of the unconscious member whom she'd knocked out before Kegan and the cloaked individual arrived, and slung it across her torso.

The cloaked individual nodded and gestured to the two to follow her as she left. Raine and Kegan obliged despite still feeling suspicious. Behind them, they could hear other members catching up and shouting nonsense at them.

At the end of the hallway was a door, and when the three made it to the other side, Raine closed the door and locked it with a nearby chair.

Kegan looked to see where Raine pulled the chair out from, only to realise the whole room was filled with chairs, neatly arranged into rows and columns. A large stage lined up at the front of the audience of empty chairs with curtains and all, and a table was positioned right in the middle of it, bearing all sorts of relics, be it jewellery, toys or accessories. A member of the cult stood on the stage, overseeing the relics, and when they saw the cloaked individual with the teddy bear, they took off their hood, revealing themselves to be a woman with tan skin and dark hair. "Lilac. So you have decided to turn your back on us after all. How unexpected of the leader's daughter." The woman smiled maliciously.

Surprised, Kegan and Raine turned to look at the cloaked individual, who also removed her hood. Her reddish-brown long hair landed on her shoulders as she spoke. "I never wanted to be a part of this," she replied, hugging her teddy bear for support.

The member began to walk down from the stage and towards Lilac. Kegan prepared to light the whole place up, and Raine took a step forward. "This is your home. This is where you belong." The member smiled at Lilac, almost in a deranged manner. "Why betray us when we've cared for you so much when you were growing up?"

"The exit is backstage," Lilac whispered to Raine and Kegan, despite looking petrified.

The locked door behind them started to throb as the other cult members from the other side tried to break their way in. Lilac flinched and Raine shouted to the member. "Alright, back away now, or else."

The member's smile turned upside down at Raine's demand, and she scoffed. "Who are you to stop me? Just because you are Revieras does not mean you are superior to all the nightmares. You are in our realm now, and I have all the relics here that can easily stop you."

Raine couldn't even do anything before her dream energy waned from the nightmare energy and relics. She grew faint and Kegan had to catch her before she collapsed. "Too much nightmare energy," she muttered, trying to breathe.

Out of nowhere, a girl appeared behind the cloaked individual. She wore a white shoulderless top and short green jeans, a tall and slim figure with her long hair half blonde half brunette, and her eyes emerald green. Kegan recognised the girl's white pupils as a characteristic of her being a dreamer, and was somewhat glad that he didn't need to see another person wearing an ugly cloak.

All the lights in the room went out, and although Kegan wasn't sure if it was intentional, he could hear fighting and struggling between the member and the dreamer. When the lights returned, the member was frozen in place, as if she had been tasered and paused in time.

"Come on, let's go!" The dreamer rushed over to the stage and back, and Lilac followed after ensuring Raine was being helped by Kegan, who sighed before accepting his role as Raine's official bodyguard and babysitter.

There was a door with an exit sign backstage, and the dreamer kicked the door open without hesitation, earning Kegan's respect as she did so. The three followed the dreamer out of the cult's base, and they were outside once again. They ran and ran until the base could no longer be seen, and none of the Remnants of Keresius were in sight.

Raine recovered from the overwhelming nightmare energy now that the pile of relics was no longer in the vicinity, although she was still out of breath. She still leaned onto Kegan, who began to wonder if she was really that weak or if she was trying to be funny.

"Soraya! It's really you!" Raine pulled away from Kegan once she recovered enough to recognise the other dreamer. Kegan put two and two together and realised that the emerald-eyed dreamer was actually one of Raine's friends, and one that she's mentioned to him about before.

"Raine! I can't believe it! You're in the Nightmare realm!" The dreamer exclaimed excitedly, still panting from running. "I was so worried about you! I couldn't contact you, and my family was in danger. I was so scared." Soraya's eyes began to tear up, and she hugged Raine in a sentimental display, as if the two hadn't just escaped the base of a mad cult.

Raine smiled and started to cry out of relief as well, despite her condition. "I was worried about you too! So many things have happened since the siren sounded." Eventually, she let go of Soraya and turned to Lilac. "Your name is Lilac. Correct? I heard you're the leader's daughter? Do you mind explaining everything?"

Lilac glanced down at the ground and hugged her teddy bear again. "Well...The Remnants of Keresius is a cult led by a leader known as Master Luranos. He took me in when..." Lilac stopped mid-sentence, losing her train of thought. "Anyway, this is Sir Bamesetton! He helped me through a lot of tough times!" She held out the teddy bear and made it wave with one of its paws. "The Remnants of Keresius have been stealing relics from nightmares."

"Well, I'm glad I don't have one then," Kegan sneered.

Raine leaned a little closer to Lilac, her eyebrows raised. "Wait, those eyes. You're a dreamer?"

Kegan and Soraya were equally surprised, and Kegan squinted his eyes at Lilac. "I don't sense any dreamer energy from you," he commented. Although they were in the Nightmare realm, where nightmare energy was predominant, he could at least detect a little bit of Raine and Soraya's dream energy, but with Lilac, he felt nothing.

"I don't need dream energy to be a dreamer, right?" Lilac asked, as if seeking for confirmation. Neither Soraya nor Raine answered her, and Kegan shrugged.

"Are you sure you're not lying?" He asked, in a more teasing tone. Raine gave a disapproving glance at him, but granted how she was involved with the very same Remnants of Keresius that just kidnapped her and Kegan, didn't interrupt.

"I'm not lying!" Lilac responded, more anxious now.

"Well, you're no different from a nightmare if you're with this shady nightmare cult, right? You're not a dreamer after all."

It felt like an invisible storm was brewing in Lilac's head, invisible for everyone else to see, and Kegan had only exacerbated said storm. Despite Kegan not recalling having said anything offensive, his constant prodding and mocking caused Lilac evident distress, pressing her fingertips against her head. "No! I am a dreamer! I am! I..." Sir Bamesetton was dropped onto the ground. "I'm not a black-dreamer, I've just been trapped here...I've been with the Remnants of Keresius for as long as I remember, but..." Her voice was shaking, and Lilac's legs gave out and she started hyperventilating. "I-I'm a dreamer...right?"

Raine and Soraya immediately kneeled beside Lilac to help her calm down, whispering little phrases of assurance and comfort. Kegan quickly looked away, feeling just ever so slightly guilty for causing the panic attack. But then his eyes went right back to Lilac as he realised:

Something was wrong.

Because just then, a surge of dream energy manifested, and within the blink of an eye, the teddy bear on the ground had turned into a beastly creature, about nine feet tall. Enormous claws, sharp as obsidian, extended from massive paws and pointed directly at the others menacingly.

Raine and Soraya screamed at the sudden appearance of the real Sir Bamesetton, getting up from their bruised knees and scattering away from the bear. Raine attempted to drag Lilac up from the ground, but Sir Bamesetton swung its ginormous paw and snatched Lilac away from Raine, scooping her up and squeezing her whilst giving a loud growl.

"Lilac!" Raine shouted. Lilac looked resigned, as if about to fall asleep, despondent to her environment. Raine gave another shout as Sir Bamesetton stomped its feet, causing a semi earthquake.

"Save yourself first, you idiot!" Kegan shouted, failing to take his own advice by running into danger and pulling Raine away from Sir Bamesetton's range of attack. He summoned a swarm of flames against the creature. This proved useless when Sir Bamesetton simply extinguished the flames with the swipe of his paws, and he roared again. "Oh, well that's not good," Kegan said to himself, having the

ineffectiveness of his elemental powers bring more
dread than he would like to admit. What was he
supposed to do now?

"Soraya, do you have any tricks up your sleeve?"
Raine asked, in a panic.

"I was just about to ask you that!" Soraya shouted.
"Lilac! Please wake up and disable your ability!"

✳ ✳ ✳

It was difficult for Lilac to remember anything about
her past.

She didn't even recall how she obtained Sir
Bamsetton in the first place, and she had convinced
herself and others that it was her relic, despite her not
being a black-dreamer. Or maybe she was? These
sorts of things drove Lilac crazy. She didn't know if
she was a dreamer or a black-dreamer anymore.

Dreamers dreamt and lived in the dreaming realms.
Black-dreamers caused chaos and evil and lived in the
Nightmare realm. Lilac dreamt, and yet she lived in
the Nightmare realm. She had no family name, and
she had no nightmare energy, but was able to
manipulate it better than dream energy. She hadn't
seen a mirror in a long time, but from the brief
interaction she's had with Raine and the others, her
eyes were that of a dreamer.

Then why did Lilac feel as if she was neither dreamer
nor black-dreamer? Was she really that broken? It felt

like a piece had been chipped away from her ever since...ever since the incident.

But now, as she lay unconscious, she felt the piece connecting back to her once more, and something brushing against her legs caused her enough discomfort to open her eyes.

Lilac stared at the night sky where the full moon illuminated, and as she turned to her side, she saw tall blades of grass brushing against her skin - the cause of the uncomfortable sensation on her body. She sat up and caught sight of Sir Bamesetton standing before her - a cute and animated bear albeit its huge size. Its marble eyes reflected the moonlight, and Lilac felt the urge to run at Sir Bamesetton to hug him and feel its soft fur.

Lilac and Sir Bamesetton were the only ones in the endless grass patch, and the strange environment helped Lilac to conclude that she was, in fact, dreaming. She found herself surrounded by tall trees with leaves darkened by the night sky - an isolated forest where she was the only dreamer around.

She tried to remember what was going on before she had her so-called panic attack, but it was hard to focus on her thoughts as Sir Bamesetton started speaking. "Are you awake, my child? I hope you are unharmed." His voice sounded like an old English story-teller with its calm and gentle speech, and immediately Lilac was put at ease.

Entranced, Lilac stood up and carefully walked over to Sir Bamesetton. Of course, she knew that he was always real, even when in wake, he was just a soft toy. But for her to see him able to talk and move by himself, it enthralled her. "What's going on? Why do I feel like this?" Lilac asked, her voice soft.

"Why don't we take a little break from reality and explore this cosy place?" With an indirect answer, Sir Bamesetton slowly turned around, prompting Lilac to turn and look where he was facing. There was an isolated cottage not too far off that appeared somewhat familiar, even though Lilac couldn't put a finger on where she saw it. Such a pretty cottage couldn't have been in the Nightmare realm. "You seem to be troubled. A little walk will help make you feel better." Sir Bamesetton strided towards the cottage, and Lilac followed along, still slightly hesitant.

The cottage was guarded by a row of flowers of all sorts, giving out the sweet fragrance of lilac flowers and whatnot. A small path led up to the door, with stepping stones made of polished rocks. Lilac half-expected Sir Bamesetton to crush said rocks with his enormous body, but it felt as if he was weightless, and as light as a regular soft toy.

Lilac was just about to question how Sir Bamesetton would manage to fit into the door frame when she found herself gripping onto the teddy bear in her hand. She stared at it and blinked for a second before deciding not to question the logic of dreams and entered the cottage.

Several paintings of scenery in vibrant colour decorated the white stainless walls, with filled bookshelves lining up against the edges of the room in neat order. The living room was furnished with a large soft-coloured sofa placed before a fireplace, with a large carpet resting on the floor. Numerous soft toys nestled onto the floor's carpet, and Lilac bent down to look at them more carefully, experiencing a strange sense of nostalgia.

"Tell me, child, what is troubling you?" Sir Bamesetton's voice echoed through the house, its origins unknown. Lilac picked up and placed the teddy bear in front of her on the carpet while adjusting her knees into a comfortable position as she sat, trying to form a concrete answer.

Her head was filled with all sorts of things, and she struggled to find a way to properly express herself. "I don't know who I am." She replied, still unsure. Lilac recalled her days where she had to spend all her time in the dark basements of the Remnants' lair wearing a filthy cloak and performing numerous rituals that she didn't even understand.

"Tell me then. Who are you?"

"Lilac," she replied, without hesitation, confused by the nature of the question. But then a thought popped into her head: Family names. Or commonly known as a surname. Black-dreamers didn't have such things, but dreamers did. If Lilac had a family name, then that would mean she was, in fact, a dreamer. She tried hard to recall what it was, but even in wake, Lilac's name was hardly ever used by anyone else. How was she supposed to remember what her own family name was when her given name was already obsolete where she lived?

"Lilac," Sir Bamesetton echoed, sending chills down Lilac's spine. It had been so long since her name had been used, much less by Sir Bamesetton himself. But as her own name carried by the voice of Sir Bamesetton reached her ears, Lilac swore that it wasn't her first time hearing it. But how was that even possible? Sure, Sir Bamesetton was real, but he had no voice as a soft toy. Yet, Lilac felt as if she's heard his voice somewhere before.

The voice went away, and a knock on the front door took her by surprise. Lilac tried to stand up to go answer the door, but she was glued to the carpet and couldn't move. The knocking grew into banging, and she remained helplessly stuck on the floor. Lilac wanted to cover her ears from the noise, but then something moved, which caught her attention.

A casually-dressed man with a blurry face walked out from one of the bedrooms beyond the living room Lilac was in and headed towards the door. Lilac flinched, surprised that there was even another being in the cottage in the first place. She watched the man with much caution, squinting her eyes at his distorted face.

The man opened the door, and it revealed a cloaked person on the other side. Lilac felt her heart skip a beat. "What are you doing here? Meetings aren't today! Are you trying to compromise what we have been doing?" The blurry-face man, whose voice perfectly emulated that of Sir Bamesetton's, yelled angrily. The cloaked person was talking, but Lilac couldn't hear anything, because the face of the man with Sir Bamesetton's voice became all too clear.

It was her father.

Lilac watched her father and the cloaked person exchanging words vehemently with a blank expression, failing to take in the information of her father's identity. Why did he have Sir Bamesetton's voice? Or rather, was it the other way round?

Lilac's father vanished, and suddenly, the invisible barrier preventing the cloaked person from entering the cottage disappeared, and he stomped over to where Lilac was sitting.

The cloaked person grabbed Lilac by her hair, lifting her up, and Lilac saw that she was in the body of a child, with her stubby legs and small torso, before the cloaked person went back to the entrance of the cottage and threw her out.

Lilac landed on the cold and dirty grass, a feeling of agony ate into her heart, but she couldn't understand why. Was she just evicted from the cottage? Why did her father leave? Why did nobody tell her anything at all?

The world transitioned from the empty grass path outside into an enclosed room that was devoid of any furniture, similar to the underground of the Remnants' lair. Lilac pulled herself up from the

ground, and found that she was in her own body
again. It was only then she realised that the
mysterious cottage from earlier bore the same interior
of her home. At least, the home she lived in before the
Remnants of Keresius took her.

  There was no source of light in the enclosed room,
and yet a spotlight from nowhere shone down on her.
A few rose petals scattered from above, slowly
descending to the ground. The walls were lined with
mirrors scaling beyond the unseeable ceiling.
The mirrors reflected a younger self of Lilac, an image
that she hadn't seen in years.
The younger Lilac held up a Sir Bamesetton in her
arms, looking timid and afraid.
Lilac found herself with the teddy bear again.

  "Tell me again. Who are you?" The voice asking was
not Sir Bamesetton's, but her own. Unknowingly,
Lilac dropped the bear as if it was on fire, and the
plush in the younger Lilac's arms vanished as well.
The moment it did, the younger Lilac was turned from
a mild and resigned girl to a confident and grand
awe-inspiring child actress, extending her arms and
head out in all directions posing dramatically.

  Lilac made eye contact with the girl in the mirror,
and everything flooded back to her. She remembered
how much she loved theatrics, and how much she
loved putting on plays with her stuffed toys for her
parents to watch. She remembered her unique speech,
and how she'd turn heads wherever she went, despite

only being a child then. All of it had been lost, but now, Lilac knew she was whole again.

"I am Lilac Rygh!" She cried out, with a grin. And then, she reached her hand out, phasing through the mirror, and extended her hand out to Lilac.

But before Lilac could feel the hand of her younger soul, she felt herself waking up. As if she had a choice, she reluctantly allowed her mind to travel from the dreaming back to reality.

※ ※ ※

Lilac found herself on the prickly ground, which had tons of scuffing scattered everywhere, leaving bits of cotton and whatnot around here. It wouldn't have been so eerie if not for the fact that it was Sir Bamesetton's corpse. Strangely though, Lilac didn't feel the urge to cry. She saw Soraya, Kegan, and Raine, with their eyes all on her.

She felt foreign in the Nightmare realm, and missed the whimsical nature of dreams. For the first time in a long time, she felt like herself again, but more than that, she felt like a true Pure dreamer. No longer was she a mould crafted by the hands of the Remnants of Keresius, and she would show everyone her true nature.

An epiphany born from the dream she just had took over her mind, and although all sorts of panic raided her thoughts not too long ago, she felt calm and composed now, if not a little tired. Everything around her used to be nothing but a stale grey, but now, the lively colours were slowly returning, and Lilac could see everything again, including herself.

She had been clinging onto Sir Bamesetton for a long time, and it practically became her 'relic' when she conformed to the nightmares taking her in, but now that the stuffings of the bear scattered like tumbleweeds in the desert, she felt herself detaching from the darkness. Lilac wanted to thrive in the light again. *In her spotlight.*

The others continued to stare at her warily, wondering if she would start crying from the ripped shreds of Sir Bamesetton or act like a dazed damsel in distress with no awareness of what had just transpired, but Lilac got up from the ground and stood confidently with her chest out, feeling taller than she had in her entire life.

"Lilac?" Revieras asked, once she saw that Lilac was up and uninjured. "Are you feeling okay?"

Lilac removed her cloak and smiled broadly, knowing that this was the start of a new play, one where she was the main actress. "Apologies for the outburst," she heard herself saying. "My name is Lilac Rygh, a Pure dreamer."

※★ ✦ ★※

Chapter 10: Dream

Raine had just gained the rare experience of fighting with a sentient doll-turned monster of a bear, and frankly, since she was playing the perpetual role of support in her strange trio, she did not expect herself to survive, especially in the Nightmare realm. She seemed to have underestimated the power of adopting a fire elemental, and Soraya, who was probably the best manager and friend in the world, had more skills than just looking pretty.

Raine tried to steady her breathing again, panting ceaselessly after exerting what little dream energy she had left trying to fight the gargantuan mammal in the Nightmare realm no less. When Sir Bamesetton was horrifyingly ripped into shreds, the bloodshed and guts turned into comical bits of stuffing within the blink of an eye, sparing everyone from watching a dismembered creature tearing to pieces, and Lilac was dropped to the ground while still unconscious.

Once everyone figured that Sir Bamesetton wasn't going to reappear anytime soon, they crowded around Lilac to check on her, and Soraya confirmed that she was just sleeping and still alive, though she doubted if Lilac would be very happy to see Sir Bamesetton gone.

When Lilac stood up and gave a very late introduction of herself, Raine was stunned to hear a different voice and personality altogether. Instead of the usual meek and quiet voice Raine heard of Lilac

while she was under her cloak, there was this
magnificent and confident voice that boomed out, like
those actors and actresses in a play. Lilac looked
completely different without the ugly cloak as well. Of
course, her hair was a mess and she was dirty, but it
wasn't wise to expect pristine condition after living in
the Nightmare realm as a member of the Remnants of
Keresius. "A Pure dreamer?" Raine asked, not sure
what to make of the sudden change of Lilac's
personality. She decided it was best not to question it.

Pure dreamers were an interesting type of dreamer.
They were known as dreamers who originated in the
Dream realm known for their creativity and
imagination, and often they carried more dream
energy than the other dreamers. As all the other
dreamers reasonably deduced that calling them
'Dream dreamers' was weird, they decided to call
them 'Pure dreamers'. Thankfully, none of the other
realms thought of it as an indirect way of calling them
impure, and the Pure dreamers accepted their new
terminology.

A familiar glow of warmth overtook Raine's instinct
and she took out the map from the bag she was
carrying around. When the map was finally in her
hands, she quickly realised that the instinct she felt
was her attraction to the dream energy emitted from
the Pure Dreamkeeper.

"Woah, is that the map to find the Dreamkeepers?"
Soraya's eyes gleamed as she looked at the map for
the very first time, the pinpoint of the Pure

Dreamkeeper shining brighter than any star Raine
had seen. "It's incredible," she whispered.

Raine was still unfamiliar with how the map worked,
but the Pure Dreamkeeper's pinpoint was now
glowing more and more, obvious that Raine was very
close to the Dreamkeeper. She glanced at Soraya and
then at Lilac. Her gut told her that Lilac was the
Dreamkeeper, but Soraya could also be a potential
candidate.

"Soraya, what kind of dreamer are you?" Raine
asked, almost sheepishly. Like accents, dreamers had
different variations of dream energy depending on
which realm they came from. Because Raine was
mostly in the Mainland amongst mixed dreamers, she
lacked the natural skill to differentiate dreamers
purely based on the dream energy they gave off, not
that regular dreamers had much energy to give off
anyway.

Speaking of accents, Soraya had an unrecognisable
accent as well, unlike So-hyun, who had a very strong
accent connecting her to the Ambition realm. Raine
had always assumed Soraya was a mixed dreamer just
like herself but had never asked in their three years of
friendship.

"Oh, I'm a mixed dreamer, why do you ask?" Soraya
slightly tilted her head, giggling. "I thought you knew
me, Raine! Three years and you don't know?" She
teased, allowing Raine to turn red from
embarrassment.

"Well, I'm looking for the Pure Dreamkeeper, and it appears Lilac is it." Raine's eyes shifted from Soraya to Lilac to see her response.

"The adopted child of a cult leader is actually a Dreamkeeper? How incredible!" Lilac cried. "Alas, I shall graciously accept this title." She gave a little bow, surprising Raine with her reaction. Raine had expected a somewhat similar reaction to So-hyun's, but maybe she had misjudged Lilac's true character after all.

"Do you know what being a Dreamkeeper entails?" Raine asked slowly, when Lilac lifted her head up again. Raine didn't want to give an information dump about her quest and the Dreamkeepers every time she needed to awaken one, and was starting to consider writing a summary on a piece of paper and giving it to them like some sort of brochure.

"Why yes, Master Luranos wanted to eradicate them," Lilac said, calmly. "I've learned that they are the backbone of the realm they represent, is that right?"

Raine gulped. "Eradicate?" She asked, wondering if So-hyun would be better off not knowing Lilac and vice versa. Of course, she would like to believe that Lilac was on her side, but the Remnants of Keresius was a different breed entirely.

"Yes! But do not worry. If I am responsible for bringing the Remnants to you, then I am also responsible for taking them out." Lilac nodded, confidently.

"Then, do we go back to find the leader of that cult?" Soraya shivered. "They have a lot of power, especially with their relics. Is it really a good idea to fight them now?" She glanced at the floor, as if wishing that the bear would come back alive to aid them in their quest to defeat the Remnants of Keresius.

"You know, I could always just set their whole base on fire," Kegan suggested, a grin starting to form on his face.

"Kegan, what did I say about setting things on fire?" Raine snapped, feeling like a disappointed mother disciplining her rowdy child. Except in this case the rowdy child was an arsonist black-dreamer. She gave a more exasperated tone than an angry one, and Soraya giggled at the two.

"We'll end up antagonising them, and it'll cause them to be more active and split up, especially if their nest gets destroyed. We should leave them all in a congregated area and come back when we're more powerful. Besides, they have a lot of power from the relics they've amassed over time. It wouldn't be wise to just...set everything on fire," Soraya explained, gaining even more respect and admiration from Raine with her wise words.

"Are you suggesting we leave them be?" Lilac asked, almost incredulous.

"No no, I think Soraya is right. We should focus on finding the last Dreamkeeper. It's not like the whole cult will just attack us all at once, right? We're almost there, anyway." Raine supported Soraya's standpoint

and felt a little excited fantasising about meeting the
Subliminal Dreamkeeper, before realising the
inevitable fact that she would have to end up in
Kolshav's Castle as the map stated. She wondered
what the ultimate weapon could be - something so
powerful that it would be able to break up the
Remnants of Keresius and restore the barrier,
hopefully.

"You do realise that we're talking about a group of
angry unhinged minions who were the ones who
probably destroyed the barrier in the first place,
right?" Kegan asked. He noticed that around him
were other fellow black-dreamers.

Raine and Soraya must have noticed it too, because
Soraya then announced: "I'll stay here to defend
against the Remnants of Keresius. You three can go
find the last Dreamkeeper!" She glanced and winked
at Kegan, who clearly missed her subtle hint of
requesting him to join her. Soraya shot him a
disappointed look when Kegan just gave a thumbs up.

"I will stay with Soraya!" Lilac jumped out, seeing
Soraya's expression. She puffed out her chest and
grinned. "I have spent countless years amongst them,
my knowledge will give us an advantage to defeat
them." She held out the bear plush. "Sir Bamesetton
will help, as well!"

The scattered stuffing had disappeared from the
ground. Raine's brain froze for a second before
shaking her head and dismissing it as Lilac's
subconscious ability to somehow revive Sir

Bamesetton. She sighed and replied, "Are you sure? You've been in the Nightmare realm for way too long. Just let Kegan do it." She grinned a little as she saw Kegan eyeing her with shock, but then he smiled, and Raine reconsidered leaving an unsupervised Kegan in the Nightmare realm.

"Hell yeah, I finally get a chance to blow people up!" Kegan smashed his fist against his other palm, making Raine seriously reconsider her initial idea. But Soraya gave her another wink and a "don't worry, I'll take care of him" look. Raine sighed and felt a little better thinking of Soraya as an older sister who could help her while she was busy. They were similar, like two cousins, and Soraya was definitely older and gave the charm of a protective sibling. Besides, she had the credentials of being Raine's reliable manager. She could handle a pyromaniac in the Nightmare realm.

Raine finally nodded. "Alright, it's settled then," she said, grabbing Lilac by her free hand. "Let's welcome you back to the realms of dreaming."

※★✦★※
Chapter 11: Reality Recess

Raine and Kegan had stuck together like glue thus
far, so she would've assumed a much more
sentimental goodbye when she decided to leave him
with Soraya in the Nightmare realm.

Instead, what happened was that Raine's presence as
well as Kegan, Soraya, and Lilac had attracted a good
number of other black-dreamers who, unlike Kegan,
had no qualms about pouncing on them like a bunch
of hungry animals. While Raine held Lilac by the arm
and dashed away on foot wishing she still had Jae's
motorcycle, screams of fury and blasts of fire roared
behind them, as if the two were in some action movie.

But after a little bit of running, Raine came to a quick
conclusion: She didn't know where she was going.
Despite her keen sense of direction, the Nightmare
realm was an unpredictable and dangerous place,
filled to the brim with nightmare energy, and she
didn't want to run around blindly when she could
hardly defend herself.

Thankfully, Lilac, who was probably the most
knowledgeable dreamer Raine knew when it came to
all things black-dreamer and knew the layout of the
Nightmare realm better than the back of her hand, led
the two of them, and after giving a quick revelation
that she knew how to manifest nightmare energy
better than dream energy, managed to lead herself
and Raine out of the Nightmare realm. Before Raine

knew it, she was standing outside of the shattered barrier once again, except this time she had Lilac with her instead of Kegan.

Despite their exit from the Nightmare realm, darkness persisted, and Raine was anxious she had been poisoned mentally by some other black-dreamer to cause her a state of blinded vision. She eventually found out that it was nighttime, and that she'd spent the last long hours without rest dealing with life-threatening beings. She wanted to do nothing but slump to the ground and pass out, but thinking about all the potential dreamers who would be attacked by the black-dreamers during her rest motivated her enough to face Lilac and say, "Let's head to the Ambition realm." To which she immediately regretted saying, because then Lilac had the bright idea of providing them both with free transportation.

The bear-creature that Raine vividly remembered defeating suddenly appeared behind Lilac, and instead of its usual hostile behaviour, it gently scooped Lilac and Raine up, placing the two in a comfortable position at least eight feet off the ground before dashing off at speed of a bullet train.

Raine screamed as Sir Bamesetton trapped her in its arms and yelled to Lilac, "Lilac! Do you even know where the Ambition realm is?"

"Our hearts shall guide us!" Lilac responded, confidently. Figuring that it was a verbose way of saying 'no', Raine calmed herself from the fact that Sir Bamesetton was carrying her and Lilac at a ridiculous speed and took a compass from her bag to lead the way.

Yeong-gu stadium appeared different when bathed in the moonlight sky compared to the usual scorching sun, and after failing to squeeze into the entrance of the stadium, Sir Bamesetton gently placed Lilac and Raine down on the ground after a nauseous albeit efficient ride, and Lilac gave the bear a little pat in gratitude. Within the blink of an eye, the creature turned back into nothing more than a teddy bear that Lilac carried in her arm, letting Raine question how Lilac's ability worked.

Raine gave a little introduction of the Ambition realm and a summary of the incident with Hyrensia while the two entered and walked around the empty stadium. Everything had calmed down compared to earlier when there were officers amidst panicked baseball players, and now all Raine could hear were crickets and the sound of her and Lilac's footsteps.

Then someone else's footsteps joined in. They were loud and quick, as if in a rush. Soraya had once told her that she could identify her family members by the sound of their footsteps, and Raine, being an only child with a single mom, Rhea, could never relate to that joke. But now, she finally understood when the mere sound of footfalls got her spirits up before she even looked up to see Jocelyn. "Hiya there, Raine!" She gave an exaggerated wave, as if emoting like a character from a video game, and Raine couldn't help but laugh. "I was starting to think that you died or something! Oh, thank the stars that you came back."

So-hyun appeared behind her. "You shouldn't say things like that so casually," she commented gently, a baseball bat in hand. She was doused in sweat, and Raine was just about to comment about it when she realised she was even more sweaty.

The four of them met in the centre of the baseball field. "I found the Pure Dreamkeeper. This is Lilac Rygh." Raine stepped a little away so that Lilac could meet Jocelyn and So-hyun, finding herself a little influenced by Lilac's introduction of her full name. "Kegan's in the Nightmare realm taking care of some things with another friend. They'll be back, hopefully." Raine added, once she saw Jocelyn's confused face from the lack of Kegan's presence.

"Pleased to make your acquaintance," Lilac bowed majestically, before standing upright and holding out Sir Bamesetton. "This is my ever-loyal friend, Sir Bamesetton." Lilac emulated a wave from Sir Bamesetton by moving its paw up and down.

Jocelyn's eyes gleamed at Sir Bamesetton. "Oh, you should totally meet Miss Maojie! She and Sir Bamesetton would like, get along so well!" She started bouncing up and down, and from Miss Maojie's name alone, Raine assumed Jocelyn had a cat plush the size of So-hyun lying around in her bedroom. "By the way, I'm Jocelyn Chua, and this is Kal So-hyun!" Jocelyn added, mercilessly butchering So-hyun's name. So-hyun, however, just gave a slight bow and smiled nervously. "She's a baseball player in this stadium and also the Ambition Dreamkeeper! Isn't she so awesome?" Jocelyn's smile widened when talking about So-hyun, whose face turned a deeper shade of red.

"Right, now we have the Ambition Dreamkeeper and the Pure Dreamkeeper. Now we just need to find the Subliminal Dreamkeeper-"

"Wait, Raine, what about supper?" Jocelyn interrupted Raine. Raine shot her a look before she remembered she hadn't eaten anything ever since the magic show, and that her taste buds were probably ruined from drinking the magic potion of the ice elemental. "Look, I mean it's totes horrible that there's nightmares roaming around, but I'm hungry! And we need at least eight hours of sleep if we want to function well." Jocelyn pouted jokingly before smiling again, raising her voice even though Raine and Lilac were standing right in front of her. "Oh, oh! How about we like, have a sleepover and everything? I managed to book a room at a luxury hotel nearby since our apartment in the Mainland most likely went kaboom." She then gasped. "Oh no! Miss Maojie! I left her in bed!"

"My condolences," Lilac said, apologetically. Jocelyn's ability to easily book a luxury hotel room stunned Raine so much she couldn't even comment.

Jocelyn took out her phone and pressed a few times on the screen with her index finger, saying simultaneously at the same time, "Okie dokie! I'll buy a new Miss Maojie and ship it to the hotel room right now, and then I'll hire a limo so we can get to the hotel in no time!"

Raine scratched her head. "Wait, what?"

"Don't worry! I got everything handled. What do you want to eat? I'll order pizza!"

"Oh, Sir Bamesetton and I would like waffles! It's been so long since we've had such a delicacy!" Lilac went over to Jocelyn and peeked at her phone.

"I'll add my order after everyone," So-hyun said, reading the menu from Jocelyn's phone.

Jocelyn looked expectantly at Raine as she waited for her order, who was more than puzzled about the sudden change in schedule. Of course, a sleepover sounded fun, but why now, of all times? Was she really just overreacting? Was she straining herself for nothing?

In the end, Raine decided to go along with Jocelyn and the others. At least, Jocelyn was right about needing sleep to function well. Besides, she didn't know how long it would take to find the Subliminal Dreamkeeper, and a little break would probably be beneficial, even if she did feel a little guilty and anxious. "Do they have pastries?" Raine asked, giving a defeated smile.

After ordering delivery and Jocelyn confirming that it was 'her treat', she directed the group to where the limousine would pick everyone up. Raine felt a little uncomfortable at first, but Jocelyn's carefree attitude and her chatting about random nonsensical things made it easier for Raine to feel relaxed, and she ended up joining the conversation.

Once they reached the hotel, everybody thanked the chauffeur while Jocelyn ran into the hotel to ask for the room keycard. She handed the keys over to So-hyun and told her to head over to the room first while she collected the food delivery and a new Miss Maojie.

There were more people in the hotel than Raine expected, but it only took a moment for Raine to realise that the ones staying in the hotel weren't Ambition dreamers. Most of them were mixed and had most likely survived the tragedy of the Mainland.

Despite the crowded lobby, Raine couldn't help but marvel at the luxurious interior. The floor, a mosaic of smooth marble in shades of cream and gold, sparkled and whispered beneath Raine's boots. Overhead, a dazzling chandelier of crystal and wrought iron cascaded from the ceiling, diffusing soft, golden light that danced upon the floor.

Expansive windows, adorned with heavy drapes of rich, regal crimson, framed a view of the Ambition realm's glittering cities, a breathtaking panorama that stretched into the infinite. Plush, velvety armchairs and settees were scattered around the room, inviting all kinds of dreamers to rest their weary heads.

Everything was so extravagant that Raine almost felt bad for merely existing inside the hotel, and it was easy to infer that Jocelyn and her family were probably millionaires.

Despite Jocelyn telling everyone else to head to the
room first, they were all so entranced by the lobby
itself that they decided to wait for her there, and once
Jocelyn came flocking back to them in surprise,
holding at least seven bags of food in both her arms,
they all travelled to the elevator and went to their
allocated room.

There were about six elevators to transport the many
dreamers, and they all attempted to predict which
elevator would be the one that carried them up. Once
Raine stepped into the elevator with the rest, she was
greeted by a hushed tranquility, with glassy floors and
soft ambient lighting. Mirrored panels plastered the
walls, with subtle music filling the air with a soothing
calmness.

The decadence of the hotel easily intimidated Raine,
who knew that at most, she would only be able to
book a one-night stay there after saving for an entire
year.

The room that Jocelyn had booked was more than
luxurious. As a matter of fact, one could easily live
here with a family of five. Like any person, Raine
scattered about the massive hotel room to marvel at
the high-quality furnishing and the incredible view
from the large window panes. On a higher floor, the
room revealed a breathtaking view of the Ambition
realm. An inviting sitting area beckoned with a
spacious couch filled with soft pillows centered on a
sizable glass rectangular table, all set upon a soft
carpet. A television mounted on the wall from

opposite the couch was already switched on, its screen bestrewed with hospitable words of welcome to the guests.

Jocelyn struggled to carry all the food she had ordered earlier, and she even had to go back down just to carry the newly arrived Miss Maojie. The other dreamers even had to travel back down just to help carry the ginormous cat plush and stuff it into the elevator, grabbing the attention of every other dreamer in the hotel. Thankfully, the elevator was large enough to fit them all, and Miss Maojie was pushed across the carpeted hallway back to their hotel room.

After settling the food onto the glass table and leaning Miss Maojie on the side of the couch (with Jocelyn and Lilac introducing their respective plushies to each other), they appointed who would sleep in which room and bed, and eagerly gathered for the long awaited supper.

Initially, Raine assumed that she would inhale her food and doze off in bed instantly, but she ended up staying up with the rest of the dreamers discussing non-serious topics while slowly chewing their food and watching drama on the television at the same time. It was a strange time for sure, but in the end, when Raine was throwing out the empty packaging of the eaten food, she smiled to herself and thought of it as a good memory she wouldn't regret making.

Raine took a long shower and got to change out of her costume she wore during the magic show. She hadn't had a chance to change into her casual outfit, and she questioned how the other black-dreamers managed to keep a straight face when antagonising what looked like a homeless street magician.

After changing, she went to grab her bag from the sitting room to her temporary bedroom, and having claimed the right side of the bed, took out the map just to see her progress. The red pinpoint marking the Ambition Dreamkeeper, So-hyun, and the Pure Dreamkeeper's pinpoint, which had turned purple without Raine's realisation, marked Lilac's presence. The two pinpoints lingered to a small spot in the Ambition realm and were hovering over each other to create a magenta overlay. Both pinpoints bore the insignia of their respective realms.

Raine tried to remember how Lilac's pinpoint appeared initially. As far as she knew, it just appeared out of nowhere, and she wasn't required to do anything but wait. So far though, there was no sign of a third pinpoint, and considering how it had been a few hours since Lilac was awakened, Raine couldn't help but worry,

"Harbouring any concerns?" Lilac peered at the map over Raine's shoulder. Her hair was down and she was wearing a plain black shirt. She placed Sir Bamesetton on the bed between herself and Raine.

"I really wish there was a manual on how this map works," Raine replied, not giving a straight-forward answer. She didn't want to share her worries to Lilac as well, especially not at this time, so Raine placed the map back in her bag and pulled the fresh white blankets over her body after laying down. "You're right that I'm worried, but Jocelyn is also right to say that we should get some rest. Could you turn the lights off?"

"Very well then. Sir Bamesetton and I shall retire from today as well." Lilac closed the curtains and placed Sir Bamesetton on her side of the bed. With the flick of a switch, the brightly lit room was sent to a state of darkness, and Raine felt Lilac climbing onto the bed to sleep next to her. Before Raine could say goodnight, she was already fast asleep.

* * *

Raine found herself in a field of dandelions under a bright blue sky, with the sun beaming down at her. There were no buildings or disruptive noises, just her strolling through the rows of flowers and grass.

Tonight was a lucid dream of some sort, but Raine knew better than to fight against the logic of dreams. Instead, she carried on wandering aimlessly, even picking up a dandelion to admire its beauty. She blew on it and watched as the seeds flew up into the sky, wishing for peace for the world.

There was no sign of any man-made structures at all, and Raine wondered if she was the only one that existed in her dream. It was an empty and desolate place, with nature being Raine's only company as she trod through the dandelion field, but she enjoyed it. It was peaceful and quiet.

In the distance, Raine saw a blurry image of two women having a picnic, the red mat sticking out from all the green like a sore thumb catching her eye. Cautiously, Raine inched closer to the women, sneaking like how a video game character does in stealth games. But her attempt of being covert was thrown out of the window when she recognised one of the women.

"Mom!" Raine ran over to Rhea, who was sitting with her legs crossed and holding a tea cup with a content look on her face. When Rhea was suddenly embraced by her daughter, she gasped and freed her hands before returning the hug, trying not to spill her tea. She stroked Raine's back gently as Raine started sobbing. "I missed you so much!" Raine cried.

After what felt like forever, Raine finally let go of Rhea, paranoid that she would suddenly be woken up from the dream or that something would happen to dream-Rhea. Raine had heard of myths where an individual's deceased loved one could reincarnate and live on eternally in their dreams, but most people were dismissive, saying that it was just the projection of an old memory and not the real person. Of course, there was no way to prove this, at least not yet anyway. Raine was one of the majorities who disbelieved the theory, but with Rhea in front of her, she now wished more than ever that it was truly Rhea and not a false image of what Raine's mind wanted to believe. Raine had so many questions and things to tell her, but when she noticed the other woman staring at her, she asked, "Who's that?"

Sitting next to Rhea was a ginger-haired woman with azure-coloured round eyes. She was elegantly dressed in white, and looked younger than Rhea, but older than Raine. The mysterious woman wore a rainflower-shaped clip on her hair, and she smiled warmly at Raine, a smile that Raine had seen many times whenever Rhea welcomed her home from a long journey out. "Hello there, love," The woman said, taking a bit too long with her gaze at Raine. "I'm a friend of Rhea. My name is Aiseura. You must be Raine." She took a small, steamed bun from the picnic basket next to her and offered it to Raine.

"Ah, hello." Raine accepted the bun but scrutinised it carefully. She remembered when she once tried to eat a bagel in a dream, only to find out that it wasn't a dream, but a nightmare, and realised too late that the bagel was filled with spiders. Ever since that incident, she abstained from eating anything in a dream. However, Raine decided it was rude to reject food from her mother's friend, and took a bite out of the bun, accepting the risk of tasting spiders again. However, it just tasted like freshly-baked bread. It was warm and delicious, and Raine felt an immediate bond with Aiseura thanks to the free food.

Raine ate the bun whilst listening to Rhea and Aiseura talk about her in a very parent-to-parent-like manner. Everything was normal, and Raine assumed she was just in a very nice dream that encouraged her to carry on in her journey to save the world. But the more she looked at Aiseura, the more she felt bothered by her presence, although she couldn't figure out why. Raine didn't think Aiseura was a villain or had any malicious intent, but it felt like she was hiding something.

Aiseura was definitely a new name, and thanks to Raine's dreaming state, her face blurred every now and then, making it hard for Raine to see any concrete features of Aiseura's face. For a second, Raine assumed that Aiseura's existence was a fictional one, but her gut told her otherwise.

Raine couldn't figure out what type of dreamer Aiseura was and which realm she came from, her inability to recognise Aiseura's accent making it all the more difficult. Though, her enunciations reminded Raine of Soaraya's speech mannerisms, so she assumed Aiseura was just a mixed dreamer as well.

When Raine finished the bun and accepted that there was no trace of any food poisoning, she turned to Rhea. "Mom, what are the two of you doing here in my dream?" She asked, hoping that her line of questioning wouldn't trigger any undesirable events. "Not that I mind, of course."

Rhea's eyes shifted from Aiseura to Raine, and her smile faded. "We're aware of what's been happening in Oneirolepsy and your endeavours to save it from the Nightmares."

Raine gulped, unsure what Rhea would say next.

"We're so proud of you for taking up the role of Revieras. You've worked so hard thus far, finding the Ambition Dreamkeeper and the Pure Dreamkeeper." Rhea moved a strand of hair away from Raine's face and held her cheek. "You've really grown up. I believe you can save the world together with your new friends. Don't give up." Rhea smiled at Raine, her eyes glossy.

Raine was stunned by the sudden encouragement, and she felt like crying again. Instead, she nodded her head. "I won't disappoint you, mom," she declared, trying not to remember the fact that she was just watching a movie about cats with Jocelyn, Lilac, and So-hyun in the middle of a black-dreamer outbreak. When she did inevitably remember about the cat movie, she pulled away from Rhea and smiled bashfully.

"What the nightmares are doing is horrible. You must've been scared this whole time. How resilient you are, my little rainflower." Raine's heart skipped a beat at her mother calling her by her endearing nickname. "I wish I could be with you to guide you, but the conditions right now are not ideal."

Raine doubted that she could say anything without her voice cracking, so she stayed silent and waited for Rhea to continue.

"Your dreams will guide you when you are in trouble. Believe in yourself and your dreams. The future is uncertain, and the worst may happen. But with you

leading the dreamers, I trust that everything will go
well. There is always light at the end of the tunnel.
Know that we'll always be supporting you." Rhea
brought Raine into another hug.

Raine closed her eyes and wished that she could hug
her mother like this forever. But she knew that hidden
in Rhea's supporting words was a harsh truth: Raine
would be burdened by the world on her shoulders,
and chances would be slim for her to be able to save
the world in her current state. But the world was far
greater than herself, and Raine needed to do whatever
it took for her to save Oneirolepsy and make Rhea
proud.

With newfound determination, Raine slowly released
Rhea and sighed. She knew eventually that she would
have to leave the dream, and potentially never see her
mother again.

Aiseura moved closer to Raine and looked her
directly in the eye with a stern expression. The sudden
movement got Raine to tense up as Aiseura was
nothing but a stranger to her, and now Raine was
starting to feel a little scared. But then Aiseura spoke.
"Listen, love. Your mother is right, so do not worry.
You need to save Oneirolepsy. It's your responsibility,
Revieras. So never falter, for the world is on your
shoulders." The blur from Aiseura's face faded as
Raine recognised her voice, the very same mysterious
voice she had heard when she was first trying to find
the map. But more than that, when Aiseura's clear
features were revealed, Raine gasped. She was wrong

about never having seen her outside of her dream before. It was so easy to recognise, and a part of her always hid in the mirrors whenever Raine looked at them.

"I love you, Raine. Our bond transcends the death of-"

Before Aiseura could finish, her voice cut off, and so did Raine's connection from her dream. She was brought from the dandelion field back to the ceiling of the luxury hotel room. Raine felt her eyes getting ready to unleash a stream of tears, but she was so numb from what she had just experienced that all she did was stare at the lightless ceiling without moving for hours.

※★◆★※
Chapter 12: Reunion

Raine watched the dark room gradually grow brighter from the sun rising, indicating morning. She had failed to do what she wanted most: Get some good sleep. Nonetheless, she was thankful that nothing horrible had happened to the hotel, nor Lilac, who was sleeping next to her and holding Sir Bamesetton in her arms. She didn't want to think about the dream she had in case it brought up more unhappy thoughts, so she got up and got ready for the morning.

Raine sat on the bed and contemplated what to do next. She took out the map from her bag to see if any new pinpoints appeared to guide her. There was nothing. Raine sighed and kept the map, before carrying her bag altogether and bringing it out to the sitting room.

Jocelyn was already in the sitting room, leaning against Miss Maojie in her onesie. Raine placed her bag on the couch and was just about to ask Jocelyn something when she noticed that Jocelyn was fast asleep. Pieces of papers with sketches and designs of buildings drawn by graphite scattered on the glass table. Raine couldn't help but admire the several sketches and marvelled at how professional the drawings were. Most of them included skyscrapers and layouts she didn't understand, with vague and messy handwriting on the side as annotation.

"Oh, I fell asleep." Raine heard Jocelyn's voice as she awoke. She rubbed her eyes and yawned before seeing Raine holding onto one of the papers. "Oh, good morning, Raine. Do you like my sketches? I woke up in the middle of the night and must have dozed off again while trying to finish them." Jocelyn crawled over and shifted through the many papers, before pulling a particular piece out. It was an unfinished sketch. "Oh well, I'll finish it later." Jocelyn took the paper Raine was holding and began to stack them into a neat pile, knocking it repeatedly on the surface of the table to even out the stack.

"What are these designs for?" Raine asked Jocelyn, who had dark circles under her eyes and a sluggish posture.

Jocelyn paused for a minute. She stood up with the neat stack in her hand. "I had a dream about Boris, and he helped me create these designs. I drew them for him." She said, her voice quiet. She folded up a paper with the sketch of a design of a monumental statue and kept it in the pocket of her skirt. "See ya," she added, turning around to head back to her temporary bedroom.

Raine watched Jocelyn leave and felt something tug her heart strings. Both of them had dreamt about people they cared about and died, and suddenly the atmosphere was attacked by an overwhelming sense of melancholy. Jocelyn probably missed Boris as much as Raine missed Rhea, if not more, but her usual cheerfulness had always made it seem that

Jocelyn was unaffected by it. Raine felt a little stupid now, having that initial assumption.

Of course Jocelyn would miss her cousin.

Raine went to wake Lilac up after checking the time, and a few hours passed while the group got fully prepared. Jocelyn ordered more food which was delivered straight to the hotel room, and Lilac and So-hyun shared about what they dreamt whilst everyone ate breakfast. Jocelyn's random rants and changing of the topic multiple times made it easy for Raine to avoid talking about her own dream, and eventually the group packed up to leave the hotel.

"Where are we going now?" So-hyun asked, when the group closed the front door behind them and were walking towards the elevator. It took longer than expected to leave, especially since the group had to debate whether to keep or leave the ginormous cat plush Jocelyn had impulsively bought and couldn't realistically keep. In the end, they left Miss Maojie in the hotel room as a little souvenir for the next person to discover.

"Uh. I don't know, actually. The map doesn't show the pinpoint of the Subliminal Dreamkeeper." Raine gave a nervous laugh, pressing the button for the elevator to avoid making eye contact with anyone in the group. The last thing she needed was a judgemental look for being clueless. "Though I assume the best place to start would be the Subliminal realm."

"Ooh, ooh, we can ask Val! He's a friend of mine!" Jocelyn raised her hand up to grab everyone's attention. "He's like, surprisingly good at finding people. If he weren't studying to be an engineer, he could totally be a spy! He should be in the Subliminal realm too, so we should like, head there right now. I'll call a ride!"

The elevator doors opened, and the group went down to ground level.

The doors opened to reveal the lobby laying in disarray, having shattered lights and fragments of glass scattered across the soiled floor. An eerie emptiness pervaded with nobody to be found anywhere. The velvety couches were overturned and paintings that initially hung on the walls now crashed onto the floor, damaged beyond repair. Nobody had to exit the elevator to see the damage.

The group stood as still as a rock, and the elevator doors were about to close again, but then Raine moved her arm in between the closing doors for them to detect her arm, opening the elevator doors again for her and the others to step out. "We can't stay here. The black-dreamers are getting more active in the Ambition realm."

The group hesitantly followed Raine out of the elevator after confirming that there were no black-dreamers to be found lingering in the wrecked lobby. They left the hotel and waited impatiently for the ride to come pick the group up.

Just as the group was starting to worry that the worst had happened to the chauffeur, the limousine came, and when it stopped right where the group was standing, a nicely-dressed gentleman with a grumpy face came out from the driver's seat to open the passengers' door.

"Help! Raine!" Just as Raine was about to enter the limousine as the others had, the familiar sound of Soraya reached her ears, and she quickly exited the car. She glanced at where the direction of the sound came from and gasped when she saw Soraya covered in scars and burns, struggling to even walk towards Raine in a limp.

Raine quickly ran over, feeling tears well up in her eyes at the thought of failing to be there for her injured friend. "Soraya!" She yelled, barely managing to reach Soraya before she collapsed onto the ground. "What happened? Where's Kegan?" Soraya's skin was hot to the touch, and she grimaced as Raine accidentally touched an open wound whilst trying to prevent her from collapsing.

Lilac and So-hyun seemed to have caught what was going on, and quickly exited the limousine. Jocelyn tried to follow, but was stopped by the driver, who insisted she stayed or else he would find another passenger to pick up. While Jocelyn tried to ask for a little more time, So-hyun and Lilac ran over to Soraya to help her.

"Kegan...he did this..." Soraya's voice croaked. She looked about ten seconds away from passing out, and the blood poured from her head onto Raine's hands, which were now trembling as she was hit with massive guilt.

"I'll get Soraya to a hospital!" So-hyun claimed. "You both go with Jocelyn to find the Subliminal Dreamkeeper. I'll be alright on my own." She nodded assertively.

Raine tried healing Soraya's wounds, but her dream energy levels were too low to do so. She sighed, allowing a fresh trail of tears to roll down her cheek. "Okay, I trust you, So-hyun." She said, her words heavier than she realised.

So-hyun nodded, and as Raine let go of Soraya, wiping her tears, picked Soraya up. If Raine hadn't been so upset, she probably would have gawked at So-hyun lifting Soraya up effortlessly, especially with So-hyun's small height. She'd almost forgotten that So-hyun possessed the athletic strength of a baseball star.

Lilac had already gone back to the limousine to inform Jocelyn on the horrible news. An ambulance was called within three minutes and placed Soraya on a stretcher with a stressed So-hyun following behind.

As soon as the ambulance went out of sight, Kegan appeared.

Raine tensed up. Kegan wasn't wearing his usual confident smirk - it was a more blank expression than anything, and suddenly Raine felt all the trust she had unconsciously placed in Kegan throughout her time with him together immediately thrown out the window.

He wasn't acting like his usual self, and Raine regretted ever leaving him unwatched. Kegan quietly walked over to her, clear of any signs of remorse or guilt. Raine could detect some lingering bits of energy Kegan had definitely used while he and Soraya were in the Nightmare realm, and she found it strange that he had even dared to come see her.

Raine suppressed the urge to start throwing her fists at Kegan. She crossed her arms and frowned. "What did you do to Soraya?" She coldly demanded an answer. He had only arrived after Soraya left with the ambulance, and she wasn't sure if he was aware that she had even met with her.

Kegan looked more confused than ever before answering in an offended tone. "What the hell are you on about? She attacked me!"

"Hurry up, Raine! The driver's getting impatient!" Jocelyn called from the limousine. The others hadn't noticed Kegan, presumably because of how the vehicle was angled. Kegan perked up at the sound of Jocelyn's voice, but Raine spoke again.

"Look, I don't have time for your made-up stories. We're heading to the Subliminal realm and you're not going with us, alright? Just stay put and don't do anything stupid. Once we're done, you'll go straight to the hospital and apologise to Soraya." Raine walked away from Kegan and entered the limousine.

"Are you serious?" Raine heard Kegan shouting from behind her. "She's the enemy here! Why do I have to apologise to her? And why are you antagonising me now?" Kegan's voice raised as he spoke, and Raine felt herself at even more danger in provoking a fire elemental.

Says the black-dreamer. Raine thought, entering the limousine. She had enough sense not to slam the door behind her, because as soon as she climbed in, the doors closed automatically.

Raine had barely managed to put on her seat belt before the vehicle sped off. Jocelyn, who had forgotten completely, had Lilac pay the price when she was thrown onto her violently. There were shouts from Jocelyn along with her apologies before Lilac managed to put Jocelyn back in her seat, and Raine helped to buckle Jocelyn's seat belt. While this all happened, the chauffeur ignored the chaos and focused on the road, which was an incredible feat, as Raine could barely make out anything from the sheer speed of the limousine.

"Why are we going so fast? I almost died!" Jocelyn cried, shaking her head like a cartoon character. Raine wanted to ask that too, but assumed the answer was obvious granted their predicament.

"Rides are overbooked, too many people want to get out of this place away from the nightmares," The chauffeur explained, in an exhausted tone. "All heading to the Subliminal realm for protection."

Raine had never been to the Subliminal realm before. From what she's heard, it was a place with very tight security, most likely due to the war that broke out between the Subliminal realm and the Ambition realm in the past. Although there was some debate about personal privacy in the Subliminal realm, for it had cameras everywhere to an invasive degree, it had its own borders to keep the whole realm and its dreamers safe, a very desirable trait in the current situation.

"The realm might close its borders to any outsiders. A massive surge of dreamers wouldn't be good for the realm," The chauffeur continued, speeding up the limousine until the outside was just a blur. Raine hadn't thought it was possible to actually speed up even further than before, but now the limousine was trying its best to emulate the world's fastest roller coaster, or the world's steepest waterslide. Raine once went on one of those - her body ended up being thrown into a ninety-degree angle where she could barely feel the surface of the waterslide against the back, her organs flying around inside her body as her heart spiked. She had vomited soon after exiting the ride and hung out by the children's area in the waterpark for the rest of the day.

Raine felt like she was about to throw up for the twelfth time this week, but then the limousine came to a halt, and all of a sudden, they were in a traffic jam. There were at least hundreds of cars in front of them, and Raine was immediately thankful for the fast-paced ride just a second ago, for she knew she was about to wait for at least two hours in the traffic jam.

Raine looked outside the window and admired the many vehicles out there, trying not to think about the amount of carbon emissions being produced. The sky was baby blue with no sight of any clouds. The sun beamed brightly, but not so bright until it was scorching hot. The kind of sun one would enjoy if they were having a picnic.

Bored from waiting, Lilac and Jocelyn started roleplaying with Sir Bamesetton and Miss Maojie, except Miss Maojie was all the way back at the hotel, so Jocelyn used her hand instead, mimicking a mouth every time she spoke. Raine closed her eyes and allowed herself to daydream, fantasising what meeting the Subliminal Dreamkeeper would be like. The limousine kept inching forward every few minutes, causing an unpleasant sensation to everyone whenever it did.

Finally, whilst the group was playing a game where they had to call out words based on a certain theme within a time limit (Lilac won), they reached the border of the Subliminal realm.

"Lilac, do you have a passport?" Raine asked, taking hers from her bag.

"Pardon?"

After another excruciating two hours of processing, the limousine was allowed to enter the Subliminal Realm. Cameras and vigilant eyes met Raine's gaze from every direction, and she wondered what would've happened if she hadn't left Kegan behind. Warmth lingered amid the reasonable number of dreamers outside, and the limousine dropped the group off in front of an academy.

"St. Mavros University? What are we doing here?" The sign next to the gates had the university's full name plastered in big capital letters and its crest beside it. It was a large institution, to say the least.

"Thankfully, school's closed for the day," Jocelyn grinned. "My friend used to attend this uni, so I figured it'd be the best place to meet, especially with nobody around." She shrugged casually. "He's not really good with people, but I'm sure he'll help us!" She began to stretch her fingers.

Raine marvelled at Jocelyn's logic. "Are you going to call him or something?" She asked, remembering that it wasn't possible because during the time they waited at the border, Jocelyn had been playing games on her phone until it ran out of battery. It was obvious when Jocelyn suddenly whined to everyone while Raine was talking to Lilac about birds: "Oh no, my phone died!" Followed by an exaggerated wallow.

"Hoho, there is a much more efficient way to summon him!" Jocelyn smirked, her hands forming into a steeple. "You see that over there?" She asked, pointing to a security camera by the school's gates. Jocelyn turned her body to face it and took a deep breath. The others watched her intensely, wondering what she was about to do.

Suddenly, Jocelyn started making random gestures with her hands and waving her arm about. Raine could have sworn some of the moves were from a popular anime where the characters would make ludicrous motions to summon an attack or spell.

In this case, Jocelyn didn't summon any superhero-esque spell, and looked like an idiot. Everyone else watched her in both shock and amusement, with those who had grown used to her antics by now facepalming at her nonsense again.

"Jocelyn, what are you-" Raine was cut off when a heavy weight seemingly from the sky crashed onto her, and her face made friends with the dusty ground. When she tried to get the weight off her back, a glittery red fabric caught Raine's eye, and after realising that the heavy weight that hit her was a person and not a random anvil that dropped from the sky, the person got up immediately, accidentally hitting her with a heavy satchel in the process.

Raine got up as well, and just as she was about to take a good look at whoever just spawned out of nowhere (she could hardly believe that Jocelyn actually managed to 'summon' someone with whatever move she pulled just now), Jocelyn threw herself at him and wrapped her arms around him.

"Val!" She called out, dragging the syllable. "I missed you so much!" The person, whose name was apparently Val, stood as stiff as a board. He didn't say anything, and after a minute, Jocelyn released him from her bear hug.

Val adjusted his glasses. "You know, the last time you so-called summoned me was because you needed someone to play a ridiculous sport you invented. I only came this time because I assume from the nightmares that it's an actual emergency and not one of your antics." Then, as if just realising that Jocelyn hadn't come alone, he cleared his throat and glanced at Raine and Lilac's general direction, not making eye contact with them.

"Oh right! Remember So-hyun? It turns out that she's the Ambition Dreamkeeper! She's not here right now, but I have new friends. This is Lilac, master of the very cute Sir Bamesetton and the Pure Dreamkeeper. This is-"

"Raine. What are you doing here?" Val asked, in more of a stern teacher-like voice than a curious one. If not for the fact that Val's eyes were shifting anywhere but at Raine, she probably would've felt threatened. Every Subliminal dreamer that Raine had ever met were either distantly polite or talked as if Raine had killed their dog. Not a single time had "Revieras" been spoken by a Subliminal dreamer's lips, but Raine liked it. She wasn't defined by her title in the Subliminal realm, even if that meant such treatment. Raine remembered the first time she came to the Ambition realm and was treated like a celebrity, whether it was because she was a mixed dreamer or because she was Revieras always remained a mystery to her.

Considering how Jocelyn was a Subliminal dreamer
as well, Raine felt grateful that she was so friendly
towards her, even if that meant that Jocelyn never
saw Raine as Revieras at all.

"We're trying to find the Subliminal Dreamkeeper so
we can save the world from the black-dreamers.
Looks like your realm doesn't need saving, though."
She turned around to see the environment - verdant
and free from chaos. In the distance, a food court just
across the road of the school caught Raine's attention,
where stalls were open with dim lights and long
queues, and many dreamers were seen dining there
like it was a normal Monday morning. "No
black-dreamers here, I assume?" She asked, almost
rhetorically.

"They would've been imprisoned or executed the
second they try to pass the realm's border," Val
replied, his voice implying some sense of pride.
Raine's mind immediately thought of Kegan, only to
remember the sensation of Soraya's blood on her
hands and felt a pit of anger in her stomach. Val
shifted his focus to Jocelyn. "I'm glad you're safe. But
why did you call me here? I can't be the Subliminal
Dreamkeeper."

Raine raised an eyebrow, but then Jocelyn elbowed
Val and grinned. "Val, you know how we were like,
BFFs, back in uni? We even ran a blog together!
Remember that one super rare time you invited me to
go to a museum? If that's not a sign of friendship, I
don't know what is!"

"More like you hired me to tell you gossip for your blog..." Val muttered, turning red. "And don't bring that up. It was only once. Get to the point."

"Please help us find the Subliminal Dreamkeeper!" Jocelyn clasped her hands together and bowed her head down. Lilac followed suit. Raine decided not to do anything in case it caused any negative reaction from Val, and trusted Jocelyn to convince her friend on her own.

"Why are you asking me? Is this how you found all the other Dreamkeepers?" Val glared at Raine for a second before looking back at Jocelyn. "You can't just go around asking regular people to help you do something like that."

"I'll treat you hotpot for a month!" Jocelyn wauled.

"Do you have rainflowers?" Val asked.

Everyone raised their head and turned to Raine, waiting expectantly for her. Rainflowers were exclusive and an endangered flower species, and were only found in the rainforest that Raine lived in. The rainforest was a protected sanctuary as well, and nobody was allowed to enter except for Raine and Rhea. As Raine vividly remembered, the rainforest had been set on fire by Kegan. Besides, the Mainland had been obliterated by Vanity. Or well, most of it anyway, but Raine didn't want to go all the way back to the Mainland to risk getting killed just for a pile of ash.

The last rainflower that Raine carried with her had been used ages ago, and she felt something die inside of her, knowing she was the only one who could and would have fulfilled Val's request. "I don't have them anymore," she said, softly, feeling the need to apologise even though she did nothing wrong.

Val gave a disappointed look, then shook his head. "Fine. I want you to help someone instead. In exchange, I'll find the Subliminal Dreamkeeper for you. But no guarantee, alright?"

Raine's eyes lit up. "Really?"

Val nodded. "So, what do you know about the Subliminal Dreamkeeper so far? Any clues?"

Raine took out the map and showed it to Val. "The pinpoints represent each Dreamkeeper, but the third one has yet to show up. Considering how Lilac's pinpoint was barely visible when I first saw it, I doubt the pinpoint will show itself anytime soon. It's been over ten hours."

Before Val could make any remark, Jocelyn stepped forward. "Yo, guys! Security alert! Let's bounce."

"Excellent point. What destination shall our path unfurl?" Lilac asked. "Sir Bamesetton says he doesn't like school."

"Sir Bamesetton and I are on the same wavelength," Jocelyn added. "I'm getting resurfacing trauma just by being here." She then turned to Val and lowered her head as if she was begging him for money. "So...could we come over to your place?"

"I have a roommate. She wouldn't like it if I brought everyone to our place," Val said, almost immediately, hiding his face from everybody's eyes.

Jocelyn's eyes lit up and her demeanour changed from a shameful girl asking for a favour to an excited child with no restraint. "Wait wait wait wait wait, 'she'? Is she your girlfriend?" She jumped up and down, watching Val's whole face turn red as he groaned.

"Damn it, I shouldn't have said anything. And no, it's nothing like that. She's just a distant family friend from the Dream realm," Val sighed and turned to Raine, adjusting the strap of his satchel. "I guess since she's the one whom you need to help, I'll allow you to stay over for a while-" his sentence was briefly cut off when Jocelyn hugged him again. "Oof, hey! I told you not to do that!"

"Oh, thank you thank you thank you thank you so much, Val! I promise I know the best place for hotpot. We should all go out to eat after we find the Subliminal Dreamkeeper! I wonder which realm has better food? I haven't eaten here in a while, or maybe you could come back to the Mainland, Val!" Before Jocelyn could go on another hour-long rant about food and hotpot, Val pushed her away gently so that she was no longer invading his space.

"Okay, okay, whatever you want. Let's just get this over with." Val pressed his palm against his head to fight against the headache he was getting from Jocelyn's clowning.

A taxi conveniently drove into view of the group, and Jocelyn reached her arm out to gesture to the taxi, which then stopped by the curb. "You can have the honour of having the front seat," Jocelyn commented to Val, opening the door to the passengers' seats at the back. She scooted in first, followed by Lilac, and then Raine. "Alright, let's go!"

* * *

After an awkward interaction between the taxi driver and Val, where there was an unreasonable amount of hesitation and suspicion from Val whilst the driver kept asking for the address (by shouting 'address?' exasperatedly every three seconds), the taxi started driving to Val's place.

The ride was slow and calming compared to the rest of the rides that Raine had been on previously, and she couldn't help but enjoy the serene view of the Subliminal realm. She pressed her phone against the car window and snapped a few pictures.

During the journey, Raine had managed to unintentionally eavesdrop on the one-sided conversation Val and Jocelyn were having, thereby finding out that Val wasn't a Subliminal dreamer and that his actual name was Valentino.

Despite Jocelyn's chatty voice trying to catch up with Valentino, who was trying to read a thick book he'd pulled out from his satchel and constantly telling Jocelyn to shut up, Raine managed to doze off. Well, to doze off would be inaccurate. It was more of a 'I know I'm sleepy so I'll close my eyes a bit, but will consciously avoid fully sleeping' sort of thing.

But before she could open her eyes again, she felt a heavy weight from above suddenly crash down on her. It hit her head with brute force, and the coldness that followed helped her realise it was water, and she felt her entire body being submerged in it. Slowly and warily, Raine opened her eyes. She could hardly see anything underwater, and her eyes soon got irritated. Her vision was a blurred blue, and with nothing particularly useful in sight.

Raine heard a voice above the surface of water, if there even was a surface, but she couldn't make out what the voice was saying. She swam up, trying to escape the water, but it felt as if she was swimming deeper and deeper into the body of water instead. The voice she heard grew louder, and Raine realised that the voice wasn't talking, but sobbing. Very loud sobbing, a grief-stricken cry, like a mother whose child went before her.

"...Lemar...I'm sorry..." Raine caught a name as the voice sputtered out incomprehensible words. She couldn't tell if the voice was even speaking the same language as she did, and it was hard to concentrate when she was being attacked by an overwhelming sadness for no apparent reason. When her eyes started to burn after being exposed to the naked waters for too long, she tried to close her eyes to content the pain. She took a few seconds to keep her eyes closed, then she opened them again, only to find out she was no longer in the body of water anymore.

"Earth to Revieras," Lilac called to Raine, whose face was all scrunched up, and her watery eyes looked as if they were about to pop out. She gave a sharp inhale and took a few seconds to adjust from the bright blue to the dull colours of the taxi's interiors. Once she recovered, a thought flashed into her head and she gasped.

"I got a clue! A name, to be exact, I think it was Lemar? That must be it, then!" She said, oddly relieved she was back to reality. Her excited voice caught everyone's attention, including the driver himself, who frowned and muttered something to himself in a foreign language.

"Did you see anything bad? Did the black-dreamers plague your mind?" Lilac asked, placing Sir Bamesetton on Raine's lap as a reassuring gesture.

"Oh, nothing happened. I was just in an infinite swimming pool. I couldn't hear anything except for a faint voice," Raine said, rubbing her eyes with her arm so they wouldn't drop any tears. She remembered what Rhea and Aiseura had said about Raine's dreams guiding her to the Dreamkeepers. "Hey Val-" she paused a little, suddenly uncomfortable calling him by Jocelyn's nickname in lieu of his actual name. "-entino. Could you look for a Lemar? I didn't get a last name, though. He was wearing some kind of football uniform, if that helps."

"Sure," Valentino replied, his head buried in his book.

The taxi reached a grey-and-white apartment complex, and after graciously leaving the taxi, where Raine insisted on paying this time instead of Jocelyn, everyone entered the void deck where it was being kept under a watchful eye of several cameras and warning signs stating the prohibitions of littering, football, or smoking, threatening with a hefty fine.

"The Subliminal realm is phenomenal! The Nightmare realm pales in comparison," Lilac commented, placing her foot on every corner of the void deck. Valentino gave her a condemnatory glare, unclear whether it was because of her implying she'd been to the Nightmare realm or because she was unreasonably excited about a dirty and dim-lit void deck. "Oh, the vast emptiness of it! Like an infinite space, making one feel so small and insignificant!" She placed the back of her palm against her forehead theatrically, closing her eyes and sighing. Raine was met with Valentino's '*this* is one of your Dreamkeepers?' disconcerted look as Lilac shot her eyes open. "And yet it makes one feel so limitless and powerful! Incredible!" Finally, she took a bow and held up Sir Bamesetton. "Don't you agree, Sir Bamesetton?"

Jocelyn began to applaud excitedly, but then stopped when she realised that the rest weren't. "O-kay, let's head to your place, then! Just up this elevator, right?" She playfully elbowed Valentino before running towards the elevator.

The elevator was reasonably small and dull
compared to the ones in the hotel. However, unlike
the calm elevator ride in the hotel, Raine felt panicked
as she waited for the elevator doors to open as fast as
possible.

The group arrived on the seventh floor, the
unfamiliar narrow corridors lining up with doors of
many small apartments and security cameras planted
on the ceiling. Valentino led the group to the front of a
mundane front door tucked away at the very end of
the corridor. The black steel door gate framed the grey
door, and beside it a small potted plant stood, though
its leaves were already wilting. Valentino took his keys
out and unlocked the doors before walking in,
followed by the rest.

※★✦★※
Chapter 13: Avolition

Everyone welcomed themselves into the living room of Valentino's house after throwing their shoes off, though it was obvious from his face that he was less than eager to host them as guests in his small and cramped living room. Raine asked herself how she managed to get invited into a stranger's house with Lilac and Jocelyn while she stood by the entrance, wondering if Valentino would ever acknowledge her.

"Where's Kari?" Jocelyn, who managed to get the name of Valentino's roommate while she was chatting with him during the taxi ride, started wandering around his house as if it was her own. Lilac, who also had no experience of being in somebody else's house, abandoned all manners and started exploring the living room as well.

"Oh my god." Valentino planted his palm on his face with a slap. Raine watched as his ears turned red, and he soon went to chase after Jocelyn. Raine decided to do the same, leaving Lilac with Sir Bamesetton as she started giving a whole monologue about the abstract concept of homes and nostalgic memories.

Jocelyn tasked herself with opening every possible door in Valentino's house, exploring the living room, kitchen, and soon, stood before a bedroom door.

"Jocelyn, don't-" Valentino anxiously chased after her, but Jocelyn had already opened the door which she probably should've knocked on or asked for permission to open beforehand.

 The air conditioning of the bedroom quickly escaped into the living room via the open door, overwhelming Jocelyn, Raine, and presumably Valentino with the sudden coldness of the air. From where they were standing, they could see a brunette female in green striped pyjamas lying on a king-sized bed with many plushies and pillows that occupied most of the room, the curtains blocking any sunlight out, causing the whole room to be dark despite the lights having turned on. The girl's disheveled hair scattered across the pillow she rested on in a tangled mess, and she slept in what could be mistaken for an acrobat's pose. Despite the air conditioning having been put on the lowest temperature possible, she wasn't covered by any blankets. She faced away from the door, with one of her many pillows squished into her nose.

 Jocelyn stared at the sleeping dreamer before realising she had probably made a mistake of bursting in. Quietly, Jocelyn closed the door and turned to Valentino. "What the heck, Val? Why do you have your roommate sleeping in a refrigerator-cold room when it's already daytime? Is she hibernating or something?" She repeatedly spun her head from the bedroom door to Valentino several times with her jaw dropped.

 "See if you could help her. I'll find Lemar." Valentino shrugged nonchalantly. He went to the door opposite of Kari's, presumably his own room, and left the group alone. Lilac bounced over to Raine and Jocelyn, curious by what was going on. Raine gently held onto the doorknob, internally debating whether it would be socially acceptable for a stranger in a stranger's house to open the bedroom door of another stranger without asking first.

Reluctantly, Raine pushed the door open, the sound of its hinges creaking echoing across Kari's whole room. Her body immediately started to shiver as the cold air pierced her skin, but went over to the side of Kari's bed nonetheless to wake her up by gently tapping her on the shoulder. That was when she found out that Kari was already awake and was staring at the wall in front of her when Raine came into her sight.

"Um, hello," Raine said. "You must be Kari, right?"

Kari stared at Raine for a few seconds, and for a moment Raine wondered if Kari was even able to speak, but then a soft voice came out of her mouth. "Revieras," she muttered. "Your energy is incredible."

Raine felt a tinge of bittersweetness in her comment, knowing that the amount of dream energy she had was very, very low compared to the usual. "Just call me Raine. I'm, uh, here to help you," Raine replied, in an almost questioning tone. She wasn't sure how exactly to help, as Valentino gave no details at all, but just then she felt a subconscious attack taking over her mind. Her vision began to blur and she closed her eyes, trying not to let Kari see what was transpiring in her head. She wasn't in much pain, but felt herself suffocating. Her ears ringing sounded like the waves of the ocean, and she could hear the formation of bubbles underwater.

After about five seconds, the attack stopped. Raine's vision returned and she could see that Kari was still staring at her with soulless eyes. Although she didn't understand anything about what just happened, it allowed an idea to pop into her head. "Hey, I think we should go out for a walk. It'll get you more energised than staying in your room all day." Raine smiled warmly to Kari, who was already falling asleep again. "We'll go with my friends. How about we head to the aquarium?"

"We're going to the aquarium?" Jocelyn, who was outside Kari's door eavesdropping the whole time, unbeknownst to both Raine and Kari, forgot to use her non-existent inner voice and squealed in excitement. But just as quickly as she got exhilarated, her excitement died down as she eyed Valentino's door. "Aww, but I wanna hang out with Val. Hmm, I'll go talk to him!" And just like that, Jocelyn vanished.

Lilac, who was right where Jocelyn was standing, raised an eyebrow. "An aquarium, you say? A magnificent and peculiar choice indeed! Why so?"

"My mom once told me she donated a generous amount of rainflowers to Aqua Kingdom some weeks ago. I'm hoping we can find some there. Besides, there's no black-dreamers in the Subliminal realm. Going out will be beneficial for everyone."

Jocelyn's head popped out of Valentino's room, its door opened a slight slit. "Yo guys, I'll stay here with Val. You guys go on without me! Oh, and bring me back some souvenirs. Preferably some edible ones." She gave a quick wave goodbye before disappearing behind Valentino's door.

"Hey, get up, come on." Raine waited as Kari slowly rolled out of bed.

After waiting for Kari to clean herself up, Lilac and Raine assisted in giving her a makeover. Jocelyn even came out of Valentino's room for a little while just to pick an outfit for Kari - A casual light cyan top with a denim jacket, and white jeans. When Kari finally got the strength to tie her own hair into a braid while Raine sprayed perfume on her, she transformed into an entirely different person. Well, almost. She slumped back onto her bed the moment she was done dressing up, and Raine had to drag her up again.

"Hey Val, come look at your girlfriend!" Jocelyn pulled Valentino from out his room and to Kari's, dragging him by the sleeve as he groaned defeatedly to showcase the newly dressed Kari.

"I told you, she's not my girlfriend. But be careful if you're going to Aqua Kingdom. There's going to be a lot of people there." Val scrutinised Kari for a second before nodding. "Stay safe," he added, just as he left. Raine was confused by Valentino's warning but decided not to pay too much attention to it.

Lilac pulled Kari out of her bedroom while Raine found the remote to turn off the freezing air

conditioner. Turning off the lights and closing the
door, Raine and Lilac dragged Kari out the front door
with Jocelyn waving goodbye for the fifth time. The
girls wore their shoes and left the building.

  The three of them exited the house and travelled
down several blocks to the nearest bus stop, where
they read the guide for the buses' routes. Jocelyn
confidently gave a tour of the neighbourhood, despite
not living there, while Lilac listened eagerly. Raine
was trying to keep Kari awake for the two minutes
they waited for the correct bus to arrive.

  The bus eventually came into view and stopped for
the three to hop on, and they scrambled to the back
where there happened to be enough seats for
everyone to sit together. There were more people than
usual, but it didn't stop the group from chatting. After
some probing, Kari gave a more elaborate
introduction to herself.

  "Family friend of Val," she started, using his
nickname. "Was sent to live in the Subliminal realm
because I was getting more negatively affected in the
Dream realm." Raine remembered that the Dream
realm was located closest to the Nightmare realm, and
that Kari had probably lived close enough for her to
be influenced by nightmare energy. There was a
popular phenomenon called the black dream effect,
causing a dreamer's mental and physical strength and
health to deteriorate. Their dream energy would get
soaked and eaten up by the nightmare energy
consuming their essence, and eventually their soul

would be lost to darkness. Although it had not been declared to be an official malady, dreamers still used the term loosely. "Val moved to the Subliminal realm because of a scholarship and left the Mainland. His family owed mine because they suffered financial issues, so they allowed me to move to Val's place. We weren't that close when we were younger, but I knew his sister-" Suddenly, Kari's eyes lowered. "Never mind. I didn't know him that well back then. Still don't."

"My condolences. Nightmare energy can be really draining," Lilac commented. She wasn't paying much attention to Kari, her eyes glued onto the window to her right. "The Subliminal realm is truly magnificent! I haven't seen any corpses or hubris yet, unlike what I've heard!" Her voice was loud enough for the whole bus to hear her, and for a moment Raine thought they were all going to get kicked out from the vehicle. Lilac placed Sir Bamesetton by the edge of the window and directed her gaze to Kari and Raine. "Losing to the nightmares is truly execrable. I wish you luck on your amelioration."

Raine decided to let Lilac comfort Kari in her own unique way and rested her back against the bus seat. Just as Lilac said, there were no corpses or hubris, only greenery vistas and a sneak peak of other Subliminal dreamers enjoying their time outside walking on the streets. It almost felt like a sanctuary.

But after a few bus stops, Raine noticed that it was getting a bit more crowded, and the dream energy around was no longer pure subliminal energy. As more individuals boarded the bus, she could hear accents of Ambition dreamers, Pure dreamers and even mixed dreamers expressing their woes to their friends and family. Most of them carried large bags and luggage, and it took a lot of squeezing for Raine, Lilac, and Kari to get off once they reached the aquarium.

Upon the entrance, Raine was stunned to see a whole stampede of non-Subliminal dreamers crowding around the aquarium. It was supposed to be a tourist attraction, but now it had turned into a refuge for those who had escaped the black-dreamers in other realms. Everyone quickly noticed Raine coming up to the aquarium, and before long, Raine, Lilac, and Kari were swamped by a crowd. They all bombarded her with questions about the black-dreamers invading the dreamer realms, shouting in a rather agitated and angry manner, and Raine couldn't escape from their judgement. She wished she had something to hide behind other than Lilac and Kari, and began to feel threatened by the amassing audience.

I should've worn a disguise, Raine thought, feeling dizzy from the staggering horde.

⁎★ ◆ ★⁎
Chapter 14: Aquarium

It didn't take long for security to arrive. The head security approached Raine after dismissing the crowd which had formed around her, and she had to pretend not to notice everyone staring at her. "What are you doing here, Raine? The aquarium is already reaching maximum capacity. If you think you're here to admire some fishes, you're wrong. This place is being turned into some shelter for the foreigners to reside while the government is deciding on whether to close the border."

Raine felt a little insulted, but then shook her head. "I'm here because I require some rainflowers to fulfil a mission. It's to restore the barrier of the Nightmare realm."

The head security eyed Lilac, who was holding up Sir Bamesetton for him to see, and then Kari, who was a second away from falling asleep and collapsing onto the ground, and then sighed. "Fine. Come with me. The rainflowers are displayed along with the Angel's Crowned fish."

"Thank you," Raine offered a smile as a peace offering and let the head security lead them into the aquarium, squeezing through the many whispering dreamers.

The sheltered dark aquarium with natural air conditioning provided a comfortable and familiar space as the blue waters displayed by glass panes illuminated the area. Many fishes in different shapes and sizes were found swimming by, and it would've been a nice view if not for the hundreds of heads blocking the glass.

It was surprisingly less crowded than Raine had assumed, considering how bad the head security had made it out to be earlier. Nonetheless, she had to make sure Lilac didn't suddenly run off somewhere to express her marvel and that Kari wouldn't drown in the sea of people wandering around.

"What's the Angel's Crowned fish?" Kari suddenly asked. "Heard it once in my dreams."

The head security gave a sound of annoyance but complied. "It's the most exotic fish around. Heard from my co-workers that it's one-of-a-kind, and imported from Psytheon."

"Psytheon?" Raine raised an eyebrow. "Isn't that the waking world?"

"Correct. It was rumoured to have been sent by an angel of the sea in Psytheon. It feeds off the rainflowers' dream energy - which were gifted by Rhea." The head security eyed Raine at the mention of Rhea. "Right this way," he added, leading the group to a small exclusive room devoid of any other dreamers.

The room, smaller in comparison to the others in the aquarium, lacked any other visitors. A water tank stood with a red stanchion preventing access in the centre of the empty space.

A large fish with red-and-blue scales resembling a dragon swam around in the tank. Its fins were like the

wings of a fairy, the back tail resembling that of a
mermaid. It had a long and round body with coloured
patterns like tie-dye painted by divinity itself.
Rainflowers were planted in and around the tank, its
white petals waving around to the rhythm of the
water's movements. They glowed as brightly as the
blue waters, and for the first time in a long while,
Raine felt hope and relief.

"We keep some spare rainflowers in the storage
cabinet here. They've never wilted, so we've always
had extras. Wait for me while I go get them. Don't
touch anything." The head security left to find the
spare rainflowers after dropping his stern warning to
everyone.

"It's the same as in my dreams," Kari muttered,
almost in awe, inching closer to the fish. It swam
slowly yet elegantly, not acknowledging its visitors
who were eyeing it with beauty.

Raine wanted to take a picture of it and send it to
Jocelyn, but a sudden scream pierced her ear, and she
let out a groan. The scream echoed in her head,
blurring the lines between reality and her
subconsciousness. The scream resonated as a
heart-wrenching cry, enveloping Raine in another
wave of sadness and despair. She dropped to her
knees and shielded her ears to no avail.

Noticing this, Lilac bent down to Raine. "Is
something the matter? What has befallen you?"
Unsure how to respond, she placed Sir Bamesetton on
the floor next to Raine. "What enemy is to face the

wrath of Sir Bamesetton?" But Raine could hardly listen to Lilac's voice.

No!

The yelling and screaming were almost unbearable, and Raine felt she was going to faint. Just as she heard the rushed footsteps of head security and his calls to her, she felt herself passing out from all the noise.

※ ※ ※

It took Raine a moment for her to open her eyes. When she did, she saw the same thing she had seen during the taxi ride. All her senses aligned accordingly, with the additional wave of sadness washing over her. Unlike before, the water felt colder with increased pressure, and Raine couldn't breathe.

I can't breathe at all...Am I dreaming?

Raine could hardly think as her lungs began to fill up. Her chest was about to explode with water and with each passing second, she inched closer and closer to death. Hardly any air remained in Raine's body, and she couldn't tell anymore if she was dreaming or truly drowning.

Just then, the water began to drain. It felt like a giant wave crashing over the shore and enveloping the sand before returning to the sea, leaving said sand behind wet and gritty. Raine coughed uncontrollably as she threw water up from her body, trying desperately to catch some air. It took her a minute to breathe normally again, but she was still mortified by the experience.

The water had completely vanished, leaving Raine unsettled by the absence of walls. A black void stretched out before her, and she couldn't even discern what she was standing on. Any step forward seemed like a perilous plunge into the abyss, so she remained still, attempting to collect her thoughts.

"Hello? Is someone there?" A voice called from behind Raine. Raine turned around to see a boy. He couldn't have been more than twelve years old, having a round and immature face. He had neatly trimmed black hair and grey eyes which met Raine's. The boy casually ran up to Raine, who was too disoriented to move. The boy stood close to Raine, his miniscule height only reaching her torso. He wore a strange football uniform that looked like it was produced at least a decade ago.

"Woah, are you really here?" He asked, mouth agape. Raine, who was still dumbfounded by the predicament she was suddenly in, looked left and right before staring at the child, unsure if he was a threat.

Figuring that Raine would be able to outpower a child, she decided to play nice in order to avoid any potential conflicts, killing two birds with one stone by trying to get some answers from the boy as well. "Yes. Who are you? Where am I?" She asked, putting on a confident voice.

"I don't know," The boy answered sadly. Raine didn't know which question he was referring to, but then the boy continued. "But this is where I live."

"You're a dreamer as well?"

The boy nodded before asking, "What are you doing here?"

"I'm not sure, but I think it has something to do with the Subliminal Dreamkeeper."

"Subliminal? I'm from the Subliminal Realm!" The boy said, excitedly.

Raine giggled at the boy, realising that he wasn't a threat after all. Her tone changed as she talked. "Really? Do you know anything about your Dreamkeeper?"

"I don't remember a lot of things, but I had a friend who could control the world! He sounds so cool, right? I think he might be a Dreamkeeper, but he's the same age as I am. My mom says that Dreamkeepers can only be strong adults who are responsible and mature." The boy stared at the non-existent ceiling as he tried to recall, but after a few seconds, he shook his head in frustration. "No! I can't remember anything! I'm sorry."

Raine gave him a reassuring smile. "Hey, it's okay. You don't have to beat yourself up over it. You already remember your friend being able to 'control the world', and it's very helpful."

The boy looked up at Raine. "Really? Am I helpful?"

Raine nodded. "You are. And you'll help save the world."

The boy broke into a cheerful grin, running around in circles happily as he cried, "Yes! I helped somebody!"

Raine watched the boy, thinking about the joys of being his age. She then thought about what was happening to her world, and she clenched her fist as she imagined what the other children had to go through because of the black-dreamers.

After the boy simmered down, Raine went over and asked him. "So, do you know how to leave this place? I need to get back to my friends."

"I've never left this place before. But I'm sure there's a door somewhere. All rooms have doors." The boy looked around. "I'll help you find it!" He started to walk further away from Raine, placing his hands in front of him like he was blindfolded as he felt about the empty place for some resemblance of a door.

How is there going to be a door when there aren't any walls? Raine thought.

"I found it!" The boy cried, much to Raine's surprise. Raine quickly ran over to the boy. True to his word, there was a door, seemingly placed in the middle of nowhere. It was grey and dull with a shiny doorknob. Raine wasn't sure if the door would explode were she to touch it. Reluctantly, she grabbed onto the doorknob, and the door opened.

There was nothing but light on the other side of the door, and Raine had to shield her eyes from the brightness of it. She took a step back from the door and looked at the boy, whose eyes fixated on the door, or rather, what was behind it.

"Guess I'll be leaving now," Raine said to the boy. She prepared to take a step, but the boy was now grabbing onto her shirt and preventing her from carrying on.

"Wait! Can I come with you?" He asked, pleading.

Sorrow struck Raine and she didn't know why, but the only thing she could say to the blissful child was, "Of course."

Hand in hand, Raine and the boy walked through the door. But as Raine moved, she realised she no longer felt a hand holding hers. Before she knew it, she was swallowed whole by the light, and everything disappeared along with it.

✳ ✳ ✳

Raine woke up in a hospital bed with the curtains undrawn, the sun rays beaming from the window into her eyes. She blinked several times to fully regain her sight, unable to sit up straight. She was alone, and felt chills run down her spine at the thought of the boy.

But after a few minutes, Raine had already forgotten his face. As Raine thought about what to do next, she was interrupted by the sound of footsteps echoing throughout the entire room as Kari and Lilac entered the room. Seeing Raine wide awake, they rushed over to her. The head security followed behind, holding two rainflowers in his hand. He moved past Lilac and Kari and approached Raine rather sternly.

"Get well soon. And leave when you do." He handed the rainflowers to Raine, and also gave her a piece of paper and a pen. "As you know, there are refugees in the aquarium. I request for you to write a speech to address the situation and calm everyone down."

Raine, albeit still a bit ill, decided to write a letter addressing the dreamers, reassuring them that she was trying to sort the situation with the black-dreamers out. After ten minutes, she handed the speech back to the head security, who nodded. "By the way, you're free to stay in the aquarium. The place will clear up soon." He left after his information was acknowledged with a nod from Raine.

Raine watched the head security leave the room before she turned to Lilac and Kari. "What happened?" She asked.

"You fainted, and I fell asleep. They carried us both to hospital beds and once they found out that I wasn't actually sick, they kicked me out of bed and had me watch over you. Lilac went to buy food for Jocelyn," Kari explained, yawning. "I wanted to see the mermaids."

"Aha, a revelation! Sir Bamesetton has just imparted news of the staff's discourse regarding the relocation of these foreigners to another domain within the Subliminal realm. This aqueous sanctuary shall be unfettered, allowing us lasses the freedom to venture and discover its mysteries." Lilac grinned widely, picking up Sir Bamesetton. "Shall we take a detour?"

Lilac and Kari looked expectantly at Raine, who considered. "Yeah, sure. I'd like that. Just don't cause any trouble for anyone." She gave a smile. Spending time at the aquarium would not only be a nice experience, but it would also give her time to get to know Kari's situation better, as well as to think about the strange dream she just had.

Lilac's eyes lit up. "Very well, then! Sir Bamesetton and I shall extend our welcomes to that of the denizens of the deep!" Before Raine could leave the hospital bed, Lilac had left the room as well, probably to offer her soliloquy to whoever and whatever was in the shark tunnel with her.

It took an extra ten minutes for Raine to be officially discharged. Kari fell asleep again during that time, and Raine had to snap her back to reality for the millionth time. "Kari, wake up. You said you wanted to see the mermaids. I was told there would be a mermaid show in about an hour. Why don't we head there?" She asked, keeping the rainflowers in her bag. She wondered if she was supposed to just give it to Kari, but decided to wait until she was back with the others at Valentino's place.

"Huh? Oh, sure." Kari lazily stumbled about, and Raine had to drag her all the way back to the aquarium from the infirmary.

This time, the aquarium was much more empty than when Raine first stepped foot in. Most of the other dreamers had left, and now it was quiet and almost eerie, the cooling air accompanied with the smell of salt water. The bag of goodies and sweets for Jocelyn which Lilac had held onto earlier was now in Raine's hand, and she was looking at a kiosk that showed the layout of the aquarium.

The jellyfish gallery sat conveniently close to where the mermaid show was taking place, so Raine and Kari decided to admire the jellyfishes there as they slowly walked. There was still plenty of time, and moving at a slow pace with Kari sounded comforting.

Kari moved slower than Raine thought, and she had to slow down significantly for the two to be able to walk side by side. As they reached the jellyfish gallery, they entered a small dark cave-like tunnel with glowing jellyfishes, illuminating the room with pink and blue.

"Hey," Raine started, wondering how she could structure her sentence to ask about Kari in the nicest way she could think of. "What do you and Valentino usually do? I don't have siblings and I've never had a roommate before, so I'm curious."

Kari took a moment to respond. "Not much. Just sleep all day and night. I don't talk much to Val, but he checks up on me sometimes," she answered, her voice clearly indicating that it hadn't been used in a long while.

"Is it because of the black dream effect?" Raine asked, in a gentle tone.

"Don't know. I just like to dream. Better than reality. Want to live in them forever," Kari replied, after another brief pause. Raine waited to see if Kari would say anything else. "There's someone I care about in my dreams who doesn't exist when I'm not sleeping. Even though she once did."

The two finished walking through the jellyfish gallery and were now exiting through an automatic glass door that led directly to where the mermaid show was. Raine looked at her reflection in the glass door and felt the air growing more heavy, contributed by Kari's forlorn words.

"I'm so sorry," Raine said, knowing how it felt to lose somebody precious. She had seen Rhea's last moments, and even saw the death of others. Were she not Revieras, she probably would have escaped into her dreams of the dandelion field forever, where she could see her mother again. "Was she a family member?"

"She's Val's- I mean, she wasn't a family member of mine, but she felt like an older sister to me," Strangely, Kari had more energy in her voice than usual, but she didn't sound too bothered by the topic, so Raine began to walk again, and Kari followed. "I don't know what happened to her, exactly. But one day, she just vanished, and now it seems like she never existed in the first place."

"What was her name?"

"Nayeli Lin."

At the mention of her name, a loud ringing sound echoed in Raine's mind, so high-pitched and loud that she almost crippled down to the floor. She grabbed her ears and squeezed her eyes shut, as if trying to shut the noise out from her head.

After what felt like a century, the sound stopped, and when Raine opened her eyes again, she saw that Kari had already gone a few steps ahead, unaware of what Raine had just gone through. Raine didn't want to worry Kari, so she caught up with her, pretending that she just needed to tie her shoelaces.

Raine and Kari made it to a relatively large room, enough to become a theatre. The cold pierced Raine's skin as she shivered. Kari had probably trained to be immune to the cold, assuming her room was always as cold as when Raine first stepped in. The enormous tank that held many underwater structures and coral reefs was empty, unlike all the other tanks Raine had seen on her way to the mermaid show.

There was a family of three already sitting in front of the tank, on the floor. It looked clean enough, so Raine and Kari picked a spot on the floor to sit while waiting for the show to start. Raine stared at Kari, who was already zoning out and daydreaming, and wondered if she should continue the uncomfortable conversation which had been cut short earlier.

"Kari, have you ever encountered a black-dreamer before?" Raine asked.

Kari looked as if she hadn't heard Raine, but after a
second, she replied, "Don't remember, but I think so.
In the Dream realm. Before the barrier broke."

That was an answer Raine didn't expect. "How long
has it been since...Nayeli went missing?" She asked,
the question leaving a bad taste in her mouth.

"Twelve years," Kari mumbled.

Raine started to feel like she was being rude for
prying or asking such questions, but she needed to if
she wanted to help Kari. "Have you been like this
since?" Her mind traced back to when she first saw
Kari lying in bed.

"What else? I'm always tired, and I can't do
anything." Kari lowered her head, not out of shame,
but out of tiredness. Raine felt guilt stabbing her,
because despite the lack of energy in the words Kari
spoke, hopelessness reeked from her sentence. Kari
spared Raine from having to ask even more questions
by continuing to speak. "I don't have anything to do.
No motivation or reason, and anyway I don't have any
talent or skill. Living is just too tiring."

Raine failed to realise that a crowd had amassed on
the floor behind her, and the empty tank was now
filled with bubbles. A dark-haired mermaid dropped
from the top of the tank and swam towards the crowd,
placing her palm against the glass pane. Immediately,
a bunch of children and adults clambered to the glass
pane, trying to get a good view of the beautiful
mermaid whose tail was the colour of a pink summer

sunset. Kari's head rose as she stared at her, allowing Raine a sigh of relief. Saved by the mermaid.

"She looks different from the ones in my dreams," Kari commented, almost to herself.

"Really? What did you dream about?" Raine asked light-heartedly, in an attempt to change the topic.

"Once met a mermaid in my dreams, and she turned me into one as well. Was fun until I got trapped in a fishnet and got captured for experiments," Kari scooted forward and pressed her finger against the glass, where a trail of bubbles lingered.

Raine nodded slowly. "How did the dream end?"

"I was saved by Val." Kari smiled, turning around to face Raine. "He's always helped me try to get out of bed and dedicates his time to research on the black dream effect just so I can get better."

Hearing that, Raine smiled as well. "So you two are pretty close, after all." She couldn't tell if it were the lights or Kari herself that made her turn red. "Do you like him?" She asked, expecting Kari to deflect, as most people would.

"I think so," Kari replied.

Just before Raine could answer, A faint singing outside the room caught her attention. Some people, including Raine, broke eye contact from the glass tank with the mermaid to glance outside the entrance. Unlike everyone else, though, Raine got up and headed to the source of the singing. "I'll be back," she told Kari.

Raine didn't remember a large crowd forming
outside the room she was in. In fact, the crowd had
formed a big circle, and a familiar reddish-brown
haired girl holding onto a stuffed bear could be seen
in the middle elegantly hopping about, having a
musical number. Her arms waved about in the air,
and she would gaze solemnly at Sir Bamesetton
occasionally as lyrics poured out from her.

Flabbergasted, Raine squeezed through the crowd
and to everyone's surprise, interrupted Lilac's
performance by grabbing her arm and pulling her into
the room where the mermaid show was taking place.

"What is this? An antagonist here to challenge my
score? Oh, Revieras! What an unexpected opponent!"
Lilac's voice caught everybody's attention, and for a
second Raine expected the head security from earlier
to suddenly teleport into the room and kick Lilac and
herself out. Raine shushed Lilac.

"What are you doing?" She asked. "This is an
aquarium, not a stage."

"But Revieras, the world *is* my stage! I am merely
providing entertainment and expressing myself
through what I do best." Lilac gave a curtsy. She was
using Raine's title in order to further her
exaggeration. Raine sighed, but then Lilac reverted to
a calmer voice. "All my life, I was trapped in a cage,
now that I am free, I deserve to fly amongst these
flightless birds." She poked at Raine gently. "You want
to give the dreamers freedom from this nightmare,

but what about freedom for I, after I worked so hard just to gain a speck of it?"

Raine was now confused by whatever Lilac just said. But after giving it a little thought, she finally understood - Lilac had spent most of her life unwillingly in the hands of the Remnants of Keresius, and was never able to embrace or express her true identity. Now that she had been freed from their grasp, it wouldn't be unreasonable for her to act out after being starved of liberty.

"There are appropriate times for you to be on stage. You know, so the show doesn't get disrupted?" Raine tried to speak in Lilac's abstract metaphors but ended up confusing herself even more.

Luckily, Lilac seemed to have listened. "Very well! I shall retire to the background cast, momentarily. Bid the audience farewell, Sir Bamesetton- Oh, a mermaid!" Lilac rushed over to the room with the glass tank, admiring the mermaid as if she had just appeared. Raine followed Lilac and was glad to see Kari still there, sitting on the floor and watching the mermaid swimming here and there. It was an accomplishment, Raine thought, that Kari hadn't fallen asleep yet.

Lilac reached a hand for Kari and hoisted her up to get a better view of the mermaid. Raine decided not to interrupt the two, and smiled as she watched the two discussing chatting amongst each other.

The audience's murmurings muffled the ringtone of Raine's phone, to which she jumped in surprise from the vibration. Luckily, everyone in the room was too mesmerised by the mermaid to pay any attention to Raine, and she eased a little as she answered the phone.

Jocelyn's voice was heard. "Raine, Raine! Dayren just goaled! What a redemption!"

"Dayren? Are you watching football right now?" Raine asked, puzzled.

"Don't worry! It's a pre-recording. Val evicted me from his room earlier, but now he says he's done! Come back now! Oh, and did you guys see any dolphins or manta rays? Could you bring back some seaweed for me?"

"We've been a little busy," Raine said, eyeing Lilac and Kari, who had somehow managed to grab the mermaid's attention and was now playing rock-paper-scissors with her. "We got a lot of snacks for you. We'll return right away, and tell him I've got some rainflowers."

"Dude, no way!" Jocelyn cried. "Someone just got a penalty!"

Raine sighed in her lack of knowledge on football. "Alright, see you soon." She ended the call and walked over to Lilac and Kari, who both greeted her with a smile. The mermaid, seeing Raine, waved as well, her tail flowing gently in the water. Raine, who was just about to keep her phone, pulled it back out and took a picture of herself, Kari and Lilac, with the mermaid behind. All of them had a smile on their faces.

The mermaid swam away to interact with the other dreamers, and Raine kept her phone. "Jocelyn just called me. We're going back now."

There was a bit of hesitation, but Kari and Lilac nodded.

Leave! Leave this place for good, and don't come back, you monster!

Raine heard the voice again. This time, it didn't hurt. Well, not physically. The words were harsh enough for Raine to feel a bit of pain in her heart, despite knowing it most likely wasn't directed at her. She considered telling Lilac and Kari about the voices, but in the end just said: "Let's take a picture of the manta rays first. Jocelyn wants to see them, and they're near the exit."

After snapping more pictures, which took longer than Raine initially expected, the three of them stepped out of the aquarium, where rainfall was underway. Luckily, the roof over their heads prevented them from getting immediately soaked. The wind brushed Raine's hair, and despite the fact that she could feel some raindrops splatter onto her pants, it was less cold than when she was in the aquarium, and the sounds of pitter-patter oddly comforted her. That was, until she remembered that the bus stop to head back was a three-minute walk with no shelter from the rain.

❋★✦★❋
Chapter 15: Lost Memory

Thankfully, Raine had kept a secret stash of money in her bag to be able to call a taxi. After Jocelyn graciously doxed Valentino's address, Raine, Lilac, and Kari were taken back to his and Kari's place.

"Heyo! Welcome back! I hope you had fun!" Jocelyn was waiting at the entrance for the three of them. And the snacks. "Did you buy the seaweed?"

Raine unzipped her bag which held the plastic bag of goods and handed it to Jocelyn. "Here you go," she said, smiling as she watched Jocelyn's eyes sparkle with joy.

"Come on, let's go talk to Val!" Jocelyn pulled Raine into the house like a magnet and brought everyone into Valentino's room.

As they entered the room, Raine took in all the details and furniture inside. The bed was much smaller compared to Kari's, and beside it stood a long white desk with a large computer resting on its surface. Raine was surprised to see it, for the type of technology she usually saw were gadgets about the size of her hand, or simple laptops with nothing but a touchpad. However, Valentino's set-up was more advanced. It had multiple monitors and a separate keyboard with an oddly-shaped mouse. Multiple bookshelves were filled with many colourful binders and organised series of books. Unlike Kari's room, there was no air conditioner, but a black fan built by

the corner of the windows opposite from the desk
instead. The windows had closed blinds, and
altogether the room felt suffocating with no sense of
natural light. Raine began to think that Kari and
Valentino were both vampires who were allergic to the
sun.

Valentino was already sitting on a swivel chair by the
computers, and he turned at the sound of the door
opening. "Where's Kari?" He asked, getting up from
his seat.

Raine noticed that Kari had vanished. "Strange, she
was behind me just a second ago." She noticed that
the door to Kari's bedroom was open, and she entered
Kari's room after knocking twice on the agape door.

Kari had taken off her denim jacket which was now
thrown on the floor. Her beautiful French braid was
now a tangled mess as the hair tie lingered
somewhere lost in the room. She laid on the bed like a
starfish and stared at the ceiling.

Valentino moved past Raine and firmly grabbed both
her arms and lifted her up from her lying position.
"What's wrong?" He asked Kari, in an
uncharacteristic soft tone.

Kari replied, in a whisper: "I wish Nayeli could've
gone to the aquarium with me."

Valentino went still, as if his brain had
short-circuited from Kari's answer, but then he
sighed. Lilac and Jocelyn read the room and left him
and Kari alone in the room, but Raine walked
forward, taking out the rainflowers from her bag. "I

got the rainflowers." She quietly passed the rainflowers to Valentino, whose eyes widened just the slightest as he took it.

"Thanks, I guess," he said reluctantly, before he slowly got up and walked out of Kari's bedroom. "Leave her alone for now. We have things to do."

Raine felt the tension between herself and Valentino ease a little as she successfully fulfilled his request. She gave Kari an encouraging smile before leaving the room. "In hopes of a better future," she said, closing the door behind her. She turned and saw Valentino talking to Jocelyn before giving her the rainflowers.

Valentino then returned to his room. "I needed the rainflowers to make an antidote to combat the black dream effect. I came up with it myself, and Jocelyn's helping me to create it because I can't see very well and I don't want to risk messing up the dosages. Anyway, I'll help you find Lemar now." He nodded, gesturing to Raine to enter his room again. Raine wished for Jocelyn to be next to her so she could make the whole situation a little less awkward, and kept the door slightly ajar so that she could still hear the faint voices of Jocelyn and Lilac working outside.

Raine was brought over to the monitors where there were thousands of texts and profiles. All of them were dreamers named Lemar, and for a second, Raine doubted she was even on the right track, but then her eyes widened when they landed on a specific profile.

Lemar Castillo.

Another loud ring in Raine's ear caused her to flinch, and she planted her palm on the computer desk to support herself. It was a similar ring to when Kari first mentioned the name of Nayeli Lin.

"Um." Valentino looked at Raine for a second but then faced the monitor, choosing to ignore her and focused on the profile of Lemar Castillo instead. "I dug a little deeper into his background. He was twelve when he died from drowning." The ringing continued.

Valentino stopped and looked at Raine again once he noticed that something was wrong with her. "What?" he asked, warily. Her shoulders slumped and her head lowered, the favour of Valentino crushing her the first time they met soon to be repaid.

The ringing was too unbearable. Raine lost all her strength and collapsed, taking down Valentino along with her.

✳ ✳ ✳

Raine found herself sitting on the bleachers in the middle of a football match. A familiar face sitting next to her stood out, amongst all the other dreamers watching the game. "Val!" She gasped. "I mean, Valentino! I'm so sorry!" She remembered tackling him in the head as she toppled down, and Valentino was now staring at her, clearly unimpressed.

"Whatever," he said, acting as if nothing had happened. "As I was saying, Lemar was once in a junior football's team with nine other players around the same age as him." He pointed at the football players on the field. Raine squinted and realised that the players were junior players, and Lemar was one of them.

"Lemar told me he had a friend who could control the world," Raine brought up. "But he couldn't remember anything else."

Valentino eyed her with doubt. "I've investigated everyone affiliated with Lemar. There's no such person. But I'm willing to bet that Lemar was referring to an elemental. What are the chances that this elemental is your Dreamkeeper?"

"This doesn't feel like any regular dream." Raine looked around. "It feels like a memory." If it weren't for the fact that Raine remembered being knocked out by the ringing, and the fact that she would never be watching football with Valentino, she probably would've believed that this whole sequence was real. The vague drowsiness Raine always felt when she dreamt was absent.

"I don't remember any of this. If it really is a memory, then it isn't mine," Valentino rebutted. He watched the football game with fascination, having accepted being sent into a dream-like state out of his will. "I can't do anything while we're in this dream. "I don't know how this happened, but we might as well investigate while we're here."

Raine nodded in agreement, although it seemed like Valentino was only staying to watch the football match and not to actually find out what was going on with Lemar and the Subliminal Dreamkeeper. Still, she didn't complain, and tried to watch the game as well, despite knowing nothing about the sport.

"Has Kari told you about Nayeli?" Valentino asked, rather suddenly.

Raine was taken off guard by the unexpected question, but nodded anyway. "She was your sister, right?"

"That's the thing, Raine. I don't have a sister."

She went numb. "What?"

"I've never had a sister. My parents never had a daughter. Only me. Kari has probably told you that she moved to the Subliminal realm because of the black dream effect, but it was her family who kicked her out because she kept insisting that Nayeli existed, and that everybody had forgotten her. We all thought she went crazy." Valentino turned back at the ongoing football match. "I can't exactly remember when it all started. Kari and I were about eight when it happened. But now, I'm not sure if I believe Nayeli really did exist, or if Kari was just mixing up her reality with her dreams. Her and my parents declared she had a mental illness and wanted nothing to do with her."

It took Raine about a minute to process everything Valentino said. "If Nayeli did exist, and nobody remembered her, weren't there any pictures or evidence of her?"

"We didn't have any," Valentino answered. "And anyway, there was an incident shortly after that almost wrecked my family, and Nayeli was the least of our concerns when we could barely find a place to sleep." The audience cheered at one of the teams scoring a goal, but Raine was too focused on what Valentino was saying to pay attention to the smell of food or the sound of football players cheering in triumph.

"I see. I'm sorry," Raine said, finding it easier to look at Valentino in the eye now.

"Don't be. You didn't do anything," Valentino pressed his palm against his cheek, as if feeling for something on his face. "Also, I'm sorry if I come off as rude or strange." He sounded genuine, and Raine suddenly felt bad for all the unspoken tension between the two when they first met. "And, um, sorry for crushing you."

"I don't think you're a bad person. Jocelyn's your friend, so I'm friends with you too." Raine said, smiling. She watched Valentino's face grow even more red and giggled slightly to herself. "You get flustered quite easily," she teased, trying to make things more light-hearted with a small comment.

"I am quite aware, yes." Valentino gave a regretful smile. "It's a bit of a problem."

Just as Raine was about to add another comment, a trickle of raindrops fell from the sky, landing on the sleeve of her shirt, causing the small spot to dampen. Another trickle fell, and another, and another. "It's

drizzling." As far as Raine recalled, the sky was clear
and devoid of any clouds. Now, the sky had grown
murky, and the clouds which had appeared from
nowhere were an angry grey.

Valentino lifted his hoodie up, shielding himself
from the rain, and allowing his whole outfit to get wet
instead. "Strange. I'm getting Deja vu from this." He
looked around and flinched when a raindrop landed
on his face. "Maybe you're right. This is a lost memory
of mine. We should explore it." He got up from his
seat. "It may be connected to Lemar. *I could've
witnessed his death.*"

Raine followed Valentino off the bleachers and onto
the field, where the rain only got heavier - a signal to
everyone of an oncoming thunderstorm, and
spectators began to depart from the place. With the
open field lacking shelter and safety from the bad
weather, the sound of a whistle was heard, along with
the declaration of the match being cancelled
temporarily. Parents of the junior football players
went to drag their children to safety. The sounds of
parents and coaches shouting fell to static as Raine
heard Lemar's voice calling out to no one.

"Zephyr! Zephyr! Where are you?"

Raine's eyes darted to Lemar, but then she heard
Valentino gasp. "What is it?" She saw Valentino
staring at another boy whom she failed to notice.

"He's...looking at us."

Raine's heart skipped a beat. The boy, who was on
the same team as Lemar and wore the same uniform,

was doused with the rain. His black hair was a drenched mess, and his cyan eyes stared into Raine's soul as she made eye contact with him. He wore a distressed look on his face that no child should ever wear, and his whole body was trembling. Raine couldn't tell if he was trembling because it was cold or because he was afraid. "That's not supposed to happen," she commented, scrutinising the boy's features to store in her own memory. "Right? We're supposed to be invisible."

"What's more is that I have never seen this person before. He doesn't exist," Valentino added. "Something is very wrong."

The clouds grouped together to overshadow the entire football field. Thunder rocked the ground after a blinding flash of lighting, causing a deafening roar which prompted more shouting and panic from everyone in the field. Another lightning struck, this time hitting a tree nearby, causing its bark to blow off and almost hit someone. Leaves of every tree nearby were now flying uncontrollably against the strong wind, and everything in an instant became foggy and cold - a disaster soon to unbound. That was when Raine remembered Rhea teaching her that the Subliminal realm didn't *have* natural disasters.

"Zephyr!" Lemar cried, running after the cyan-eyed boy. His shoes made a squelch sound as he made his way through the rising waters. Lemar grabbed onto Zephyr's hand and started to run away, but stopped when Zephyr refused to move. Lemar turned around. "What are you doing? We need to leave!"

"I'm sorry," Raine could hear Zephyr stammer, as tears began to form. Lightning flashed once more, and she had to close her eyes to shield herself from its blinding light.

For a moment, everything disappeared. The world shifted and moulded itself whimsically, like a mould of clay, shaped by lost memories. Then, everything returned, but it wasn't the same anymore. Something had changed.

When Raine opened her eyes again, the typhoon ended, and everything went dark. It was dead silent, and everyone had vanished except for Raine and Valentino. The rain had stopped, with the ground still damp and the environment wet. The air was still and moist, windless and frozen in time. Raine saw a full moon hovering in the night, accompanied by the stars. "Is this...the aftermath?"

Valentino didn't answer. He stood still, as if lost in thought.

Something glistening caught Raine's eye. The stars above formed the shape of fishes as they began swimming in the sky's canvas.

But the two were woken up before Raine could point out the stars to Valentino, and they ended up back in Valentino's room. As the two slowly got up from the floor, they quickly realised that Lilac and Jocelyn were staring at them, mouths agape. "What in the flying funk is going on? Raine!" Jocelyn rushed over to

Raine and shook her dumbfounded. "I'm trying to set Kari and Val together! Don't do anything weird!"

"*Jocelyn!*" Valentino grew so red that Raine could feel the warmth of his cheeks, only for her to realise she was blushing too.

"I'm so sorry! I passed out and knocked him over!" Raine immediately distanced herself from Valentino.

"You have a really hard head," Valentino commented, shaking his head.

"What a shocking turn of events! But regardless, we have accomplished concocting the vial to save Kari from her inner demons!" Lilac held out a small glass vial coloured pink.

"Zephyr's our Dreamkeeper. I just know it," Raine said, still mildly embarrassed. "Let's help Kari and then we can go to Psytheon." Her heart skipped a beat at the mention of the waking world.

"Why Psytheon? How do you know he's there?" Valentino asked, ignoring Lilac and Jocelyn's dramatic gasps.

"Before the dream ended, I saw the Angel's Crowned fish," Raine answered. She realised he wasn't with her at the aquarium and that he probably needed more context than 'weird fish in a dream'. "It's a unique fish that was imported from Psytheon. It's trying to tell us that Zephyr's in the waking world. That's why the map didn't show his pinpoint - he wasn't in Oneirolepsy in the first place."

This revelation stunned everyone, and for a moment, nobody spoke anything, but then Valentino broke the silence. "Well, I already know what the Angel's Crowned fish is, so you didn't have to explain. But anyway, congratulations. You've located your Dreamkeeper." He walked over to Lilac and took the vial before leaving to find Kari. "Let's wrap this up."

Excited, Raine, Jocelyn, and Lilac followed Valentino as he opened the door to Kari's room. Raine was expecting for Kari to still be in bed and be welcomed with a warm gift that would help erase all the bad memories and depression away from her life so that she could be finally free. In a way, it was a vicariously pleasing ideal to at least help a dreamer out in times like these, and she craved to see Kari's delighted expression and joy when the vial reached her.

But when the door opened, not only was the group met with the familiar chill of Kari's room, but also the unfortunate familiar energy of a black-dreamer lingering. Detecting nightmare energy was the last thing Raine expected upon entering, and instead of Kari resting in bed, she was up by the bed and held helplessly in a choke hold by a black-dreamer in dark clothes. Kari was already looking in Raine's direction, as if she had been pleading for someone to come to the rescue for a while now.

Raine noticed a bit of silver in the black-dreamer's hand - a blade, and it was pressing against Kari's throat. Instead of a mortified expression, Kari wore a blank one, if not peaceful, as if she had resigned her life already, and that there was nothing left to keep her going. But as she glanced at Valentino, some kind of realisation dawned upon her, and immediately, her eyes screamed: *I don't want to die.*

The group was so focused on the turquoise-haired black-dreamer that they failed to notice another black-dreamer hiding by the door. Immediately, the other black-dreamer yanked Raine's hair and pulled her forward, causing Raine to lose grip on the vial. The glass vial hit the floor and shattered into a million pieces, causing the precious contents to seep out.

But that was the least of everyone's concern. "If any of you moves, this dreamer will choke on her own blood," threatened the turquoise-haired black-dreamer.

"No attacking, either!" Adding to his ally's threat, the other black-dreamer, who had blond hair covered by a black top hat, threw Raine to the carpeted floor, and pressed his heel against her head. His voice had a tone similar to Raine's when she was performing her magician shows, and now that she was on the ground, she could see the black-dreamer dressed in a white magician's suit.

Valentino, Lilac, and Jocelyn all froze, and the magician continued. "Now, all of you might be wondering: How did two nightmares break into the Subliminal realm? That, my friends! Is because of Koshalv's magnificent ability for the shadows to submit to his will. Now, isn't that amazing? Any nightmare can just pop out from the darkness at any time!" He gestured his hands as he spoke, one of them carrying some sort of a card-gun. "Now then, allow us to introduce ourselves! I am Ralisrok, and that lass over there is Slevlyeot. We come on behalf of the Nightmare King." Ralisrok took a bow, whereas Slevlyeot rolled her eyes, clearly unamused by his performance.

Valentino, seemingly tired of Ralisrok's verbose villain-speech, vanished from the door and reappeared behind Slevlyeot. Knocking Slevlyeot from behind, he managed to separate her and Kari, and the silver blade dropped to the ground.

Jocelyn and Lilac took this as a chance to step forward, but before they could do so, Ralisrok aimed his gun at the two, and fired. Instead of bullets, two cards shot out, and sank deep into the skin of Jocelyn and Lilac. It wasn't hard to deduce that the card had been laced with some poison or dark magic that knocked out its victims, for the two immediately crippled to the floor, where the shattered glass from the vial sank deep into their legs and causing more pain, but their voice had been taken away from them, and they were unable to scream.

Ralisrok shifted his attention from Jocelyn and Lilac onto Valentino, giving Raine the opportunity to kick him as he attempted to shoot. Her kick lacked power, but it was enough to catch Ralisrok off-guard and flinch, causing the card to fly at a wall.

Kari was still on the floor, and sustaining some injuries before the group had entered, was unable to stand. Raine's kick only caused Ralisrok to exert more force on his heel, and Raine felt her skull crushing slowly and excruciatingly. "How dare you interrupt my show," he muttered, begrudgingly toward Valentino, who was too busy struggling to fight Slevlyeot in the cramped room to acknowledge his comment.

Raine noticed the blade that Slevlyeot had dropped, and tried to grab it, but the pain and the cold numbing her made it impossible to move her muscles to stretch her arm outward. Ralisrok, noticing her attempts, stepped on her arm with his other foot, and Raine had to keep in a pained groan.

Slevlyeot tore away Valentino's glasses and scratched at his face, causing him to stumble backward. He grabbed her clothes and pulled as they both collapsed to the floor. The two were struggling for survival, right in front of Kari, who had a front-row seat to their clash. Raine could hardly see anything, and her vision was starting to blotch up with darkness. She could faintly make out Slevlyeot retrieving her silver blade and with a clean slice of her blade, blood started pouring out from Valentino's throat, his life seeping out along with the red.

There was complete silence, and for a second the only thing Raine could hear was the loud buzzing of the air conditioning, and the faint gushing sound of the blood. Some of it had splattered onto Kari. Death shook her awake, and just as Raine was about to lose consciousness, a loud, grief-stricken yell from Kari shook her awake, the cry reverberating across the whole house, and even across the whole building.

A blinding light appeared from out of nowhere, but it turned out to have manifested from Kari. Dream energy poured out from her core and eliminated any source of nightmares around. The light was filled with nothing but raw dreams, matched only by the purest of dreamers, and slowly, the whole room transformed.

✳ ✳ ✳

Raine stirred and found herself free of Ralisrok. She was no longer crushed in between his heel and the carpeted floor, and she sat up in surprise. Unlike the moody atmosphere and colour of Kari's room, the place was filled with bright energetic colours, its palette warm and welcoming, but also kind and gentle on the eyes. A fuzzy warmness replaced the usual freezing temperature of the room, and Raine felt herself being hugged by the safety of the room.

Kari's entire room had its whole colour palette changed from a mundane grey to a vibrant rainbow, but everything else had stayed the same. Raine didn't get the sense that she was dreaming, but she also wasn't grounded as well.

She was quick to find Jocelyn, Lilac, Kari, and Valentino in the room as well, all wearing the same confused expression as Raine did. Except, Valentino was glowing, and almost translucent, like a ghost. Luckily, the injury to the throat was missing, and he looked fine...for now at least.

There was also another ghost-like individual, who
was a new face Raine had never seen before. She had
long ginger hair and a colourful palette, much like the
room itself. Raine felt like she was looking at an older
female version of Valentino. "Oh, hey there, Kari! It
seems you've brought all your friends along to your
space." She was sitting by the edge of the bed, and
gestured to everybody to sit on the bed like some sort
of meeting whilst she inched further back to make
space. "All of you must be so confused right now, but
don't worry. I'm here to tell you everything." She gave
a warm smile. Everybody, including Jocelyn, Lilac,
Valentino, Kari, and Raine sat cross-legged on the
bed, eyeing the individual suspiciously, except for
Kari, who immediately threw her arms around her in
a hug.

"Nayeli!" Kari sobbed, hugging the ghost.

Raine and Valentino stared at Nayeli, their mouths
agape, while Jocelyn and Lilac eyed each other,
unaware of what was going on. Once Kari released
Nayeli, Raine took the opportunity to scrutinise her.
Nayeli's eyes were a dark brown, unlike Valentino's,
which were a dark grey, but they shared the same
nose and mouth, and their jawlines were both angled
sharply. "You're his older sister?" Raine asked,
without thinking.

There was silence across the room. Everyone had
different expressions - Kari and Nayeli wore surprised
looks while Valentino had a curious glint in his eyes,
which were now clearer to see without his glasses on.

Jocelyn and Lilac gasped in shock. "You have a sister, Val?" Jocelyn's jaw dropped open, incredulous by the sudden revelation. "I never knew!"

"Neither did I," Valentino replied, almost humorously.

Nayeli suddenly scooted closer to him and started touching his cheeks, shoulders, and neck. "Wow, you've really grown up! I remember when you were still in primary school, you were so small and cute! Now you're what, eighteen?" She continued examining Valentino, who was getting more and more uncomfortable by the second. Unlike Nayeli, who had seemed to know Valentino for a long time and was very familiar with him in a sibling manner, Valentino saw Nayeli as nothing but a stranger who had the title of his older sister. One that he had no memory of.

"Nineteen," he corrected, pulling away from Nayeli.

"Did you find a home? Are you safe? You're not living on the streets anymore, right? Is our family okay?" Nayeli continued bombarding Valentino with questions.

"Our family is okay. So am I. I live in the Subliminal realm now, where I study engineering," Valentino stated, still feeling dubious of Nayeli.

"But Val, you're glowing! What happened?" Nayeli's proud smile dropped to a sad one, before it turned into shock, and she let out a gasp. "Did you die? Was that why Kari brought you all here?"

"Whatever, Raine can heal me," Valentino replied, nonchalantly, exchanging faces with Raine, who gulped. "Explain all of this," he said to Nayeli.

Nayeli cleared her throat and sat up straight. "This is known as Reverie's Space. Kari can enter this space whenever she dreams, and I would be here to hang out and comfort her. Whatever happened earlier, which I assume was a horrible event, allowed Kari's ability to mix in Reverie's Space with the space of her bedroom. So you could say we're being held by Kari's ability. Though it's not necessarily a bad thing. Think of it as a haven - nothing bad ever happens here. It's a daydream mixed with real life."

Kari was always so tired and sluggish that Raine hadn't expected her to be able to possess such a powerful ability. Nayeli continued to explain. "Right now, anyone outside of Kari's ability can enter this room, but not enter Reverie's space." Raine imagined a neighbour entering Kari's room to find two black-dreamers and a lot of blood and shattered glass, but none of her friends' bodies. "If you wanna leave, just open the door right there." Nayeli pointed at the bedroom door that would lead to the living room, or in this case, outside of Reverie's Space.

Valentino waited for anybody else to acknowledge Nayeli's explanation, and once he figured that nobody was going to ask any questions, he asked his own. "Nayeli, why don't you exist? Why does nobody but Kari remember you? What happened to you?" He paused, as if trying to keep himself from asking too many questions at once.

Nayeli's face fell a little. "Oh, um. I died," she said, vaguely.

"I know that, but it doesn't explain why nobody remembers you. How did you die, exactly?" Valentino questioned further.

Nayeli paused, and her eyes darted over to the ceiling for a split second while she recalled. "I drowned, I think."

Just as Raine believed that she was free from the painful callings, she could feel the ringing pierce her ears again. *So much for a haven*, she thought, trying to hide the pain from everyone else, who was all paying attention to Nayeli now.

"Where?" Valentino asked, his tone eager for the answer.

"A football field, if I remember correctly. There was a typhoon. You were there too, you know?" Nayeli tilted her head slightly and smiled regretfully. "How unlucky. I was the only Lin who died during the disaster. I hope our family is doing fine without me."

"Raine," Valentino called urgently. The ringing got even worse, but Raine tried to focus on him. His eyes were widened, and he was waiting for Raine to say something.

Ignoring the pain in her ears, Raine matched Nayeli's words to the memory-dream she experienced with Valentino and connected all the pieces together. "Oh

my dreams," she whispered. "We have to find
Zephyr!"

A flick of horror appeared on Nayeli's face, at least,
that was what Raine caught from her peripheral
vision, but then Nayeli was smiling again, and Raine
doubted that what she saw was even real. Probably a
side effect from the ringing and the fact that her
vision was starting to blur a little. "Zephyr? Aune?
The one with the cyan eyes?"

"You know him?" Raine and Valentino asked,
simultaneously.

Nayeli paused. "He was someone really special to
me," she replied, nodding affirmatively. "Anyway, I
think you should leave now. You all are in a hurry,
right?"

Jocelyn, who was closest to the door, stretched her
arm out to grab the doorknob. She pulled. "Huh? The
door's not working. Is it locked?" She pulled again,
with more force this time. When it refused to budge,
Jocelyn decided to stop being lazy and shifted her
entire body closer to the door to exert more strength
onto the knob. She gave a little huff as she pulled as
hard as she could, and for a moment Raine thought
the doorknob was going to break. Instead, Jocelyn
released her grip on the doorknob, her palm red.
"Nope, the door's, like, totally broken."

"We are trapped!" cried Lilac.

Nayeli's face filled with disappointment. "That
means Kari doesn't want to leave," she said, letting
everyone turn to Kari.

"Kari-" Valentino said, in a half-stern, half-resigned tone, but then Kari suddenly hugged him, letting him flinch.

"I don't want you to die. What's the point in returning to reality if there's nothing left for me there? There's no reason for me to live anymore," instead of loudly sobbing, Kari lowered her head and mumbled. "Why can't we all just stay here? I want to be with you and Nayeli in this space forever. Nothing bad will happen to us, and we can be happy."

Everybody else held their breath, their gazes kept on Kari and Valentino. "That's unhealthy escapism, Kari, you need to be strong and face reality head on," Valentino said, lowering his volume to match that of Kari's. "Every dreamer out there also has to face it. Even if it's bad. You can't wallow in despair." His words were sharp, yet his tone was gentle - it was his way of comforting others.

"I feel hopeless," Kari said, her words weighing heavily down on her.

"Find hope. I'll be here with you, I promise." Valentino pulled Kari away from him. "Everything will be okay. I won't leave you."

Raine nodded. *Everything will be okay*, Valentino said, and Raine wanted to believe it. In the time Raine had spent with Kari at the aquarium, Raine had developed a desire to help her change for the better and find meaning in life. Seeing Kari regain her liveliness would give her the hope and relief she needed, knowing that she helped a dreamer. If Kari could break free of the darkness because of Raine's help, then it would give her enough strength and motivation to help Oneirolepsy break free of the nightmares.

"I want you to be by my side." Kari gently squeezed Valentino's hand with hers.

"I will be," he said softly.

Jocelyn hesitantly reached for the doorknob again. This time, the door opened without a sound. "Hey, the door's open!" She turned to face the others, excitedly. But when she looked at Valentino's ghost-like form, she suddenly jumped onto him and forced him into another hug. She started sobbing and wailed, "I wanted to treat you to a hotpot! We still have to visit the library and watch football matches at three in the morning!" Her tears fell onto the bed, driving a spear of pain into Raine's chest as she watched Jocelyn saying goodbye to her friend. "I already lost so much, I don't want you to leave as well!"

Valentino struggled to break free of Jocelyn's hug, though after a certain point where he saw how distraught Jocelyn was, accepted it. "I won't die, Jocelyn, I promise. We can spend time together after everything is over."

"Don't break your promise." Jocelyn wiped her tears and finally pulled away from him. Lilac patted her on the shoulder for reassurance.

"Well, I suppose we have to leave now," Valentino said, getting up and heading towards the door. "Don't worry about me anymore. Just move on and save the world. I trust you can accomplish that."

Everyone had worried looks on their faces, and Raine spoke. "I'll heal you as much as I can," she promised, hoping her healing abilities would pull through.

He nodded, and Kari went up to him, grabbing him by the hand. "I want to face reality head on with you. Together," she said, looking up at him.

Valentino returned her gaze and smiled. "Together."

The two exited through the door side-by-side, and as Kari's presence disappeared from the dream-like world, her ability ceased, and Nayeli faded away along with the bright colours and warm atmosphere. Just like that, Jocelyn, Lilac, and Raine were returned to the harsh reality. The reality that Raine needed to save.

✳★✦★✳
Chapter 16: Reignition

The return back to the same dull, chilly room of
Kari's outside of Reverie's Space was less than
appealing, especially with Valentino severely
wounded and the others injured. Raine hardly missed
the throbbing pain in her head caused by Ralisrok.

A surge of dream energy still lingered ever since
Kari's ability unlocked an entire tsunami of pure
dream, and whilst everyone was still in Reverie's
Space, the dream energy had wiped out any remaining
nightmare energy around, including the two
black-dreamers, Ralisrok and Slevlyeot.

Raine went over to Valentino, and while Kari went to
assist Jocelyn and Lilac, Raine prayed that she had
enough dream energy to heal Valentino enough so he
wouldn't die. Time had seemed to freeze while
everyone was in Reverie's Space, and the after effects
of Kari's ability gave Raine some additional support of
dream energy.

She closed her eyes for concentration, and lingered
her palm over Valentino's injury, leaving a bit of space
between her hand and the unsightly gash on his neck.
She felt dream energy manifesting from within her
and pressed her eyelids shut as her body tensed. She
pulled in all the dream energy she could from her
surroundings for extra power, and after pulling and
pulling, she used all her strength and mind to push it
all out from her hand. She felt a glowing sensation

emitting from her palms and out onto Valentino. She didn't trust that she would like what she would see if she opened her eyes, so she kept them closed, and waited until she was too drained to heal anymore.

Raine heard movement and slowly opened her eyes. The bleeding had stopped, and the wound had healed. Not completely, but enough for Valentino to live. Raine heaved a sigh of relief and let her shoulders slump.

The others quickly gathered over to them. "I'll get Val to a hospital," Kari said, assertively. Her voice was louder now, and there was more energy in it unlike her usual mumbling. Her once blank eyes were now filled with determination. "I can do this on my own. Please go find the Subliminal Dreamkeeper."

The mention of a hospital reminded Raine of somebody else. "We need to find Soraya and So-hyun," she said, before another person popped up in her head. "And Kegan," she added, her head lowering.

"They must still be in the Ambition realm, those poor lasses," Lilac sighed. Raine remembered that she still hadn't explained to everyone what had become of Kegan and felt mixed emotions about telling Jocelyn about him hurting Soraya.

Jocelyn perked her head up. "I'll-"

"No, I'll call the ride this time," Raine cut in, interrupting her offer to give everyone more free transport.

Miraculously, none of Kari's neighbours had heard or felt any disruption, and after confirming that Ralisrok and Slevlyeot were the only black-dreamers that had slipped in because of Koshalv and not because of the Subliminal realm's borders being infiltrated, everybody left the house. Raine, Jocelyn, and Lilac waved goodbye to Kari, who was holding onto Valentino as the two departed from the group.

Raine caught Jocelyn closing her eyes and mumbling a small prayer for Valentino in a foreign language. When Jocelyn opened her eyes again, she faced Raine and said, "There we go. Now Val will definitely live."

The private transport arrived, and Raine, Lilac, and Jocelyn all clamoured into the blue cab. Raine allowed Lilac the privilege of taking the front seat, where she began playing with Sir Bamesetton and talking to herself about the front view, while she and Jocelyn sat at the back. "Raine, back then, when So-hyun went to go help your friend, I couldn't see anything. But Lilac told me that she was hurt very badly when she was in the Nightmare realm with Kegan," Jocelyn said.

Raine hesitated. "Yeah?"

"If your friend already came back from the Nightmare realm, where's Kegan?"

"Um...I don't know." Raine's eyebrows furrowed at her upcoming answer. She knew she would have to confront Kegan again eventually, but she still felt betrayed and upset. "He was the one who hurt my friend, Soraya. I left him behind when we went to the Subliminal realm."

Shock crossed Jocelyn's face. "Huh? That doesn't
sound like him at all!" She gave a disapproving shake
of her head. "Are you sure you didn't misunderstand
anything? I don't think Kegan is a bad person, and
Soraya is your friend, right? Maybe something
happened in the Nightmare realm."

Raine shifted uncomfortably in her seat, fidgeting
with her seat belt. "I don't know. I've been friends
with Soraya for several years, and Kegan is a
black-dreamer. I trust Soraya with my life. We'll find
Kegan eventually, if that's what you're worried about,
but it'll be dangerous, and I don't trust him."

Jocelyn pouted. "But we're friends! I thought you
and Kegan were always together!"

"Apparently not," Raine answered, and left it at that.
She didn't want to push the topic any further, and
Jocelyn nodded understandingly.

The conversation took a turn for lighter topics
between Raine and Jocelyn, and after a couple of
hours, the cab reached the Ambition realm once
again. Raine felt grateful that she didn't need to go
through another lengthy process just to get into the
realm like she had when entering the Subliminal
realm, and her conversation with Jocelyn ended just
as they reached the hospital So-hyun and Soraya were
in.

The hospital loomed before Raine, a towering
monolith of concrete and glass. Its facade, a mosaic of
muted grays and whites, reflected the overcast sky,
mirroring the somber mood that seemed to envelop

the building. An array of large windows punctuated the exterior, allowing glimpses of the bustling activity within, where life and death danced an unending waltz. Though, Raine felt that it was more of death stepping on life's foot constantly, watching the steady stream of people ebbing towards the entrance.

"Hang on," Raine said, allowing the scent of antiseptic in the air to fill her lungs once she left the cab along with everyone else. "I don't think I should enter the hospital."

"Why not?" Lilac inquired.

The last time Raine went to a hospital with Rhea five years ago, the two ended up stuck there for eight consecutive hours healing sick patients and practically being hired to do the doctors' jobs without any pay. Raine shuddered at the memory of being dragged to numerous rooms and having to use her ability on many wounded dreamers, and some of their injuries weren't very pleasant to see. When she and Rhea had gone home, Raine collapsed onto her bed and slept for an entire day, too tired to have even dreamt.

"I just don't want to cause any disruptions," she said, slowly backing away from the hospital.

"Very well, then. Allow Sir Bamesetton and I to take up the honour of reuniting with our fellow Dreamkeeper." Lilac casually strolled into the hospital unsupervised, humming a little tune whilst she swayed her arms back and forth, throwing the stuffed bear about.

"I'll go make sure nothing bad happens." As if she had the reputation of being a mature and responsible dreamer, Jocelyn quickly chased after Lilac.

Ten minutes flew by. Raine spent that time wandering in the small garden outside the hospital, observing the vibrant flowers and fishes in the pond. Eventually, she sat down on a bench and took out the map from her bag just to examine it to occupy herself while she waited for the two to appear out of the hospital with So-hyun.

The Pure Dreamkeeper's pinpoint glowed purple, forming the insignia of the Dream realm with pride. It was placed accurately at where Raine was - the hospital, and she expected the Ambition Dreamkeeper's pinpoint to glow right by the Pure Dreamkeeper's, but instead, it was placed somewhere far east from the hospital.

Well, that's odd, Raine thought. *Wait, then So-hyun's not at the hospital? What about Soraya?* She tried to rationalise her thoughts. So-hyun had probably gone to buy some food for Soraya. But So-hyun didn't need to go that far just for some food. As a matter of fact, there were plenty of restaurants around, and even the hospital itself had some food stalls and vending machines.

Just then, she heard footsteps. Lilac and Jocelyn were back, except they had no So-hyun, and no Soraya. The only thing they brought back was worry on their faces, and a bag of chips Jocelyn had bought from one of the vending machines in the hospital. "A dark spell has been cast upon the two! They have vanished and are nowhere to be found!" Lilac hugged Sir Bamesetton. "The hospital claims that they never saw the two exiting the hospital, and yet, they have completely disappeared from the surface of the world! Could this be the work of evil?" She turned her head left and right, searching for any traces of any black-dreamers.

A feeling of trepidation struck Raine, but she wasn't surprised by the news. "I just took a look at the map earlier. So-hyun's pinpoint is somewhere far away, but still in the Ambition realm. She's in the eastern part of the realm, maybe with Soraya? At least she's not completely gone off the radar," Raine informed.

Just then, Raine felt someone place a hand on her arm. She jumped in surprise and found an Ambition dreamer covered in minor cuts and bruises. His dark hair swept over his eyebrows, just barely meeting the tip of his eyelashes. He had eyebags and was wide-eyed, and pulled Raine's arm so that he could steal her attention away from Jocelyn and Lilac. "Revieras! You need to help us!" It was as if he was demanding for help, instead of requesting it. Raine couldn't deny helping a fellow dreamer despite needing to deal with the strange disappearance of Soraya and So-hyun.

"What's wrong?" Raine asked, feeling influenced by the Ambition dreamer's worry.

"There's an elemental war going on in Yulion! All of the residents in the city have already evacuated, but my younger sister is still there, and it's too risky for me to go in to help her," The Ambition dreamer was practically trembling from the whole event. "Please, we need you to restore peace in Yulion! And find my sister, if you see her."

Raine nodded. "Hey Jocelyn, Lilac, take this." She handed the map over to them, and Jocelyn took it. She felt immediate regret, as it was an incredible risk to part ways with it, but considering that the map was of no use to her at the current moment, and Jocelyn and Lilac needed the map to show So-hyun's location, Raine felt it was necessary. "The two of you go find So-hyun and Soraya. I'll see what's happening in Yulion."

"Got it! You can trust us!" Jocelyn gave a confident thumbs up, and after glancing at the map with Lilac, the two departed as soon as possible, without even a chance to say goodbye.

Raine nodded reassuringly to the Ambition dreamer. "I'll find your sister. And also resolve the fighting."

The Ambition dreamer bowed deeply in gratitude. "Please be safe."

✳ ✳ ✳

The trip to Yulion was a brief one, and with each second, Raine's imagination only got worse. Elementals in general had notoriety for being extremely dangerous and powerful, especially when provoked. Many incidents and disasters had happened in the past involving elementals, and Raine already had too much on her plate to have an additional elemental crisis on top of everything. Dread followed in each step Raine took as she approached Yulion with the scent of death hovering in the air. While Jocelyn and Lilac went to find So-hyun and Soraya in the east, Yulion was located in the west, and Raine felt more alone than ever.

Raine had a sneaky suspicion that any elemental whom she'd met wouldn't be very friendly, and in case she met any black-dreamers, there would be nobody else but her to fend for herself. She fell short of breath after consecutive minutes of running, and after stopping for a second to rest, she noticed something strange beneath her feet.

Sand.

Gravelly, soft sand that spread across the ground. As Raine stepped forward, the sand only got deeper, and she remembered that the nearest beach that consisted of sand was twelve bus stops away, so it was *very* strange to have sand around in Yulion. That being said, Raine could only guess that the sand wasn't natural.

She walked a little further and scoured the streets of Yulion - sand everywhere. Though broken windows and overturned cars were the new norm, an entire collapsed building blocking the road with melted base didn't seem so usual. The building was covered with so many smashed materials and scraps that Raine failed to picture its original state. As she traced the contours of the building, she noticed a young girl ensnared underneath the rubble. Her leg had been caught and trapped under a pile of heavy debris, preventing her from moving at all. Her body hid well amidst the wreckage, and Raine almost missed her, if not for the fact that she scanned the building twice for any threats around.

Sorrow struck Raine as she saw the helpless dreamer. How long had she been trapped there? Possibly long enough for any hope for help to have waned long ago. It bothered her to know that she could have possibly left the girl to die in a slow and awful manner without even realising it. But now she could help. And she did.

Raine ordered her legs to tread through the heavy sand as if it were deep water. The sand beneath her was extremely soft and unstable, and she felt like she could sink in at any given second. Luckily, that didn't happen, and she safely made it towards the girl.

"Help me," the girl softly whined, with hardly any energy or life left in her.

"Hey, you'll be fine. I'm here now," Raine replied, taking a minute to analyse the situation. The girl's left leg was trapped between a large concrete block and an iron girder, and to make it worse, more sand had fallen in between the small cracks to make it impossible to pull the leg out. An open wound poured a fair amount of blood out, staining the sand a light pink.

Raine used her ability to heal the girl's wound but couldn't help with freeing the leg. The girl grew more unresponsive, and Raine found herself calling for help on her phone. Raine sat by the girl and waited until an ambulance arrived.

The responders exited the vehicle with a stretcher and tended to the girl, and one of them cleared a safe path for Raine to move further into Yulion. "We'll take care of her," the responders guaranteed. After exchanging more information about the girl's brother at the hospital waiting for her, Raine turned her back and sank deeper into the sand-bound city.

It didn't take long to realise that the air around her had become polluted and dusty. The smell reminded Raine when she was in the burning rainforest where she met Kegan for the first time, and her body forced her into a coughing fit. Raine covered her mouth and nose. She remembered using her handkerchief, and immediately clawed into her bag to search for it, only to realise she had dropped it back then, too. Filled with disappointment, she continued on, blinking more than usual to expel sand particles from her eyes. Some had gotten into her mouth, and she could hear a small crunch whenever her jaw moved in the slightest. The sand leaking into her boots pulled against her movement, slowing her down significantly. Despite that, Raine did not concede.

The silhouette of a person appeared in the distance, allowing Raine to feel a mix of relief and fear. *That must be the elemental.* The silhouette hopped about,

pacing everywhere, clearly unaffected by any sand resistance. The unclean air made it hard to see, and Raine moved closer to the silhouette. The soft sand had hardened, making it relatively easier to walk.
 As Raine took a step forward, she noticed that there was not just one silhouette, but two - the other silhouette being someone she knew all too well. "Kegan?"

※★✦★※
Chapter 17: Elements

The two individuals turned at hearing Raine's confused voice, clearly unexpecting a third person to interfere with their battle. Kegan had an unreadable expression, while the other person (presumably an Ambition dreamer) whom Raine didn't recognise scanned her for any injuries, weapons, and malice with a half-frown worn on his face, his eyebrows slightly furrowed and eyes sharp as a blade. His fair skin dusted with ash and his scarf billowed in the wind like a silken stream of purple, the bright fabric contrasting his beige hair.

While the Ambition dreamer was distracted by Raine, a fireball shot out from Kegan's hands. The former, despite being caught off-guard, managed to swerve around it, allowing Raine to get hit by the attack instead. The fire scorched her face and she let out a pained yell.

"Ohoho, straight to the face!" Kegan called out, watching Raine wipe her face several times with her hand. His words were laced with mockery, and sand showered down his jacket from his shoulders. With a clap of his hands, Kegan launched a fire-missile targeting Raine and the Ambition dreamer.

A large solid wall made of sand shot up in between the missile and the two, allowing the missile to strike the wall instead of its intended target. There was a loud crash on the other side before the sand-wall

softened and crumbled down into a pile of sand
beneath the Ambition dreamer's feet, some of the
sand resting on his brown khakis.

Raine could feel an unnatural amount of dream
energy emitting from the Ambition dreamer, and it
was easy for her to conclude that the dreamer Kegan
was fighting against was none other than a sand
elemental.

"Leave. You have no place in this fight," the sand
elemental said curtly. The pile of sand that
constructed the wall earlier was recycled into a flight
of stairs, its tiles forming just a second before he took
his step. Towering over Kegan, who was trying to
shoot him off the flight of stairs with his flames, the
sand elemental used the stairs to gain momentum and
finally jumped down on Kegan with a solid punch in
the face. This caused Kegan to step back a bit, but now
that the sand elemental was close in proximity, it gave
him the opportunity to swallow the dreamer in his
ring of fire.

Raine was still standing afar, and the sight of Kegan
and the sand elemental was replaced with tall, angry,
flames. "Hey, stop fighting! We can talk this out!"
Raine shouted, hoping her voice was loud enough for
everyone to hear. She wasn't sure how any of this
happened, who the sand elemental was, and why he
and Kegan were fighting. The only thing she knew was
that Kegan was not happy with Raine, or anyone for
that matter.

A mountain of sand shot up from behind Raine and flew over to engulf the ring of flames, burying both Kegan and the sand elemental. While Kegan struggled to break free from the sand, the sand elemental dug his way out like it was nothing, and retreated back to Raine after realising it wasn't a very good idea to stand too close to Kegan when attacking. "I don't know why you think you can talk your way out of this. Especially when we're dealing with a nightmare elemental." He possessed the telekinetic ability to move sand however he pleased, and whenever he saw Kegan managing to escape the mountain of sand, he would hurl more buckets of sand to create a new layer to prevent Kegan from getting out. "Seung Jeo-sa. I'm from the Subliminal's Elemental Academy. I assume you know the nightmare?"

This took Raine by surprise. She had hardly heard anything of the Subliminal's Elemental Academy, and only knew of it as a private school on a faraway deserted island where students, who were elementals and dreamers with powerful abilities, resided. Knowing that Jeo-sa was one of these students, Raine felt rather alarmed.

She debated whether to call Kegan a friend of hers. "Yeah, I was supposed to keep an eye on him, but he got upset at me and ran away. I'm sorry for the trouble he's caused," Raine sighed. "What are you doing here in the Ambition realm? What happened to those at the academy?"

"Most of us are returning to our homeland to fight the nightmares. But there's also been a problem. A lot of elementals are being kidnapped by those under Koshalv's command."

A ripple of fire burst out, eliminating the mountain of sand. Kegan was free again. "Alright, enough exposition. I'm getting sick of your sandcastles." He cracked his knuckles and took his stance. "I'm not gonna go easy on you, Revieras. Soraya's my enemy, and if you side with her, that makes you my enemy as well."

Raine couldn't comprehend what Kegan was saying. "What do you mean, Soraya's your enemy? You attacked-" But the sensation of gushing heat pouring onto her cut her off, filling her vision with bright orange. Was this what it felt like to be standing inside a furnace? Raine quickly manifested a shield made of dream magic wrapping her entire body and shot out blasts of dream energy at Kegan. The multiple shots of Raine's attacks stopped Kegan's attack and Raine started to pace around the sandy battlefield like Jeo-sa to dodge potential oncoming attacks.

"Alright, fine. We'll fight this out." Raine took a deep breath and prepared for a battle against Kegan, the fire elemental and black-dreamer whom Raine had spent most of her time with up till now.

Jeo-sa glared at Raine, who was bouncing about and taking multiple deep breaths to psych herself up. She and Jeo-sa now shared an unspoken rule that the two were now teammates and fighting against Kegan, despite Raine knowing nothing about Jeo-sa, except that he wasn't very friendly. "What?" Raine asked, unnerved by his glare.

"Nothing. Your attacks are boring, is all. I mean, they're just spheres made out of dream energy. Not very versatile."

"They're effective in dealing damage and are direct hits," Raine replied, offended. But then she realised that her counter-argument was only half-true. Kegan may be a black-dreamer, but as he stated before, he had 'neutral' energy. That meant that Raine's attacks would be less effective than if she were to deal with actual nightmare energy.

Raine groaned. The last time she stood against Kegan, she had won by becoming that of a businesswoman promising something greater than fire. Of course, that tactic wouldn't work now.

Kegan was the first to charge. He speedily propelled himself forward with his flames, preventing Raine from interfering as he started delivering punches to Jeo-sa. Raine watched in horror while Jeo-sa got simultaneously burned by the surrounding flames and having his face receiving punches by Kegan's fists. Kegan pushed Jeo-sa back, taking step by step as he switched fists left and right, for as long as possible, until Raine picked up the courage to interfere by launching an energy blast when Kegan was switching fists again. The blast caused a small explosive force, interfering with Kegan's attack, and he paused briefly to recover himself.

That small pause was enough for Jeo-sa to free himself from Kegan's trap. His hands commanded the sand beneath him to fly up and douse the surrounding flames. Now angered, Jeo-sa also used the opportunity to blind Kegan by hurling sand at him, prickling his face like hail. Gaining the upper hand, Jeo-sa now stepped forward and started beating Kegan up in return, and Raine had to suppress the instinct to tell Jeo-sa to stop hurting her friend. After a few hits to the stomach and face, Jeo-sa collected a mass of sand to finally propel Kegan back with a strong force of massive sand directed at him.

There was no time for Raine to use her words to get Kegan or Jeo-sa to back down. It was too late to resolve things peacefully. She watched Jeo-sa wince in pain, his face bruised from the former attack. Raine stood in front of Jeo-sa, getting ready to face Kegan head-on. Her nerves were starting to get the better of her, but she launched her energy spheres at Kegan, before realising that Jeo-sa was right about her lack of utility in her attacks.

Raine retreated from taking on the role of offensive and turned back to heal Jeo-sa's wounds. Her energy was now significantly drained, but a worthy trade-off since Jeo-sa was now able to fight again.

Within the blink of an eye, the sight of Jeo-sa was blocked by a giant pillar of flames standing upright and shooting to the sky, the heat caused Raine to jump back, only to realise that about thirty of these columns had been placed across the battlefield to limit movement. Raine could no longer see Kegan or Jeo-sa and channelled her energy to create a protective layer around her body to prevent herself from melting.

There was a loud shake beneath all the sand, and Raine could see a shockwave of fire, the orange ring expanding with its rising flames. Raine knew she wouldn't be able to jump over it in time and resorted to calling out to her teammate. "Jeo-sa!" She called, alerting him of the shockwave. Jeo-sa recreated his sand staircase which rose beneath Raine's boots and his own, connecting the two separate staircases together from above, avoiding the fire columns and dodging the shockwave.

Multiple of these fiery shockwaves are dished out from beneath the two, causing the staircase to be 'chopped' off several times. Raine could feel herself sinking down as each shockwave passed, but Jeo-sa took the chance to make it rain sand, eliminating the fire columns and thickening the layer of sand below, which at that point had crystallised.

Kegan started shooting at the buildings around him. It took a few seconds for Raine to realise that he was trying to start more fires to gain an environmental advantage. The surrounding buildings caught on fire and collapsed with a loud thud, and now the desert-like battlefield had turned into one of a volcano-scape. Raine shot out her dream blasts at Kegan while he was preoccupied with the buildings, and he ended up getting hit.

Raine felt a stab of guilt watching Kegan groan in pain, but she also felt the staircase melting off. Soon, there was nothing beneath her feet, and she fell into the pit of sand below. Raine created another magic shield for Jeo-sa, and he lifted himself off the battlefield again to charge at Kegan. All too soon, the entire place was ignited, and there was fire everywhere. Raine felt like an ice cream out in the sun, and her vision was beginning to blur.

The fire, being controlled by Kegan, grew bigger and bigger, as he threw more of his flaming attacks against his opponents. Raine couldn't see anything, and she was attacked from all directions at once. Her whole body ached with pain and burns, and she had to suppress a scream.

Jeo-sa covered the whole of the streets with sand, inadvertently dumping a bunch of sand on top of everyone's head. Though this annoyed Raine, the fires were extinguished, and Kegan lost his upper hand.

Raine attacked again. The depth of the sand made it difficult for her to move, and Kegan found himself facing the same issue. Jeo-sa, who seemed to be immune to sand resistance, freely rushed against Kegan and threw more sand-bombs at him. The speedy projectile caused more damage than the sand itself.

Kegan tried to ignite the surroundings on fire again. This time, the sandy ground turned into unbalanced solid crystals. In some way or another, he managed to cause his flames to arise again.

Jeo-sa, taking note of Kegan trying to manipulate the surroundings to his advantage, decided to do the same as well. The sky above darkened as thick sand particles clouded the sun, polluting in the air and restricting breath. Raine's eyes grew irritated and watery beyond control, and suddenly, the fiery sensation was replaced with gravel-like bits swirling around in the air.

Kegan was evidently taken aback by the increase in sand, which was now rising to his knee level. Raine found it harder to see and started coughing, lacking oxygen and she began to feel lightheaded. "Jeo-sa, stop! I can't-" *breathe*, Raine tried, but failed.

Jeo-sa didn't listen. Kegan wasn't affected by the dust as much as Raine was, presumably from being exposed to all the smoke in the past. But he noticed Raine struggling to keep her head up, and threw a glance at Jeo-sa, who was busy creating mounds to use against Kegan. "Yo, you planning on suffocating your friend?"

Jeo-sa ignored Kegan's remark. Raine tried to say something to him, to tell him to stop, but she could no longer speak. She only coughed and coughed, trying to inhale oxygen, but the oxygen has been dirtied by sand and ash, so she coughed even more, her throat restricted and filled with everything except fresh air.

What was becoming a sandstorm grew more vigorous, and Raine dropped to the floor. Jeo-sa was unaffected by the sandy disaster, and even Kegan was starting to find it hard to conquer the sandstorm. He barely managed to shoot out flames to clear the sand away, only for more sand to replace and smother his flames.

In Raine's blurred vision, she saw a glowing orb that Kegan pulled out, presumably a relic, and despite his weakened state, he wore a smirk on his face while the orb emitted energy. It was his trump card, or as Raine would describe it - a trick up his sleeve. For in one moment, Jeo-sa was standing boldly in the middle of the sandstorm, and in the next, he was blasted by what Raine could only process as the largest flamethrower in the world, and despite all the sand in the world, it wouldn't stopped the massive jet of fire aiming right at Jeo-sa. And then, she passed out.

※★ ✦ ★※
Chapter 18: Deception

The first thing Raine saw once she woke up again was Kegan. Slowly, she got up and wiped off sand from her shoulders, only to find out that the entire back of her body was practically showered with it. As she tried to contort her arm to rid her clothes of any lingering particles, she noticed that the whole battlefield had been fully crystalised. Still delirious, she shook herself awake. It was now much easier to breathe, and the sandstorm had completely dissipated. "Jeo-sa!" She searched for him.

"Here," his voice called from behind. There was no sign of injury and he looked fine, albeit irritated as usual. "The attack missed."

"What? How?"

"Manipulating, merging, creating a barrier, and counter attacking using sand... It's really not that hard," Jeo-sa shrugged, directing his glare at Kegan. "Challenging someone from the Subliminal Elemental's Academy was a mistake."

"Your entire existence is a mistake, sand-boy." Offended, Kegan prepared to hurl more fire attacks at Jeo-sa when Raine stepped in between the two.

"Alright, alright! Stop fighting, please. That's enough sand and fire for one day, thank you very much." Raine held her arms out to distance the two elementals apart, and she sighed.

Jeo-sa scoffed and crossed his arms. "Whatever. If Revieras herself allows this crazy pyromaniac to run around free, then I won't bother wasting my time and effort to stop him. Just leave the Ambition realm alone."

"I am not a pyromaniac!" Kegan shouted, for the millionth time, but a small whirlwind of shifting grains swirled around Jeo-sa in harmony, and he swifty vanished, bringing all the sand with him. The battlefield was quickly deprived of pure sand.

Although Jeo-sa had already left, bits of glass and crystals still remained - the aftereffects of a clash between fire and sand. There was a long silence as the two stared at each other, waiting to see who would apologise or at least say something first.

Finally, Raine took a deep breath and asked, "Are you still mad at me?"

Kegan took a second to answer. "Well, yeah, sorta." He hesitated before adding, "But I don't want to kill you for it."

She felt both surprise and relief from his answer. "Really?"

"Yeah. Don't feel like it. Plus, it feels like cheating with this thing." He held out the orb for Raine to see. It glowed bright with passion and strength, though the energy it emitted was neither dream nor nightmare - just raw energy.

Raine eyes widened in fascination and leaned closer to admire the orb, then glanced up at Kegan. "I thought you said you didn't have a relic?"

Kegan shrugged. "It's a long story, but I got it back in the Nightmare realm." He hid the orb away from Raine.

There was another pause before Raine spoke again. "Kegan, I want to believe that you would never betray us, so-"

"Oh, you're the one feeling betrayed?" Kegan laughed, cutting Raine off. "Soraya's playing you, and you all fell for it. Now I'm the bad guy, right? Who's the one feeling betrayed here, huh?"

"Look, I know you keep saying that, but I don't understand! She was injured by you, and I held her in my arms, she wasn't faking it!" Torn between believing Soraya and believing Kegan, Raine made aggressive hand gestures in the air, trying not to let the stress overtake her rationality.

Kegan inhaled, as if he was about to go into a long-winded explanation to justify his claim. But instead, he stated: "She's with the Remnants of Keresius."

Raine froze as she heard his words, but then doubt made its way through Raine's mind. "Wait wait wait, what? That can't be right." *Are you lying to me?* She would ask, but she assumed the question would just anger Kegan again, and the last thing she needed right now was a second round of battling against him.

"It's the truth. Now apologise for doubting me," he demanded, despite Raine fumbling about in confusion.

"What? No, I need you to tell me what happened in the Nightmare realm! You can't just accuse Soraya like that. I mean, I can understand if it was somebody else, but I've known Soraya for three whole years!" Raine remembered when she and Soraya would meet up at their favourite café and talk about all sorts of non-serious things. Not only as a friend, but as a manager, Soraya was always reliable, helpful, supportive, and kind. She couldn't believe that Soraya would be affiliated with the black-dreamers.

But right at that moment, both Raine and Kegan heard footsteps approaching.

"Kegan! You-" The voice of Soraya echoed across the vacated street of Yulion. Her footfalls were quick and heavy, and the moment she saw Raine, her face was filled with relief, horror, surprise, and disappointment all at once. "Raine!" She immediately switched her focus from Kegan to Raine, and as Soraya got closer to the two, Raine could feel an increase in temperature and even without looking at Kegan, she could tell that he was not very happy upon seeing Soraya.

Raine grabbed Soraya's hand and pulled her away from Kegan before he was agitated enough to shoot more fire at the two. She was far enough for Kegan to not be able to hear her and Soraya, but close enough to see him still glaring at the two with hatred. Shaking her head, Raine turned to Soraya. "Soraya, why are you here? I thought you were at the hospital. Where's So-hyun?"

"I recovered and went to chase Kegan down because he mentioned burning down the dreamer realms. I didn't see So-hyun at all when I was at the hospital. Weren't you in the Subliminal realm?" Soraya asked, worriedly, scanning Raine's face. "What are you doing with Kegan? He didn't hurt you, did he? Was all of this-" Soraya gestured to the very destroyed Yulion "-his doing?"

There were so many questions that Raine had, and she was thinking so much that she failed to realise Kegan was already next to her and reprimanding Soraya, cursing her out with words that Raine didn't want to repeat. "You're even worse than me, y'know? And that's coming from a nightmare to a dreamer."

"Shut up, nightmare. You're just trying to trick us," Soraya spoke with such venom in her voice that Raine could hardly recognise her. Her tone switched so fast, from a sweet friendly tone to a harsh and malicious one. Of course, Raine had seen Soraya as a whimsical friend and Soraya as a stern manager, but never Soraya as...whatever was happening in front of her.

The atmosphere had grown dark again, and Raine felt as if she was back in the Nightmare realm. Even the reassuring aura of Soraya that Raine had grown fond of and used to couldn't overpower the strong sense of foreboding she was feeling, and the arguing voices of Soraya and Kegan only got louder and sharper.

Raine began to feel faint again. Initially, she thought it was because of the arguing, but then she felt a vertiginous drop in dream energy, and nightmare energy began filling the streets. Many cloaked members of the Remnants of Keresius had surrounded the three.

"You see, Raine? Soraya brought all her minions here!" Kegan shouted, trying to prove his point. He noticed that Raine was feeling unwell, and was just about to say something else, except Soraya suddenly attacked Raine, and the latter was pushed to the ground.

That single attack was all it took for Raine to realise Kegan was right, and in that instant, her entire world was turned upside down.

About ten of the Remnants pounced on Kegan immediately, and he started blasting more flames, but given that he just fought Jeo-sa not too long ago, he was in a rather weakened state.

While Kegan was busy fighting for his life, more and more cloaked individuals surrounded Yulion. Soraya took out a small penknife and knelt down to Raine, who was wounded with betrayal. "Why?" Raine asked. Soraya was her friend. Her manager. Her partner. All the best memories of Raine's life included either Rhea or Soraya, and now that the former was gone, Raine had to find that the latter was alo lying to her the whole time Raine knew her?

All the happy moments and things Soraya and Raine shared were now tainted with the fact that Soraya was a traitor. Raine doubted that any of it was ever real,

and that, infinitely hurt more than any pain the
Remnants of Keresius could inflict.

Soraya held the penknife near Raine, bearing a face
of indifference. "My allegiance to Keresius surpasses
mine to you," she answered, with little remorse in her
voice. "We are to fulfil his last wishes - to eradicate
the dreamers and rebirth this world into one where
nightmares reign supreme." She brought the tip of the
knife to Raine's chin, but then pulled back her arm.
"Zira will take care of you." Soraya stood up and
handed the penknife to another member, who was
wearing roller skates, before leaving. Her hood was
unveiled, revealing a silver-blonde haired nightmare.
She had a round face and a wolf cut, her dreamless
eyes gazing upon Raine. Zira held out a finger and
almost teasingly, gave a gentle poke on Raine's
shoulder. "I hope you like freeze tag," Zira teased, as
Raine felt all her muscles stiffen. Just as Zira implied,
Raine was now practically a statue. Even her voice
chords wouldn't work. With a drop in body
temperature, Raine couldn't even shiver.

Zira brought the pen knife closer to Raine and made
a slit on her arm. Raine's eyes were frozen too, and all
Raine could see were more black-dreamers blocking
the view of the sky. Despite the flowing of her blood,
she still couldn't move, and could only feel the
stinging of the open wound as Zira collected some of
the blood.

That was when Sir Bamesetton came into view. Not
the stuffed bear, but the same monstrous entity that

Raine had seen and fought when Lilac was
unconscious. With a single swing of its paw, Zira was
sent flying. More ruckus ensued at the sight of the
horrific bear, and the earth shook with each step Sir
Bamesetton was taking.

  Raine felt another touch on her shoulder, and in an
instant, she was unfrozen again. She winced at the slit
on her arm. It was still fresh, and Raine was far too
weak to heal herself. The person who untagged her, as
expected, was Lilac. However, instead of her usual
grin, she was frowning. "Oh, how could I have failed
to discern that Soraya was in verity, aligned with the
Remnants of Keresius? The fault lies with me! The
shrouded cloak of anonymity donned by the cult
obscures even those who were once kin to me!"

  "It's alright," Raine said, translating all of that to a
simple apology for failing to realise that Soraya was a
member of the Remnants of Keresius. "What are you
doing here? Where's Jocelyn?"

  "We were led to this spot by the pinpoint marked
upon the map. A certain quandary did arise, causing
Jocelyn and me to part ways momentarily. Fret not -
for said quandary has since been resolved, and
Jocelyn will grace us with her presence soon." Lilac
showed Raine the map to prove that it hadn't been
torn or anything of the sort and helped return it back
into the safe confines of Raine's bag. "Also, I bear a
gift for you."

  A member who slipped out of Sir Bamesetton's wrath
caught Lilac and Raine talking in the middle of a

battle and decided to strike Raine. Raine, who was too slow and weak to dodge or defend herself, was hit in the face, and she was knocked down.

Lilac turned and swung her fist. She was a little weaker in terms of physical strength, but was faster, and got in several extra punches. She ended her combo with a final jab to the jaw. The member was knocked unconscious. "Are you alright?" Lilac assisted Raine, who was struggling to stand up. "Not only have the remnants sought your demise, but they have also striven to procure your blood for a new incantation. I perceive from the wound upon your arm that they have indeed achieved their dark goal."

An eerie sensation crept up on Raine as she realised her blood would be used for their ritual. "I'll be fine, but I don't know why I feel so sick and weak. I was just fine a moment ago." She felt as if she had run four miles, and her legs were that of jelly.

"It has possibly got to do with the abilities possessed by the members." Lilac pointed at Zira, who was speeding about on her skates trying to avoid the bear. "That one likes to play freeze tag." She then pointed to another member who was wearing a purple pendant trying to attack Kegan, only to be instantly rewarded with burns. "That one can transmute dream energy into nightmare energy. Perhaps it's why you and Jocelyn are currently unwell. Or it could be because of that one." Lilac pointed to another member wearing a gold watch, who was charging right at her. Lilac punched said member and kicked him in an extremely vulnerable spot before shoving him aside. "That one has a passive ability to weaken his enemies - which are dreamers. That ability even affects yours truly."

"We'll need to deal with the pendant and the gold watch," Raine replied, already mixing up every member that Lilac just identified.

Lilac promptly left to fight alongside Sir Bamesetton and Kegan, dealing with the Remnants of Keresius. Even though Lilac was a dreamer, she had spent enough time in the Nightmare realm to be able to use nightmare energy herself without any repercussions.

Kegan was attracting most of the Remnants of Keresius, mostly because he had the relic that Soraya was trying to steal back. He blamed the fact that he couldn't obliterate them all within three seconds not on how he was severely weakened by Jeo-sa earlier, but because if he did use a hundred percent of his power, it would affect his own teammates as well.

He summoned a few of the fire pillars right beneath the feet of some unfortunate members, instantly turning them into ash. Soraya, who had spent enough time with Kegan at the Nightmare realm to learn and recognise his fighting style, was dodging his flames left and right, getting closer to him to steal the orb. A year ago, Soraya had impressed Raine by showing off the results of her kickboxing practice. That was before Raine found out Soraya's true identity.

Raine felt the effects of the relics slowly disappear as Sir Bamesetton and Lilac eliminated the respective members. Zira circled around the field, avoiding Sir

Bamesetton and trying to snatch the orb from Kegan every few rounds, and when she circled around Raine, she tagged her once again.

Zira skated her way to Lilac to freeze her as well. Lilac pulled out a card-gun - formerly Ralisrok's - and shot out a card which was aimed at Zira's skates. Upon landing, the card exploded, and Zira was thrown back.

As if on cue, Sir Bamesetton stomped over to Lilac to act as her bodyguard while she went to unfreeze Raine, who was curious as to why, how, or when Lilac obtained the card-gun. "I acquired this whilst in Kari's abode." She handed the card-gun to Raine. "We have to save So-hyun!"

"So-hyun?" Raine looked about. Lilac had mentioned that she came to Yulion because of the map. If Soraya was last seen with So-hyun, then Raine could only assume something bad had happened to her. "Alright, Kegan and I will deal with Soraya, you find So-hyun," Raine said, gripping the card-gun and running to Kegan. "And ask Sir Bamesetton to deal with the roller skating black-dreamer and the other members!"

Although Zira's skates could easily overtake anyone on foot, they were futile against Sir Bamesetton. Zira's ability didn't work on it, and within a few seconds, it caught up to Zira and prepared to crush her. However, in that very second, Lilac ran out of energy to fuel the sentient beast, and the stuffed bear reverted to its cute and harmless state. Zira fled the battlefield and was nowhere to be found.

Meanwhile, Raine and the others were winning against the Remnants of Keresius, and soon only a few of them were left to fight.

Kegan was using the orb to supply fuel for his flames - something an elemental would almost never do, considering how they already had a ludicrous amount of energy. Even though Soraya had no weapons, she was still somehow able to dodge all of Kegan's flames and fought through with her limbs alone.

The battlefield now littered with cloaks that belonged to the fallen members, and the nightmare energy made way for the dream energy. Soraya and Kegan exchanged kicks and punches, the losing party being unclear. Wanting to help, Raine aimed a card and shot at Soraya. The card was similar to Raine's usual energy blasts and exploded upon hitting her. Soraya took a step back and coughed.

"Attack me and your Ambition Dreamkeeper is dead," she threatened, backing away from Kegan and Raine. "I have that little dream-blinded freak with me, and I won't hesitate to kill."

"Where's So-hyun?" Raine asked, trying to hide her shock from Soraya's sharp words.

"Give me the relic," demanded Soraya.

"Do not comply," Lilac warned, gripping onto her teddy bear.

"Those who betray Keresius shouldn't talk."

Kegan glanced at Raine, giving her a 'I don't think I can go on any longer' look. Raine eyed the orb in his hand, feeling conflicted as to whether she should just

surrender the relic. As far as Raine knew, relics were
only used as storage for nightmare energy, and she
didn't want to risk So-hyun's life for it. "Raine,"
Soraya called, once no decision was made. "You've
never seen my ability before, have you?"

Raine gulped.

"Don't stress. It's not a very good one. If it was, I
wouldn't have had to spend three years doing spy
work." Soraya met eyes with Raine, and all of a
sudden, it seemed that everything had faded away
except for the two.

Raine blinked, and Rhea stood before her. She wore
her favourite black cardigan, and Raine could smell
the perfume she would always wear. Her forehead
bore slight wrinkles, curtained by strands of her curly
hair. "My sweet rainflower," Rhea smiled warmly. "I
know you want to save Oneirolepsy. You were always
a brave hero, and I'm forever proud to have you as my
daughter."

Raine's feet glued to the ground. Each word spoken
by Rhea's voice was like a stab to the heart, and Raine
was so stunned that she couldn't even cry, speak, or
move. She could only listen. "Won't you hand your
mother the relic?" Rhea asked politely.

"Raine!"

Raine felt something sweep by from behind her, and
when she turned her head, Lilac, who was next to
Raine, had been tagged by Zira. Zira stylishly
manoeuvred her way to Rhea, before dragging out an

unconscious and frozen So-hyun who had been hidden behind a building nearby onto the ground.

Even though Raine hadn't been tagged by Zira, the sight of Rhea walking towards her still rendered her legs useless. Rhea stood just an inch away from Raine and held her cheek. "Let's go to the Nightmare realm and eliminate the king, then we can spend every day together again, just like before. I just need the orb, but your friend won't let me have it." Rhea gave her reassuring-mom-face and gently took the card-gun from Raine, who didn't resist. "Won't you get it for me?"

Kegan scoffed. "Boo! You're copying off Vanity!"

Rhea moved aside to let Raine walk over to Kegan. Zira was still holding So-hyun captive, and pulled the pen knife against So-hyun's neck.

Raine stopped when she was just standing in front of Kegan. His legs were slightly trembling, and he looked as if he would fall to the ground after being hit once. "Don't be stupid," Kegan said.

Rhea walked over to Zira and had a little discussion whilst they waited for Raine to retrieve the orb. Kegan didn't move and was still holding the relic in his hand. There was much less glowing of the relic now, and it just looked like an orange sphere made from glass.

Raine reached out to take the orb from his hand, but he pulled his arm away. Unimpressed by this move, Raine attempted to snatch it a second time. This repeated several more times, and finally, when Kegan's arm got tired, he simply accepted parting

with his relic with a defeated sigh. He was too
exhausted to fight, and all he did was stare at Raine
disapprovingly. She examined the orb for a few
seconds. There was no energy left in the orb, but
Raine handed it over to Soraya anyway.

Zira, who was knelt to So-hyun, poked at Raine's leg.
"They're all frozen now," she said to Rhea, who had
the orb.

Rhea went over to Kegan, and Raine could hear him
getting beaten by Rhea, and in her frozen state, she
couldn't see anything, since they were out of her view.
But Raine didn't want to look at them anyway.

Just as it seemed like everything had been lost, Raine
heard footfalls.

"So-hyun?" Jocelyn's voice called out, as she saw her
best friend being held by a black-dreamer on roller
skates.

From where Raine was facing, she could see Jocelyn
walking up to them. Her hands trembled as her skin
grew pale.

Soraya's ability faded, and the image of Rhea
disappeared forever. "Move and she's dead," Soraya
said, gesturing to Zira.

Zira brought the blade of the pen-knife to So-hyun
and ever so slightly pressed against her skin, releasing
a slit of blood.

Raine tensed as she heard Jocelyn gasp in horror.
Raine wanted nothing more to stop Soraya, but all she
could do was observe. Observe that something in
Jocelyn had snapped.

"I've had enough of you hurting my friends," Jocelyn said, in a cold, quiet voice. "Come fight me, you coward."

The threat and insult seemed to have worked. Soraya and Zira stepped forward, leaving So-hyun behind. "Tag her, and we can use her back at the lair," Soraya ordered.

Light slowly diminished as the day concluded. A strong wind swept through, rustling the nearby leaves. It caused a small slip of folded paper to fall out of Jocelyn's skirt. Raine remembered it from when they were back at the hotel, and she'd found Jocelyn designing something for Boris.

Zira was a second away from ending So-hyun's life. Jocelyn got into a fighting stance and prepared to charge at them, screaming at the top of her lungs.

That was when a large shadow formed on top of them.

Raine noticed the small piece of paper glowing before it slowly dissipated, and a large statue made out of bronze with a blue-green shade was formed from above the heads of Soraya and Zira.

The shadow got bigger and bigger, and just as Soraya and Zira raised their heads, the statue crushed them.

In that instance, everyone whom Zira had tagged were now unfrozen, her ability expiring as her life had. Raine felt her muscles softening, and she could turn her head again. However, just like all her friends, they remained still anyway, stunned by the sudden appearance of the statue.

Jocelyn retracted her fighting stance and shared an equally dumbfounded expression, unsure what just happened, but when she saw So-hyun stir, Jocelyn immediately gasped and went up to her.

So-hyun laid on the ground, gasping for air. Raine, Kegan, and Lilac followed behind to check up on their friend. "Are you alright?" Jocelyn asked.

"I'm alright. What happened?" With Jocelyn's help, So-hyun stood up from the ground. "I remember being taken by Soraya, and some strange people in cloaks. I couldn't tell if they were nightmares, but they took my baseball bat away."

"I'm so glad you're okay, So-hyun!" Jocelyn broke into sobs and embraced So-hyun into a tight hug, squeezing the air out of her.

"Ow! Jocelyn, I'm still hurt!" So-hyun groaned.

Jocelyn immediately pulled away and looked at Raine, who then used her remaining energy to heal So-hyun.

Once everyone concluded that they were fine, they gathered around the statue to marvel at its strange origin. Raine cautiously pressed her finger against it and confirmed it was a tangible material.

Lilac took the card-gun by the statue which Soraya had taken earlier. Luckily, it had been spared from being crushed, and she handed it to Raine, who was examining the statue with curiosity. "This shall aid you on your voyage to Psytheon. My knowledge of this strange weapon is limited, save for the fact that it shoots."

Raine took Ralisrok's card-gun and claimed it as her own, "Well, I guess a change of attacks could be a good thing," she replied, remembering Jeo-sa's criticism of her sphere blasts. She pulled a card out from the gun and inspected the object, gaining the knowledge of how to manifest more of them using dream energy. She could apply different effects to these cards, and for the record, Raine thought, playing cards fit her aesthetic much better than energy spheres.

Raine kept the card-gun in her bag and looked below the statue where the blood of Zira and Soraya spilled. The betrayal cut deep, and the fact that Soraya had weaponised her love for Rhea against her made Raine feel even worse, but she didn't want to waste any more time processing her own heartbreak. There were more members of the cult than Raine had expected, and they all had invaded the Ambition realm with no issue, some of them with relics and abilities to cause even more harm. She needed to find the Subliminal Dreamkeeper now, as fast as she could. And she needed to get to Psytheon.

But before Raine could do any of that, she had to do one last thing. She turned to Kegan, who was exhausted and lying on the floor, gazing at the sundown. "Are *you* alright?" She asked, reaching out her hand to Kegan, but he pulled away.

"Pfft, do you really think I'd be defeated by Soraya that easily?" Kegan laughed. Raine could tell that he was avoiding the question and that he was not alright, but decided not to say anything.

Raine lowered her head and spoke with genuine remorse: "I'm sorry for doubting you, Kegan."

Kegan paused for a second, then smiled. "Glad to hear you admit your fault."

※★ ◆ ★※
Chapter 19: Alignment

"I can't believe this." So-hyun walked around the statue and placed her palm on it to confirm its authenticity. She turned to Jocelyn. "This is your ability?"

Jocelyn gawked at the statue, then suddenly broke into a fit of excitement and happiness. "Oh, I did it! I found my ability! Oh, Boris would've been so proud!" She started dancing and circling around the statue.

Raine and Lilac applauded at Jocelyn's newfound ability. It was certainly a strange discussion, but once Raine brought up how she noticed the piece of paper from Jocelyn's pocket glowing and disappearing, Jocelyn gasped and confirmed that the statue they were seeing was completely identical to her sketch and how she envisioned it to look.

"The statue is an effigy for a famous architect that Boris was fond of. He was a very important founder of the Subliminal realm. I originally wanted to make a statue for Boris, but he told me that it was too tacky," Jocelyn explained, looking at the flawless carving of the statue's face.

Raine sat next to Kegan on the ground, and the two watched the sun fully set. "I have a surprise for you," Raine said to Kegan, once the sun disappeared. She placed her hands behind her back, and then pulled out his relic. "Ta-da! Magic."

Kegan responded with a pleasant surprise. "Woah, how did you do that?"

"Soraya didn't completely fool me with her ability. I'm a magician, so I know how to make things disappear and reappear," Raine explained, deciding to keep the fact that she switched the orbs with a fake projection when giving it to Soraya a secret. "I'm Revieras for a reason. I think." She winked, jokingly, and handed the orb to Kegan. It was glowing brightly again, illuminating Yulion with its bright light. "We found out that the Subliminal Dreamkeeper, Zephyr, is in the waking world, Psytheon - a parallel world to ours," Raine brought up.

Lilac, Jocelyn, and So-hyun sat down next to Raine and Kegan, and they all formed a group circle. "Oh, oh! Wait, I wanna explain! I learnt this back at the Subliminal realm!" Jocelyn raised her hand up, as if she was in a classroom discussing with her schoolmates. Raine nodded, giving Jocelyn the green light. "In order to get to Psytheon, we have to wait for an astral alignment. I dunno much about it, but I remember the time being around midnight. Also, we need a large open space and an element." Jocelyn pointed finger-guns at Kegan. "And we have to chant something. I forgot what it was."

"It's an Orael phrase," Raine contributed. "Rhea told me about it. We still have about five hours before midnight though. What do we do?"

"There's an open field near here in Yulion," So-hyun said. "If we need an open space, we could go there, I think. Maybe we could set up a temporary campsite there."

"Wait, we aren't going to Psytheon with you?" Jocelyn asked Raine, almost disappointed.

"Psytheon is a very dangerous place for dreamers. There's this phenomenon that's described by an unending urge of an echo that beckons the dreamer to return to Oneirolepsy. They'll get these constant sleep attacks and if they're not careful, they will be stuck forever in the waking world, their comatose body lying uninhibited and asleep until the end of time." Raine eyed Jocelyn and had a sneaky suspicion that she already knew all this. "I don't want to risk any of your lives. I'll go alone."

"And are you certain in your capability to locate a single soul in a realm unfamiliar to yourself?" Lilac inquired. "What if *you* succumb to this phenomenon? You'll be beyond the reach of help."

"Have some trust in me, okay? I'll be extra careful," Raine gave a reassuring smile, then turned to Kegan. "Are you well enough to help us with the portal? We need an element, so-"

"Hell yeah! I've totally got to summon a kickass portal from my fires!" Kegan's eyes lit up with excitement. "Just, uh, a little intermission. I need some time to reignite my flames."

"Do you need me to heal you?" Raine asked, concerned.

Kegan laughed. "You forgot abilities don't work on me. I'll be fine! A little injury won't kill me." He stood up to prove his statement, and Raine made a face, making no effort to mask her doubt.

"Okay then! Let's move out!" Jocelyn hadn't noticed Kegan being injured and shot up like a rocket with the intention of leaving as soon as possible, but she was too eager and got up so fast that she got dizzy, and Lilac had to stand up and support her before she fell again. "Woah! I just saw the stars just now! Anyway, who wants s'mores? Let's get the extra fluffy marshmallows!"

✳ ✳ ✳

A dark purple permeated across the sky, and a million stars littered on the canvas that was the night, with a full moon illuminating the world. The cooling night breeze comforted Raine as she helped carry a large pack of marshmallows and sleeping bags for her friends who were planning to spend an unspecified amount of time in the field. For all Raine knew, she could be spending at least a week or two in Psytheon searching for the lost dreamer, maybe even a year if she was placed in a whole other continent from her Dreamkeeper.

Somehow, the group had managed to acquire the necessary equipment for camping, as well as food and snacks to last for days. They even had sleeping bags, much to Raine's surprise. Going camping with friends sounded fun, and Raine almost wished she could delay going to Psytheon just to spend time with her friends. But saving the world was more important than toasting marshmallows while telling horror stories, so she tried her best not to feel jealous.

So-hyun led the group to the field where Kegan would open the portal for Raine to enter Psytheon while the others waited at the camp. Jocelyn made a deal with Raine that if she hadn't come back in seven days, she would get Kegan to open the portal for her at the next astral alignment. Despite much hesitation, Raine agreed.

Settling the campsite on the field, Kegan ignited the campfire (with Raine's guidance in case he burnt down the entire field) while Jocelyn and So-hyun set up the tents. Lilac organised all the food and picnic mats, using Sir Bamesetton as weight to prevent them from flying away with the wind.

The campsite was finished setting up with an hour left to spare, so Raine decided to spend it with her friends. Lilac handed out a bamboo skewer to roast their marshmallows over the campfire, and their chatter filled the otherwise quiet field with their laughter.

Before Raine knew it, it was five minutes to midnight, and the stars began to align. Finishing her bit of chocolate Jocelyn had shared to everyone, Raine and Kegan stood up and marched far away from the campsite. With each step, Raine found it harder to move, attacked by fear and uncertainty. She liked being in the dreaming world. She liked the hour she had with Kegan, So-hyun, Jocelyn, and Lilac. She

liked the familiar environment of Oneirolepsy. And
she wasn't ready to leave.

But her mind changed when she remembered how
the black-dreamers were still terrorising Oneirolepsy.
Sure, things had calmed down since the first time the
siren rang, but she needed to make sure all the
dreamers were safe. And she would sacrifice her life
for that.

"Let's hope your Subliminal Dreamkeeper will be
able to bring you back, because I sure as hell won't be
able to," Kegan warmed up his knuckles and wrists,
addressing Raine.

"He should be an elemental," Raine replied,
"Although all signs suggest that his element is water."

"Ah, unlucky."

Jocelyn, So-hyun and Lilac went over to Raine and
Kegan. "Sir Bamesetton is keeping a watchful eye for
any miscreants around. We are here to bid you
farewell, Revieras." Lilac opened her arms to give
Raine a bear hug, but then Jocelyn also rushed in with
a hug from behind Lilac, as well as So-hyun. Raine
almost lost her balance as she was overwhelmed with
support from her friends.

"Please be safe," Raine said, when everyone finally
let go of her.

"You too," they replied.

Raine took a deep breath. "Okay. Time to open the
portal."

She closed her eyes and channelled her dream
energy. Lilac and Jocelyn assisted by unleashing their

dream energy as well. So-hyun couldn't do anything because she was dream-blind, but she held onto Raine's hand for moral support.

Raine started chanting the Orael phrase, and eventually everyone started chanting along with her. She couldn't help but feel a bit of guilt, like she was sinning. Rhea said that in the past, chants and spells belonged only to the black-dreamers, and that dreamers shouldn't ever use them. Nonetheless, the glowing orb was being used to provide more energy and fuel, and using Kegan's element of fire as a medium, a small portal began to form in front of everyone. The portal increased in size gradually, until it was about the size of a door. A mesmerizing display of crimson and gold hues danced within its edges, as though liquid flames swirled and cascaded within its fiery embrace. The heat emitting from the portal was a signal for everyone to open their eyes and all at once, they stopped the chant, and the orb disintegrated.

Raine stood before the portal, her friends behind her watching her departure. It was no different than walking into straight fire, and even though Raine wanted to get in, her survival instinct and legs begged otherwise.

"Hurry up, dude." Kegan said.

"I-" Raine retorted, but Kegan had run out of patience. In an instant, Raine felt herself being pushed from behind and she was thrown into the feisty portal. Her body was burning in one second, and in the next, she was in another world.

※★✦★※
Chapter 20: Awaken

The rough texture of the uneven cobblestone pressed against Raine's skin as she lay flat on the ground, leaving indents on her body and little bits of pebbles which she dusted away when she stood up. It turned out that she wasn't just on the ground, but in the middle of the rocky streets. At midnight.

A gentle drizzle enveloped the atmosphere, casting a hazy veil. The pitter-patter of raindrops created a soothing symphony as they ricochet off the streets. Raine was quickly soaked in the drizzle, but that was the least of her concerns. She found the chilling air to be comforting, and the lack of people around made it feel as if she were in a dream. A tranquil one.

Raine inhaled the damp air and investigated her current predicament. It was almost pitch-black under the watchful eye of the moon, and the droplets of rain shimmered like stars. The entire experience exuded a sense of escapism, and despite Raine's circumstances, she found herself surprisingly calm.

However, her serene mood quickly shattered when the sound of a car's engine grew louder and louder from behind, and with a swivelled gaze, yellow headlights blared in her eyes. Raine was rooted to the spot as the black car grew closer.

With a loud screech of the tires, the car came to a halt, just an inch away from touching Raine. For a second, there was nothing but the sound of rain, until

the driver of the car decided to come out of their
vehicle to check on Raine.

Her car stood alone on the road with no other soul in
sight. Raine found it a little strange that the two of
them were the only ones awake in the city, but didn't
question it. The driver had a young complexion,
holding an unnecessarily large umbrella. Raine made
eye contact with the driver, whose eyes were a
pastel-like pink, giving off the resemblance of an
azalea. Her soft-angled eyebrows gave her a look of
mischief. She scanned Raine with an expression of
wonder and curiosity, two things that Raine wouldn't
expect from someone in a situation the two of them
were in.

"I'm sorry I got in the way," Raine apologised. Her
first words to a being who was not belonging of
Oneirolepsy were spoken out, and now she was a little
afraid of how someone from a parallel universe would
behave. For all she knew, the driver could hold the
malice of a black-dreamer. At least she hadn't been
run over.

The driver smiled. It was more of a mocking smile
than an apologetic one. "No worries." A light-hearted
voice spoke before she scooted a bit closer to Raine, to
an uncomfortable degree. Her expression slowly
changed into one of surprise as she stared at Raine.
"You're a dreamer, right?"

Raine was caught off-guard. "I didn't expect people
from Psytheon to know about Oneirolepsy. Yeah, I'm
a dreamer. My name is Raine."

The driver laughed. "Oh, that's not true at all! Most people aren't aware that there's another parallel universe in the land of dreaming. They're just so self-centred, believing they're the superior beings because they can talk," she gave a small shrug. "I was half-joking about that last bit, by the way. I only know about Oneirolepsy because I'm an exception. How lucky we are to have met! But I kinda guessed that you were a dreamer anyway. There's been a little problem where everyone has been in a coma-like state and has been unable to wake up. That's why it's so empty out here. Hold this for a second." The enigmatic driver handed the umbrella to Raine so she could untie her jacket from her waist to wear it on her person. She wore many layers and showed little skin. "Rain is nice and all, but water and me don't really make a good match. I break out into rashes and start wheezing all over," she added, taking the umbrella back and gripping on the handle, the canopy casting a shadow over her head.

"Right," Raine commented. "You mentioned that everybody's asleep? I don't think that's a 'little' problem. How long has this been going on?"

"A week or so. You wouldn't believe the number of possibilities there are when the whole city of Kyronami is asleep."

Raine didn't know what that entailed and began to wonder if she was speaking to a criminal. "A week? That's not normal, is it?" She recalled that the outbreak of the black-dreamers had also occurred during that time frame, and questioned if the two events were somehow connected. Even though she was in the so-called waking world, everyone in it was asleep, apparently.

"Yeah, not normal by Psytheon standards. But there's not much I can do about it." The driver went back to her car, and Raine instinctively followed without realising. "Hey, you should stop by. I promise I'm not a serial killer or anything." She giggled at her own comment, opening the car door.

Raine hesitated. "Actually, I came here to find someone. He's a dreamer too, just like me."

The driver stopped. She faced Raine and a big smile formed on her face. "Does he by any chance go by the name of Zephyr Aune?"

"You know him?" Raine's heart skipped a beat.

"Oh, I do! But you and I need to talk. Sit down. We're going to my place first." She gave a small pat on the passenger's seat next to her, and Raine, albeit hesitantly, sat down as the driver kept her umbrella, trying her very hardest not to get any raindrops on her. Raine closed the car door and hoped that she wouldn't get kidnapped.

The driver played soft ambient music from her phone and started driving. "You're not allergic to cats or anything, right?"

"No. Do you have one at your place?"

"Seven, actually." She grinned.

Raine pictured the driver being swarmed by seven fluffy, adorable cats and got jealous, despite knowing it would be impossible for her to take on the responsibility of caring for seven cats herself. "Who are you, by the way?"

"Hm...you can call me Umbral. I was born in Psytheon, right here, in Kyronami City. Nice to finally meet you, Raine," Umbral spoke, not taking her eyes off the car windscreen, where the windscreen wipers worked furiously against the drizzle. "How well do you know Zephyr?" She then asked.

"I've never met him before. I had a friend find him so we could save Oneirolepsy from the black-dreamers with the Dreamkeepers. Zephyr's the last one." Only after Raine finished her sentence did she realise how weird she sounded.

"Could you elaborate, maybe? I've no idea what a Dreamkeeper is, sorry." Umbral offered a sheepish smile.

Raine explained everything to Umbral, from the beginning when she was performing her usual magic show. She wasn't sure how accurate her storytelling was, nor if Umbral actually understood everything, but when Raine finished, Umbral nodded. "Uh huh, so your subconsciousness led to you finding Zephyr in Psytheon? Have the voices gone away yet?" She was referring to the strange echoes of crying Raine had been hearing.

"I'm not sure, but I haven't heard anything yet," Raine sighed, feeling parched from talking.

A sudden wave of fatigue washed over Raine like a heavy blanket, enveloping her entire body. It felt like a magnet was pulling her towards sleep, the powerful force barely overpowering her will to stay awake. Raine tried to lift her eyelids up to prevent herself from closing her eyes, but she found herself too weak and sluggish, her body surrendering to fatigue. Raine lost the ability to stay aware and focused, and the voice of Umbral talking to her became nothing but muffled white noise.

No, don't fall asleep, don't fall asleep, or you might never wake up again, Raine warned her body to stay awake, but her thoughts just made her more tired, and now everything around her felt hazy and foggy.

In an instant, a surge of intense pain radiated through Raine's abdomen, causing a sharp and jarring sensation. She was shaken awake and gasped for air, her mind taking a few seconds longer than needed to process that Umbral had just struck her in the stomach. Raine let out a groan of pain. "That was too much, Umbral!"

"That's not a very nice way to thank someone for saving your life," Umbral grinned. "But anyhow, I apologise."

Raine gripped her stomach and sighed. She didn't enjoy the sudden attack of sleepiness and expected for it to happen again later on. "I know I said I'm not allowed to fall asleep, but next time just nudge me gently instead of attacking me directly, okay?"

"How ineffective, but your call, I guess."

The conversation fell short, and Raine looked out the windows. Earlier, she had observed several cars remaining stationary in the middle of the streets, and even collisions between vehicles. Some individuals were sleeping right in the middle of outside, unreactive to the rain showering their cold bodies. If the problem had been ongoing for a week, it would mean that the sleeping bodies hadn't been moved for that amount of time. Raine wondered how hungry they must be, or how it would feel to move their muscles after a week of not using them.

The car came to a stop, parked at the side of the road. "We're here," Umbral said. Raine exited the car and waited for Umbral, who was fumbling around awkwardly with the umbrella as she tried to open it in the car. Raine offered to assist Umbral with the umbrella, opening it from outside and then holding it over Umbral's head as she scooted over from the driver's seat to the passengers to get out. She closed the door with a small thud and took hold of the umbrella handle.

A row of shops lined up with shelter protecting them from the rain. Raine peered into one of the restaurants' glass windows and saw that some customers had their unfinished food on their tables, their heads lying on the table unmoving. Raine assumed the owner was asleep as well and felt chills run down her spine.

Umbral went into a suspicious-looking building with dim lighting, closing the umbrella as Raine followed her. There were flights of staircases that led up to nowhere, and Umbral began walking up, using the umbrella as a walking stick as she ascended the stairs. Raine followed her carefully, reconsidering if maybe this was a kidnapping attempt after all.

After climbing for what felt like an eternity, the staircase led to a small glass door with stickers of cats and a wooden open-closed door sign from inside. The sign had the words 'CLOSED' facing Raine and Umbral, and the lights were all off. A poster pasted on the wall served a pictorial guide on how to take care of cats and how much it cost to have one.

"Welcome to Maui Planet," Umbral grinned, unlocking the glass door and entering. Raine followed into the darkness, and for a second, thought that Umbral had vanished, but then the lights turned on, and Umbral appeared behind Raine. "I'll give you a complimentary iced chocolate, you can enter after taking off your shoes," she added, then disappeared again.

A shelf next to the counter brimmed with an assortment of cat-themed accessories, ranging from cat toys to phone holders. A giant plush of a grey cat reminded Raine of Jocelyn's Miss Maojie. On the counter sat a cash register and a menu showcasing various beverages and their corresponding prices. A small countertop display housed keychains and souvenirs.

Apparently, Umbral's home was a cat café.

The white walls were decorated with framed paintings and posters about what not to do with cats in the café, with the wooden floor blanketed by a fuzzy cat-shaped carpet. Raine did as Umbral asked and took off her boots, placing them neatly on the shoe locker by the corner of the entrance.

Raine entered through a sliding glass door that led to the main space of the café. Inside, she found a spacious area filled with empty tables and chairs for accommodating guests. Many playing structures and beds for the cats hogged the space, and as Raine looked around, she caught four different cats sleeping around. Some toys were playfully scattered on the clean floor, serving the purpose of both aesthetic and function.

A restricted area had been cordoned off with a 'staff only' sign. Large windows revealed the nighttime sky and the streets beneath the building. Raine surveyed the entire place with wonder, before taking a seat on a cream-coloured floor sofa attached to the wall with a complementary low coffee table.

Umbral entered through the sliding glass door with two iced chocolates with black silicone coasters. She placed the drinks down on the table and sat next to Raine. "The cats are asleep right now, unfortunately," she said, with a disappointed tone.

"You know, when you said you owned seven cats at home, I didn't think you meant a cat café," Raine replied, taking the iced chocolate. The drink was cold to the touch and she took a sip. It was just the right amount of sweet.

"Yeah, well, I live here. There's a closed off room here which is my bedroom. I co-run this place with a

friend, Kaymi, who's also fallen to the sleep-spell."
Umbral pulled out her phone. "I've been trying to call
Zephyr for a few days now, but he hasn't answered
me. I haven't seen him for a while now."

"Do you think he might be asleep as well?"

Umbral let out a small chuckle. "No, he's definitely
not asleep." She pointed outside the windows, where
the rain had gotten heavier. "You know how he's a
water elemental, right? The thing is, his powers are
connected to his emotions. So whenever he's agitated
in one way or another, it starts raining." she gave a
small shrug. "Kyronami city is known for having a lot
of rain and cold weather," she added in a
non-insulting way, holding the phone to her right ear.

Out of curiosity, Raine took out the map from her
bag. The outline of Oneirolepsy had completely
vanished, as well as So-hyun's and Lilac's pinpoints,
leaving a blank map. But a bright white speck had
appeared in the middle of it, indicating a presence of
the Dreamkeeper. It didn't help much as Raine
couldn't know where exactly the speck was located,
but she was relieved to know that the Subliminal
Dreamkeeper was indeed in Psytheon, and alive.

"Huh, no reply. How unsurprising." Umbral placed
her phone on the table in defeat and drank her own
iced chocolate. "Hey, why don't you find Zephyr? You
two probably share some dreamer link or whatever,
and it's too bothersome for me to go out in this
weather." Umbral left for a second, but then returned
with the umbrella. "Return this to him too, please?"

Raine was unsure if she was able to trust herself to find Zephyr without either getting lost or falling asleep, but she grabbed onto the umbrella nonetheless. "Where do I start finding him? I don't even know this place."

Umbral took her phone and handed it to Raine. There was a digital map on the phone. "I don't have Zephyr's location exactly, but I know where he lives. It's a beach house near the sea. Wherever the wind or water goes, you follow."

"You're trusting me with your phone?" Raine asked. Umbral's phone case depicted a night sky with stars and pink clouds, with a finger ring holder the shape of a black cat pasted right in the middle of the phone.

"Well, no, but yes," Umbral said, drinking the rest of her iced chocolate. "Bring him back here so we can talk. I'll be waiting for you here."

With a sigh, Raine got up, taking her half-finished iced chocolate with her for support, lifting her bag up and double-checking the new map on Umbral's phone. "Okay, I'll see you soon." She waved her goodbye and turned to leave the cat café, using the umbrella handle to hook on her arm as she tried to open the glass door with her full hands, only to place them all down on the floor as she had to put her boots back on.

Raine stepped out of the building and onto the pouring streets. She opened the umbrella and began making her way towards the beach house which had been marked on Umbral's map. Without a vehicle and

with public transport ruled out, she inhaled the moist
air and pressed forward, enduring the downpour for
about two more hours. The further Raine walked, the
more evident the resemblance between Kyronami City
and the modern Mainland became, albeit with a
duller and less colorful ambiance. Additionally, a
conspicuous absence of vitality prevailed, which,
given the coma situation, was understandable, but
venturing out alone past midnight in the darkness felt
eerie. In retrospect, Raine considered whether she
should have persuaded Umbral to accompany her
after all.

She took additional sips of her iced chocolate, and
when all that remained was the melted ice, she found
a trash can to throw away, and out of pure boredom,
found Umbral's music playlist to play so that she felt
less alone and afraid.

The rain would have been less piercing if it weren't
for the strong wind that came with it. The
questionably oversized umbrella prevented the
uncomfortable sensation of the raindrops getting
Raine's sides wet, but the wind completely negated all
of that in an instant, and while Raine tried to grip
onto the umbrella so that it wouldn't fly away, her
entire body became so drenched that the viscosity
even managed to hinder her movements.

Umbral definitely foresaw this, Raine thought.

But a clear view of the beach helped provide Raine
with hope, and she checked Umbral's phone. She had
reached the beach house. The rain muted the distant

crashing of the waves against the shore as she walked towards it, hoping for the sight of anyone. "Hello?" She called out, hoping she wouldn't be mistaken for a burglar. But there was nobody.

Raine went even closer to the beach house, peering through the windows. She knocked on the front door and called out Zephyr's name a few more times. Raine felt a little tense, granted that she didn't know what kind of a person Zephyr was, but nobody replied.

Then, as if her entire body had shut down, Raine sank to the sandy ground below. She could scarcely hear the faint callings wishing her back home, and her eyelids were feeling heavy again.

No, no, no! Don't fall...

Suddenly, Umbral's phone, which had been in Raine's hand and playing soft, lo-fi music, started blasting heavy metal at the volume akin to a volcano eruption, snapping Raine awake. Both irritated and thankful for her eardrums being damaged, she switched the music off and got up. She wasn't sure where to go now, and wondered if she should return to the cat café without Zephyr.

Raine searched in the downpour around the beach for another half-an-hour. Still nothing. Not wanting to risk falling asleep on the beach and potentially never waking up, she decided to leave and ask Umbral to do another search after the rain subsided.

Her legs were now incredibly sore from the excessive walking, and she felt as if she was about to collapse

any minute, even without the help of a sleep attack.
Retracing her steps, she returned to the city.

Raine entered autopilot mode as she kicked a pebble
along the pavement she traversed. Her boots
produced a squelching sound with each step, but over
time, the noise disappeared.

The water beneath her had disappeared too. In front
of Raine, where raindrops had been falling
incessantly, were now all devoid of time and gravity,
stuck frozen in the air. The sound pellets of rain
hitting the umbrella over Raine's head had stopped,
too.

Slowly, Raine lifted the umbrella from her head
and looked up at the sky. All the raindrops remained
motionless in the air. Then all at once, they began to
scatter in various directions, all converging toward a
specific point in the center of the street. The
raindrops congregated together to form a block of
water with the dimensions of a vending machine.
Strangely, despite the water's liquid form, it bore an
established shape with distinct edges and defined
edges hovering from the ground.

And then, she saw him.

※★ ✦ ★※
Chapter 21: Sublimation

It could have been because seeing him meant no more walking, or the fact that another dreamer existed who could understand and empathise with Raine, but upon seeing him, she felt profound catharsis and recognised the Subliminal Dreamkeeper instantly.

Her drowsiness had all vanished, and her senses could detect a high spike in dream energy. In the waking world.

Zephyr approached the strange block of water and Raine, who watched intently, wondered if he would do any cool elemental tricks with it, like some sort of performance. She stood a considerable distance from him and the water-cube, but she could faintly see his expression. An expression of sadness, anxiety, and confusion mixed all into a single face.

He stopped right by the water-cube. Raine couldn't tell what he was trying to do, but then she noticed something moving inside the water-cube. Her distance prevented her from making anything out other than a blob of water inside an even bigger blob of water, and she grew more curious about its nature.

After an entire minute of nothing else happening, the water-cube popped like a balloon, its definite shape held by whatever elemental power bursting into a wave of thick water which poured everywhere,

including on Zephyr himself. The water reached
Raine's boots, and she decided to approach him.

Raine closed the umbrella and walked over to
Zephyr, gazing into nothing, staying perfectly still, as
if in the midst of processing whatever just occurred.

"Excuse me," she said, grabbing Zephyr's attention.
He blinked and looked at Raine, unexpecting
someone to talk to him.

"Oh, hello," Zephyr replied, slowly. When he
confirmed that he and Raine were the only ones
around, he asked, "How did you wake up? Is everyone
not asleep anymore?"

"Uh, I'm not from around here, and no. By the way,
what was that giant water thing?"

"Oh, you saw that?" Zephyr turned around, as if the
water-cube had yet to reappear again, but it didn't,
and the empty pavement flooded with puddles
remained as its original state. "Um, I'm not sure what
that was either. I saw something moving inside, but it
was very vague and blurry. A bunch of small figures
moving around with a ball." Then, as if Zephyr
realised what he just said, he quickly shook his head.
"Ah, I'm sorry. I sound strange, don't I? You're
probably not used to elemental powers and magic, so
I understand if it's a little shocking or confusing.
I...promise I'm not a demon. Or an alien. Or a god."

"Oh, I'm actually used to those things." Raine
scratched her head, "Hang on, do you know who I
am?"

"Have we met?" His hands fidgeted around, a little alarmed. "I'm sorry, I don't know who you are. Am I supposed to know you?"

"I don't think so." Raine quickly realised that Zephyr was not so much of a dreamer than she'd originally assumed. "My name is Raine. I'm from Oneirolepsy, which is why I'm awake...for now." Her drowsiness had still yet to make a reappearance, but for now, Raine enjoyed not having to worry about falling asleep, even if only briefly. She could feel the water beneath her seeping into her boots. "By the way, I met your friend, Umbral. She told me to bring you back to her cat café once I found you." She held up Umbral's phone for proof, and then offered the umbrella. "She also wants to return this to you."

Zephyr took the umbrella, his expression slightly changing at the mention of Umbral's name. "Oh. Um, we're not currently on speaking terms right now. But I suppose we can talk things out." He scanned Raine for a moment, and then his eyes lit up as he came to a conclusion. "Ah, I think I remember who you are. You're a dreamer, right?"

Raine nodded, feeling oddly proud. "I'll explain everything while we get back to the café."

＊ ＊ ＊

The hour of walking felt like nothing while Raine spilled her entire story of the Dreamkeepers and the black-dreamers' breakout to Zephyr, who listened

intently with sympathy and shock at the whole thing
(almost too much sympathy; Raine felt as if her
stories might bring him to tears).

She decided to keep some conversation topics for
when the two reunited with Umbral so that the three
of them could keep up with everything going on.

Raine felt gross, considering that her boots were wet,
and she had been walking for a long time now, and
she admired Zephyr's natural ability to dry up within
the hour since he had been so rudely doused in water
by his own weird magic water cube. She thought it
would bring some comfort to meet a like-minded
dreamer such as Zephyr, but throughout the talk she
had with him, she only realised her misbelief.

"You just met Umbral, right? What do you think of
her?" Zephyr asked. The two made it back to the cat
café's building, and now scaled the endless loops of
stairs.

"She's kinda eccentric, but she's helped me
somewhat, and either way she's the only other person
awake in this city." She glided up the stairs with
Zephyr following reluctantly behind. "Did you two
have a fight or something? I thought you were
friends."

Zephyr stopped for a second, and Raine turned
around to face him, stopping mid-step as well. "We
had a disagreement," he stated, before climbing up
the stairs again, speeding up a little this time. Raine
caught up to his pace and after a moment of silence,

except for the sounds of their footsteps, they reached the café's door.

Raine pushed open the door, which opened with its familiar jingle of the bell. She and Zephyr skipped through the empty lobby after taking off their shoes and pushed the sliding glass door open, finding Umbral still sitting at the same spot Raine left her at. Her empty half-smile turned into a full grin as she shifted her attention from a sleeping cat in front of her to Raine and Zephyr. "Hey hey, welcome back! And hi again, Zephyr! Hope you didn't miss me as much as I missed you." She winked at Zephyr, gesturing for the two to sit down.

Raine sat next to Umbral, admiring the peacefully resting black Manx cat next to Umbral. Zephyr tucked the umbrella into a corner and sat next to Raine, deliberately avoiding Umbral on the right. Umbral noticed he had sat away from her on purpose and gave a slight frown directed at him. "Are you still mad at me, Zephyr?" She asked, almost teasingly. "I haven't done anything yet, you know? You should calm down a little."

"I am calm," Zephyr stated, leaning slightly so he could look at Umbral without staring at Raine unintentionally. "Is it really my fault for being worried? You were serious about murdering someone."

"Hang on, what?" Raine interrupted.

"Oh, but he tried to kill me first! His stupid lackeys tried to waterboard me and I almost died! As a matter of fact, I'm being the good Samaritan here, giving him a peaceful death, unlike his torture." Umbral sat up straight and leaned even closer to Zephyr.

"Killing him isn't the right thing to do, you won't be any better than him," he answered.

"True, but it's what *I* want to do. And it's not about being better than him, it's about getting my revenge," Umbral refuted, but then she clapped her hands together. "Anyway, Raine, now that everyone is here, we should start discussing some things, right?"

Raine raised her eyebrow at the sudden change of topic, but dismissed it anyway, feeling a little bit awkward now. "You both are aware of the situation in the dreaming world, and about the Dreamkeepers." She turned to Zephyr. "You're the Subliminal Dreamkeeper. I need you to come back to Oneirolepsy with me so we can save the world."

Zephyr took a few seconds to answer. "How?"

"The other Dreamkeepers are waiting. We'll work together to restore the barrier and eliminate the black-dreamers for good." Raine noticed that Umbral was glaring at her, even though she was still wearing her smile.

"I mean, I wouldn't let loose an elemental who can't control his powers into a world of helpless dreamers, but pop off, if you will," Umbral commented, before Zephyr could respond. "Hey, can I come with you? This entire thing sounds fun."

Raine started to feel a little bit intimidated by Umbral, and almost bumped into Zephyr in an attempt to scoot away from her. "I don't think it's a good idea for a normal human to go into the dreaming world."

"Umbra isn't a normal human. She's a Vortex," Zephyr claimed.

"Oh, come on!" Umbral suddenly raised her voice. "You weren't supposed to tell her that. Can't you understand when you're supposed to stop talking, or are you so socially disconnected that you forgot what cues to take?"

"You were also not supposed to tell Raine that I couldn't control my powers. You don't have to undermine me by saying those things." Zephyr's rigid posture betrayed the calm composure he tried to maintain, revealing some of his annoyance.

"Umbral, can you relax a little? What do you mean by Vortex? I'm not familiar with that term." Raine gently tugged Umbral's sleeve, getting her to sit back down. Umbral's erratic behaviour filled Raine with discomfort, but she complied and gently stroked the black cat, who managed to remain asleep despite the commotion.

"It's a term for those who are half human and half dreamer or nightmare," Umbral explained. "Which by the way, are very cool people." She added.

Raine connected the dots and figured Umbral being a Vortex would explain why she deviated from everyone else's comatose state. "You kept that from me?" She asked, almost feeling betrayed.

"I like to keep the element of surprise," Umbral replied, paying more attention to the cat than Raine. "Want another surprise? I've been to Oneirolepsy before, so I know how things work. I know who you are, Revieras."

Raine went motionless at the revelation, in contrast to Umbral, who was still lovingly petting the Manx. A cat brush lay on the floor, and she retrieved it to groom the sleeping cat. "What? You knew who I was the entire time?" Raine asked, cautiously watching Umbral peacefully grooming the feline.

"Of course I knew. Frankly, I'm surprised you're still alive. Usually dreamers drop dead asleep within a few minutes alone. By the way, can I have my phone back?"

Raine begrudgingly handed the phone back to Umbral, who started playing an instrumental of heavy metal on her playlist, scaring Raine half to death with the sudden volume. Zephyr didn't even flinch.

Startled by the music, the cat immediately jumped up with a fright, and hopped onto Umbral's lap. She quickly turned off the heavy metal and switched back to calmer music. "Huh, I thought you were in a sleep coma too. I'm sorry, Miso." Umbral patted the cat's head and began comforting it as it meowed.

Out of the four cats Raine could see, Umbral had managed to awaken three of them with her phone. A ginger cat walked into the open floor and Raine took this as an opportunity to get away from the awkward tension between Umbral and Zephyr. She got up and walked over to the ginger cat and sat down next to it. The ginger cat curiously sniffed Raine before allowing her to be in its presence and got into a loaf position.

"You shouldn't come with us," Raine told Umbral.

"Hm?"

"You shouldn't come with us," Zephyr repeated.

"Yes, I heard her the first time." Umbral picked up the brush which she had dropped on the floor in surprise when the cat woke up, "But why?"

"It's too dangerous, even if you are a Vortex. And besides, this is my first time going from Oneirolepsy to Psytheon. I'm not sure how well it'll work if I bring you and Zephyr back to Oneirolepsy."

"Oh, I've done that multiple times. I'm a shadow elemental," Umbral stated, grooming the cat once again.

Raine did a double take and quickly realised that Umbral was not joking about keeping the element of surprise. "Okay. Did not see that one coming." She looked back at Zephyr, who was gazing outside the window. "Could you leave for a while? I need to talk to Zephyr," she asked Umbral.

Umbral shrugged and picked up her phone, brush, and the cat all at once, getting up and leaving. "Don't get too comfortable with him, okay?" She grinned, before leaving through the glass door.

The tension eased significantly as Umbral left, and Zephyr went over to Raine to sit. Raine didn't want to make Zephyr uncomfortable by asking about his relationship with Umbral and decided to focus on more important matters. "Zephyr, was what Umbral said earlier true? About you not being able to control your powers?"

The ginger cat got up from its loaf position and brushed itself against Zephyr, successfully making Raine feel jealous. "I suppose so. I don't know why, though. I can control air, but not water."

"Wait, you're also an air elemental?"

Zephyr nodded.

"I... also did not see that coming," Raine mumbled to herself, recalling all of Valentino's research and seeing if he had ever mentioned Zephyr being an air elemental along with a water elemental. "Woah, two elements?"

"Is that alright?" Zephyr asked, worried about what Raine would think.

"Oh, it's completely fine," Raine instantly reassured him, ignoring Kegan's existence. "May I ask when and how you ended up in the waking world? It's not typical for a dreamer to be here."

Zephyr looked away for a second, leaving Raine's question lingering in the air for a few seconds before answering apologetically. "I'm sorry, I don't remember. All I know is that I've been here for about twelve years now."

"You don't remember?" Raine echoed, the phrase sounding familiar. She shook her head, dismissing the non-answer and asking a new question. "Do you remember anything from when you were still in Oneirolepsy?"

"Oh, hmm. I remember that I lived in the Subliminal realm, and as a child, it was difficult for me to control my elemental powers, so a lot of people were afraid of me. I think I left because I was causing everyone trouble. My parents were also scared of me." Zephyr placed his hand on his chin, staring at the ginger cat as it started circling around him and Raine.

Raine grabbed the opportunity to gently stroke the cat while it circled around her, and if it weren't for Zephyr's extreme melancholy of a statement, she probably would have squealed in joy. "It must've been rough, I'm sorry."

"It's alright. Like I said, I don't remember a lot of things, so it doesn't matter."

Raine recalled all the knowledge she gained with Valentino's help, hoping that nothing slipped from her mind. She then remembered the dream at the football field. "I think I saw your past in my dreams," she said, forgetting how strange that sounded to anyone else.

Zephyr stared at Raine. "Excuse me?"

Raine sighed. "Okay, well, I've been hearing callings prior to coming here. I've had fragments of dreams where a boy named Lemar would appear in an empty void. He told me that the two of you were best friends, and I had another dream taking place at a football field. I saw you and Lemar playing on the field, and all of a sudden a typhoon occurred, and my dream ended. I think you were the one who caused the typhoon."

Zephyr fell silent for a while, and then spoke. "I think I saw something similar earlier too, with the strange water-cube. I..." He looked away for a moment, and his tone lowered. "I didn't hurt anyone, did I?"

The vision of Lemar flashed in Raine's mind. "I think you did," she answered, hesitantly, watching Zephyr's expression change to one of sadness and guilt. Surprise did not register though, and Raine wondered if he had done something similar before. "But from what I saw, you definitely didn't do it intentionally."

"It's still my fault that someone got hurt," Zephyr sighed, looking outside the window, where it started to drizzle again, the faint sound of raindrops getting more audible the heavier the rain got. "I'm a monster."

"No, no, that's not true at all! You're not a monster." Raine placed a reassuring hand on his shoulder, but she could tell that it hardly helped him at all. "You have to believe that it's not your fault. You didn't want anyone to get hurt, and you didn't ask for your elemental powers."

"The world would be better off if I didn't exist at all," Zephyr muttered, then shook his head. "I'm sorry, I didn't mean to sound so pessimistic...But you agree, right? That elementals are all just dangerous people."

Raine tried to find words of comfort, but there were none. She had always been hearing others complain about elementals being too powerful and posing a threat to other dreamers. Elementals, from what Raine heard, had either been feared or hated throughout the history of Oneirolepsy. What Zephyr said remained true, especially given what Raine had gone through with Jeo-sa and Kegan, but she didn't feel that way. She found it impossible to visualise Zephyr as a heartless monster wrecking the world with his powers. "I don't agree," she finally responded. "Even if you have dangerous powers, that doesn't inherently make you a bad person. It's not your fault if you can't control your powers."

Zephyr nodded a little, not believing Raine's words, but he didn't argue. "I know I have lost memories from the past, and I haven't tried to retrieve them, but...I think doing so will help," he began. "Actually, I've been hearing callings too. And I saw Lemar in the water-cube. I think I should talk to him...or at least, try to remember what I did."

The ginger cat settled down between Zephyr and Raine, staring at both of them intently before purring and closing its eyes again. "How about we go back to the football field? Maybe we can use the power of dreams to restore some of your lost memories." Raine suggested.

"The...power of dreams? What does that mean?"

Raine briefly remembered the first time she entered the strange memory-dream with Valentino via passing out from a deafening ringing and falling on top of him and decided it wouldn't be a good idea to repeat the process with Zephyr. Also, she quickly remembered that she wasn't in Oneirolepsy, and being in the waking world would make oneiromancy more dangerous by tenfold. However, she placed her trust in Zephyr's elemental-ness and closed her eyes. "We both have to be connected to the same dream. Hold my hand," Raine instructed, feeling a little sad from the absence of the cute ginger cat.

A few seconds went by, spent on giving goodbye pets to the ginger cat. Raine then felt a cold touch on her palm. She grabbed Zephyr's hand, and still with her eyes closed, shifted her concentration over to her subconscious mind, allowing the dream to take over.

Hopefully, Raine would be able to wake up again safe and sound.

Chapter 22: Traceback

Raine felt both alarmed and relieved when she saw
the familiar sight of the football field. Alarmed,
because of her dreaming in Psytheon, meaning that
there might be a chance for her to be perpetually
trapped inside this dream forever. Relieved, because it
meant that she had succeeded in hopping over to the
correct dream. Zephyr stood next to her right, looking
around the place, clearly unfamiliar with the scene.

The game had yet to start, and on the sidelines, the
football players were either playing, training, or
chatting with one another. A few were being doted on
by their parents, and some had yet to see theirs arrive.
Raine quickly spotted Lemar practising passes with
one of his teammates, the younger Zephyr nowhere to
be found.

"What is this?" the current Zephyr asked.

Raine explained the process of oneiromancy and how
dreaming worked to Zephyr. After a lengthy
discussion, Zephyr finally understood. "We're
invisible to the others, so we can freely investigate.
Find your younger self, I guess," Raine said. She
didn't know how Zephyr would regain his powers by
reliving his undesirable past, but she needed to try
anyway. Even though Raine had already experienced
the event from Valentino's perspective, seeing it from
Zephyr's would unlock something new, though by the

looks of it, the latter exhibited a greater tendency toward forgetfulness.

Zephyr left to do some searching, leaving Raine behind. Just as she took a step, a family entering the bleachers and locating an open seat nearby caught her attention. At first, she paid no mind to them because nothing about them stood out and assumed they were irrelevant to Zephyr, but the more Raine eyed the two dreamers with their parents, the more Raine felt something connecting in her brain. She let out an audible gasp once she recognised the familiar faces.

The parents of the two dreamers left their children alone to purchase some snacks. "Oh, Val! My coordinates say that I'm close to my soulmate!" The female dreamer, around her late teens, tapped on her younger brother's shoulder when her parents were fully out of range. Nayeli's hair and clothes remained the same as when Raine first saw her in Reverie's Space. Unlike in Kari's dream, Nayeli was fully opaque, and still alive, talking to a younger version of Valentino who wore no glasses.

Raine gauged his age to be around eight and found it mildly amusing to see a child version of someone she knew. His stoic expression turned to excitement as he heard Nayeli speak. "Really? You'll find your soulmate?"

Raine tried listening in from a distance, only to remember the advantages of invisibility. She casually made her way towards the two and spied on them shamelessly. The topic of Nayeli's soulmate rendered

Raine utterly confused until she gathered more
information by listening in.

"That's right! You remember what I said about my
ability, right? If I follow the coordinates and find my
soulmate, our shared dreams will be able to come
true! It means we can finally be rich and happy and
live well!"

"Does that mean I'll be able to get my own room?"
the younger Valentino's eyes sparkled at the thought.

Nayeli grinned. "You can have your very own house if
that's what you want. I just need to *get* with my
soulmate after I find him, and then we can live
happily ever after." She stood up and glanced around.
"I'll go look for him right now. When mom and dad
return, tell them I just went to the restroom."

Raine's eyes followed Nayeli as she walked away and
off into the distance. *So it's Nayeli's ability.* She
thought, trailing her from behind. While Raine
followed Nayeli, she spotted Zephyr still searching
and gestured to him to come over. "I think I found a
lead," Raine said, pointing to Nayeli. "Do you
recognise her?"

Zephyr caught up to Raine and peered at Nayeli from
the front before stepping back to where Raine was.
"No, I don't think so."

Raine followed Nayeli and assumed that Zephyr
would be walking closely beside her, but when Raine
turned around to check, she noticed that he was just
standing still, refusing to follow the two. "What's
wrong?"

"I'm sorry, but I don't think I can follow you," Zephyr replied, glancing away. "I just...I can't."

Raine watched as Nayeli walked further and further away. She scanned what was in front of her to see what could possibly make Zephyr so reluctant to follow, but there was nothing threatful as far as she was aware. "Oh, well." There was a bit of disappointment in her voice, but she gave a smile. "That's alright. I'll go check it out myself then."

Raine said that, but she couldn't shake off the feeling that something was incredibly wrong. Her subconsciousness was telling her that it was extremely important for Zephyr to follow Nayeli, and it felt like her head would explode if she didn't listen to her inner voice. "No. Actually," she met eyes with Zephyr, and traced back to Nayeli's mention of him being *someone special.* "This is important." She saw that her words made Zephyr feel incredibly anxious, and she regretted having said anything. "Nothing bad will happen to you. We're in a dreaming state, so it's virtually impossible for us to get hurt." She added, though it was more to assure herself than Zephyr.

Zephyr paused. He looked as if he wanted to argue, but he just nodded silently and began moving forward. Raine quickly took the lead in silence.

Thankfully, the two were still able to find Nayeli not too far off. They followed her to a secluded area of the football field, which housed nothing more than shadows. Nobody would ever come here unless they were purposely trying to hide in order to do some inconspicuous things. Nayeli turned her head left and right, searching for something. Or rather, someone. "Oh!"

A young boy with cyan eyes ran up to Nayeli. Raine and Zephyr immediately recognised him as Zephyr's younger self. "What are you doing here, sister?" Completely ignoring Raine and Zephyr's existence, the child ran up to Nayeli casually. Raine almost had a heart attack when he called Nayeli sister, but then remembered that everyone in the Subliminal realm addressed each other that way. Still, for some reason, she felt some sense of foreboding horror as Nayeli and the younger Zephyr met.

Nayeli's eyes widened as she saw the younger Zephyr. "Zero," she whispered. "Zero metres." She stared at the child in front of her. "I found you." She took a step closer to the child, her footsteps setting off alarms in Raine's head. She suddenly felt threatened by Nayeli but couldn't figure out why. "I can finally...be free." Her hands trembled relentlessly, and she had a crazed look on her face. Raine felt her stomach twist as the sense of impending trouble hung in the air. She distanced herself from Nayeli subconsciously, unable to take her eyes off her.

"Zero metres?" The young Zephyr asked, looking up at Nayeli, who shook her head, and went back to her warm and compassionate mood.

"It's my ability. I can see how far away my soulmate is, and if I find him, I can turn my dreams into reality.

But that's only if my soulmate shares my dreams as well." Nayeli offered a smile.

"Oh, that sounds cool!" The child's eyes lit up in excitement.

Nayeli inched closer to him, nodding. "It is! What are you doing here, by the way? Are you alone?" Her lips curled upwards, trying to be as friendly as possible. She looked to her left and right, as if double checking to see if the two were truly alone.

The child swallowed, as if Nayeli had caught him doing something wrong. "I'm hiding because it's too noisy outside, and I feel weird, but I don't know why. It's like a scary storm is inside that's making my heart beat very fast."

Nayeli didn't seem to be paying attention to anything he was saying. "Do you have an ability? Are you an elemental or anything of the sort? You won't hurt me, right?"

He paused. "...*No*. I'm not...I would never hurt you, sister."

"Good." She stepped closer. "That's good."

The child gave her a confused look, still unable to understand anything. "That's...good?"

"Yes, I've spent so many years cooped up in such a small house, with barely any food, but I've always taken care of my younger brother, because I care about him. And now, I can give him everything he ever wanted. And I can finally be happy. I don't have to be trapped anymore. And you know why?" Nayeli asked, almost in a whisper. "*Because I found you.*"

Nayeli took another step and backed the child into a corner, her smile fading as she mumbled. "I just need to...just for one moment...and then my future...I can be free." She grabbed onto him, making sure he couldn't escape if he wanted to.

"W-what are you doing? You're scaring me." the younger Zephyr tried to pull away from Nayeli, but she held onto his wrists.

"For my family. For me. Everything will come true..." Nayeli's eyes met the young dreamer, who had by now began to realise that she held no good intentions for him. "Our shared dreams will set me free."

Nayeli closed the space between herself and the dreamer, forcefully pulling him onto her. Before Raine could see anything else, her view was blocked by Zephyr's hands. Raine stared blankly at his hand, frozen in shock and unable to move. She had forgotten that the current Zephyr was standing next to her and watching the whole scene unfold the entire time. She tried to force her ears to drop off her head so she couldn't hear the sobs that the child wept out, but all she could do was listen. And she heard everything.

※ ※ ※

Zephyr turned Raine around and walked her out of the secluded area, both of them quivering all over. They were outside again, where the bleachers were visible, and hundreds of people were gathered, unbeknownst to the horror that just occurred. Zephyr removed his hand from Raine's eyes, before collapsing onto the grass field.

"What...? Nayeli-...she...she's a monster." Raine's voice barely squeaked out from her dry lips. She couldn't imagine a dreamer to be as bad as a black-dreamer. No, Nayeli was even worse than a black-dreamer. And for her to be Valentino's older sister, and Kari's best friend, the two who looked up to her. Raine felt her legs giving out, and she ended up collapsing next to Zephyr as well.

Zephyr didn't reply, and the two sat in silence, staring at nothing. Even though Raine had her vision blocked by Zephyr just then, she could tell that he had seen everything. It was his lost memories. And all of a sudden, it made sense why Zephyr didn't remember anything. Why would anyone want to remember such a horrifying event?

Zephyr hugged his knees to his chest and buried his head down. Raine anticipated hearing Zephyr sobbing, but instead, he was silent, and that made it all the worse.

Raine's emotional state mirrored his own, far from a decent state. She offered a sympathetic pat on Zephyr's back.

He lifted his head back up, and he looked at Raine defeatedly. "I'm sorry."

Raine hugged Zephyr tightly. "You don't have to apologise. It's not your fault at all."

Zephyr nodded solemnly and pulled back from Raine after a few seconds. Hearing footsteps, Raine found Nayeli returning to the bleachers. She had a blank expression, numb and indifferent. The young Zephyr unseen.

Raine felt disgusted looking at Nayeli. She had no trace of remorse or guilt at all.

The clear sky persisted without interruption, with nobody aware of Nayeli's crime. Raine watched Nayeli scoot back to Valentino's side as if nothing had ever happened. She could see Valentino trying to talk to her, but she left him without any reply, just staring blankly at the grass field, and Valentino returned to watching the football match after realising his sister was ignoring him for whatever reason. Both their parents sat next to them, blissfully unaware of the sin their daughter just committed.

Raine wanted to leave the dream, but she couldn't. A few minutes later of idle silence, she saw the child version of Zephyr come out onto the field, limping back towards a group of his teammates whilst staring at his shoes. She saw Lemar approaching him and trying to talk to him, asking where he went.

Their coach came up to Zephyr and reprimanded him for something Raine couldn't make out, probably having to do with his disappearance and lack of enthusiasm. She could hear his piercing voice from afar, and were she in Zephyr's shoes, she would've burst out crying a long time ago in a broken mess.

But then the game started.

With the blow of a whistle, the football match began, and everyone was cheering and rooting for their children or relatives. Suffocating noise filled the air. Raine wanted to leave the dream, but she couldn't take her eyes off child Zephyr, who struggled to match the energy of his other teammates on the field. He hadn't even touched the football yet, and when the other team scored a goal, everyone got irritated by his unenthusiastic behaviour. Raine could hear his teammates booing him, insulting him in front of his face, and even their coach was glaring at him with a displeased glare.

Thunder roared, and it began to drizzle. Raine remembered this segment of the dream, except this time, things changed, and instead of the dream making an abrupt time skip, it continued, and she couldn't run away.

"Zephyr!" Lemar cried, running after the cyan-eyed boy. His shoes made a squelch sound as he made his way through the rising waters. Lemar grabbed onto Zephyr's hand and started to run away, but stopped when Zephyr refused to move. Lemar turned around. "What are you doing? We need to leave!"

"I'm sorry," Raine could hear Zephyr stammer, as tears began to form. Lightning flashed once more, and she had to close her eyes to shield herself from its blinding light.

The typhoon came as if on cue, and for a moment, the coldness and fear sank deep into Raine until she could no longer differentiate dreaming from reality, completely disoriented and scared of everything at once.

Water filled her vision, followed by even more water. The strong wind overtook her vision, causing everything to go blurry, her body soon to blow away like insignificant leaves in the storm. Muffled screams echoed, unable to be heard over the chaos, but something gripped tightly onto Raine's arm.

A small sense of safety comforted Raine just a little as Zephyr held onto her. She kept her eyes closed and waited for it to end.

"Zephyr! Zephyr-" Lemar's voice cut off as he gurgled in the water, which submerged his small body in an instant. He wasn't seen by anyone again.

The typhoon caught Raine in its flood, and the unlucky victims barely managed to escape its wrath. The torrential rain refused to cease, powering on with agony and despair as its fuel, its angry waves crashing against the universe.

Raine could hardly breathe, and it felt like an ice bucket had just been dumped onto her. This was only to find out that there was no 'like' about it, for the vision of the typhoon in the football field disintegrated into the recesses of her memory as the present took over her consciousness, and she returned back to the waking world.

The view of the serene cat café did not welcome her back. Her arms were tied around her back, detained by heavy rope as dust gathered on the ground she sat on. Raine found herself in a dimly lit space stacked

with large boxes everywhere, with cobwebs hanging
on the walls.

"Oh, good morning, Raine! Did you sleep well?"
Standing just one feet away from Raine was a gleeful
Umbral, holding on to an empty bucket. "Sorry for the
interruption, but you've just been kidnapped."

※★ ✦ ★※
Chapter 23: Vortex

The last thing Raine needed after finding out about Nayeli and what really happened in the football field was a kidnapping from someone whom Raine considered a friend.

But really, a shadow elemental and a self-proclaimed Vortex wearing a cat-smile should have been an obvious sign of a lack in sanity.

"What the...where...why...?" Raine tried to ask. Her thoughts entangled into a disorderly web, unable to form anything remotely coherent. Umbral placed her hands behind her back and started pacing around Raine like a bird circling their prey.

"I have no idea what you just asked, but I'll answer anyway." Umbral abruptly stopped walking and pointed to herself. "I'm Umbral, a shadow elemental and a Vortex who is currently helping Katz out with stopping the Dreamkeepers. You're currently being tied up in a factory far away from the cat café because you're not supposed to head back to Oneirolepsy, as Katz instructed, and in any case, I'll be leaving you to rot and tell Zephyr that you were tricking him all along." She placed the empty bucket on the ground. "I saw the two of you unconscious, and assuming it was some dreaming shenanigans, it was the perfect opportunity! So defenceless, so vulnerable!"

Raine felt tempted to punch Umbral, only to remember her locked-in wrists. "Katz? Who is Katz?"

she asked, with water trickling down her forehead onto her chin. Her body shivered relentlessly from the cold water thanks to Umbral, and she could only glare at her in return. The storage room was unbelievably musty, and she decided that the moment she returned home, if she returned home, that is, her priorities would include a long shower and a delicious meal.

Umbral's smile faded. "Oh, you don't know? He's the King of nightmares." She snapped her finger in a sudden realisation. "Right, right! You all call him Koshalv, just like how you're also called Revieras. But just like how your name is Raine, his name is Katz. I'm helping him get rid of you."

Raine failed to understand Umbral's intentions or her reasoning. "But still, why do you want to help him? Aren't you Zephyr's friend? Why hurt the dreamers if you're friends with one?"

"Do I need a reason to help him? I do it because I want to, and because I'm also Katz's friend." A sombre demeanour coloured her smile. "The nightmares won't accept me because I'm half-human, and the humans here won't accept me because I'm half-nightmare. It's not anyone's fault though. I'm quite aware of my own actions and how I behave."

Umbral took a sharp inhale and stared at Raine. "It would be a lie to say that I don't care about other people, but that shouldn't stop me from doing what I want. Sure, I could be labelled as apathetic, and even evil. But what's wrong with that? It's not like I'm actively going out on a serial killing. I just want to have some fun."

"Was your friendship with Zephyr 'just for some fun' then? Are you manipulating him, too?" Raine asked, getting more upset on behalf of Zephyr rather than herself.

Umbral crossed her arms. "No. That's just friendly teasing. I wouldn't do anything to hurt him."

"It may not be intentional, but you're still hurting him." Raine expected a petty attack from Umbral, but she merely scoffed and left the storage room, leaving Raine alone with the potential spiders that crept inside. The door didn't close all the way, allowing sound to leak through to Raine's ears.

"Revieras is in there. Katz- I mean, Koshalv said not to kill her, and I instruct you not to hurt her either. Just leave her alone until she falls to the Oneirolepsy effect," Umbral's muffled voice could be heard, before she walked away.

Raine peered to the silt of the door and noticed two shadowy figures facing one another. "I don't remember seeing her in the castle," one of the figures said. Raine assumed it was one of Koshalv's black-dreamer guards summoned from Umbral's shadow and grew increasingly worried from the confirmed possibility of black-dreamers appearing in the waking world.

"She's Koshalv's new right-hand-woman, so to speak," the other guard explained, in a hushed manner. "A shadow elemental from this world came over to the castle demanding to 'befriend' the King. Unbelievable. She's reckless and bold but proves to be competent. Koshalv is using her as nothing more than a tool."

"Wait, is the door not locked?"

The door shut with a slam from the other side. Raine lowered her head with a sigh and tried to struggle with her wrists in a futile attempt to free herself, holding in her breath as she used all her might to twist and wear out the rope so it would loosen up. After a while, she gave up and exhaled, taking in a new deep breath before trying again.

After trying again and again for what felt like an eternity, Raine accepted defeat and slumped against the back of the wall. Her wrists burned as her fatigue proliferated. She missed Zephyr's dream energy, and Raine figured there was nothing else to do but to refrain from falling asleep.

※ ※ ※

Raine stared at the unmoving door for a long time. Everything around her stood motionless except for her breath. Time remained still, and she began to wonder if Kegan and the others would have to come to her rescue after all. After being with Zephyr and having gone through a lot with him despite only knowing him for a brief while, she was practically immune to the Oneirolepsy effect. However, that didn't help much in her current state, and she almost wished that it would come to take her, since she would rather dream forever than to be stuck in a stale room for an indefinite amount of time.

The door of the storage room gently opened. Even though Raine had been zoning out and staring at the door frame for a good while now, her body jolted by the sudden wailing of the door's hinges and the sight of Zephyr gave Raine a shock. "Zephyr!" She called his name, each syllable providing her with relief, but noticed his downcast gaze and grew worried.

"Raine," he walked up to her and helped to untie the rope. The aggression in his movements surpassed her expectations, given his personality, and for a split second Raine almost feared Zephyr breaking her wrists, but the rope eventually came loose, and Raine shook her hands free, massaging her bruised wrists. "Are you okay? Did anyone hurt you?" Zephyr asked, lifting Raine up from the floor. He held onto Raine's bag, and he handed it to her once she was free.

Raine had a lot of things she wanted to discuss, especially because of that dream, but there was currently another issue at hand. "Umbral kidnapped me," she said, now doubting Umbral's very name. "She didn't hurt me though. I heard she's working for the King of black-dreamers, Koshalv." Raine peered outside the storage room. "Where are we? Is anyone out there?" she pointed to the open door.

"It's a factory. Specifically for books, I think." Zephyr closed the door so that he and Raine could talk in private. "It's very far away from where the cat café was. I'm sorry if I took a long time to find you."

Raine began exploring the storage room while Zephyr spoke. "It's alright," she said, inspecting a large box on the ground. Inside were stacks of blank papers, left untouched that a thin layer of dust had begun to form around the edges of the box. "How did you know where to find me? And why a book factory, out of all places?" Raine asked the last question rhetorically, but Zephyr looked deep in thought.

"Umbra approached me once I woke up," Zephyr replied. "She told me that she left you at her other home."

Raine stopped her inspection of the storage room in mild surprise. "Really? This factory is her other home?"

Zephyr shook his head. "Umbra told me that she was abandoned by her parents and thrown here a long time ago. I figured that's what she meant by 'other home'." He looked away for a brief second. "When I came in, there were two sketchy individuals who tried to attack me. I had no choice but to...disable them. Do you know who they are?"

Raine predicted that he was one word away from apologising again, and while she did feel sorry for Umbral's unfortunate past, it didn't give her the justification to kidnap someone. "All I know is that they're black-dreamers working for Koshalv. And you don't have to apologise. It's a good thing, you know? You saved me."

Zephyr nodded before opening the door. "We should leave now. I don't know where Umbra is, but I don't want to leave her alone. Something bad might happen."

To her, or because of her? Raine debated if she should tell Zephyr not to involve himself with Umbral anymore, especially since from what she's seen, her friendship fell short of being a good one, and her lack of empathy made her all the more dangerous. "Do you know where she is?" Raine asked, finally leaving the suffocating storage room. Zephyr shook his head.

The factory's interior differed from the storage room. Despite the conventional nature of book manufacturing, the place exhibited a remarkably futuristic quality, leaving an impressive impact. Being Raine's first time in a factory, fascination overcame her. Unlike the cramped and small storage room, the factory itself sprawled expansively, its bright lights reflecting off the glistening walls of the factory with machines and structures dotting the surroundings.

"Woah." Raine couldn't help but gaze around. If it weren't for Zephyr, she probably would have already been running around the place and checking out all the machines and tools lying around. "This is a nice place," she commented, beginning to dislike Umbral, not because she kidnapped her, but because she decided to kidnap her and put her in a dirty, unappealing storage room when such a nice place existed right outside the closed door. The smell of dust had completely disappeared, and a cooling and

refreshing chill took over. Though, that was most
likely due to Kyronami's constant state of rain and
wind. "Where do you think she went? Any ideas?"
Raine asked, peering at a strange device lying on a
spotless white table.

"I'm right here," Umbral said. Raine let out a gasp
and saw Umbral standing across the table, her hands
placed behind her back and staring at Raine.

Raine backed away immediately and retreated over
to Zephyr. Umbral circled around the table and
strolled towards the two. Raine felt a rising panic
inside of her. "Were you here the whole time?" Raine
asked Umbral, getting into a defensive stance. But
Umbral didn't look interested in fighting at all.

"Of course, why would I leave you for anyone else to
find? There's a thunderstorm outside anyway, and it's
too bothersome to go out, even with this." She held
out her oversized umbrella and attempted to do a cool
spin with it, but failed and dropped it instead. She
quickly picked it up and cleared her throat. "I saw the
two of you leaving the storage room. Quite an
anti-climactic breakout, I must say. It's not fun at all."

Raine had failed to realise there had been an ongoing
thunderstorm, where being in the factory muted out
the outside noise. Hearing Umbral talk, Raine calmed
herself down with deep breaths, and pulled out from
her defensive stance. Although Umbral already
proved herself to be unpredictably dangerous,
reasoning with her sounded possible enough to try,
and even if it failed to work, Raine still had things she

needed to tell her. "Umbral, I overheard from the two guards that Koshalv is using you as a tool. You shouldn't work for him!" For a moment, Raine wanted to grab Umbral's hand and pull her over to her side with Zephyr, but then Umbral started laughing, leaving her in a confused state.

"It doesn't matter if he's using me," Umbral replied, her laughter a mask. A subtle undertone of contemptuous mockery tinged her voice. "It doesn't matter," she echoed again, trying to collect her thoughts. "I'm doing what I want, and what I want is to help Katz, regardless of what he thinks of me. Besides, he's the only one who can understand me."

"Understand you? You're the one being inscrutable," Raine argued. "And what do you mean by him being the only one who can understand you?"

Umbral sighed, as if it was something a toddler would know. In a '*do I really have to spell it out for you?*' voice, she responded. "Katz is also able to manipulate the shadows, and he accepts that I'm a Vortex. He doesn't see me as an evil incarnate or a weak halfie. And besides," her voice lowered a little as she mumbled, "I don't have anywhere else to belong."

"Umbra, you have the café," Zephyr refuted, in a semi-desperate tone. "You have Kaymi and me." He tried to approach Umbral, but she took a step back.

"You won't let me do anything. I have to force my 'nightmare' side back just for you to be happy, because otherwise I'm just a monster." Umbral's voice shook a little, but then she let out another laugh. "Oh,

but we're getting sidetracked! How about I
demonstrate my shadow element to you, Raine?"

In a split second, Umbral became one with the floor.
She 'melted' into her shadow and vanished,
reappearing again behind Raine, and attacking her
with the umbrella before she could do anything.
Umbral had more strength than she let on, and Raine
was knocked backwards, the sharp point of the
umbrella causing harrowing pain.

A torrent of water sent in Umbral's direction, and
she quickly dissolved back into the shadows again in
retreat, only appearing again once the water
disappeared. "Ah, I'm sorry!" Zephyr turned
everywhere to search for Umbral, and sighed in relief
when she appeared once again with a satisfied
expression.

"Unnecessary apology unaccepted," commented
Umbral, before trying to attack Raine again. A
waterfall circled around Raine like a protective shield,
stopping Umbral almost in an instant. She changed
her target from Raine to Zephyr, and to Raine, all she
could see was a blurry mass of white and blue moving
backwards and forwards.

Raine tried to think of how she could help stop the
fight, or at least contribute to prevent a worst-case
scenario. The battle reminded her of Kegan and
Jeo-sa's, where it included two elementals and a
helpless Raine as well. At this point, she embodied
nothing but the weakest link of Zephyr's chain. "Wait,
Umbral! Can't we just talk this out?" She begged, only

to find that the shadow beneath her feet started to contort.

An arm suddenly emerged from Raine's shadow and gripped onto her leg, pulling Raine down to the floor. Umbral came crawling out from the ground, a majestic yet horrifying sight, and pushed Raine to the floor. "Talking things out is *boring*," she said, in an almost sarcastic tone.

The waterfall surrounding Raine and Umbral turned amorphous and like a burst balloon, spilled on top of Raine and Umbral. Umbral disappeared into the shadows again. This time Zephyr tried to layer the ground with water so that she wouldn't be able to pop up again. He went over to Raine, who was drenched, and offered to lift Raine back up, who accepted the help.

Inadvertently, he yanked her up with an abrupt force. A slight soreness lingered in Raine's arm, but she didn't want to bring it up in case Zephyr felt bad.

An inky blackness had permeated throughout the whole of the factory, spreading and gobbling everything in its shadows. It felt like the whole world had been blanketed by a large shadow, rather than pure darkness, but Raine still felt an eerie sensation crawl up her spine. She and Zephyr retreated to the corners of the factory where the shadows had yet to spread, the sounds of their shoes kicking against the water on the ground echoing throughout the otherwise silent factory.

Raine hugged herself against the wall opposite from the oncoming shadows, only to realise that the wall behind her had casted a shadow of her own. By that time, however, Raine had her neck gripped by Umbral's arm, which then pulled back into the shadows, causing Raine to be strangled. Raine felt her entire body in pain as she failed to phase through the wall, and instead had to be pushed against it as hard as humanly possible.

The layer of water on the ground threw itself at Raine. Although the water slightly pricked and choked her, it allowed her to break free from the hand and she dropped to the ground with a cough. Umbral appeared and was on top of a conveyor belt, bent down so that her head wouldn't hit any machines above her.

"Umbral, are you even allergic to water?" Raine asked, remembering that her own body was covered in water, yet had still somehow managed to be the victim of Umbral's attack. She wondered if hugging Umbral would be considered assault.

Umbral shrugged, ignoring the question.

Raine realised that directly asking Umbral was about as useful as herself in the fight. She signalled Zephyr to attack Umbral with his water elemental powers, but he shook his head.

Raine didn't have to try to convince Zephyr anymore though - Umbral had jumped at the opportunity to strike the two again. This time, she had Zephyr as her target and shot out tendrils of shadows about to consume the seemingly unsuspecting dreamer, but there was suddenly an influx of water, like the waves of an ocean riding behind a surfer's, went over Zephyr's head and splashed onto Umbral.

Fortunately, Raine stood far enough to have avoided the water. Even if she had no problems with water itself, she could tell the pressure would have broken something.

When the water cleared, Umbral vanished, and Raine assumed she went back to hiding again. She remembered that she had Ralisrok's card-gun from Lilac, and immediately rummaged in her bag for it.

She let out a satisfied gasp as she held onto the gun. The deck of cards belonging to Ralisrok which were used as ammunition had been depleted during Soraya's fight, but Raine could use her dream energy to manifest new cards on the spot, thanks to being in the presence of an elemental dreamer.

When Umbral popped out from one of the large printers' shadows and onto a conveyor belt, Raine aimed at her and shot a card filled with dream energy. Umbral took a direct hit to her arm and winced, underestimating the pain from a mere card.

Raine doubted the effectiveness of dream energy against a Vortex but continued shooting at her anyway. Raine's new weapon took Umbral by surprise, but she used her umbrella to deflect the cards, and the factory grew dark again.

Umbral disappeared once more, and darkness rendered Raine's vision useless. She couldn't see

Zephyr either, and in a second, was met with a smack on the head with the umbrella.

Raine groaned in pain and knocked Umbral with her elbow, then shot at her once more. Opening her umbrella and using it as a shield, Raine marvelled at how resistant the umbrella was when its canopy blocked the blast from her card.

Umbral backed away and took some unfinished books from a pile before hurling it at Raine, who quickly retreated behind a machine twice as big as her. She saw Zephyr hiding as well and gestured to her cards. He nodded, and Raine shot multiple cards at once in Umbral's general direction.

A gust of wind formed simultaneously, conveniently redirecting the flow of the cards and hitting Umbral, despite her holding the umbrella out to protect herself. "Ow! Hey, that's cheating!" she yelled.

"I'm sorry!" Zephyr called out again.

Raine went over to Zephyr and whispered to him. "Look, I know you don't want to hurt Umbral, but can you summon water so that she doesn't hide in the shadows again? I don't want her running away."

Zephyr gave Raine a concerned look, but agreed, and the thinnest film of water formed on the floor and the walls. Umbral had to retreat to the conveyor belts again.

Raine continued shooting at Umbral with her cards, and Zephyr used his elemental powers to create strong wind to amplify the card's speed and precision.

Eventually, the wind got so strong that Umbral's umbrella was ripped out of her hands.

Annoyed, Umbral shot out a flurry of sharp razors made from shadows, effectively breaking the machine which shielded Raine, and hitting her. A barrier of murmuring, unintelligible whispers, attacked Raine, along with a sense of dread and suffocation.

A massive explosion of dark energy engulfed the area, and Zephyr had to quickly pull Raine away from its radius. Raine felt even more drained, and the whispers of the shadows prevented her from hearing anything Zephyr said.

Another high-speed, concentrated burst of shadow energy propelled at both Zephyr and Raine, but it was blocked by a wall of water, which combined with wind, turned into a water swirling tornado and flew at Umbral.

The whispers went away, and Raine could hear Zephyr say, "I should stop her."

Raine nodded. "Hey, could you combine your water elemental with my cards? It'll be like a water balloon that bursts upon hitting her. I'm not sure if she's lying about being allergic to water, but from the way she's moving and fighting, it should be true."

She handed a couple of cards to Zephyr, and while he concentrated some of his elemental energy into them, Raine stuck her head out to find Umbral, but everything swirled black and white, where elusive shadows raided her vision. Additionally, a severe headache quickly developed, and her head spun like a carousel.

Filled with disarray, she felt Zephyr placing the cards onto her hand, and despite being unable to see, she managed to load the cards into her gun, and relying on Zephyr, shot them all in a random direction, hoping he would be able to redirect them correctly.

Feeling another strong wave of wind, followed by the sounds of water falling and explosions, Raine found herself able to see again, and saw that Umbral had been attacked directly with water hitting her. Her entire body went limp and she collapsed immediately.

Zephyr gasped and immediately ran over to Umbral. Raine, also worried for Zephyr, kept her card-gun and ran up to Umbral. Although she had suspicions of it potentially being a trap to let both their guards down, when Raine moved closer and saw a blank, lifeless expression on Umbral's face, she realised that there was no trap.

With shallow breaths, Zephyr slowly moved his hand over to Umbral to check her pulse. His shaky movements hinted that he teetered on the brink of a panic attack, mere seconds away. But then he heaved a sigh of relief, indicating that Umbral was still alive. Open, yet vacant, her eyes stared into the void, as if she had been frozen. "Umbral...? Are you there?" Zephyr asked, gently shaking Umbral.

She didn't respond. With more hesitation, Zephyr asked again. "...Ann?"

The girl's eyes shot up at Zephyr when she heard her name.

Raine looked at Zephyr with a puzzled expression. "Uh...I'm sorry." Zephyr apologised in a soft tone, lifting Umbral up. The water beneath her quickly evaporated. At that moment, Umbral's body, a mere hollow vessel, held no life. Raine figured that Ann was her real name, but knew she had pieces missing about Umbral's past.

Meanwhile, Umbral remained in Zephyr's arms, still unresponsive, like the remains of a crab's moulted shell. It seemed as if she had surrendered her existence entirely; despite the steady rhythm of her heartbeat, her mind echoed with a profound emptiness and void of thought. Even though Zephyr had lifted her back to her feet, she immediately slumped back down to the floor. Eventually, Zephyr gave up trying to get Umbral to stand upright and sat on the floor with her, supporting her back so she wouldn't completely lie down on the cold floor.

Raine assumed that Zephyr would've at least tried talking to her, but he just looked solemnly at Umbral, as if waiting expectantly for something. Raine started to wonder if this was the first time Zephyr had seen Umbral in such a state. Zephyr summoned a breeze which helped to dry Umbral's clothes, and after a few seconds, when all water had been gone, she blinked, and returned back to her usual self.

"Damn it," Umbral muttered under breath, when she saw Zephyr and Raine in front of her. "I guess I lost."

Chapter 24: Return

Zephyr, Raine, and Umbral gathered on the floor and stared at one another. Raine spoke first, and she crossed her arms while addressing Umbral. "Tell me the truth, Umbral. And no more lying. Who are you, exactly?"

Umbral sighed and spoke reluctantly. "The name of this body is Ann. She had resigned her life and allowed me, her shadow, made sentient from nightmare energy, to take over. It's why I can't handle water. I'm just a shadow using Ann's body as a puppet, so I disappear whenever her body gets in touch with a lot of water." She noticed Raine and Zephyr's puzzled expressions and decided to elaborate. "Seventeen years ago, a nightmare arrived in the waking world and got a human pregnant. The human already married another human and didn't want the child, and although she tried everything to kill the child inside of her, she failed. Eventually, she decided to end her life instead of taking care of her daughter, and her husband threw the newborn into the garbage dump of this very factory. The newborn had an older sister conceived by the two humans prior, and she had the ability to turn invisible. She took the newborn in and raised her in secret. That newborn was Ann."

"Wait, humans have abilities?" Raine asked.

"No. Now that I think about it, it is quite strange. She probably found a relic or something." Umbral shrugged. "She always wore that weird necklace. Anyway, the sister, named Liang, decided to tell her parents one day about Ann's existence. But she never returned after. She probably got killed." Umbral's words rendered Raine shocked, more so from how casually she said them. Zephyr looked equally as shocked, but neither of them interrupted. "After Ann realised that Liang would never come back, she allowed me, her shadow, to take over her body as Umbral. I am Ann, but Ann isn't me. The last time I saw Liang, she told me that she had a friend named Kaymi who ran a cat café in Kyronami city, and that I should go there if I ever left the factory. I eventually found Kaymi. She let me work at the cat café and even let me live there."

Raine could hardly speak. Meanwhile, Zephyr looked at Umbral in disbelief. "Umbra, is all of that true?"

Umbral nodded. "A while ago, I went to Oneirolepsy to talk to Katz. I've heard of him as the King of nightmares and was interested in meeting him. I used my shadow elemental powers to get to his castle, and I ended up befriending him." She smiled at the thought of befriending the King of black-dreamers, and Raine looked at her as if she was insane. "Only recently, he told me about a 'Revieras' coming to the waking world and asked me to help him stop her. I agreed."

"Why would you agree to help the King of black-dreamers, Umbral? I know you're a Vortex, but still, you're trying to assist in the destruction of Oneirolepsy," Raine sounded irritated, but managed her composure. "I just want to save the world so that my friends and I can live peacefully, and I need the Dreamkeepers to do that. I can't have you stop me from doing that. Please, don't work with Koshalv anymore."

Umbral paused, taking the time to consider everything. "I don't want to disappoint Katz. I've already told him that I'll help him stop Revieras. And he won't want to be my friend anymore."

"Umbra, will you do it for me then?" Zephyr spoke up. "I don't know how important I am to you...but I hope that I can convince you to come over to my side instead of his. I want to help Raine save the dreaming world." He inched closer to Umbral and the two stared at each other. "I don't want you to get hurt, Umbra. This King of nightmares sounds dangerous, and I know you may consider him to be your friend, but what kind of friend is he if he's only going to be your friend if you work for him?"

"He understands me," Umbral refuted. "Do you?"

"I do," Zephyr said, in a quiet tone. "I recently remembered everything about myself, Umbra. It was really bad, and I know now why I had lost my memories of my past self in the first place."

Umbral's eyes widened. "You got back your memories?"

Zephyr nodded. "I remember all the times where I'd overhear my parents talking about how they were afraid of me. How their lives would be easier if I were never there to burden them. How dangerous I was to everyone as an elemental. How I never belonged, and how my home was never home to me." He grabbed Umbral's hand. "But Umbra, now that I'm here, in Kyronami city, I feel right at home. And you are a part of it too. You're one of my only friends. And just now, when you told us everything about your life, I realised that the two of us share the same feelings and experiences. How similar we had it, where we were only seen as monsters and not for who we really are. And I'm sorry if you felt that I was rejecting your nightmare side. But I understand you, Umbra, I really do. More than anyone else."

Umbral stared at Zephyr in silence, strangely moved by his words. Then, all of a sudden, she let go of Zephyr's hand. "Wow, that was really cheesy."

"Oh, um...I'm sorry." Zephyr backed away from Umbral.

Umbral laughed at Zephyr's response. "Even though it was cheesy, it made me feel very happy. I think you're right. Maybe you understand me more than I gave you credit for. And yeah, I suppose you were never really rejecting my 'nightmare' side. You're just making sure I don't end up hurting anyone, which is boring as hell, but I get it." She then turned to Raine. "So, I won't stop you anymore. I'll support you and

Zephyr, okay?"

Although Raine had her reservations about Umbral and Zephyr, it appeared everything had been resolved, and as long as Umbral no longer antagonised Raine, she decided to accept it. "Sounds great."

"Well, then! Let's get going. I don't want to be in this factory anymore." Umbral began departing, gesturing to Zephyr and Raine to follow behind as she led them out of the factory. With the complicated layout of the factory, Raine was glad Umbral hadn't decided to just leave the two and disappear into the shadows, and soon, the three made it out and stepped outside, where the thunderstorm had calmed. The sun rose above the sea, lighting up the sky.

"Umbra, Raine, look," Zephyr gestured towards many individuals slowly waking up with a dazed expression, presumably with a million questions in their heads with nobody to answer them. "Everyone's awake now."

Raine couldn't understand the phenomenon at all, but she assumed it had something to do with either Umbral or the situation with the black-dreamers back in Oneirolepsy. "That's right! We need to get back home." She turned to Zephyr.

"Oh, yes! About that," Zephyr said, sounding reasonably excited. "I think it's because I got back my memories, but I can control my powers reasonably well now.

That means we can go back to Oneirolepsy now, Raine."

"That's great!" Every fibre of Raine's body begged to see her friends again back home. Ensuring no one lingered nearby, she then asked, "Do you know how to create a portal?"

"It's significantly easier to get into the dreaming world from Psytheon than it is the other way around," Umbral commented, speaking from experience. "You don't need to chant or wait for any astral alignment, just need an element. Zephyr has two of them, so you'll be fine."

"Ah, that's convenient." Raine smiled. "Ready then, Zephyr?"

Zephyr nodded. "I'll be back soon, Umbra."

"No need to rush. I'll be working with Kaymi at the cat café. See you two soon!" Umbral waved with thrice the speed of a normal wave before melting into her shadow on the floor and disappearing. *Being able to move around with shadows must be convenient,* Raine thought, imagining Umbral just casually popping up from the floor back at the cat café.

"Um, to be honest, Raine, I'm not really sure how to make a portal," Zephyr told her, once Umbral left.

"Oh. Er, well. Just imagine a portal in front of you and concentrate your energy there, I guess?" Not being an elemental herself, Raine wished she had asked Kegan for a how-to guide on portal summoning before.

Zephyr nodded, and within a few seconds, a portal made from water formed, swirling and swishing about. Raine marvelled at Zephyr's abundance of dream energy and stood before the portal. The cool water promised a more comfortable method of travel between the two worlds compared to a portal of straight fire, and a wave of accomplishment swept through her. She had found the last Dreamkeeper. And now she could finally go home.

* * *

The moment she planted her feet back on Oneirolepsy soil, Raine's body felt lighter, the catharsis of a burden lifted from her weary bones, like when one of Raine's magic shows ended and she could finally rest without having to worry about it anymore. In this case, however, Raine knew that she would not be able to close the curtains until the barrier was restored.

But for now, the collective gasp of Jocelyn, So-hyun, and Lilac welcomed Raine back home, and the three of them immediately ran to her in a big group hug. The world lit up as the first light of morning painted the sky with its embrace, where dawn brushed away the remnants of night and unveiled a new day. It was perfect weather for Raine to reunite with her friends once more. "We missed you so much! I was so worried," So-hyun spared Raine from dying by an excessive group hug. Her eyebrows raised as she registered the unfamiliar face of Zephyr, who awkwardly fidgeted about while standing next to Raine.

"Um...hello. My name is Zephyr." Zephyr gave an uneasy smile but relaxed a little once he saw Jocelyn waving at him excitedly with a cheerful grin.

"Oh! You're the Subliminal Dreamkeeper, right? Right? We're like, from the same motherland and all, so we're automatically cool, yeah? I'm Jocelyn!" She handed out a fist bump to Zephyr, who returned it reluctantly. Discomfort gnawed at him, evident from his darting eyes. Jocelyn then burst into a loud gasp. "Wait! I was right! The Subliminal Dreamkeeper *is* a guy! Yo, where's my hundred bucks? Dude, thank you so much!"

"Bucks? I thought we used dollars?" Zephyr asked, unable to keep up with Jocelyn's enthusiasm. "And um...you're welcome, I guess?"

Lilac introduced herself and Sir Bamesetton to Zephyr, and So-hyun, being more formal, gave a small bow.

Thrown off by the fact that Raine had yet to hear Kegan's whining of a water and air elemental being in the same proximity as him, she glanced around the campsite, his absence weighing more heavily than she'd realised. A subtle unease crept over her; he didn't know whether he had gotten in trouble or was causing some, and either way didn't like the sound of a fire hazard going unsupervised. "Where's Kegan?"

"You took a while to return. Kegan left then, saying he could sense that something was wrong in the

Nightmare realm, and that he'd go there to check for himself first. He hasn't returned yet," So-hyun explained.

"Oh, that's right! Raine, we need to hurry and help Kegan! I know he's like, super powerful and stuff, but still! I don't like not seeing him around. We need to go find him! Let's go to the Nightmare realm, like ASAP!" Jocelyn started tugging at Raine's arm impatiently.

"Wait, what? Kegan's in the Nightmare realm?" Raine doubted Kegan's capability of learning from the past, especially with the incident of Soraya and the Remnants of Keresius. Though impossible, Raine had hoped she could've at least had some time for a rest in bed and some good food. Instead, she had to travel from one hell to another. She let out a sigh. "We have to go to the Nightmare realm. But Jocelyn," Raine said in a serious tone, "You're not a Dreamkeeper. You don't have to come with us. And you shouldn't. The Nightmare realm is extremely dangerous."

"I concur. My desire is that my comrade remain unscathed whilst embarking upon this odyssey!" Lilac held up Sir Bamesetton in her arms. "Sir Bamesetton sides with me! Heed his wishes!"

Jocelyn shook her head and grabbed onto So-hyun's hand. "No. I'm going with So-hyun. I want to make sure my best friend is safe," she insisted in an unusually serious tone.

So-hyun stared at her hand holding Jocelyn's, unable to make eye contact with her. "Jocelyn, I want to make sure you're safe as well. I think you should listen to Raine."

"But wait!" Jocelyn let go of So-hyun's hand and rummaged through the pockets in her skirt. She pulled out a folded piece of blank paper and a short pencil and shouted,"Look, look! I have my ability, so I'm like, totally safe! I can like, draw a bazooka, or a rocket launcher! Or, or, or, oh, a machine gun!" She frantically started waving her paper about, trying to prove her worth to the rest of the group.

Raine didn't want to waste any more time trying to argue with Jocelyn about her going. "Okay, fine! You can come with us. But please stay safe. We all need to be careful when we're in the Nightmare realm." Something about Jocelyn being in the Nightmare realm sent Raine's heart racing, but she ignored it and decided to worry about something else. "Now, how do we get to the Nightmare realm as fast as possible?" She glanced at Lilac's bear plush, but Jocelyn raised her hand. "Ooh! What if Zephyr created a waterslide in the air, all the way from here to the Nightmare realm! Or like, I could draw out a tank, or a helicopter!"

Raine immediately regretted letting Jocelyn travel with her to the Nightmare realm.

"Um...I don't think a waterslide is necessary," Zephyr said, failing to recognise the rhetorical nature of her suggestions. "I have an alternative, though."

Jocelyn paused in her tracks. "What is it?"

"A sea serpent."

Within that very sentence, a sea serpent shot up from out of nowhere and soared into the sky, its movements like a ribbon as it swerved through the clouds and performed spins while flying towards Zephyr. The serpent's scales were a jaded turquoise, its body resembling that of a snake. It was a massive yet beautiful creature, and Raine could hear the other Dreamkeepers gasp at the sea serpent.

"You mean we get to ride that thing?" Jocelyn's jaw dropped, her entire body quivering with excitement.

Zephyr nodded and spoke as if owning a sea serpent was the most common thing in the world. "If you want to. His name is Cady." The sea serpent, having heard its name, flew over to Zephyr from above, gently landing on the grass patch like an idle aeroplane waiting for its passengers to hop on.

"Oh, yes, yes, yes, yes, yes, yes! I love you, Zephyr!" Jocelyn, without hesitation, ran over to admire Cady, ignoring the fact that she just made Zephyr incredibly flustered.

So-hyun and Raine helped to clean up the campsite while Lilac and Jocelyn chatted with Zephyr about his elemental powers. In about ten minutes, all of them were on the sea serpent, and Cady flew off.

The ride was slower than Raine initially assumed. She had thought that she was subscribing to a rollercoaster ride which was fast enough to cut through space itself, but they were all moving at a reasonable pace. Their altitude was just right, not reaching such heights that breathing became difficult,

and their speed was moderate, allowing for a calm
journey. The gentle breeze, rather than tumultuous,
provided a soothing embrace. Soon, all of them had
made themselves comfortable and were laying head
down on the serpent's back, easing their muscles and
minds. The smooth scales of the serpent made for an
easy mattress to sleep on.

Jocelyn and So-hyun slept next to each other, and
Lilac placed her head against Raine's shoulder as she
rested with Sir Bamesetton clutched in her arms. Only
Raine and Zephyr did not lose to sleep. Despite
Raine's lack of rest, and her recent dissension with
Umbral, the inclination to sleep eluded her entirely.
Her anxiety served as her caffeine, providing her with
enough stimulus to keep her fully awake.

Zephyr's gaze descended below, almost in a subtle
way of mocking those with a fear of heights, admiring
the whole of the dreaming world from above. He
hadn't been back in Oneirolepsy for twelve years now,
Raine recalled, and she could see from the look on his
face that its landscape and beauty did not disappoint
him.

Raine opened up her bag and took out her map to
ensure that everything remained in order. Surely
enough, a cyan blue pinpoint appeared, symbolising
the Subliminal Dreamkeeper. There were now three
glowing points - the Ambition Dreamkeeper, the Pure
Dreamkeeper, and the Subliminal Dreamkeeper, all in
the same proximity.

A strange new pinpoint appeared on the map directing to the Nightmare realm, specifically, the castle. Raine kept the map and focused on the present, remembering she'd yet to discuss with Zephyr.

"Zephyr," Raine started, avoiding eye contact with him. "You remember everything that happened on the football field, right?"

Zephyr didn't look back at Raine, but his expression grew solemn. "Yes, I remember. What about it?"

"It's strange. There were many people there, but nobody remembered the incident. Nayeli wasn't even remembered by Valentino, her younger brother, and you couldn't remember your best friend. Neither Jocelyn nor Valentino remembered anything about a flood in the Subliminal realm."

"Oh. I think that was my fault. Do you remember the water-cube from before?"

Raine traced back to when she first saw Zephyr in Psytheon and nodded. "I couldn't see very clearly, though."

Zephyr turned to Raine. "The water from it holds the memory of the event. It was stolen from everybody, including me. That's what I was seeing when I stared into the cube. Remnants were playing football on a grass field, but one of their faces was blurred. It was Lemar's." He rubbed his eyes, then looked up. "You said Nayeli had a younger brother?"

"Yeah, Valentino is one of Jocelyn's friends. He doesn't remember anything. But strangely enough,

Kari, who's friends with Nayeli and Valentino, could remember her. I didn't see her in the field though." Raine adopted the guise of a detective, delving into a mystery known solely to her. How did nobody remember Nayeli or Lemar? And why could Kari?

"The only thing I can think of is either a black-dreamer cancelling out your dream energy with its nightmare energy in Kari's presence, or that she was in Reverie's Space, her ability, when it happened." Raine finally decided. Despite the barrier, it had been proven with Hyrensia's story that a black-dreamer hiding in the dream realms was plausible. Besides, Kari herself told Raine she had met one before.

Zephyr nodded. "Then...Do you think you should tell them the truth?" He shifted about, uncomfortably. "I mean...I don't think I'd want to know...If my best friend, or my sibling, ever did such a thing...But it doesn't sound right either, to hide it."

Raine sighed. "I don't know. I don't think I should be the one telling them." She remembered the Nayeli she saw in Kari's pocket of reality, and she suddenly realised something. Raine had seen Rhea before in her dreams, and while Rhea had passed just like Nayeli, the former bore no ghost-like state, unlike Nayeli. Did that mean that the Nayeli in Kari's reality was nothing but a false projection?

It must be. Just an image, created from the fragments of faulty memory of a blissful child who looked up to her. Raine could hardly associate the

Nayeli she saw in Reverie's Space to be the same
Nayeli from Zephyr's memory.

Two different people, with memories of the same
individual in completely different ways, affected in
completely different ways. As much as Nayeli's
presence was a comfort to Kari, she had left Zephyr
with so many horrors and unpleasant feelings. Nayeli
wanted nothing more than to remember her, while
Zephyr's memory wanted nothing to do with her at
all, causing him to lose his memories. Either way,
both were burdened with great pain that nobody
could understand, not even themselves, leaving their
lives to be derailed in a way that could never be
justifiable.

"Do you think I'm a bad person, Raine?" Zephyr
asked, almost in an abrupt manner.

"No. Why would I think that?"

"Because I killed Lemar," Zephyr looked away. "I
only got my memories back recently, but I spent a lot
of time with him as my best friend. I hurt a lot of
people in that football field as well. I caused that
typhoon and made everyone forget the incident."

Raine thought about it for a moment, and imagined
if her loved ones had been in that football field. She
imagined if Rhea had taken Lemar's place, but she
couldn't find it in her to hate Zephyr for anything.
"It's not your fault, Zephyr. I don't want you thinking
that, either."

Zephyr nodded. "Thank you, Raine."

At least, Raine thought, Zephyr could be free from his own nightmares that hid in his lost memories. She shook her head, refusing to think about it anymore. She noticed that Jocelyn had shifted positions while she and Zephyr were talking. Was she awake the whole time?

Raine didn't know if Zephyr would ever meet Valentino or Kari, so she let it go. Before she knew it, the sky had grown dark, and the atmosphere changed drastically to one of misery and disdain - the familiar stench of the Nightmare realm. Jocelyn shifted in her 'sleep' before sitting up, her movement disturbing So-hyun from her rest as well. Lilac sensed the welcoming nightmare energy and rose too, while Raine groaned softly, knowing the next few hours would be filled with discomfort. She decided to stay as close to Zephyr as possible for his elemental nature.

Cady slowed down significantly, the nightmare energy gnawing at the serpent. Soon, all of them landed on the ground, and it disappeared into nothing more than water vapour.

"I didn't see Kegan at all when we were flying," Raine said. "Do you think he's been captured?"

"The cult regards Kegan as a menace, given his triumph over a pivotal figure within their ranks. It's not improbable that he's now become the focus of their malevolent intent," Lilac said, a rough translation being a 'yes'.

"I'm sorry, but who is Kegan?" Zephyr asked.

Raine was just about to answer him, but the air had suddenly gotten thick, and fog started to spread. Visibility dwindled as the air thickened with a ghostly mist, and soon, the strange fog swallowed the group into its embrace. The fog reeked of nightmare energy, and when Raine saw a faint silhouette of a stranger, she quickly put two and two together and realised that the fog was the result of a black-dreamer's ability being used deliberately against the Dreamkeepers.

Raine began to feel sleepy, and as her vision began to blur, she saw her friends slowly dropping to the ground, before she collapsed and blanked out.

※★ ✦ ★※
Chapter 25: Nightmare Realm

Raine panicked when she found herself in a field of dandelions, only to remember the familiar scenery from the previous dream she had. Frantically, she got up and went to find Rhea.

The sky had grown more sombre than Raine remembered, the dandelions nowhere to be found. The sun hid amongst the overwhelming clutter of stormy clouds, exposing Raine to the cold. Raine grew worried and tried to find her mother.

The picnic mat caught Raine's eye, and she ran up to it, expecting to see Rhea and Aiseura again. But only Aiseura appeared. "There you are, love," she said, as if expecting her. She patted on the picnic mat next to her, gesturing for Raine to sit down.

Raine sat down next to Aiseura. "Why am I here?" Raine asked, trying to recall what had occurred in the Nightmare realm. "Am I dreaming? Where's my mom?"

Aiseura looked at the sky. She was calm and collected, unlike Raine. "She isn't here right now. But she's alright, love. No need to worry."

Aiseura's answer hardly satisfied Raine. "I need to get back to my friends. We were in the Nightmare realm, and suddenly passed out because of an ability, and-"

"Calm down, Raine," Aiseura interrupted. "In times like these, we must gather our thoughts and face our enemies with a clear mind. It is a mistake I had made, and a lesson I learned too late."

"What do you mean?"

Aiseura took a deep breath and looked at Raine. "Do you know who I am, Raine?"

Raine stared into her eyes. She couldn't put her finger on it, but somewhere in the back of her mind, she knew the answer. She had seen Aiseura before but had never recognised her. Only a fleeting second in the past, inaccessible by Raine's memory of infancy.

Aiseura broke eye contact with her, and instead pulled a necklace which had hidden under her dress. The other half of Raine's heart-shaped necklace twinkled faintly.

Raine's shoulders slumped as Aiseura took Raine's own necklace and pieced the two halves together, forming a complete heart. "I'm your birth mother," Aiseura said, in a low voice. Her lips parted into a sad smile. "Rhea took you in as her daughter, but I am your biological family. I'm sorry I never got the opportunity to meet you."

Raine's voice trembled as she spoke, her life having been turned upside down. "What...happened?"

Aiseura pulled back from Raine, letting the two necklaces split into half again. She sighed and looked beyond the clouds. "Do you know what realm we come from, Raine?"

"The Mainland," Raine said, instinctively.

Aiseura shook her head. "The Love realm."

"Love realm? What is that?"

"There used to be seven realms, a long time ago.
There was the Mainland," Aiseura traced in the air
with her finger, outlining the shape of the Mainland.
Raine remembered spending most of her time there.
Although most people wouldn't define it as a realm
itself, Raine considered it her home. "And then the
Subliminal realm," she traced the Subliminal realm,
just slightly above the Mainland. Raine's first time in
the Subliminal realm involved her meeting with Kari
and Valentino, and she remembered the time she'd
spent at the aquarium with Lilac and Kari fondly,
wishing she could've spent more time with her friends
there.

Raine offered her own finger and traced the other
two realms she knew. "The Ambition realm, and the
Dream realm," she added, moving her finger in the
air.

Aiseura smiled. "That's right," she said, beginning to
trace an unfamiliar realm, right next to the Dream
realm. "This is the Nightmare realm," she added, in a
neutral tone. "And here is the Love realm."

The Love realm neighboured dangerously close to
the Nightmare realm. "There is also the Future realm.
Ah, I think I have a map," A map appeared next to
Aiseura on the picnic mat, seemingly from thin air.
Aiseura held out the unfamiliar map for Raine to see.
"It's an obsolete map, so there are some slight
changes compared to the map you have now," she
explained. "The reason why nobody remembers the
existence of the Love realm and the Future realm is

because both were destroyed, and the King of the Future realm had the ability to wipe out history."

Raine stared at the map in Aiseura's hands. Though she could accept the Love realm as her birthplace, she would never accept it as her home, for her heart only belonged in the Mainland where she grew up. "What happened to the Love realm and the Future realm?"

"A lot of things happened that involved betrayal and the Nightmare realm. It is not for you to know," Aiseura stroked Raine's hair and placed down the map in her lap. "I only need you to know the truth of who you really are, Raine."

"That I'm a Love Dreamer?" Raine asked, the words feeling like ash in her tongue.

"That you are the daughter of the Love realm's queen."

Her words stunned Raine.

"Your father, the King of the Love Realm, Aymeric, fell to megalomania and corruption, manipulated by Keresius, the King of nightmares," Aiseura said, a familiar name registering in Raine's mind.

"The King of black-dreamers? Isn't that Koshalv?"

"Back then, it was Keresius. I can only assume he had been killed after the Love realm met its end," Aiseura said.

The Remnants of Keresius. The cult was formed by the remnants of the former ruler of the black-dreamers? Raine thought. "Why do I need to know all this? What's going to happen?"

Aiseura smiled. "I'm very proud of you, Raine. You've come so far. You have gathered and awakened the three Dreamkeepers and made some friends whom you've helped along the way. And now you're at the final chapter. Many things will happen, and I need you to stay strong. The fate of the world is in your hands."

Raine felt afraid of having to deal with the Nightmare realm. At first, she was suspicious of Aiseura, for she had been a stranger, but now, Raine was depending on Aiseura for answers. She seemed to know more about Raine than herself, and the Love realm was just as a mystery as before. "I wish you had seen what the Love realm was like, Raine. It was beautiful," Aiseura commented, with a nostalgic look in her eye. "But I'm glad to have met you regardless."

Raine fell silent.. She had too many questions but couldn't find the voice to ask any of them. "Ah, this is important, Raine," Aiseura said, suddenly remembering something. "As you know, the Dreamkeepers contain a key fragment in their souls. There is a room locked away in the Nightmare King's castle in which lies several chambers that will be used to merge the keys together and unlock a powerful tool that will help you save the world." Aiseura shifted her body and her eyebrows furrowed, looking at Raine with a stern and almost resentful expression. "*I need you to eradicate the Nightmares and their realm.* It is the only way Oneirolepsy will find peace. The tool will help you accomplish that. Do not fail."

Raine felt the air thicken. Aiseura wore the face of a
bitter queen. One that failed to protect her realm,
people, and family. "They are all bad individuals,
Raine. Eliminate the Nightmare realm. Remember the
date where Love was torn apart, the same day you
were born, and taken away to safety in Rhea's arms."
Her voice sent chills down Raine's spine. "Do you
understand, Revieras?"

Raine resisted the urge to gulp and kneel before
Aiseura. "I understand," she said.

"Then you shall go, and save this world."

✸ ✸ ✸

Raine snapped back to the Nightmare realm. She felt
annoyed, considering she had about a thousand
questions left answered and had herself kicked out of
her own dream. She was now in a silent and foreign
space, its eerie vacancy disturbing Raine, along with
the smell of decay which lingered in the air. Confined
within a barren cell, fatigue made a home in Raine's
body. Handcuffs tethered Raine to the floor,
restricting any movement at all.

Raine tried to break free of the handcuffs by
squirming her wrists around and trying to loosen
them. She'd seen other magicians tied up to train
tracks and successfully breaking out before the train
could run them over, but alas, she lacked experience
and couldn't escape.

Her legs were bound to the floor as well, and despite the numerous attempts of kicking around, it only served to exhaust her without achieving any liberation from her restraints.

Raine sighed and thought about the other Dreamkeepers. She had yet to see anyone else, friend or foe, and loathed the isolation. Even when she had been kidnapped by Umbral, she wasn't completely alone. But here Raine rested, on the cold floor, left to rot.

The parasitic nature of nightmare energy leeched off Raine and sucked up what little remained of her dream energy, preventing her from doing anything. Panic rose as she imagined the potential torture her friends could face, and she grew restless.

It had not even been confirmed whether Raine was even in Koshalv's castle. For all she knew, her kidnapper could have no affiliation with the King at all. Enfeebled by nausea, her mind clouded with negativity.

Raine tried to shout for help, but even her voice had abandoned her.

In the end, Raine accepted the futility of seeking help, and she stared longingly at the exit door in front of her. Raine didn't like the idea of waiting for an indefinite amount of time for somebody to come to her aid, but what else could she do? She worried that if she did wait and do nothing, danger would only come to the Dreamkeepers and Kegan. She didn't even know if they were in the same place as her. What

if the black-dreamers separated her from them? She
was doubtful that they knew what to do. Raine also
didn't know what to do. Raine found it hard to trust
anything, and any optimism had been stamped out a
long time ago.

Raine's mental fatigue caught up to her, and she
stared down at her own shadow, exhaustion
preventing her from thinking anymore. At this rate,
her shadow reigned more free than her physical body.
She wondered if she should just fall asleep and try to
find Aiseura, but she didn't like the sound of that
either, so all she did was focus on the dark, empty,
hollow shadow beneath her.

Suddenly, the shape of her shadow started to contort,
and just as Raine accepted that she had gone insane, a
smirking Umbral popped out, and when she laid her
eyes upon Raine, she let out a happy, "Hi again,
Raine!"

Raine couldn't believe it. "Umbral?" Her voice failed
to project the extent of her disbelief, and instead, she
sounded disappointed and tired. Umbral frowned at
Raine's lack of enthusiasm for her welcome, but let it
slide. "What are you doing here, Umbral? I thought
you were back at Psytheon at the cat café."

Umbral shrugged. "Do you really think that I'd just
pass up the opportunity to hang out with you, Zephyr,
and Katz- I mean, Koshalv? Besides, I have some
reverse kidnapping to do."

"Reverse kidnapping?"

"Y'know, I kidnapped you earlier and everything. Yeah, I'm making up for that now that we're here. I mean, seriously, how many times have you been kidnapped, Raine?"

"More than enough for a lifetime. Could you help me out of these, please?" She shook her wrists and feet, letting the cuffs make a jingle.

Umbral kneeled down and scrutinised the cuffs that Raine was bound to. "Sure, just give me a minute or two."

Raine suddenly felt suspicious of her, but Umbral freed her from her shackles without any tricks. "Thank you. Do you know where we are?" Raine attempted to stand up, but her body immediately toppled over.

Umbral cocked her head, uncharacteristically worried. "How are you going to get around the castle in this state?"

"I don't know. I don't have anything on me." She missed the map, her bag, and her dream energy. "Never mind, I think I'll be alright." She tried to stand up again. This time, Umbral helped her up, wrapping Raine's arm around her shoulder for support.

"Don't worry, Raine! I'll be your bodyguard!" She beamed with much confidence.

Raine hardly believed her.

She stumbled along with Umbral, fumbling with the lock of the cell door. Somehow, she felt even worse with Umbral supporting her. Once they figured they would need to break the door down, Umbral immediately dropped Raine and attacked the door with shadow blasts.

Once the door ripped apart, Umbral picked the unhappy Raine up from the floor and they both stepped out. "We need to find Zephyr, right?"

"We also need to find Jocelyn, So-hyun, Lilac, and Kegan," replied Raine.

"Alright, I don't know who any of them are, but let's go!" Not a minute had passed after Umbral promised to help Raine did she immediately leave her behind and started exploring the castle's interiors.

Raine sighed and clutched her stomach while following Umbral, who had already taken the lead. *Best bodyguard ever,* Raine thought, watching Umbral carelessly frolicking around the dark hallways.

The air weighed heavily with a palpable sense of dread, and Raine felt uneasy walking through them. Umbral, on the other hand, acted no less than a child at the circus. Her quick footsteps echoed across the empty halls, clearly not worried at all if somebody were to hear her. "Aren't there any guards around? I think we should lower our volume," Raine suggested.

"Hm? I work for Koshalv, they won't attack me," Umbral said, nonchalantly.

Raine was dumbfounded by her logic. "We're walking together, they're going to attack *me* if you grab their attention!"

The two of them swerved to another hallway, and Raine let out a gasp when she saw a group of guards in armour lying unmoving on the floor. Evidently, someone else had already taken care of the threat.

Umbral kneeled down to inspect one of the fallen guards. She lifted up his helmet after examining his injuries and the scratches on the armour. "That's odd. He was mauled to death."

Raine raised her eyebrow and bent down to check for herself, but the sound of footsteps from the opposite end of the hallway made her flinch back up, and she pulled back to hide by the corner of the wall. "I can't fight at all," she whispered to Umbral. The nightmare energy around exacerbated Raine's condition, as well as the fact that her only weapon, the card-gun, was not currently in her possession. She couldn't pull any magic tricks to slip herself out of the situation either, with her barely being able to stand.

Somebody turned the corner, and Raine was met with a familiar face. However, Umbral, by instinct, decided to throw a punch, and her eyes met the wrath of sand. "Ah! What the hell?" she cried, scraping the sand particles off her eyes.

"That's your own damn fault for trying to punch me," Jeo-sa replied, crossing his arms. "We meet again, Revieras." next to him was Lilac, who gripped onto one of the guard's swords. Raine frowned at Jeo-sa's presence and Sir Bamesetton's absence.

Lilac gasped. "Ah, there you are! I harboured grave concerns for your safety. When we fell into the clutches of those nightmarish fiends, I dreaded the worst fate for the esteemed leader of dreams!"

"I was worried about you too, Lilac. Why is Jeo-sa with you?"

"A group of elementals and I went to infiltrate the castle to find a friend of ours from the academy. I just happened to find her in one of the cells, and now she wants me to help you and the Dreamkeepers," Jeo-sa explained, although he didn't sound very happy upon seeing Raine again.

"Thanks for the help," Raine turned to Lilac. "Where's Sir Bamesetton?"

"It is a bold and strategic choice to part ways with Sir Bamesetton in pursuit of our missing comrades. His reputation for both reliability and prowess doth indeed grant some solace in these perilous times. May fortune favour your separate quests, and may our reunion be swift and triumphant!"

Jeo-sa rolled his eyes. Meanwhile, Umbral eyed Raine with a confused yet amused grin. "You gonna introduce me to your friends?"

"No time. We have to find the rest."

"Behind you, Revieras!" Lilac shouted.

A guard creeped up behind Raine, bringing down a sharp sword at Raine. Umbral acted quickly and pulled Raine away from danger, while also kicking the guard down. Unfortunately, all Umbral managed to do was injure her foot by kicking against heavy armour.

Lilac charged and clashed swords against the guard, while Jeo-sa started to fill the inside of the guard's armour with sand. The guard gave a muffled yell and collapsed after suffocating from the sand.

"Take his sword, there's more guards coming," Jeo-sa demanded.

Raine picked up the sword and looked in front of her. True to Jeo-sa's words, there were now about five or six guards charging at the four of them with swords.

Raine felt herself getting sick from the nightmare energy, and when Lilac managed to knock out a sword from a guard's grip, the latter decided to fight using nightmare-energy channelled attacks, practically liquifying Raine's muscles.

Umbral pulled Raine away while Lilac and Jeo-sa dealt with the guards.

Lilac wielded her sword and refused to falter, her living in the Nightmare realm allowed her to be nullified to its effects, unlike Raine. Jeo-sa had the upper advantage, being an elemental, and fought hard without mercy.

Jeo-sa ended up being the only one who actually managed to kill the guards. The hallways littered with sand and corpses dressed in armour. "You all are useless," he commented, receiving immediate complaints from all three girls.

The ground shook with each footstep. Lilac, who immediately recognised it, had her eyes light up when she saw Sir Bamesetton running toward her in the distance.

Ignoring Umbral's shriek of horror, Lilac and Sir Bamesetton reunited. "Sir Bamesetton's counsel

shines as a beacon of hope in this dire situation. A
hallway leading to cells where our companions may be
confined has been unfurled! It is a path we must tread
with haste and determination. Let us press forward
and rescue our friends from their lamentable
captivity!"

Raine found it progressively difficult to understand
Lilac, but then the bear picked the four of them up
(with Jeo-sa and Umbral giving a horrified shout) and
immediately charged on.

Once Sir Bamesetton reached the aforementioned
hallway, Raine and the others hopped down and
began to investigate each and every room available.
Despite lacking any defence, Raine entered each door,
hoping to see her friends. However, she only saw
angry black-dreamers confined in dirty jail cells
behind thick bars and dirty mattresses on the
bug-infested ground. Raine grimaced every time she
found a prisoner in their respective cells, feeling
horrible for her friends who were trapped in the very
same filthy cages.

"Hey, I think I found them!" Umbral called.
Everyone followed her voice into another cell room,
where Umbral had already managed to tear the door
off its frames. Raine almost fainted from relief when
she saw Jocelyn sketching on a piece of paper with her
pencil, and So-hyun, who immediately ran up smiling
at the sight of Raine and the others coming to their
rescue. Sir Bamesetton ripped the bars apart and
granted the two freedom once more.

"Oh, thank goodness you came to save us, Raine!" Jocelyn immediately kept her sketching materials and trapped Raine into a hug. After a brief moment, she let go and turned to Umbral. "That was impressive, kicking down the door to take down the guard at the same time."

Umbral smiled. "What guard?"

The six of them caught sight of a crushed guard with the broken door resting on top of him. Nobody had even noticed he had been killed by Umbral, much less acknowledge his existence. "Oh. That guard." Umbral shrugged. "Anyway, we need to find Zephyr."

"And Kegan!" Jocelyn pointed out.

"Who?"

"They're both elementals, so I'm pretty sure they'll be locked up somewhere else in another section of the castle," Raine said. "We have to go explore the rest of the castle. It'll be dangerous. Are you feeling okay, Jocelyn?"

"Not gonna lie, I feel like I'm about to topple over like some playing blocks," Jocelyn sighed. "But I'll be fine! I just sketched the sickest piece of work without a reference, too! Isn't that like, awesome? Let's go find the elementals! Ah, by the way, who are you guys?" She pointed at Jeo-sa and Umbral.

Raine sighed as Jocelyn spent the next five minutes getting everyone to introduce themselves in the dimly lit cell.

✳ ✳ ✳

"You are aware of the punishment that comes along with high treason, yes?" Andrei paced left and right with a perpetual frown on his face, holding onto a blade laced with intimidating spikes and sharp edges. Kegan tried to hide his impressed reaction towards Andrei's effortless blade spinning tricks, feeling more entertained than afraid. In fact, Kegan would have felt more threatened if Andrei held a fire extinguisher instead.

"Sorry man, I'm not good with how the constitution works here. Do you go around tying people up and giving them villain speeches or am I just that special?" Kegan responded. He had managed to piss off Andrei when he discovered that his ability didn't work on Kegan, and instead of Kegan falling asleep to the fog, he riddled Andrei with mockery.

"You're tied up and covered in blood, take this a little more seriously or else I'll kill you instantly." Andrei pointed the blade at Kegan.

Kegan scoffed, refusing to let go of his snarky attitude despite being strapped onto a torturing instrument which stretched and probably dislocated his limbs enough to never visit a chiropractor. He only managed to escape having his joints completely dislocated by acting as if he'd enjoyed it (because he's totally not a masochist) and had Andrei reward his arousement with a hundred cuts from his blade. Usually, by now, Kegan would have reduced Andrei's body to ash, but a relic hidden in the room prevented fire from igniting in the room, according to Andrei himself. "Whatever," Kegan replied, getting annoyed.

He really wished his ability included the nullification of relics as well as abilities.

"You have no escape, and you are at my mercy. At least beg for your life." Andrei kicked Kegan several times, pulling his blade against his skin. "Koshalv has given me permission to execute you when I wish. But I prefer torture. Death is merely an easy way out of your crimes."

Kegan stifled a cry of pain and glared at Andrei. He knew he had limited time to escape, and he grew irritated by his lack of power. He had only wanted to return to the Nightmare realm temporarily because he had a hunch that something was wrong, and after meeting Vanity and Andrei, he ended up in the castle.

"You're aware that I actually enjoy torture, right? I'm having a lot of fun right now," he let out a chuckle and grinned happily, trying to ignore the burning pain from his open wounds.

Andrei didn't look impressed at all. He withdrew his blade. "Do you want me to waterboard you, elemental? Should I drag you to a waterfall and push you off the edge as you drown?"

"Oh no, water, I'm so afraid," Kegan replied, in a mocking tone. He already had his fire elemental powers ripped away from him, so being threatened with water seemed hardly necessary. "How are you going to get enough water to scare me, hm? There are no waterfalls around here."

Suddenly, the doors opened. Andrei turned, and gasped, because in a moment, about a hundred waterfalls burst into the room, and a sea serpent shot out to strangle and attack Andrei. The serpent let out a roar and pulled Andrei into the rising water, letting him drown.

The sea serpent disappeared with the sudden flood of water, and Kegan felt thankful for the height of the torturing instrument saving him from getting drenched. A dreamer he didn't recognise stood before him.

"Oh, um, was that too much? I'm sorry, I really didn't mean to cause a flood like that." He closed the doors behind him and walked towards Kegan. "Are you alright? You look like you're about to die. I don't really know how to help. Um..." The dreamer searched around anxiously and found some keys which had been washed onto the floor. He picked it up and freed Kegan by unlocking the cuffs.

Kegan immediately hopped off the rack, only to forget that he had been severely tortured just a minute ago, and was hardly in the condition to stand. The dreamer managed to catch him before he fell, and he tried to hide his embarrassment with a joke. "Woah, I think you're getting too comfortable with a nightmare now," he laughed.

The dreamer hardly seemed threatened. "Oh. You're a nightmare?" He asked, surprised. "You're not going to hurt me, are you?"

Kegan recollected Andrei drowning about a minute ago and decided he didn't want that happening to him. "Nah, we're cool. I'm friends with Revieras. The name's Kegan. Who're you?"

"I'm Zephyr. You said you were friends with Raine?"

"Yeah. Hang on, are you the Subliminal Dreamkeeper?"

Zephyr nodded hesitantly.

"Sounds awesome. You're a water elemental, right?"

"And air."

Kegan raised his eyebrows. "No way. You're a double elemental, and both elements are against my own? Dude, how dare you."

"Um, I'm sorry about that. Does that mean you're a fire elemental?" Zephyr asked, rather uncomfortable now.

"The best fire elemental you'll ever get to know," Kegan said, proudly. "Now, let's find Raine and take down Koshalv for good!" He proceeded to pull away from Zephyr and attempted to march out the door, only to slump back to the floor.

Zephyr ran to Kegan and lifted him up, this time ensuring he wouldn't suddenly run away from him. "Do you want me to bring you out of the castle?"

"Nah, I'm fine- ow!" Kegan winced as Zephyr turned his arm so that he could take a proper look at his wounds.

"Oh, I'm sorry," Zephyr quickly apologised, looking at the blood spilling from the wound. "Um, I could try to use my elemental magic to help with the wound."

Kegan didn't like the sound of a water elemental dumping his magic on a fire elemental such as himself. He sighed and wished he could swap abilities with Raine.

* * *

Raine sighed and wished she could swap abilities with Kegan. Not because she wanted to be a crazy pyromaniac, but because she didn't want to deal with the nightmare energy in the very air she breathed, and she also felt bad about not being able to properly fight against the king's guards. Jeo-sa led the group, being the most competent fighter out of all of them. He wore his usual frown on his face, but even Raine could recognise his exhaustion. She felt guilty that he had ended up helping the Dreamkeepers when he really wanted to find his missing friend.

They went down a flight of stairs, the floor covered with a carpet in a dark shade with strange patterns and symbols. Raine let out a sigh of relief, free from walking in narrow and foreboding hallways. "No sight of anyone," Raine commented.

The entrance gates stood boldly across the flight of stairs. Despite how much Raine loathed the castle, she had no motivation to leave the place. She had things to do.

Jeo-sa rushed through each room without wasting any time, unlike everybody else who bothered to turn their heads like owls just to admire the castle's beauty. The group made their way to a new room and walked past an archway, revealing a shifting mosaic of swirling shadows that painted the overhead ceiling, like a turbulent sea of darkness, occasionally revealing glimpses of starless skies. Raine could've sworn she heard whispers within the walls.

"I think we're in the throne room, guys!" Jocelyn pointed in front of her, where a regal throne sat on a dais. An opulent curtain veiled the large window behind the throne, with large intimidating pillars towering over everyone's heads.

Earlier, Jocelyn had been running around with Umbral and Lilac, going on a tangent about the architectural structure of the castle. Although Raine couldn't make out all the technical terms Jocelyn spewed out, she couldn't deny the elegance and beauty of the castle. Had she not been so sick, she probably would have run around with Jocelyn too.

"Ah, the throne room, a chamber resplendent in its regal splendour, indeed does it captivate the senses with its majestic beauty. As we stand within its grandeur, let us remain vigilant and steadfast, for beauty often conceals treacherous secrets in realms such as these," Lilac dramatised, giving a tour of the throne room to Sir Bamesetton, who had now returned to a stuffed toy.

Large chandeliers suspended in the ceiling brightened up the throne room. Raine glanced back and saw Umbral throwing her legs up as she rested on the throne, leaning back comfortably with no care in the world. "Umbral, I don't think you should do that,"

she said, watching Umbral crossing her legs on the
armrests.

"Why not?" Umbral asked.

Just then, the sound of the entrance gates from the
main hall opening could be heard. Before anyone
could figure out what to do, a black-dreamer stood by
the open doorway. He wore all black, allowing his
sharp purple eyes to stand out. His tousled black hair
had a few strands falling casually across his forehead,
complimenting his framing features. He looked just as
surprised as Raine and the rest of the group upon
seeing one another. Within the spur of the moment,
Lilac and Umbral recognised him instantly.

Raine felt nightmare energy overwhelming her entire
body, and she collapsed. Jocelyn held onto So-hyun
for support when her legs failed her. The stranger
pulled out a gun and aimed it at Jeo-sa.

"'Sup, bro!" Umbral greeted enthusiastically, with a
hint of rebellion in her voice. She didn't seem
threatened at all and hadn't left the seat of the throne.
She leaned forward and gave a casual wave.

Everyone was surprised to find Umbral still alive
within the next two seconds. "Umbral. Don't call me
that," the black-dreamer spoke with an annoyed but
calm voice. He sounded more tired, if anything. As a
matter of fact, he looked like he had just climbed a
mountain without any gear in stormy weather.

"What? We are siblings though. Well, half-siblings.
We have the same father, Katz."

Silence overtook the room, and for a second, it seemed that Umbral had discovered a way to paralyse everyone using her words alone.

Koshalv's eyes widened for a second, but after a second they lowered again, and he spoke in a resigned voice. "Of course. And you didn't tell me."

"I like to keep the element of surprise," Umbral grinned, finally getting up from the throne, but she had barely managed to walk down the dais before Jeo-sa charged at Koshalv, only to be met with firing bullets from Koshalv's gun. The bullets shot out with a loud bang, but Jeo-sa created a barrier using his sand to stop them.

The loud gunshots caused tears to well up in So-hyun's eyes, with Jocelyn gripping onto her for dear life as the room around her spun endlessly. Raine knew that she wouldn't be able to hold out for any longer.

Lilac ran and helped her up. "Lilac, the two of us will find the chamber room," Raine instructed, standing up and gesturing to So-hyun, whose entire body trembled with fear, but still trying to assist Jocelyn. "The two of you find Zephyr and Kegan."

"Good plan, me and the sand-guy will stay here to fight Katz- I mean, Koshalv!"

"Don't you dare call me-" Jeo-sa started, but he stopped himself, and ducked away from the scene.

Raine wondered if Jeo-sa would really retreat from the fight, but then she noticed his hair standing on its ends.

A burst of purple illuminated the surroundings, nearly blinding Raine. A loud crash followed, with a crater-like depression replacing the ground where Jeo-sa once stood.

Raine glanced at Koshalv by the open doorway, wondering if it was an ability of his, but then she saw another dreamer standing by his side. "Jeong!" Jeo-sa called, in shock.

A red-haired dreamer, supposedly the friend Jeo-sa had been looking for, wore an oversized purple jacket and although being a dreamer, sided next to Koshalv with a grim face. He hardly acknowledged Jeo-sa and instead ran at him.

"Jeong-i! What are you doing?" Jeo-sa dodged Jeong-i's attack, but Koshalv snuck up to him while Jeong-i distracted him and managed to kick Jeo-sa down, shooting at him.

"Go, now!" Raine shouted.

Lilac quickly dragged Raine away, and So-hyun carried Jocelyn out of the throne room, allowing everyone to split paths. Raine felt a pang of guilt tug at her heart as she heard Jeo-sa yelling in pain from the gunshot.

Jocelyn and So-hyun fled the throne room, and just as Lilac barely touched the exit, she quickly backed away. A crash of lightning appeared right in front of the doorway, almost killing Raine and Lilac instantly.

Rapid strikes of lightning flashed, causing everything to go bright every few milliseconds. Raine only realised now that Jeong-i was a lightning elemental.

"Hiyah!" Umbral threw a kick at Jeong-i and bounced up and down, teleporting everywhere with the help of shadows. Distracting Jeong-i, Jeo-sa got up and attacked Koshalv.

Raine and Lilac managed to leave the throne room right before Koshalv shot up at the chandelier, allowing it to fall right where Umbral, Jeo-sa, and Jeong-i were fighting.

※ ※ ※

Umbral immediately dissipated back into the shadows the moment the chandelier dropped. The chandelier's delicate crystal and glass components, previously bathed in soft light, fractured into countless shards, each glinting malevolently as they cascaded downward. A mesmerising spectacle of destruction unfolded, as if stars themselves were plummeting from the heavens. It gave a crash louder than the sound of the initial gunshot as the glass shattered everywhere, causing Jeong-i to get scrapped. Luckily, some last-second built sand structures protected Jeo-sa, but now a bigger issue had surfaced.

Sparks ignited by the bullet's impact smouldered dangerously near the flammable carpet, and thanks to Jeong-i's previous strikes of lightning, the throne room caught fire almost instantly.

Umbral didn't want to risk walking into fire just to save an elemental she didn't know. And besides, she couldn't use her shadow travelling ability on others. In the end, she backed out to the main hall and crawled out of Katz's shadow.

"Seriously, Umbral?" Katz groaned as he watched her appear beneath him.

Umbral quickly stood up to Katz's level and watched the once empty archway now completely filled with orange flames. She kept her eye there, waiting for either Jeong-i or Jeo-sa to run into view, but all Umbral could hear was unintelligible screams blocked by the cackling fire, before they ceased. "Why do you look like you're on death's door?"

"Remnants of Keresius."

"Oh." Umbral paused a little. "Are you going to fight me, then?"

"Should I?"

Umbral shrugged. "I don't know whose side I'm on, to be honest." she watched Katz's face for any sign of emotion. He remained unfazed, and Umbral took it as a sign to talk to him. "I didn't manage to follow your orders, and I didn't capture Raine. I don't want to stop her anymore."

Katz's expression remained neutral. "Does that mean you're going to actively stop me from accomplishing my goal?"

Umbral's eyes were fixed onto his right hand, which was holding his gun. "Raine told me you were using me." she said, wondering if she would meet one of his bullets in the next minute or so.

"Umbral, I never intended to use you. And anyway, you were the one who approached me in the first place. I merely gave you a role. But it seems now that you're objecting to said role. I won't force you to do anything you don't want to do, Umbral, but if you try to stop me, I won't hesitate to hurt you."

"Then you're saying that we're friends?" Umbral asked, excitedly, her eyes lighting up. When Katz gave her an irritated glare, Umbral giggled and changed her question. "Hey, I never said anything about stopping you. I don't want to choose one or the other team, okay?"

Katz nodded, seemingly satisfied with Umbral's answer.

"Want a half-sibling hug?"

"Stop that."

Umbral pouted, but then saw Katz's expression go blank. She tilted her head, watching him cautiously, like a cat waiting to pounce on a rat. A few moments flew by, and Katz shook his head, returning to his senses. Before Umbral could say anything, Katz spoke in an urgent and unusual panicked tone. "I need to go. Umbral, please just go back home."

Umbral stood idly as she watched Katz leave the main hall. *Did he get another vision?* Umbral knew that Katz possessed multiple abilities - something she's always found cool about him. One of these said abilities included being able to see a fragment of the near future, either in a dream or a vision. Umbral assumed something less than pleasant would soon occur, evident by his uncharacteristic anxiousness. She only wished he would've told her what he'd seen.

Umbral shrugged and decided not to question it - the fate of Oneirolepsy was hardly any of her business. *I guess I'll just go home, like Katz said.* She thought back to Zephyr. Even though she had come back for Raine, part of her worried about Zephyr, even though she knew the amount of power he held.

She let out a sigh and decided to put her trust in Zephyr and the others. Anyway, if she never saw Zephyr again, Raine would be the first person she would go after. With a final glance of the castle and the burning throne room, Umbral melted into her own shadow, leaving Oneirolepsy's fate in the hands of the Dreamkeepers.

※★✦★※
Chapter 26: Chambers I

"Are you sure you're alright?" Zephyr asked Kegan for the thousandth time. It had been amusing at first, watching a dreamer worry needlessly for a nightmare, but once Kegan practically turned into a broken record by repeating the same 'don't worry about it' over and over again, he found the idea of running away from Zephyr to be a tempting one.

The two exited the torture room long ago and now ventured into the depths of the unexplored castle, scaling the tight halls. Kegan recovered enough to walk on his own again, and while he still lacked enough energy to use his elemental magic, he trusted Zephyr to take down whatever enemy that the two would face.

Although Zephyr originally wanted to try helping Kegan recover by using his elemental powers, Kegan denied vehemently, not wanting to deal with any water or air that could potentially extinguish him. In fact, Kegan would rather take multiple infected wounds than to have Zephyr touch him with his water elemental magic. "Where do you think the others are?" Zephyr asked nervously. They had been walking alone for a good ten minutes now.

Kegan imagined what Raine and the others were up to. He lacked information, but having Zephyr next to him at least told Kegan of their presence somewhere

in the castle, and that Raine had already returned
from Psytheon.

That made four dreamers together in the castle, and
possibly Jocelyn. Kegan knew of Jocelyn's
unreasonable eagerness to step foot into the
Nightmare realm, despite the nightmare energy
potentially ailing her, and he also knew that Raine
would not allow Jocelyn to be faced with unnecessary
danger. Kegan wasn't sure who got their way in the
end, but having Jocelyn around, albeit a stupid idea,
sounded nice.

"Knowing the nightmares around, they've probably
already tried capturing them. And knowing the
dreamers, they've probably already taken them
down," Kegan replied, confidently. "Oh, hey, stairs."

The stairs in question referred to the stone steps
hidden by the corner of a lonely room, leading down
to a dark and claustrophobic underground. From
where Kegan was standing, he could smell the cold
and damp air, the steps releasing haunting echoes and
a feeling of isolation. Perfect for a mini adventure
with his new best friend. "Let's head down!"

"I don't think that's a very good idea," Zephyr gently
opposed, peeking down the stairs. The darkness
shrouded much of the surroundings, leaving little to
be discerned. "Why would they be in a basement?"

Kegan shrugged. "The place that'll be looked for the
least is the place that's the most unexpected."

Zephyr didn't seem very convinced, but he didn't
argue. Kegan himself also didn't really believe what he

had just said - he just spilled random nonsense to convince him, though now he felt a little bad for misleading the duo. Nonetheless, Kegan began descending the stairs, holding his hand up against the wall for support.

Zephyr hesitantly followed behind him, but eventually quickened his pace so that he could walk next to Kegan to ensure he didn't fall. Kegan could feel anticipation revolting against his chest, like how he always felt when he prepared to set things on fire.

Each footfall echoed through the confined space, the sound reverberating like ghostly whispers in the hollow chamber. The ceiling, once high above, began to descend, forcing Kegan to stoop slightly as he continued his descent into the depths.

Finally, the two reached the basement. Darkness clogged the space, accompanied by a musty aroma. Kegan accepted it as the norm, while Zephyr on the other hand, looked extremely worried for both him and Kegan. "Are you sure this is a good idea?" Zephyr asked, seeing Kegan's injuries.

"Why are you whispering? This is the best part of our exploration so far," Kegan stated, walking as if he had been commanded to. A heavy wooden door presented itself to Kegan, and he opened it without hesitation. "Oh, hey, I found their wine cellar."

Zephyr's head perked up, hearing the hinges creak in protest. That seemed to have worsened his concerns, but Kegan had already entered the wine cellar, and he had no choice but to follow.

Coolness pervaded within the air, carrying with it the earthy scent of ageing wood and the faint aroma of wine. Cobwebs draped across corners, and the play of torchlight and shadow danced upon the stone walls, creating an atmosphere that felt both ancient and alive.

The heart of the wine cellar revealed itself in rows upon rows of oak barrels, each one bearing the weight of history and the promise of time's alchemy. They stood like sentinels, their curved surfaces marked with vintages and labels long since faded. Dusty bottles lay nestled within wooden racks, their shapes distorted by years of ageing, the contents within hidden treasures.

Kegan picked up a bottle of wine, a layer of dust immediately transferring onto his fingers. He examined it, even though he had barely any knowledge of alcohol, before handing it over to Zephyr. "Want a drink?" he asked jokingly.

"Um, no," Zephyr said, pushing the bottle of wine back to Kegan. He then gave an inquisitive look. "Are you even old enough to drink?"

Kegan frowned. "I'm only like three years younger than you."

Zephyr took a few seconds to do the calculation in his head. "You act younger than you are," he commented. Kegan could hardly discern whether the remark was intended as a compliment or an insult, and Zephyr gave no implication whether it was one or the other.

Just then, Kegan noticed a shadow appearing by the wooden door. He looked up, and in a split second, the guard by the door had thrown a spear, its sharp edge directed at Zephyr. It flew by too soon for Kegan to be able to do anything about the spear, and he watched as the spear plunged into Zephyr's chest.

A nightmare in armour narrowed his sharp eyes, the scar on his right cheek grabbing the attention of anyone who looked at his face. "You're not supposed to be here." He wore a strange gadget on his head akin to goggles, presumably his relic.

Zephyr screamed and dropped the bottle of wine in his hand onto the ground. It shattered and spilled its contents everywhere, and one of the glass pieces managed to find its way into Kegan's skin.

With the spear out of the guard's hands, Kegan took another wine bottle closest to him and threw it at the guard as an attack. The guard easily dodged it by backing away, but then Kegan ignited a fire right there, allowing the alcohol to fuel the fire, which let it rise quickly to create a barrier dividing the entrance of the wine cellar from the guard.

Kegan went over to Zephyr and pulled the spear out of his chest, feeling a little sorry upon seeing him resist tears from leaking out. "Can you summon your weird water dragon thing to get us out?" He asked, holding onto Zephyr to and for support.

Zephyr looked at the raging fire at the entrance, then at Kegan, who nodded. "I can try."

The sea serpent manifested itself from Zephyr's elemental magic and broke several wine bottles as its body grew bigger than the room could hold, its water-like shape solidifying into scales. Zephyr and Kegan got on, and the sea serpent charged right into the fire.

At the same time, Zephyr used his air elemental powers to summon a vortex-like magic to push the flames away from the two, allowing the sea serpent to flow through. The guard, who had been standing by, didn't even get a chance to react, for the sea serpent then attacked the guard with a direct hit. Kegan then used the remaining fire combined with Zephyr's magic to create a fire-whirlwind spell and launched it at the guard, scorching him into oblivion.

The fire eventually died out, and the sea serpent reduced to evaporating water. Zephyr and Kegan landed on the ground, now out of the wine cellar, with the wooden door now gone and several priceless bottles shattered, and a corpse lying next to them. "Oh, it's hardly a fair fight against two elementals," Kegan laughed, amazed by how well the two coordinated their moves together.

Zephyr gave a slight nod, still hurt by the spear attack from earlier. Kegan was about to offer him an 'are you okay' before he heard noises from upstairs, and prepared for more guards to descend, but he gave a happy gasp once he found Jocelyn and So-hyun walking down the stone steps.

"Kegan! Zephyr!" Jocelyn smiled brightly, but her face fell when she saw the injured state of the two. The moment they reached the end of the staircase, Jocelyn let go of So-hyun and immediately ran to hug Kegan, though it was more of a collapse than an embrace. "Oh my dreams, I'm so glad you're still alive!" she cried, changing the 'okay' to 'still alive' for obvious reasons.

Kegan didn't really know how to react to her hug and remained frozen until Jocelyn finally pulled away to hug Zephyr as well, who also had a similar reaction to Kegan, acting as if he had never been hugged before. "We have to find Raine and the others now! Maybe she can heal the two of you," Jocelyn pulled the two back to the staircase, where So-hyun waited.

"I just told Raine," So-hyun stated, not looking up from her phone. After a few seconds, it seemed she got a reply, for her eyes had widened. "She found the room. We have to head back up."

Although Kegan desperately wanted to explore the rest of the basement, he knew the Dreamkeepers took precedence over his desires. "Right, let's go then!"

❋ ❋ ❋

Katz ran down to the basement as fast as he could, panic growing within each second. He received a vision whilst talking with Umbral, and what he saw hardly pleased him. Although he knew that his visions always came true, a part of him hopelessly prayed that it wouldn't, despite him knowing of its impossibility.

But he didn't want to think about that. Even if Katz couldn't stop the vision from coming true, he still wanted to be by his best friend before he died. The vision of Alaric being killed by the two dreamer elementals haunted his mind and pushed him to move even faster.

For the past week, he had been out of the castle, making sure the nightmares didn't end up blowing the entire dreaming world into smithereens. He had met and saved Vanity from getting killed, even though he didn't really want to - he just needed to make sure she didn't cause any more trouble.

Katz had gotten Alaric, the head of the guards, to fix whatever had been lost in the explosion in the Mainland, and to immobilise any other roaming nightmares who wanted to further worsen things. He had also gotten Slevlyeot and Ralisrok, Alaric's twin and his eccentric friend respectively, to take care of the Dreamkeepers, but that obviously failed, granted they were now in the castle. For Andrei, he had been instructed to deter the fire elemental, using Vanity as bait.

He assumed that Slevlyeot and Ralisrok were killed, and though he worried initially of telling Alaric of the fate that had befallen his sister, anxiety now took over his mind as he worried for Alaric's life.

The twins held a special place in Katz's heart from an early start. Keresius brought them in as infants, when news of a nightmare and a dreamer giving birth to them reached his ears. The nightmare, seen *as a traitor, ultimately met the blade of Keresius, while the dreamer slipped away using her ability.*

The twins were raised alongside Katz to become his personal guards, although now, Alaric became his right-hand man, and Slevlyeot became somewhat of an informant.

Alaric had the ability to calculate the perfect aim of his spear within the blink of an eye, and Slevlyeot had the unique ability to exchange the ability of two individuals but could only be used once. Katz had her use her ability on him.

The twins and Katz had grown quite close, and even though the term 'friend' was hardly ever used in the Nightmare realm, Katz wouldn't deny that he considered the two his closest friends.

But now, they would be killed by the dreamers.

Katz finally reached the stairs that led to the basement, and made his way down, almost tripping as he skipped down, jumping over multiple steps at a time. He searched for any sight of the dreamers, his gun ready to fire. Yet, no one lingered in that space. Silence prevailed.

Then, within the shadows, Katz saw Alaric on the ground.

With a curse under his breath, Katz ran to Alaric and kneeled to him.

Too late. The vision came true. Katz checked his pulse. Nothing at all.

Katz sighed. Even if he knew that this would happen, he at least wanted to hear his last words. He took his relic to keep as a memoir - one that allowed its user to see the past of whoever he was looking at.

Katz always thought of it as ironic, granted how he could see the future, while Alaric could see the past.

The demands of his hectic schedule left him distressed, preventing him from properly grieving the loss of his best friend.

Katz wanted to just sit by Alaric's corpse and talk to him, but instead he stood up, preparing himself to deal with the dreamers. He stumbled a little, still exhausted from having to fight off the Remnants of Keresius earlier, but forced himself to leave the basement.

There were far bigger threats than the Dreamkeepers.

* * *

Raine didn't feel the relief she expected she'd feel upon seeing Kegan and Zephyr again. Jocelyn and So-hyun were there too, all of them looking like they were about to die, and Raine felt bad that she had to put her friends through such an ordeal. She reached her hand out to Zephyr first, trying to gain as much dream energy as possible from his elemental presence.

Raine healed Zephyr's wound, and she didn't bother to inquire where he had gotten it from. She didn't want to hear the details, and when she turned to Kegan, she remembered that her healing ability wouldn't work on him, and her eyebrows furrowed.

"Don't be too upset, Raine. I'll be fine," Kegan assured with a chuckle, although Raine could easily recognise his lies. He continued to grip onto Zephyr for support and had limped on his way to Raine earlier, being the slowest of everyone.

"Don't push yourself too hard," Raine said, gently. She trusted that Zephyr would be able to take care of him, although a part of her was still very confused about the friendship dynamic between the two.

The six of them stood outside a locked door marked with several faded symbols. The door looked about a thousand years older than Raine, and for some strange reason, a foreign familiarity struck Raine when she gazed upon them.

She stared at the symbol which heavily resembled the shape of a heart, and assumed it signified the Love realm. She figured that the other symbols also signified their own respective realms, but looked different from the modern emblems Raine recognised.

Lilac had originally found the door to the chamber room, which had been hiding away in an isolated part of the castle. No trace indicated that the room had been accessed by any visitors, not even Koshalv himself, but Raine knew it was where the Dreamkeepers needed to enter. She brought her hands to the doorknob, and found little surprise when it didn't open.

Dust landed on her fingers as she twisted the doorknob, and as she stepped back to wipe them off, Kegan kicked down the door with a loud bang. "Kegan!" Raine shrieked. She knew he was in no shape to kick down such a heavy door, and grew upset at his reckless move.

Despite that though, Kegan succeeded in his attempt to unlock the chamber room, and now nothing stood in between the Dreamkeepers and the chamber room. It felt like gazing into an alternate universe; the room's interiors were a complete contrast to the castle, and from Raine's view, she could see a few large glass chambers placed in the centre of the room, presumably for the Dreamkeepers to enter in.

Raine made her way in cautiously, but there were no booby traps or any hidden black-dreamers waiting to strike. The rest followed behind and each took a careful examination of the chamber room.

There were five chambers in total, and when Raine first counted them, her heart jumped a beat, for there were only three Dreamkeepers. But two of the chambers were deactivated and were covered in grime and dirt. The chambers had little symbols marked on them, each designating each Dreamkeeper. Raine saw that one of the deactivated chambers had the emblem of the Love realm on it, the other being an emblem Raine had never seen before and could only guess that it was the Future realm.

Raine could hear Lilac and Jocelyn chattering about the chamber room, their voices echoing. Zephyr and Kegan observed a strange panel device planted in front of the six chambers, curious of its intentions.

The six chambers hooked up to a mechanism which linked to the control panel. The lack of buttons made

it hard to operate, and something resembling a slot in
an odd shape was placed in the centre of the control
panel. Raine slowly untied the necklace from her neck
and placed it inside the slot. It fitted one half of the
slot, and Raine's eyes widened as she realised she
would need to get Aiseura's other half. But how would
she accomplish that?

Raine picked her necklace up and brought it close to
her chest, holding it carefully by the strings. Just as
she prepared to retie it around her neck, a bullet shot
through and shattered the necklace, its little pieces
dropping onto the floor.

Everyone heard the bullet loud and clear, and when
Raine turned, she saw Koshalv's gun directed at her.
"Cease," he demanded, his eyes narrowed. Raine was
frozen and didn't dare to move. Raine saw that all her
friends wore tense expressions on their faces, mixed
with fear, anger, and powerlessness. Immediately, the
whole of the chamber room was filled with nightmare
energy, and Raine felt herself succumbing to the
nightmares.

✳★✦★✳
Chapter 27: Black Dream

Pushed back into the darkness which consumed everything with nothing to spare, Raine accepted that her life had succumbed to its end. Immersed in nothing but her own thoughts, it seemed more and more likely that the remainder of her consciousness would be spent in this perpetual state of sleep paralysis.

Then, a voice echoed, unmistakably hers, despite having uttered no words. In fact, Raine doubted she still had a mouth to speak from.

Revieras.

The name didn't sound like hers at all. But she still acknowledged it. Just a single word, yet it allowed a million thoughts in her head to pour out like from a broken pipe. All of her fears and nightmares, wrapped into negative thoughts which filled her head.

Had Raine only been spared as the last Love dreamer just to be placed into the role of Revieras? Why had she even been pushed so hard to save the world? What had obligated her to? Why did the Nightmare realm even break free from their barrier in the first place, and why did Raine have to be responsible for a global crisis, when she just wanted to live a normal life?

Engrossed in her thoughts, she failed to notice a sob. She finally noticed it when it occurred a second time, and once she realised it wasn't hers, she chased the cloud of bad thoughts away, trying not to think of everything. She just needed to hear another voice.

Another sob.

A faint cry from afar, barely audible to where it could be mistaken for Raine's own delirium, but still loud enough for her to pursue the noise. She lacked a physical form, allowing her to traverse through nothingness indefinitely, but her heart told her that she was progressing.

Raine could feel a presence somewhere, and then she remembered something. Her friends had been caught by the black dream too. Were they also in the darkness with her?

Raine finally discovered the source of the initial sob - So-hyun. Despite the lack of anything, not even a body, or light at all, Raine could feel her presence in front of her. The Ambition Dreamkeeper, crying softly in the nightmares that surrounded her.

So-hyun? Raine called. Her voice couldn't travel, but she knew the message had been conveyed. She decided to treat the black dream as nothing but a simple nightmare, and just like dreams, nightmares could be manipulated in a nonsensical manner, and that meant that voices could be heard even in the medium of nothingness. So-hyun responded.

I can't get it out of my head.

Raine didn't know what she meant by 'it' at first, but she figured that the nightmares plaguing her mind had made their way into So-hyun's head as well. She remembered that every other dreamer also faced the same horrors she did, if not worse, and she knew she needed to help So-hyun break free. Although she didn't know the exact details of So-hyun's troubles, she could empathise with her emotions.

They won't stop laughing at me. I can see Hyrensia cursing at me from hell. I can hear the Diamond Cutters scoffing at me. I can hear Jocelyn yelling at me for taking Boris away from her. I can see the corpse of my coach wide-eyed staring at me with contempt. It won't stop.

The nightmares are real.

For the first time, Raine could see her physical body forming again. The darkness waned a little, then she saw So-hyun as well, with tears flowing down her face.

Raine grabbed So-hyun and hugged her. She didn't know what to say. She couldn't deny that So-hyun was dream-blind, nor could she reject all the ceaseless torment she had been through her entire life because of it. She couldn't just ignore the fact that Hyrensia and Boris were dead, and that So-hyun had gone through so much. Raine couldn't say that things were okay, because they weren't, and the nightmares would just keep crawling and crawling into So-hyun's mind until nothing remained. Instead, Raine spoke her truth: *We're here for you, So-hyun.* She could feel So-hyun clinging to Raine as she wept louder. *You're the Ambition Dreamkeeper for a reason, So-hyun, and I know why.* "It's because you're strong-willed and powerful, even without dream magic or any abilities. Because you're you. You've been strong *despite all the taunting and troubles in your life, and I don't want you to give up now."* Raine heard her own voice talk again, and she offered So-hyun a smile, knowing she was one step closer to defeating the nightmares.

So-hyun looked up at Raine again. She stopped crying, and wiped the remaining tears off her face with her sleeve. *The thoughts are gone. "I can see it again. My dreams."* So-hyun narrowed her eyes. "My ambition."

Raine let out a shaky exhale. She had freed So-hyun from the nightmares. She lent out her hand to So-hyun and said reassuringly. "Let's find the others."

So-hyun accepted Raine's hand. "All I could hear were sharp words about how I couldn't accomplish anything. But then I heard yours, and my mind calmed down a little," she said. "I know your words won't magically make all my troubles disappear, but they can help me face them."

Another presence caught Raine's attention. "I heard something," So-hyun gasped, pulling Raine over to an unknown direction.

The two kept walking and found Lilac.

"Lilac!" Raine and So-hyun called out. It felt much easier to speak this time, with the support of a fellow Dreamkeeper. But the blank expression on Lilac's face followed by the absence of Sir Bamesetton dispelled her optimism.

Who is Lilac?

The three words hit Raine like a truck. Even though Lilac grew up with nightmares in their realm, she was also experiencing the same turmoil brought upon by the black dream, just like Raine and So-hyun.

Is the role of your character just a facade, or are you just a mould created by somebody else's palms? Regardless of what you think, you're nothing but a fraud.

Lilac's idiosyncrasy melted away, leaving the residue of an empty vessel, the same vessel Raine met when she first encountered her back at the lair of the Remnants of Keresius. The ugly cloak which the members wore concealed Lilac's smart attire, blending her in with the void. Just as before, her identity was stripped away from her.

Are you a dreamer or a nightmare? Or are you just a flightless bird aiming for the skies? The world is your stage, and you put on a display, yet you're nothing but a puppet, one who'll soon meet her doomsday.

Lilac failed to recognise her own name, evident from her ignoring Raine and So-hyun's constant cries. Lilac's cadence of nightmares continued to spill out in second-person, and as Raine continued to listen to its sorrowful stanzas, she realised that the narrator's voice belonged to Sir Bamesetton, rather than Lilac. Although, Sir Bamesetton didn't sound right either. Rather, the voice belonged to somebody who symbolised the comfort of Sir Bamesetton.

"You're still loved," Raine whispered. Lilac perked up, having heard another voice other than the

nightmares beckoning her to yield. "It's okay if you
feel you don't fit in. We're still with you. We're still the
Dreamkeepers. Your identity isn't set in stone; it's a
journey, and you have the power to shape it." Raine
stepped closer to Lilac and offered her a hand as well.
"We're here to support you every step of the way.
We'll figure it out together. You can take your time
and be whoever you want to be. As long as you feel
happy and free."

So-hyun suddenly pulled Raine back from Lilac,
right before Sir Bamesetton - the beast, not the teddy
bear, came jumping out from the darkness and
attacking Raine. Lilac stood by her place, her face
empty, as if wearing a mask.

"Lilac, please!" Raine called, as So-hyun dragged her
away, running in circles to escape Sir Bamesetton.
"Isn't the world your stage? Don't you want to show
the audience who you truly are?" Raine panted, trying
to call out to Lilac while escaping the bear. So-hyun
practically dislocated Raine's arm with her pulling as
she dragged the two to safety, but soon it became
evident that even an athlete couldn't escape the beast,
and Sir Bamesetton caught up to them. Raine let out
one last plea to Lilac. "You are in charge of your own
play, your character, and your voice! Wake up, Lilac
Rygh!"

Raine and So-hyun hugged one another as they
prepared to get mauled by the bear, lowering their
heads and shutting their eyes. But after a few seconds
of painless silence, Raine slowly lifted her head and

saw that only a teddy bear appeared beneath her feet. Slowly, the two let go of each other and Raine picked the bear up. She and So-hyun then walked over to Lilac.

Raine handed the teddy bear over to Lilac, who took it with a sombre expression. "My father gave me this. It was my favourite toy," she muttered. "The Remnants of Keresius took him away, and I never saw him again. I was so young, I didn't remember anything except for his voice. He would always tell me bedtime stories and play with my toys with me. He was my light."

Raine peered at the button-eyed stuffed animal. As she recalled all the times she'd seen Lilac's ability, she realised that it all had been manifested to protect Lilac, just like how her father would have. "I don't know why he was ever with the Remnants of Keresius. But I never thought anything bad about him. I loved him despite everything."

"Did you hear the voices?" So-hyun asked. Lilac nodded, hugging the stuffed toy close to her.

"I heard Sir Bamesetton- no, my father's voice. Crying in the distance. I heard my own voice too, telling me that I was a nobody, and would never find an identity to call my own. But I know that's not true." Lilac closed her eyes and smirked, before loudly announcing to the nightmares. "Lilac Rygh, a name that resonates with valour and purpose! With thy noble quest to rescue the dreamers from the clutches of nightmares, thou art a beacon of hope in this world of shadows. May thy determination and courage lead us to victory, and may the dreamscape be free from the terrors that plague it!"

Raine looked at So-hyun, confused by Lilac's shift in vocabulary, but shook it off with a laugh. "Yes, you're the Pure Dreamkeeper, and the most quintessential Pure dreamer I know."

"Let us embark on our valiant quest to seek out and rescue our companions from the clutches of darkness. Together, we shall illuminate the path of dreams and banish the nightmares that beset our friends." Lilac smiled, taking both Raine and So-hyun's hand.

Raine could feel the nightmares growing weaker and weaker, and she felt more in control of the nightmare she and her friends were in now. But she was too hopeful, because within an instant, a gust of wind, strong enough to knock over an entire building, swept Raine off her feet, and somehow, Lilac and So-hyun were left behind, spared from the sudden wind. Despite Lilac and So-hyun holding on to Raine, it fell nothing short of gripping onto butter, and Raine was sent flying.

She now soared in the non-existent air, with So-hyun and Lilac nowhere to be seen. She shivered as the cold pricked her. The gust of wind forcefully threw her around, screaming in her ear.

Another voice sounded. Unlike So-hyun or Lilac's faint cries, this one was incredibly potent, sending Raine back to the time where painful ringing and subliminal callings plagued her mind back at the aquarium. But this time, the voices resounded not only within her mind, but also externally.

This is all your fault!

It's all your fault!

It's all your fault!

It's all your fault!

Those words echoed after one another, stacked upon each cry and ringing that continued ceaselessly. Raine's eyes watered and her heart bled in pain, but she didn't know why. The gust of wind grew even colder and harsher, and in a second, Raine was dropped into a flood of freezing water.

She could see the figure of Lemar floating under the water, before his image eddied away. All the water then vanished, before congregating into the sea serpent, which now circled around Raine, letting out a monstrous yell.

This is Zephyr's nightmare, Raine thought, eyeing Cady. She didn't need to hear his voice to recognise his pain. She had seen it for herself before.

The agony was too much to bear, especially for a child, and Raine understood why Zephyr had lost his memories. It would've been too painful to remember that too, alongside everything else, and now Raine felt even more guilty for letting Zephyr go through it again, after trying to block it out for so long.

But Raine knew that the current guilt she was feeling could never match the guilt Zephyr felt for killing Lemar, for hurting everyone at the stadium, for erasing the existence of Lemar and Nayeli. For hurting everyone he'd ever met with his elemental powers.

Heavy downpour commenced. Raine didn't know if she'd be able to save Zephyr with her words alone. She rubbed her eyes, trying to find Zephyr in the darkness, but only the sea serpent made its appearance, who now sounded angrier and more aggravated than ever, soaring around and flying, though it hadn't attacked Raine yet.

I'm sorry.

Raine crumbled to the floor, bringing her knees to her chest, watching the water slowly rise to her boots. She didn't know what to do. She didn't know how to help at all. And she could feel her emotions acting out of control.

"My own life should have been left forgotten by everyone, including me." Raine heard Zephyr's voice. She lifted her head and saw Zephyr sitting next to her, meeting her gaze. "I thought it was awful that I couldn't even remember my own life. But now that I remember, it doesn't feel any better."

Raine hesitated to speak. "I'm sorry."

"You don't have to be. It was my fault that it happened anyway." Zephyr turned away. "Why didn't I run away? Why did I spiral out of control? Why did I choose to be in that stadium in the first place? Why is it me?" He listed out the many questions he had. "I can't blame anybody but myself. I killed Lemar and...her. It's my own fault I had to go through this. Everyone was right to think of me as a monster." His voice started to crack. "I'll be alone forever because of me."

"Zephyr..." Raine watched as he tried to hide his tears away from her. "Please don't blame yourself for this. You didn't choose for those things to happen."

The sea serpent flew closer to Raine and Zephyr, swooping down and eventually picking them up on its back, roaring into the emptiness, its wings moving sharply at high speed. Raine jumped a little by the sudden movement and placed her hands on the serpent's scales for support, but Zephyr was still curled up and crying silently.

Raine scooted closer to Zephyr but made sure she wasn't touching him. "You didn't ask for everything that happened, and you definitely didn't deserve it. You have to realise that the responsibility lies with the person who hurt you," Raine stammered a little, not wanting to say her name. "You're not to blame for her actions."

Zephyr nodded slowly. "I just can't stop thinking about it. Even if I don't want to."

"We're here to help you. You're not alone." Raine glanced down beneath the sea serpent and noticed Lilac and So-hyun on the ground, searching for Raine. It had stopped raining, and the sea serpent let out a more tamed sound, alerting So-hyun and Lilac to look up. The serpent made a turn and picked the two up, and Raine smiled when she saw the two again. So-hyun and Lilac noticed Zephyr and immediately went over to comfort him.

"Fear not. This is nothing but the babbling of the nightmares. All shall be well," Lilac stated, offering Zephyr the teddy bear. So-hyun didn't say anything, but her presence alone consoled Zephyr enough. He stopped crying and welcomed their comfort.

The sea serpent dropped all four of them down as it dissipated into nothingness. There was no definite ground, so they all landed with the soft cushion of darkness itself. Wondering where the serpent went, Raine searched, but then saw more familiar faces.

"Kegan! Jocelyn!" Raine called. Everyone turned and saw Kegan and Jocelyn running up to them, and suddenly, everything got brighter and warmer. It felt like all the nightmares had completely gone away.

"Dude, call me a certified therapist, because I just totally undoed Kegan's pyromania," Jocelyn announced, clearly proud of herself.

"I am not a pyromaniac! And she should thank me for helping her dreamer ass out of that nightmare space," Kegan crossed his arms, evidently annoyed from being labelled a pyromaniac, but he could tell that Jocelyn was just kidding, and returned her quip with a smirk.

"We're all together now! Let's break free from this black dream!" Jocelyn attempted to hug all her friends at the same time, her short arms failing her miserably.

The presence of Jocelyn and Kegan lightened up everyone's mood, including Raine's. Granted that they all just faced their own personal nightmare, seeing

Kegan and Jocelyn joking around brought warmth, although Raine could never begin to imagine what sort of nightmares the two would have.

"Wait, Kegan, if you're here, then that means this black dream isn't an ability," Raine pointed out. "I still don't know where we are, or how to get out of here."

Kegan shrugged, but then something shiny by Raine's foot caught her attention. She gasped. "The other half of the necklace!"

The others watched as Raine bent down to pick up the shiny object, barely aware that Raine even had a necklace in the first place. "What is that?" So-hyun asked.

Raine didn't answer. She just held Aiseura's half of the necklace in her palms and stared at it longingly, wishing for answers. She took her own half of the necklace and linked it to Aiseura's half. The completed heart emitted a light so bright that it overtook the darkness with ease, and Raine could feel herself leaving the black dream.

✳★ ✦ ★✳
Chapter 28: Chambers II

Koshalv had already left by the time Raine escaped the black dream, but she didn't care about that.

Her other friends laid on the floor unmoving. Worried, Raine crawled over to them, and let out a sigh of relief to find that they weren't dead, just unconscious.

Kegan had gone, and Raine swallowed as she imagined the worst had happened to him. She had assumed that by leaving the black dream herself, everybody would follow, and they would all awake at the same time, but she had obviously been proven wrong. How long had it been since Kegan woke up before her?

Raine's thoughts were cut off by a loud sound that made her flinch. The sound of a metal gate crashing, along with more clamouring came from outside of the castle, deafening in intensity that Raine could hear it from the chamber room. She gazed worryingly outside the chamber room. Should she stay with her vulnerable friends who still had yet to wake up, or should she go investigate and try to find Kegan?

Raine's knees wobbled as she left the chamber room. She could hardly justify her decision to leave, considering her weakened state surrounded by nothing but nightmares. Mixed feelings rose in her chest when she figured her irrationality sprouted from her concern for Kegan.

Sneaking to the entrance of the castle, Raine could hear a multitude of footsteps, shouting, and gunshots. Her anxiousness spiked as she inched closer to danger, and carefully peered out to see what was going on, only to be met with a shocking view.

The metal gates defending the entrance of the castle had been knocked down and torn apart, and at least thirty nightmares in cloaks were charging at Koshalv, who fought them off alone. Raine recognised the opposers to be the Remnants of Keresius, and just as she tried to think of a reason why they would attack their own King in the first place, she peered too far out, and Koshalv caught sight of her.

Raine quickly pulled her head back and covered a gasp, but then looked back after a second. She knew he had seen her, but the fight with the cloaked nightmares kept him occupied, and after Raine realised that she had since stopped filtering them out with the euphemism of black-dreamers, caught the sight of guard-like figures emerging from pure darkness alone, commanded by Koshalv. They all manifested and bred from the absence of light, and charged at the Remnants of Keresius, where they all were forced to drop their target on the King and focus on the sentient creatures of darkness.

Koshalv ran back into the castle, and Raine went back to hide by the corner, but he immediately dragged her out. Raine let out a yell from shock, the nightmare energy pooling onto her again as the King of nightmares stared at her unimpressed, then kicked

her down and began dragging her back to the
chamber room.

Raine winced as she felt the impact of the kick linger
in her stomach, and the friction burned against her
back as Koshalv mercilessly pulled her like a sack of
heavy potatoes. "Let me go! What are you doing?" she
yelled, trying to kick free from him, her efforts all in
vain. "At least tell me what's going on! Where's
Kegan?"

"Oneirolepsy's future is being compromised thanks
to your incompetence." Koshalv let Raine go and
allowed her to stand back up, but only because he had
to free his hands to pull his gun out. He aimed in
Raine's direction, and before she could say anything,
shot out a bullet just an inch away from her face.
Raine turned around and saw one of the Remnants of
Keresius members dropping to the ground with the
bullet hitting his skull. "As you can see, the Remnants
of Keresius have begun their plan. As for the fire
elemental, he is fighting against Vanity somewhere
outside."

Raine tried to catch her breath and failed to speak in
a steady voice. "What? Vanity? And what plan? I
thought that the cult's plan was to kill me and the
Dreamkeepers. Why do you have a gun when you're
the King of nightmares?"

"That is because they want to deter you from saving
Oneirolepsy from the nightmares. Their plan is to
overrule the dreaming world with nightmares and

create a new King whom they will be able to control -
the Eperlithian. And just so you know, guns kill."

The Eperlithian? Raine could have sworn she had
heard that name before when she was first captured
by the Remnants of Keresius, but never knew what it
meant. "They want to overthrow you?"

"The Eperlithian is an entity created from pure
nightmare energy alone. I do not condone
Oneirolepsy becoming a playground for nightmares,
but the Eperlithian will allow it."

Raine blinked. "Wait, you *don't* condone the
nightmares roaming free?"

Koshalv paused. "Oneirolepsy would not survive if
such a thing were to happen. I have been using the
power of other dreamer elementals and my own
power to keep them in check ever since the barrier
was destroyed."

Raine stared at Koshalv, who turned around,
ignoring Raine's sudden epiphany. "Now, you will go
back to the Dreamkeepers and bind all the key
fragments into one, and unlock a weapon that will be
able to take down the Eperlithian," he said, almost
commanding Raine. "I doubt that you are capable
enough to do such a thing, so I will temporarily assist
you. Don't waste my time."

Koshalv began to walk, and Raine had to catch up to
him with her jelly legs, still feeling very unsure and
confused. Had she mistaken him for an antagonist the
whole time? "Your ability knocked the Dreamkeepers
out, including me. I don't know why they haven't

woken up yet," Raine said, immediately regretting speaking to Koshalv. She expected him to either ignore, insult, or glare at her, but to her surprise, he replied in a calm and steady voice.

"On the contrary, that was *your* ability, under the influence of nightmare energy. I merely took advantage of their unconscious state to make sure they wouldn't hinder my plans."

Raine frowned, finding it making no sense. "My ability is to heal."

Koshalv glanced at her. "No, that ability belongs to Raine. Your ability as Revieras allows you to manipulate the dreams of everyone, including nightmares. Your subconscious was affected by my nightmare energy, so you ended up having possibly one of your worst nightmares, dragging your friends along. Though, I wouldn't consider it an ability. It's merely Revieras' gift."

Raine took the following silence as an opportunity to process the new information Koshalv provided. So far, it seemed that he knew more about Raine than she did herself, and she couldn't help but feel a little inferior to him. "Does that mean you have multiple abilities too? As both Koshalv and..." she trailed off as she remembered what Umbral called him, but she decided against calling him by his name.

Koshalv didn't bother to finish her sentence for her. "My gift allows me to control both the nightmares and the darkness which they come from. My ability lets me see the future."

Raine expected the first answer but was surprised by the last part. "Is that what you meant by Oneirolepsy's future being compromised? You saw the future where the Eperlithian took over?"

The two turned a corner, and Raine found that the chamber room seemed further away from the castle's entrance when she was walking with Koshalv. "From what I saw, you end up disrupting Oneirolepsy's balance by eradicating the nightmares and their realm. It would've been ironically amusing if it wasn't such a world-threatening concern."

Koshalv appeared to be more aware of Raine's future plans than she herself. Raine recalled Aiseura's words: *Eliminate the Nightmare realm.*

Raine only wanted to restore the barrier and save the dreamers, but now that she put more thought in it, she probably would have done what Koshalv said she would do. "But Oneirolepsy's balance has already been disrupted when the nightmares broke into the dream realms," Raine argued, abandoning her long-used euphemism. The word 'nightmare' felt foreign when she used it.

"You think I haven't noticed?"

Although Koshalv spoke in a low and steady manner, his laboured breathing with slight expansion and contraction of his chest juxtaposed his composure, his fatigue almost palpable, somehow in a worse condition than Raine. She initially thought of his lack of vigour as natural for the King of nightmares, but she reconsidered as she watched the pattern of his breathless gasps. Perhaps Koshalv hadn't killed her yet not because he didn't want to, but because he couldn't.

Raine decided to ask a rather bold question. "Are *you* planning on taking me and the Dreamkeepers down?"

"If I planned on doing that, you would not be speaking to me right now," he replied, sounding irritated by her questioning. "And, if you haven't gotten the hint yet, I'm telling you not to eradicate the Nightmare realm."

"But-"

Suddenly, Koshalv looked up at the ceiling and shot with his gun aimed up at what Raine thought to be nothing, but then something swung by from above and crashed into him with a harsh kick, throwing him off the ground. His gun was knocked away from him as he got caught off-guard. A cloaked offender landed on the floor and began to charge at Koshalv again.

Raine broke from her brief shock to pick the gun up and tried shooting at the mysterious offender, but being unfamiliar with the weapon, she ended up throwing the gun back at Koshalv, probably breaking every commandment of firearms in the process.

Somehow, he managed to catch it, but instead of shooting at the cloaked being, he used it as a hand weapon and hit the attacker in the face with it. Raine finally figured that the gun had run out of ammo and felt mildly embarrassed for throwing an empty gun at Koshalv.

Still, the physical hit rendered the attacker delirious, and Koshalv pulled the cloak off the individual. "Damn it, Zelgia. Of course it was you," he cursed, recognising the attacker.

"Oh, shut up, Katz. Why ask me to call you Koshalv if you're not going to call me Luranos anyway?"

Raine hardly expected to hear the name 'Katz' and 'Luranos' coming out from the now unveiled attacker, exposing their messy white hair and golden eyes. At first, Raine wasn't sure of their gender, their androgynous face and neutral voice hardly being any help, but she then grew more concerned as she remembered hearing the name Luranos before.

Luranos was the leader of the Remnants of Keresius.

But everything happened too quickly, and for once a nightmare who had stronger nightmare energy than Koshalv himself made its welcome. For only a second, Raine could see Luranos hoarding a myriad of stolen relics, and the remaining members of the cult surrounding Koshalv and Raine.

And in the next, the Eperlithian summoned from the darkness, and nightmare energy emanated across the whole room.

The pure nightmare lacked a fixed form, constantly shifting and contorting as if it were composed of living shadows. The moment Raine met eyes with the being, she felt her soul paralysed, and unsettling cheers reverberated from the remaining members who had defeated Koshalv's summoned guards from the entrance.

Raine felt a suffocating aura, and she collapsed onto the floor. *The Eperlithian is here.* It didn't help that Koshalv looked equally as tense and worried, and Luranos' cackle echoed across the whole castle.

The Eperlithian charged at Koshalv, initiating the other members to tackle him as well, and as Koshalv barely managed to escape, large orange flames sharply rose, illuminating the darkness as screams rolled out, setting the members' cloaks on fire.

A hand reached out to Raine, and she almost cried tears of joy when she saw Kegan. "Kegan!" Raine gasped, filled with relief. She took his hand and almost collapsed into his arms. Kegan smirked at her before pulling her away from the scene.

"Revieras!" Koshalv called, throwing something at Raine. She caught the sparkling object and saw that it was her heart necklace, fixed and binded with Aiseura's other half. "Use that and get the key, *now.*"

Raine nodded and turned her back to Koshalv as Kegan dragged her back to the chamber room. "Kegan! Where were you?" Raine asked, once she and Kegan were far away from the Eperlithian. Raine struggled to run alongside Kegan and marvelled at how her legs still functioned - an even bigger miracle being her ability to complete sentences without butchering her words.

"I woke up and saw that you all were still knocked out, so I went out after hearing some weird noises," Kegan answered, leaving walls of flames behind him as he ran to serve as barriers to shield the two from

any tailing nightmares. "And then I found Vanity. She
was helping Koshalv, so I fought her, and fast
forward, saw you in trouble like always, and saved you
again. You better thank me later," he added, teasingly.

"Oh, well, I don't know how to tell you this, but I
think Koshalv isn't actually who we're supposed to
fight against?"

Kegan stared at her blankly. "...Okay, let's just get to
the chamber room."

❋ ❋ ❋

Raine panted as she arrived back in the chamber
room with Kegan, still uncertain if leaving had been a
good choice in the first place. Expecting that her
friends might still be unconscious, she felt a surge of
relief upon seeing them awake.

Although they were reasonably lost and confused,
they could easily tell that Raine was panicking and
possibly one second away from fainting again. "Hey,
what happened, Raine?" So-hyun asked. "I mean, I
remember everything in the black dream, but you
woke up sooner than us, and you look very stressed.
Where did you go? What's going on?"

"We need...to...get the key...now," Raine's words got
caught in her breath, and she pointed at the chambers
in front of her. "Get in the chambers now!"

Although she hadn't explained anything with
Koshalv or the Eperlithian, the Dreamkeepers could
recognise the urgency in Raine's voice, and didn't

question anything. Lilac was the first to move and
stepped into one of the chambers. The moment she
did, the chamber closed and lit up a bright purple. "I
can sense it. The Eperlithian will consume us all anon.
We must make haste," she claimed, her voice muffled
behind the glass chamber.

Jocelyn held onto So-hyun tightly, and it took a few
seconds for So-hyun to break free from her and enter
her respective chamber as well. It lit up with a bold
red.

Zephyr entered his chamber too, and a blue light
emitted.

All three of the chambers were lit up, and Raine
inserted the heart necklace into the empty key slot on
the control panel and pressed the only button
available on it. The necklace locked into place, and a
small sound signalled to Raine that it had started. The
chambers brimmed with overflowing light and dream
energy, and she had to close her eyes to protect them
from being blinded.

All the key fragments lying hidden within each
Dreamkeepers' souls were pulled out in that brief
moment of pure white, and once the light
disappeared, the chambers opened up again,
welcoming the three Dreamkeepers back out. A
wind-up key appeared in Raine's palm now, her
necklace free to be reclaimed. "Is everyone alright?"
Raine asked, momentarily placing the wind-up key
down as she wore back her necklace.

"We're alright," they affirmed, walking out the chambers and clamouring to Raine.

The control panel had opened and revealed a secret compartment inside - an old small box, with a small but effective lock, the type which had no keyhole in it, but a passcode instead.

"Do you know the passcode?" Jocelyn asked Raine.

Raine took the box with her hands and turned it around slowly as she scrutinised it. *Remember the date where Love was torn apart, the same day you were born, and taken away to safety in Rhea's arms.* Aiseura's voice looped in her head.

1603. Raine keyed the numbers into the lock at the same time.

Click.

The box opened and revealed an alarm clock, and Raine let out a small gasp. Its circular face adorned with seemingly a mosaic of galaxies, each one glimmering with its own unique cosmic colours. The clock's outer casing fashioned from a lustrous, silvery metal that seemed to shift and shimmer like the night sky, and Raine knew that she was gazing at no ordinary alarm clock.

There were no traditional clock hands to read the time, as if the object itself exceeded such a concept. Instead, there were constellations that slowly rotated around the clock, tracing the passage of time with their celestial patterns. There existed an almost rhythmic quality to it, and Raine knew she beheld divinity itself.

Everyone had their eyes on the divine alarm clock and failed to realise that Koshalv had entered the chamber room. He shoved Raine, and before anyone could attack Koshalv, he swiped the alarm clock and the key, his eyes narrowing as he quickly inserted the key into the alarm clock, winding it up as fast as he possibly could. "It's here," he mumbled to himself repeatedly, as if he was purposely trying to stress himself out just so that he could work faster.

Raine looked out the door to the chamber room, and saw the Eperlithian arriving, flooding the entire room with darkness once more. It lunged at both Raine and Koshalv, with its claws out, and just as the entity of pure darkness scorched Raine, the alarm clock sounded just in time.

※★◆★※

Chapter 29: Dream Weaver

Raine would never be able to shake off the feeling of having been attacked by the Eperlithian. It would forever etch into her soul, a part of her corroded with nightmare energy spread by the anomaly of pure chaos and strife.

But when the alarm clock sounded, Raine could feel everything fade away, including her own heart and soul, and she hovered amongst the stars. She knew she was dead by now, yet at the same time, she felt that her consciousness strayed beyond the concept of life and death.

She could see galaxies swirling around her, like wet paint swishing around by a paintbrush, mixing vibrant colours together to form bold and mesmerising patterns. In front of her, two cosmic stars rammed into each other at the speed of light, causing a collision which let out a bright light, and the fragments that produced a perfectly spherical fireball of blue and red that were created from the result of the crash slowly transformed into an entity, antithetical to the Eperlithian.

The entity appeared as an ageless figure, neither old nor young, with an aura of boundless wisdom. Their form shimmered like moonlight on water, ever-changing and elusive. They wore a robe made of woven moonbeams that trailed behind them like wisps of night fog, and their eyes gleamed with the infinite depth of the cosmos.

"Good morning, Revieras," they welcomed, despite it not being morning, and it not being good. "You too, Koshalv."

Raine jumped as she saw the King of nightmares next to her. "Don't look at me like that," he said. "I'm here to make sure you don't do anything stupid."

"You snatched the alarm clock away from me! I thought you had betrayed me or something," Raine crossed her arms.

Koshalv rolled his eyes and directed his attention to the entity. "You're one of the Dream Weavers, correct?"

"That is correct. For what purpose have you conjured my presence?" Their voice resembled a lullaby inviting anyone who heard it into a deep sleep, echoing with the tranquil moonlight.

Raine froze when she heard the term 'Dream Weaver'. When she first heard that the Dreamkeepers would be able to unlock an ultimate weapon that could restore the lost and rescue the world from nightmares, she assumed that it would be some sort of a blade that could tear down any and every nightmare in Oneirolepsy.

But now, she realised that the weapon wasn't any of the sort. The weapon was the ability to command the gods of Oneirolepsy. A Dream Weaver. They were beings responsible for creating the dreaming world, Oneirolepsy, weaving dreams within a single motion of a finger, from the top of the sky to beneath bedrock. They were essentially deities in Oneirolepsy, and although Raine never really paid attention to the Dream Weavers, she now stood before a deity, and one who fell under her command at that.

"Can you eliminate the nightmares?" Raine asked, managing to get Koshalv to raise his voice at her.

"Are you serious? After what I told you?"

Raine argued back. "I'm not listening to the King of nightmares! You're just going to trick me!"

"You are going to cause the world to be destroyed!"

"No, I'm saving it from your kind!"

"Now, now, there is no need to argue," the Dream Weaver spoke, silencing both Koshalv and Raine, though the two were still glaring at each other to death. "The roles of Koshalv and Revieras were meant to intertwine, harmonising rather than opposing each other's essence. We are Dream Weavers, not omnipotent gods. Anything you wish into reality must be weaved into the world in a consistent flow. Now, do not argue and tell me what it is you both wish."

Reluctantly, Raine spoke. "Give us some time to decide."

The Dream Weaver nodded, and disappeared into one of the many stars, allowing Koshalv and Raine to have a nice little debate. "Look, I know we have different goals, but a common one is to make sure the Eperlithian doesn't destroy Oneirolepsy," Raine started, trying to calm her voice. "I want to restore the world to its previous state where the nightmares never broke free from the barrier."

"I would like that too," Koshalv added. "I am not against restoring the barrier, all I am requesting is that you do not completely erase the nightmares and the realm itself."

"The world would be a better place without them, though," Raine mumbled, earning another glare from Koshalv. She cleared her throat and spoke again. "What does the Dream Weaver mean by our wishes being woven in a consistent flow?"

"If we wish for the Eperlithian to be eliminated, then there must be a narrative to why and how it happened. The Dream Weaver will not just magically wipe it from existence."

"Summoning a Dream Weaver is not enough narrative?"

"The Dream Weaver is not going to go hand-on-hand combat with the Eperlithian."

"But can they restore the barrier?"

"Possible, but we will need to gather all the nightmares who have escaped, and the damage they dealt will be irreversible."

Raine lowered her head. "We can't reverse time, can we?" she asked, feeling bad for all the lives that had been taken by the nightmares, but then she shook her head. "We can destroy the Eperlithian on our own. We'll defeat the Eperlithian and command the nightmares back to where they belong."

Clenching her fist, Raine turned to Koshalv. "The
Dream Weaver is right. We should work together, not
against, if we want to save the world," she said.
Although she didn't like the idea of working with the
King of nightmares, she knew she had no choice. And
besides, now that Raine thought about it, he seemed
more reasonable than she initially assumed.

"Fine. But you have to listen," Koshalv considered
Raine's idea. "Your ability allows you to tap into the
subconscious of anyone, and my ability allows me to
command anyone verbally. Once we defeat the
Eperlithian, we will combine our abilities and bring
the nightmares back to their realm, and then have the
Dream Weaver restore the barrier."

"How will we defeat the Eperlithian and the
Remnants of Keresius?"

"We fight."

Raine stifled a laugh. "I think you forgot the part
where I'm probably dead."

"We can change the narrative."

Raine's smile faded as she realised that Koshalv was
serious, and that they were going to have to fight the
Eperlithian. "The Dreamkeepers will be there, right?"

"They'll be there."

"Then we'll kill the Eperlithian."

Revieras and Koshalv called upon the Dream Weaver
and stood before them. Amidst the swimming stars,
their hopes and dreams were weaved seamlessly into
the world:

"A surge of ethereal energy coursed through them, neither dream nor nightmare, but a potent force that fuelled both Revieras and Koshalv's unwavering determination to rescue the world.

Empowered by the world itself, Revieras emerged from the shadows, accompanied by the Dreamkeepers. In the grand hall, they confronted the Eperlithian, while the Remnants of Keresius rallied to safeguard and serve their newfound sovereign.

Though the malevolent energy of nightmares recoiled, Revieras harnessed the power of dreams within her, and Koshalv deftly manipulated his own, aided by the Dreamkeepers' support. With this unity, they found greater stability on the precipice of conflict.

At that very moment, the battle commenced."

※★◆★※
Chapter 30: Eperlithian

Raine found herself holding her card-gun, with the
Dreamkeepers by her side. And although it was mildly
amusing for a magician with playing cards to be up
against the personification of pure nightmare itself,
she felt confident that she would win. She had to.

The Eperlithian towered over everyone, and
immediately the other members guarded it like fence
posts. Kegan did what he was best at and started
shooting his flames, propelled by Zephyr's wind
elemental magic. Raine questioned when the two
decided to complement each other's elements so well,
but shot a card directly at the Eperlithian anyway.
Thanks to the Dream Weaver, both Raine and
Koshalv's guns had their ammunition reloaded.

The card exploded upon impact, dealing minute
damage to the Eperlithian, although it proved to be
more effective than Koshalv's bullets. Him trying to
fight the Eperithian was like trying to put out a fire
with even more fire, and the Eperlithian chased after
Koshalv, commanded by the Remnants of Keresius to
eliminate their former ruler.

Lilac had Sir Bamesetton fare up against the
Eperlithian, fighting claw-to-claw with grunts and
growls. Raine shot more cards at the Eperlithian,
trusting that the others would deal with the
surrounding enemies.

"You!" Luranos called out to Koshalv, who held out his gun and ceaselessly shooting at the cloaked members of the cult he so despised. Luranos didn't appreciate his underlings being killed, and threw light orbs made from magic that would scorch anything upon impact at Koshalv.

Koshalv retaliated with his own black magic, cutting the light with darkness. "The ability suits you," he commented.

"Oh, shut up. If it weren't for you and those stupid twins, I would've kept the cooler power," Luranos pointed accusingly at Koshalv, who scoffed and attacked Luranos again with his magic, as if taunting Luranos.

Raine couldn't help but overhear the two and raised an eyebrow. But that split second of distraction sufficed for the Eperlithian to shoot out a wave of nightmares at her.

Sir Bamesetton stood in front of Raine and blocked the attack, sacrificing itself to save Raine. Lilac let out a wail as she watched the bear collapse. "Master Luranos! How could you?"

"You are a traitor, child. I should have never taken you in." Luranos replied, before getting hit by Koshalv again.

"Oh, shut it, you stupid cultist," he rolled his eyes. "You sound like an idiot."

From above, the sea serpent swooped in and struck the Eperlithian, and Zephyr showered the monster with water. It took Raine a few seconds to figure out why pure water damaged the Eperlithian, but then she saw steam flowing out, and realised it was boiling water.

She stepped back in case she ended up scorched from the water and continued shooting at the Eperlithian with her card-gun from afar, still filled with dream energy. She had made several promises with the Dream Weaver and one of them included a copious amount of dream energy supplied to Raine. Her dream energy supported her fellow dreamers as well. Jocelyn and So-hyun, who had grabbed swords from earlier fights with the castle's guards, were swinging left and right at the remaining members of the Remnants of Keresius.

The Eperlithian attacked again, this time aiming for Jocelyn and So-hyun. The two let out screams as they were thrashed and thrown across the main hall, wounded by the pure nightmare with their skulls bashed against the floor.

This alone angered Kegan, who didn't appreciate watching his friend getting thrown like a ragdoll. He launched a volley of fiery projectiles into the air, allowing Zephyr to manipulate the air to keep them suspended, and created a storm of burning embers that rained down on the Eperlithian.

Zephyr flew about on the sea serpent, which bit at the Eperlithian. He made eye contact with Kegan and the two nodded, and Raine quickly backed away from the Eperlithian even more.

A powerful whirlwind formed around the Eperlithian, and Kegan infused this cyclone with scalding water, turning it into a swirling, boiling tempest that engulfed and burned the Eperlithian, which let out a screech.

Raine and Lilac watched incredulously as the unconventional duo collaborated three elements together to cripple the ginormous creature, and Raine couldn't help but feel like a proud mother upon seeing Kegan work together with a dreamer.

The members of the Remnants of Keresius were all knocked down now, and as Lilac went over to help Jocelyn and So-hyun, Raine turned to see Koshalv and Luranos duking it out with both light and darkness, their abilities polar to each other.

Raine shot at Luranos too, deciding to help Koshalv out, but still maintaining a distance from him. "Random question, but are you two related?" she asked. From the way Koshalv and Luranos were acting, she couldn't help but get the hint that the two were siblings.

"Never!" The two yelled at the same time, so vehemently that it convinced the two were, in fact, siblings. Koshalv unleashed bullets over and over again, and as if he had predicted where he would aim at, Luranos dodged all of them like second nature, shooting out his own light magic back.

Raine found it impossible to aim at Luranos without his light scorching her retinas to oblivion, but Koshalv remained hardly affected at all. Quickly though,

Koshalv's gun ran out of bullets, and he watched as
Raine tried to shoot at Luranos with her card-gun,
missing her target completely.

"Give me that, you incompetent fool!" Without
warning, Koshalv marched over, took the card-gun
from Raine's hands, and started shooting at Luranos
with a faster and more accurate grip.

Raine sighed, leaving Koshalv to finish Luranos off.
She figured that she fit best as a healer and went to
find Jocelyn and So-hyun so she could heal the two.

The infuriated Eperlithian thrashed Zephyr off the
sea serpent, causing him to drop from the ceiling
while it ripped the sea serpent to shreds, tearing apart
and mutilating Cady.

Kegan winced as he heard Zephyr hit the hard
surface of the floor, running over to help him, but he
was tripped over by the Eperlithian and hurled into a
pillar.

Raine finished healing Jocelyn and So-hyun, who
witnessed the two elementals being torn apart by the
Eperlithian. So-hyun took the two swords belonging
to her and Jocelyn and launched them at the
Eperlithian like a javelin and stabbed the Eperlithian,
stunning it and giving Zephyr and Kegan time to
recover back to their feet.

"That gives me an idea," Kegan said, looking at the
two blades stuck in the Eperlithian. A strange sight to
behold, granted it lacked a fixed form, but it
significantly weakened the Eperlithian, and it

appeared smaller than before. He made a gesture to Zephyr and a thumbs up.

That alone assured Raine that the two had invented their own sign language within the hour they'd first met.

Little sparks of fire were shot out from above, combining Kegan's intense heat and Zephyr's rapid cooling to create a hail-like projectile that pricked the Eperlithian like a million tiny needles with a shattering effect.

Letting out a blood-curdling screech, the Eperlithian contorted itself and knocked both Kegan and Zephyr onto the ground and crushed them, before hauling them up into the air and hurling the two at the wall.

Jocelyn and So-hyun went to Kegan while Raine went over to Zephyr to help him, but he was still injured and harmed in ways other than physically, and she couldn't completely heal him.

She turned to Jocelyn and So-hyun, who were panicking when they saw Kegan injured and unable to move. Raine couldn't heal him and watched in despair as the Eperlithian let out another screech.

Jocelyn turned to the Eperlithian and removed the piece of paper she had in her skirt. Raine recognised it as the same paper she had been sketching with when she had been jailed with So-hyun, and at that moment, Raine realised that she wasn't joking about creating a bazooka.

The paper dissipated into nothing, and using what remained of the dream energy lingering around,

Jocelyn now held onto an oddly-shaped metallic bazooka. It looked slightly inaccurate as Jocelyn claimed she had no reference, but it still functioned, and before everyone knew, Jocelyn aimed at the Eperlithian, and shouted as she squeezed the trigger. "I have no idea how to use this, but you're done, fool!"

With an explosive roar, the rocket streaked through the hall, leaving a fiery contrail in its wake. It homed in on the Eperlithian, which futilely attempted to evade the impending impact.

Cataclysm unleashed. The rocket struck the Eperlithian, unleashing a colossal eruption of energy. Shadows and fragments of the nightmare entity scattered in all directions, dissipating into the void. A shockwave rippled through the hall, and a blinding light momentarily engulfed the area.

The Eperlithian's form fractured, its shadowy, amorphous mass breaking apart into countless smaller fragments. The darkness surrounding it weakened until it completely vanished, turning to nothing but wisps of dim, pale light that rise and disperse like ethereal smoke.

Raine felt a profound sense of relief, as if she had finally released from everything that had been burdening her since the start of the journey. The remnants of the Eperlithian faded away, like mist evaporating under the morning sun. As it dissipated, an eerie and haunting sound, like a symphony of tormented whispers and wail, was released - the

ghostly voices echoed and reverberated as a mournful
cry.

"No!" Luranos shouted in defeat, before getting
stomped to the ground by Koshalv. He pointed
Raine's card-gun menacingly at his head, with a stern
look on his face.

"Meet your end," Koshalv said, blasting a card
brimming with dream energy into Luranos' skull.

✳ ✳ ✳

Everyone gawked at Jocelyn, who immediately
dropped the heavy weaponed and turned back to
Kegan, whose eyes were widened. "Wow," he said,
despite his condition. Jocelyn and So-hyun proceeded
to help him up, and having Raine manifest another
blank piece of paper, Jocelyn sketched a first aid kit
and used her ability to turn it into something tangible.
She and So-hyun then proceeded to wrap Kegan up in
bandages and helped him to recover.

Having the many bodies of the dead Remnants of
Keresius members on Koshalv's floor, it annoyed him
more to still find Raine and the Dreamkeepers
trespassing in his castle. He effectively chased them
back out to the castle gates. So-hyun, Jocelyn, Kegan,
Zephyr, Lilac looked at Raine once they were all out,
wondering what to do next.

"We defeated the Eperlithian, right? But the barrier
is still broken. It doesn't change anything," So-hyun
said.

"We planned for that," Raine answered. "We made a promise with the Dream
Weaver earlier. They'll restore the barrier for us."

She could hear the Dream Weaver speaking in the back of her mind, talking to her from her subconsciousness. *"I see you have succeeded in saving what we have spent millennia weaving. As a token of our gratitude, and in return for your efforts to wake me up, the barrier will be restored."*

"We have to call all nightmares back to their realm before it is sealed once more," Koshalv said, not bothering to hand Raine back her card-gun. But Raine directed her focus on Kegan rather than the weapon. She went up to Kegan, who eagerly talked to Zephyr about their combined elemental attacks earlier.

"Hey," Raine said, disrupting the two.

"'Sup. I'm still alive, somehow. You're lucky you had me to help kill the Eperlithian." Kegan gave a confident smirk. But knowing that it was probably the last time Raine would ever have to deal with his snarky attitude, she felt more sad than annoyed compared to usual.

"Kegan, we're going to restore the barrier soon. I think we'll never be able to see each other again."

Kegan spoke after a small pause. "I don't mind staying in the dreamer realms. Besides, I have neutral energy and all that, I won't hurt anyone with my presence."

Raine turned to Koshalv for any input, but he just shrugged. "You don't want to stay in the Nightmare realm?" she asked, looking back at Kegan.

He chuckled. "I mean, sure, it's fun as hell to be able to burn things and mess with other nightmares, but it's way more fun to hang out with you. Besides, I could go on so many adventures and explore the other realms!"

Jocelyn chimed in. "Yeah! We could go on more adventures together with Kegan! I refuse to leave him in this horrible realm! No offence," she said the last bit to Koshalv, who didn't look the least bit fazed.

Raine sighed. Although she knew it could potentially be dangerous, a part of her didn't want Kegan to leave, especially when Jocelyn and Zephyr were his friends too. "Okay. But don't you dare try to set my rainforest on fire ever again."

Kegan gave an unconvincing thumbs up.

Raine returned to where Koshalv negotiated with the Dream Weaver. "To bring the nightmares back...we have to combine our abilities, right?"

"Yes. Are you ready to begin now?"

Raine nodded. Reluctantly, she held her hand out to Koshalv. He placed the card-gun back on her palm, and Raine looked up at him annoyed. "Don't we need to make contact for our abilities to combine?"

"Nonsense. Just do your job for once."

Raine frowned and closed her eyes for focus. How was she supposed to know what to do without any guide? *Come on, Revieras, do your thing...* she chanted internally, hoping that somehow, she would be able to tap into the subconsciousness of every nightmare in Oneirolepsy.

A familiar sense of despair washed over her as she felt herself connecting with the thousands of egregious nightmares out there, her mind flooding with dread and horrid thoughts as she sensed the malice of every nightmare at once. But having dealt with the Eperlithian, she learned to control herself, and she calmed herself down with slow breathing.

After a few seconds, she could hear Koshalv's voice in her head. *Understand that both dreams and nightmares have their roles in shaping the world, and a balance must be always maintained.*

Raine could feel the anger and protest of the many nightmares who refuse to listen to Koshalv. But she strengthened the subconscious link between her and Koshalv, and both their abilities intertwined together to send out a resounding command to every nightmare in the world:

I want to go home.

Immediately after Koshalv's command, the nightmares underwent a subtle transformation, their darkness mellowing and their malevolent influence lessening. She could hear movement around her, and a change in the atmosphere, but she hesitated to open her eyes, uncertain of the safety in unveiling the scene before her.

"Open your eyes," the Dream Weaver spoke to Raine.

Raine found herself standing right outside the Nightmare realm, the thin but powerful layer of the magical barrier restored right in front of her eyes. There was nothing ostentatious about its appearance - it remained the same as before, a mere translucent wall fuelled by power beyond the world's comprehension, this time more potent and more reinforced to ensure the barrier wouldn't break again, but it meant the entire world to Raine.

I did it. It's finally over.

Not far from the barrier, she could faintly see thousands of nightmares slowly but steadily marching toward where they belonged, obedient to their King's commands.

Even though the damage was irreversible, it had stopped.

Raine's friends were around her, marvelling at the restored barrier, and watching the nightmares' irregular subdued and submissive state. She let out a sigh of relief when she saw Kegan next to her.

The Dream Weaver had returned to the galaxies, where they would gaze at the world from below, weaving hopes and dreams into the world evermore. Koshalv was all the way back at the castle, and balance had officially been restored.

Raine looked down at her heart necklace - a beautiful gold that shined brightly, and after all these years, she had found the missing piece. After a bit of thinking, she removed her necklace. "Hey," she said to Kegan, and held out the necklace to him. His eyes darted to the accessory.

"You're giving this to me?" He asked, surprised.

"Think of it as your new relic. And uh, I told you I'd show you something greater than fire, so...here you go." Raine placed the necklace in his hands and nodded. "There, I fulfilled my end of the deal. Thanks for keeping yours."

Raine could see a wave of happiness wash over Kegan from his eyes alone. They glimmered brightly, like stars in the night, and he looked like a happy child who got the candy he wanted from the store. He let out a chuckle. "Oh, you and your cheesy antics, Raine. I like you, so I'll accept this silly jewellery of yours."

She offered him a smile and turned to the sky. The sun ascended, heralding the arrival of tomorrow. Raine watched as the endless night began to surrender to the gentle touch of dawn. The horizon became an artist's canvas, painted in hues of rose and gold. The world awoke from its slumber, and the first light of day slowly permeated the darkness, casting a spell of enchantment over the landscape.

Beneath the vast, sapphire canopy of the heavens, the eastern horizon lay in waiting, a sliver of silhouetted trees, valleys, and distant peaks. The stars still twinkled, their brilliance fading one by one as the sky transformed from midnight blue to a softer, more delicate shade.

The first golden arc of the sun's radiant face broke free from the horizon, bathing the land in a warm, honeyed light. It kissed the earth with a gentle caress, igniting the dew-kissed grass with a shimmering, ethereal glow. The leaves of trees, still heavy with the morning's dew, seemed to dance in celebration.

It felt like the world had finally taken a deep breath for the first time in forever, after having been polluted by terror for so long. Raine and the others embraced the gift of a new day - a gift that everyone worked so hard to realise. The sunrise promised a fresh start, a chance to begin anew and let the past fade into the night; a testament to the enduring beauty of the world and the timeless cycle of life, where endings were but preludes to new beginnings, and each sunrise symbolised hope and endless possibilities. The future had changed for the better.

Raine was free. And so were the dreamers.

THE END

Made in the USA
Las Vegas, NV
25 January 2024

84628736R00262